May Agnes F

The Actress's Daughter

May Agnes Fleming

The Actress's Daughter

1st Edition | ISBN: 978-3-75232-677-2

Place of Publication: Frankfurt am Main, Germany

Year of Publication: 2020

Outlook Verlag GmbH, Germany.

Reproduction of the original.

THE
ACTRESS' DAUGHTER.

BY

MAY AGNES FLEMING.

CHAPTER I.

CHRISTMAS EVE.

"Heap on more wood! the wind is chill;
But let it whistle as it will,
We'll keep our Christmas merry still."—SCOTT.

"

r! Lor! what a night it is any way. Since I was first born, and that's thirty-five
—no, forty-five years come next June, I never heern sich win' as that there, fit
to tear the roof off! Well, this is Christmas Eve, and we ginerally do hev a
spell o' weather 'bout this time. Here you Fly! Fly! you little black imp you!
if you don't stop that falling asleep over the fire, and stir your lazy stumps,
I'll tie you up and give you such a switchin' as you never had in all your born
days. Ar-r-r-r! there I vow to Sam if that derned old tabby cat hain't got her
nose stuck into the apple sass! Scat! you hussy! Fly-y-y! you ugly little black
ace-o'-spades! *will* you wake up afore I twist your neck for you?"

And the speaker of this spirited address—a tall, thin, pasteboard female, as
erect as a ramrod and as flat as a shingle, with a hard, uncompromising face,
and a hawk-like gray eye, caught hold of the drowsy little darkey nodding in
the chimney-corner, and shook her as if she had been a flourishing little fruit
tree in harvest time.

"P-please, Miss Jerry, 'scuse me—I didn't go for to do it," stammered Fly,
with a very wide-awake and startled face. "I wasn't asleep, old Mist—"

"Oh! you wasn't asleep, old Mist—wasn't you," sneered Miss Jerusha Glory
Ann Skamp, the sonorous and high-sounding title claimed by the antiquated
maiden lady as her rightful property; "you wasn't asleep wasn't you? Oh, no!
in course you wasn't! *You* never sleep at all, do you? Betsey Periwinkle never
runs off with the meat, and the cold vittals, or drinks the milk, or pokes her
nose into the apple sass, or punkin slap-jack, while you're a snoozin' in the
corner, does she? Ain't you 'shamed o' yourself, you nasty little black image,
to stand up there and talk to one as has been a mother to you year in and year
out, like that? Ar Lor'! there ain't nothin' but ungratytood in this 'ere world.

2

Betsey Periwinkle, you ugly brute! I see you a lookin' at the apple sass, but just let me ketch you at it agin, that's all! Oh, my stars and thingumbobs! the way I'm afflicted with that lazy little nigger and that thievin' cat, and me a poor lone woman too! If it ain't enough to make a body go and do something to themselves I should admire to know what is. Here, you Fly! jump up and fry the pancakes for supper, and put the tea to draw, and set that johnny-cake in the oven, and then set the table, and don't be lazin' around like a singed cat all the time."

And having delivered herself of these commands all in a breath, with the air of a Napoleon in petticoats, Miss Jerusha marched, with the tramp of a grenadier, out of the kitchen into the "best room," drew several yards of stocking from an apparently bottomless pocket, deposited herself gingerly in the embraces of a cushioned rocking-chair, the only sort of embrace Miss Jerusha had any faith in, and began knitting away as if the fate of nations depended on it.

And while she sits there, straight, rigid, and erect as a church steeple, let me describe her and the house itself more minutely.

A New England "best room!" Who does not know what it looks like? The shining, yellow-painted floor, whereon no sacrilegious speck of dust ever rests; the six stiff-backed, cane-seated chairs, standing around like grim sentinels on duty, in the exact position to an inch wherein they have stood ever since they were chairs; the huge black chest of drawers that looms up dark and ominous between the two front windows, those windows themselves glittering, shining, flashing, perfect jewels of cleanliness, protected from flies and other "noxious insects" by stiff, rustling green paper blinds; the table opposite the fireplace, whereon lies, in solemn, solitary grandeur, a large family Bible, Fox's Book of Martyrs, the Pilgrim's Progress, and Robinson Crusoe.

Miss Jerusha, being frightfully sensible, as ladies of a certain age always are, looked upon all works of fiction with a steady contempt too intense for words; and therefore Robinson Crusoe had remained as unmolested on the table as he had in his sea-girt island from the day a deluded friend had presented it to her until the present hour. In fact, Miss Jerusha Skamp did not affect literature of any kind much, and looked upon reading as a downright waste of time and patience. On Sundays, it is true, she considered it a religious duty to spell through a chapter in the Bible, beginning at the first of Genesis, and marching right through, in spite of all obstacles, to the end of Revelations—a feat she had once performed in her life, and was now half way through again. The hard words and proper names in the Old Testament were a serious trial to Miss Jerusha, and, combined with the laziness of her little negro maid Fly, and the dishonest propensities of her cat Periwinkle, were the chief troubles and tribulations of her life. Miss Jerusha's opinion was that it would have been just as easy for the children of Israel to have been born John Smith or Peter Jones as Shadrack, Meshach and Abednego, and a *great* deal easier for posterity. Next to the Bible, Fox's "Book of Martyrs" was a work wherein Miss Jerusha's soul delighted, and wonderful was her appreciation and approval of the ghastly pictures which embellished that saintly volume. "The Pilgrim's Progress" she passed over with silent contempt as a book "nobody could see the pint of."

Besides the best room, Miss Jerusha's cottage contained a kitchen about the size of a well grown bandbox, and overhead there were two sleeping apartments, one occupied by that ancient vestal herself, and the other used as a store-room and lumber-room generally.

Fly and Betsey Periwinkle sought their repose and shakedown before the kitchen fire, being enjoined each night before she left them by Miss Jerusha to "keep an eye on the house and things;" but as Fly generally snored from the moment the last flutter of Miss Jerusha's dress disappeared until a sound shaking from that lady awoke her next morning, and Betsey Periwinkle, after indulging in a series of short naps, amused herself with reconnoitering the premises and feloniously purloining everything she could lay her paws on that seemed to be good and eatable, it is to be supposed the admonitions were not very rigidly attended to. There was not much danger of robbers, however, for the cottage was situated nearly two miles from any other habitation, on the very outskirts of the flourishing township of Burnfield, a spot lonely and isolated enough to suit even the hermit-like taste of Miss Jerusha.

The back windows of the cottage commanded a view of the sea, spreading away and away until lost in the horizon beyond. From the front was seen the forest path lonely and silent, with the dark pine woods bounding the vision and extending away for miles. In the rear of the house was a small garden, filled in summer with vegetables of all sorts, and the product of this garden formed the principal source of Miss Jerusha's income. The old maid was not rich by any means, but with the vegetables and poultry she raised herself, the stockings she knit, the cloth she wove, the wool she dyed, the candy she made and sold to the Burnfield grocers, and the sewing she "took in" she managed to live comfortably enough and "lay up something," as she said herself, "for a rainy day"—a figure of speech which was popularly supposed to refer to times of adversity and old age.

A strong-minded, clear-headed, sharp-tongued, wide-awake, uncompromising specimen of femaledom "away down east" was Miss Jerusha. Never since the time she had first donned pantalettes, and had "swopped" her rag doll for

Mary Ann Brown's china mug, could that respectable individual, the oldest inhabitant, recollect any occasion wherein Miss Jerusha had not got the best of the bargain, whatever that bargain might be. Though never remarkable at any time for her personal beauty, yet tradition averred that her thriftiness and smartness had on one or two occasions so far captivated certain Jonathans of her district, that they had gallantly tendered their heart, hand and brand new swallow-tails. But looking upon mankind as an inferior race of animals, made more for ornament than use, Miss Jerusha had contemptuously refused them, and had marched on with grim determination through the vale of years in her single blessedness up to her present mature age of five-and-forty.

The personal appearance of the lady could hardly be called prepossessing at first sight, or at second sight either, for that matter. Unusually tall, and unusually thin, Miss Jerusha looked not unlike a female hop-pole, and her figure was not to say improved by her dress, which never could be persuaded to approach her ankles, and was so narrow that a long step seemed rather a hazardous experiment. Her hair, which was of a neutral tint between red and orange, a vague hue commonly known as "carroty," was disfigured by no cap or other sort of headgear, but tethered into a tight knot behind, and then forcibly secured. Her face looked not unlike that of a yellow parchment image as she there sat knitting in the red firelight, rocking herself back and forward in a rheumatic old chair that kept up a horrible crechy-crawchy as she squeaked back and forth.

The night was Christmas Eve, and unusually wild and stormy, even for that season. The wind blew in terrible gusts, shrieking wildly through the bare arms of the pines, drifting the snow into great hills, and driving the piercing sleet clamorously against the windows. Miss Jerusha drew closer to the fire, with a shiver, and paused for a moment to listen to the wild winter storm.

"My gracious! what a blast o' win' that there was. Ef the old Satin ain't been let loose to-night my name's not Jerusha Skamp. Go out and bring in some more wood, Fly, and don't let Betsey Periwinkle eat the tea things while you're gone. My-y-y conscience! how it blows—getting worse and worse every minute too. If there's any ships on the river to-night the first land they make will be the bottom, or I'm no judge. And I oughter be, I *think*," said Miss Jerusha, administering a kick to Betsey Periwinkle, as that amiable quadruped began some friendly advances toward her ball of stocking yarn, "seein' I've lived here since I was born, and that's forty-five years come next June. I should not wonder now if some shiftless, good-for-nothing vagabones was to 'low themselves for to get ketched in the storm and come to me to let 'em in and keep 'em all night. Well, Miss Jerusha, don't you think you see yourself a-doing of it though! People seems to think I was made specially by

Providence to 'tend onto 'em and make yarb tea for them to swaller as is sick, and look arter them as is well, whenever they get ketched in a storm, or a nightmare, or anything. Humph! I guess nobody never seen any small sand, commonly called mite stones, in *my* eyes, and never will if I can help it. What on airth keeps that there little black viper now, I wonder. *You*, Fly!"

"Yes, old Mist, here I is," answered Fly, coming blustering in like a sable goddess of the wind, loaded down with wood. "An' oh, Miss Jerry, all de ghosts as eber was is ober in dat ar inferally ole house 'long the road."

"Ghosts! ugh!" said Miss Jerusha, with a contemptuous snarl, for the worthy spinster despised "spirits from the vasty deep" as profoundly as she did mankind. "Don't make a greater fool o' yourself, you misfortunate little nat'ral you, than the Lord himself made you. Put some wood on the fire, and be off and hurry up supper."

"Miss Jerry, I 'clear I seed it own bressed self," protested Fly, with horror-stricken eyes. "I jes *did*, as plain as I see you now, an' if as how you doesn't believe me, Miss Jerry, go and look for yourself."

"Lord bless the child! what is she talking about?" said Miss Jerusha, turning around so sharply that little Fly jumped back in alarm.

"Ghosts, Miss Jerry," whimpered the poor little darkey.

"Ghosts! Fly, look here! You want me to switch you within an inch o' your life," said Miss Jerusha, laying down her knitting and compressing her lips.

"Miss Jerry, I can't help it; I jes can't. Ef you're to kill me, I *did* see 'em, too, and you can see 'em yerself ef you'll only look out ob de winder," sobbed Fly, digging her knuckles into her eyes.

Miss Jerusha, with sternly shut-up lips, glared upon the unhappy little negress for a moment in ominous silence, and then getting up, went to the window and looked out.

But the window was thickly covered with frost, and nothing was to be seen from it.

"Ef you'd only come to de door, Miss Jerry," wept Fly, taking her knuckles out of one eye, where they had been firmly imbedded.

With the tramp of an iron-shod dragon, Miss Jerusha walked to the kitchen door, opened it, and looked out.

A blinding drift of snow, a piercing blast of wind, a cutting shower of sleet, met her in the face, and for one moment forced her back.

Only for a moment, for Miss Jerusha was not one to yield to trifles, and then, shading her eyes with her hands, she strove to pierce the darkness made white by the falling snow. No ghost met her gaze, however, but something that startled her quite as much—a long line of red light streaming along the lonesome, deserted road. There was no one living save herself all along the way for two miles, and no house of any kind save the ruins of an old cottage, long since deserted, and popularly supposed to be haunted.

"Great Jemima!" exclaimed Miss Jerusha, as, after her first start of astonishment, she came in, closed and locked the door, "who can be in the old house? Somebody's bin caught in the storm, and went in there for shelter. Well, lors! I hope they won't come bothering me. If they do, I'll pack them off agin with a flea in their ear. You, Fly! ain't them pancakes fried yet? Oh, you lazy, shif'less, idle, good-for-nothing little reptyle! Ef you don't ketch particler fits afore ever you sleep this night! And I 'clare to man the kittle ain't even biled, much less the tea adrawin'! *You, Fly!*"

Fly came rushing frantically out, and dodged Miss Jerusha's uplifted hand, which came down with a stunning force on the table. With a suppressed howl of pain, the enraged spinster shook her tingling fingers, and was about to pounce bodily upon her unlucky little servitor, when, in a lull of the storm, a knock at the door arrested the descending blow.

Both mistress and maid paused and held their breath to listen.

The wind and sleet came driving in fierce gusts against the house, shaking the doors and rattling the windows; then came a lull, and then the knock was repeated, this time more loudly.

"Oh, Miss Jerry, it's a ghos'! Oh, Miss Jerry, it's a ghos'! an' 'deed a' 'deed I don't want for to go!" shrieked the terrified Fly, clinging wildly to Miss Jerusha's dress.

With a vigorous shake the spinster shook off the clinging hands of poor little Fly, and laid her sprawling on the floor. Then approaching the door, she called, loudly and threateningly:

"Who's there?"

Another knock, but no reply.

"Who's there?" repeated Miss Jerusha, sharply.

"It's only *me*—please let me in," answered a faint voice.

To Miss Jerusha it sounded like the voice of a child, but still suspicious of her visitor, she only called:

"What do you want?"

"Oh, please open the door—I'm *so* cold!" was the answer, in a faint, shivering voice that was drowned in another shriek of the storm.

Miss Jerusha was no coward; so, first arming herself with a pair of tongs, having some vague idea she might find them useful, she pulled open the door, admitting a wild drift of wind, and snow, and sleet, and, blown in with it, the small, slight figure of a child—no one else.

Miss Jerusha closed the door, folded her arms, and looked at her unexpected visitor. Little Fly, too, so far recovered from her terror as to lift her woolly head and favor the new-comer with an open mouth and eyes astare.

It was a boy of some thirteen or fourteen years of age, wretchedly clad, but so white with the drifting snow that it was impossible to tell what he wore. His face was thin, pinched, and purple with the cold, his fingers red and benumbed, his teeth chattering either with fear or cold.

As Miss Jerusha continued to stare at him in severest silence, he lifted a pair of large, dark, melancholy eyes wistfully, pleadingly, to her hard, grim face.

"Well," said the spinster, at last, drawing a deep breath, and surveying him from head to foot—"well, young man, what do *you* want, if a body may ask?"

"Please ma'am, I want you to come and see mother—she's sick," said the child, dropping his eyes under the stern gaze bent upon him.

"Oh, you do? I hain't the least doubt of it!" said Miss Jerusha, sarcastically. "Should hev bin 'sprised if you *hadn't*. I was jest a sayin' I 'spected to see somebody comin' for me to see their mother or something. Nobody could die, of course, unless I trudged through the snow and storm to see 'em off. Of course, it wouldn't do to let a particerlerly stormy night come without bringing *me* out through it, giving me the rheumatiz in all my bones and a misery in the rest o' my limbs. Oh, no, in course it wouldn't. And who may your mother happen to be, young man?" concluded Miss Jerusha, changing with startling abruptness from the intensely ironical to the most searching severity.

"Why, she's *mother*," said the boy, simply, lifting his dark, earnest eyes again to that set, rigid face; "she is in that old house over there, and she—is going to die."

His lip quivered, his eyes filled and saddened, and he drew a long, shivering breath, and swallowed very fast to keep back his tears. Brave little heart! hiding his own grief lest it might offend that sour-looking gorgon and keep her from visiting "mother."

Miss Jerusha's face did not relax a muscle as she kept her steely eyes fixed unwinkingly on that sad, downcast young face. It was a handsome face, too, in spite of its pinched, famished look; and Miss Jerusha, to use her own expression, "couldn't abide" handsome people.

"And what brings your mother to that old house that ain't fit for a well-brought-up dog to die in, let alone, a 'sponsible member o' society?" asked Miss Jerusha, sharply.

"Please, ma'am, we hadn't any place else to go."

"Oh, you hadn't! I *thought* all along that was the sort of folks you was!" sneered the old lady; "there allers is tramps about, dropping down and dying in the most unheard-of places. There, be off with you now! I make a pint o' never encouraging beggars or shif'less char-*ak*-ters. I hain't got nothin' for your mother, and I ain't a public nuss, though people seems for to think I'm paid by the corporation for seein' sick folks out of the world. There! go!"

"Oh! *please* come and see mother! indeed, *indeed* we ain't beggars, but mother was so tired and sick she could not go any farther, and now she is dying there all alone with only sis. Oh, *please* do come," and the childish voice grew sharp and wild in its pleading agony.

The heart beating within Miss Jerusha's vestal corset was touched for a moment, and then arose thoughts of vagrants, impostors, and "shif'less" characters generally, and the heart was stilled again; the voice that answered his pleading cry was high and angry.

"I won't, you little limb! Be off! It's my opinion your mother ain't no better than she ought to be, or she wouldn't come a dying round promiscuously in such a way. There! March!"

With an angry jerk, the door was pulled open, and the long, lean finger of the spinster pointed out.

Without a word he turned to go, but as he passed from the inhospitable threshold the large dark, solemn eyes were lifted to hers with a long look of unutterable reproach; then the door was closed after him with a sharp bang, and securely bolted.

"Shif'less vagabones," muttered Miss Jerusha; "ought to be whipped as long as they can stand! Well, he's gone, and he didn't get much out of me anyway."

Yes, Miss Jerusha, he has gone, but when will the haunting memory of that last look of unspeakable reproach go too? It rose like a remorseful ghost before her as she stood moodily gazing on the red spot that glowed like an eye of flame on the top of the hot little kitchen stove—that furnished sorrowful childish face—those dark, sad, pitiful eyes—that silent reproach, far keener than any words.

Miss Jerusha strove to still the rebellious voice of conscience and persuade herself she had done exactly right, but never in all her life had she felt so dissatisfied with her own conduct before. As usual, when people are irritated with themselves, she felt doubly irritated with everybody else; so, by way of relieving her mind, she boxed Fly's ears, and kicked Betsey Periwinkle, who came purring affectionately around her, to the other end of the room. And then, with her temper no way sweetened by those little marks of endearment, she tramped back to the best room, and dropped sullenly into a comfortable seat by the fire.

But owing to some cause or another, the seat was comfortable no longer. Miss Jerusha turned and twisted, and jerked herself round into every possible position, and "pooh'd" and "pshaw'd," and listened to Fly, who, out in the kitchen, had lifted up her voice and wept, and ordered her fiercely to bring in tea and hold her tongue. And poor little ill-used Fly brought it in, dropping tears into the sugar-bowl, and cream-jug, and "apple sass," and snuffling in great mental and bodily distress. And then Miss Jerusha sat down to supper, and great and mighty was the eating thereof; but still the canker within grew sorer and sorer, and would not be forgotten. Do what she would, turn which way she might, that sorrowful, childish face would rise before her like a waking nightmare. Conscience, that "still, small voice," would persist in making itself heard, until at last Miss Jerusha turned ferociously round and told conscience to mind his own business, that "she wasn't going to be fooled by no baby-faced little vagabones." And then, resuming her work, she sat down with grim determination, and knit and knit, and still the steam within got up to a high pressure, until Miss Jerusha got into a state of mind, between remorse and conscience and the heat of the fire, threatening spontaneous combustion.

Woe to the man, woman, or child who would have presumed to cross Miss Jerusha in her present mood! Safer would it have been to

> "Beard the lion in his den,
> The Douglas in his hall,"

than the young tornado pent up within the hermetically sealed lips of Miss Jerusha Glory Ann Skamp at that moment.

But all would not do. Louder and louder that clamorous voice arose, until the aged spinster bounded up in a rage, flung her knitting across the room, and, striding across to the hall, returned with an immense gray woolen mantle, a thick black silk quilted hood, a red woolen comforter, and a pair of men's strong calf-skin boots. Flinging herself into a seat, Miss Jerusha, with two or three savage pulls, jerked these on, and having by this means got rid of some of the superfluous steam, burst out into the following complimentary strain to herself:

"Jerusha Glory Ann Skamp, it's my opinion you're a nat'ral born fool, and nothin' shorter! Ain't you ashamed of yourself in your 'spectable old age o' life to go trampin' and vanderblowsin' through the streets at sich onchristian hours of the night to look arter wagrets as ought for to look arter theirselves? I'm 'shamed of you, Jerusha Skamp, and you ought to be 'shamed o' *yourself*, going on with sich reg'lar downright, ondecent conduct. Don't tell me bout that there little fellar's looks! He's an impostor like the rest, and has done you brown beautifully, Miss Jerusha, as you'll soon find out. 'A fool o' forty 'll never be wise!' To think that Jerusha Skamp should be took in by a boy's looks at your age o' life! His looks! fudge! stuff! nonsense! You're nothing but a old simpleton—that there's what you are, Miss Jerusha! Here you, Fly! you derned little black monkey you!"

Thus pathetically adjured, Fly, in a very limp state of mind and body, caused probably by the showers of tears so lately shed, appeared in the door-way, her eyes full of tears and her mouth full of corn-cake.

"Here, you Fly, I'm going out, and you and Betsey Periwinkle has got for to sit up for me. Give Betsey her supper, and see that you don't fall asleep and set the house afire."

"Yes'm," said Fly, in a nearly inaudible voice, as she returned to her supper.

Then Miss Jerusha, putting a small flask of currant wine in her pocket, wrapped her thick, warm mantle around her, and her hood closely over her face, and resolutely stepped out into the wild, angry storm.

CHAPTER II.

THE ACTRESS—LITTLE GEORGIA.

"Death is the crown of life."
"She was a strange and willful sprite
As ever startled human sight."

e road to the old house was as familiar to Miss Jerusha as a road could well be to any one, yet she found it extremely difficult to make her way to it to-night. The piercing sleet dashed into her very eyes, blinding her, as she floundered on, and the raw, cutting wind penetrated even the warm folds of her thick woolen mantle. Now and then she would have to stop and catch hold of a tree, to brace her body against the fierce, cutting blasts, and then, with bent head and closed eyes, plunge on through the huge snow-heaps and thick drifts.

She had not fully realized the violence of the storm until now, and she thought, with a sharp pang of remorse, of the slight, delicate child she had turned from her door to brave its pitiless fury.

"Poor little feller! *poor* little feller!" thought Miss Jerusha, piteously. "Lor', what a nasty old dragon I am, to be sure! Should admire to know where I'll go to, if I keep on like this. Yar-r! you thought you did it, didn't you? Just see what it is to be mistaken."

This last apostrophe was addressed to a sudden blast of wind that nearly overset her; but, by grasping the trunk of a tree, she saved herself, and now, with a contemptuous snarl at its foiled power, she plunged and sank, and rose and floundered on through the wild December storm, until she approached the old ruined cottage, from the window of which streamed the light.

The window was still sound, and Miss Jerusha, cautiously approaching it, began prudently to reconnoiter before going any farther.

Desolate indeed was the scene that met her eye. The room was totally without furniture, the plastering had in many places fallen off and lay in drifts all along the floor. A great heap of brush was piled up in the chimney-corner, and close by it crouched a small, dark figure feeding the slender flame that burned on the hearth. Opposite lay extended the thin, emaciated form of a woman, wrapped in a shawl, almost her only covering. As the firelight fell on her face, Miss Jerusha started to see how frightfully ghastly it was, with such hollow cheeks, sunken eyes, and projecting bones. So absorbed was she in gazing on that skeleton face, that she did not observe the little figure crouching over the fire start up, gaze on her a moment, and then approach the window, until, suddenly turning round, she beheld a small, dark, elfish face, with wild, glittering eyes, gleaming through masses of uncombed elf locks, pressed close to the window, with its goblin gaze fixed full upon her.

Miss Jerusha was not nervous nor superstitious, but at the sudden vision of that face from elf-land she uttered a shriek that might have awakened the dead, and shrank back in dismay from the window.

While she still stood, horror-struck, the door opened, and a high, shrill voice called:

"Now, then, whoever you are, come in if you want to!"

It was the voice of a mortal child, and Miss Jerusha was re-assured. Thoroughly ashamed of herself, and provoked at having betrayed so much fear, she approached the open door, passed in, and it was closed after her.

"So I scared you, did I? Well, it serves you right, you know, for staring in people's windows," said the shrill little voice; and Miss Jerusha, looking down, saw the same small, thin, dark face, with its great, wild, glittering black eyes, long, tangled masses of coal-black hair, high, broad brow, and a slight lithe figure.

It was a strange, unique face for a child, full of slumbering power, pride, passion, strength, and invincible daring; but Miss Jerusha did not see this, and looking down only beheld an odd-looking, rather ugly child, of twelve or thirteen, or so, with what she regarded as an impudent, precocious gaze, disagreeable and unnatural in one so young.

"Little gal, don't be sassy," said Miss Jerusha, sharply: "you ought to hev more respect for your elders, and not stand there and give them such empidence. Pretty broughten you must hev got, I know—a sassy little limb."

The latter part of this address was delivered in a muttered soliloquy, as she pushed the hood back from her face and shook the snow off her cloak. The "little limb," totally unheeding the reprimand, still stood peering up in her face, scanning its iron lineaments with an amusing mixture of curiosity and impudence.

As Miss Jerusha again turned round and encountered the piercing stare of

13

those great, dark, bright eyes fixed so unwinkingly on her face, she felt, for the first time in her life, perhaps, restless and uneasy under the infliction.

"My conscience! little gal, don't stare so! I 'clare to gracious I never see sich a child! I don't know what she looks like," said Miss Jerusha.

The latter sentence was not intended for the child's ears, but it reached those sharp little organs nevertheless, and, still keeping her needle-like gaze fixed on the wrinkled face of the spinster, she said:

"Well, if you don't, I know what *you* look like, anyway—I do!"

"And what do I look like?" said Miss Jerusha, in rising anger, having a presentiment something impudent was coming.

"Why just exactly like one of the witches in Macbeth."

Now, our worthy maiden lady had never heard of the "Noble Thane," but she had a pretty strong idea of what witches riding on broomsticks were like, and here this little black goblin girl had the audacity to compare her to one of them. For one awful moment Miss Jerusha glared upon the daring little sinner in impotent rage, while her fingers fairly ached to seize her and pound her within an inch of her life. Her face must have expressed her amiable desire, for the elf sprang back, and throwing herself into a stage attitude, uttered some words in a tragic voice, quite overpowering, coming from so small a body.

The noise awoke the sleeper near the fire. She turned restlessly, opened her eyes, and called:

"Georgia!"

"Here, mamma; here I am," said the elf, springing up and bending over her. "Do you want anything?"

"No, dear. I thought I heard you talking. Hasn't Warren come yet?"

"No, mamma."

"Then who were you talking to a moment ago? Is there any one here?"

"Yes, mamma, the funniest looking old woman—here, *you!*" said the elf, beckoning to Miss Jerusha.

Mechanically that lady obeyed the peremptory summons, too completely stunned and shocked by this unheard-of effrontery to fully realize for a moment that her ears had not deceived her.

She approached and bent over the sufferer. Two hollow eyes were raised to her face, and feeling herself in the awful presence of death, all Miss Jerusha's indignation faded away, and she said, in a softened voice:

"I am sorry to see you in this wretched place. Can I do anything for you?"

"Who are you?" said the woman, transfixing her with a gaze quite as uncompromising as her little daughter's had been.

"My name is Jerusha Skamp. I saw a light in this here cottage, and came over to see who was here. What can I do for you?"

"Nothing for me—I am dying," said the woman, in a husky, hollow voice. "Nothing for me; nothing for me."

"Oh, mamma! oh, mamma!" screamed the child, passionately. "Oh, not dying! Oh, mamma!"

"Oh, Georgia, hush!" said the woman, turning restlessly. "Don't shriek so, child; I cannot bear it."

But Georgia, who seemed to have no sort of self-control, or any other sort of control, still continued to scream her wild, passionate cry, "Oh, not dying! oh, mamma!" until Miss Jerusha, losing all patience, caught her arm in a vise-like grip, and, giving her a furious shake, said, in a deep, stern whisper:

"You little limb! Do you want to kill your mother? Hold your tongue, afore I shake the life out of you!"

The words had the effect of stilling the little tempest before her, who crouched into the corner and buried her face in her hands.

"Poor Georgia! poor little thing! what will become of her when I am gone?" said the sufferer, while a spasm of intense pain shot across her haggard face.

"The Lord will provide," said Miss Jerusha, rolling up the whites, or, more properly speaking, the yellows of her eyes. "Don't take on about that. Tell me how you came to be here! But first let me give you a drink. You look as if you needed something to keep life in you. Wait a minute."

Miss Jerusha's hawk-like eye went roving round the room until it alighted on a little tin cup. Seizing this, she filled it with the currant wine she had brought, and held it to the sick woman's lips.

Eagerly she drank, and then Miss Jerusha folded the shawl more closely around her, and, sitting down on the floor, drew her head upon her lap, and, with a touch that was almost tender, smoothed back the heavy locks of her dark hair.

"Now, then," she said, "tell me all about it."

"You are very kind," said the sick woman, looking up gratefully. "I feared I should die all alone here. I sent my little boy to the nearest house in search of help, but he has not yet returned."

"Ah! you're a widder, I suppose?" said Miss Jerusha, trying to keep down a pang of remorse and dread, as she thought of the child she had so cruelly turned out into the bitter storm.

"Yes, I have been a widow for the last seven years. My name is Alice Randall Darrell."

"And hain't you got no friends nor nothin', Mrs. Darrell, when you come to this old place, not fit for pigs, let alone human Christians?"

"No; no friends—not one friend in all this wide world," said the dying woman, in a tone so utterly despairing that Miss Jerusha's hand fell soothingly and pityingly on her forehead.

"Sho, now, sho! I want ter know," said Miss Jerusha, quite unconscious that she was making rhyme, a species of literature she had the profoundest contempt for. "That's *too* bad, 'clare if it ain't! Are they all dead?"

"I do not know—they are all dead to me."

"Why, what on airth hed you done to them?" said Miss Jerusha, in surprise.

"I married against my father's consent."

"Ah! that *was* bad; but then he needn't hev made a fuss. He didn't ask *your* consent when he got married, I s'pose. Didn't like the young man you kept company with, eh?"

"No; he hated him. My father was rich, and I ran off with a poor actor."

"A play-acter! Why, you must hev bin crazy!"

"Oh, I was—I was! I was a child, and did not know what I was doing. I thought my life with him would have been all light, and music, and glitter, and dazzle, such as I saw on the stage; but I soon found out the difference."

"'Spect you did. Law, law! what fools there is in this 'ere world!" said Miss Jerusha, in a moralizing tone.

"My father disowned me." ("And sarved you right, too!" put in Miss Jerusha *sotto voce*.) "My family cast me off. I joined the company to which my husband belonged, and did the tragedy business with him; and so for eight years we wandered about from city to city, from town to town, always poor and needy, for Arthur drank and gambled, and as fast as we earned money it was spent."

"And *you're* a play-acter, too!" cried Miss Jerusha recoiling in horror.

Miss Jerusha, trained in the land of "steady habits," had, from her earliest infancy, been taught to look upon theaters as only a little less horribly wicked than the place unmentionable to ears polite, and upon all "play-actors" as the immediate children and agents of the father of evil himself. She had never until now had the misfortune to come in contact with one personally, having only heard of them as we hear of goblins, warlocks, demons, and other "children of night." What wonder, then, that at this sudden, awful revelation she started back and almost hurled the frail form from her in loathing and horror. But a fierce clutch was laid on her shoulder—she almost fancied for an instant it was Satan himself come for his child—until, looking up, she saw the fiercely blazing eyes and witch-like face of little Georgia gleaming upon it.

"You ugly, wicked old woman!" she passionately burst out with, "if you dare to hurt my mamma, I'll—I'll *kill* you!"

And so dark, and fierce, and elfish did she look at that moment, that Miss Jerusha fairly quailed before the small, unearthly looking sprite.

"I'm not a-going to tetch your ma. Get out o' this, and leave me go!" said Miss Jerusha, shaking off with some difficulty the human burr who clung to her with the tenacity of a crab, and glared upon her with her shining black eyes.

"Georgia, love, go and sit down. Oh, you wild, stormy, savage child, what *ever* will become of you when I am gone? Do, pray, excuse her," said the woman, faintly, lifting her eyes pleadingly to Miss Jerusha's angry face; "she has had no one to control her, or subdue her wild, willful temper, and has grown up a crazy, mad-headed, half-tamed thing. If you have children of your own, you will know how to make allowance for her."

"I have no children of my own, and I thank goodness that I haven't!" said Miss Jerusha, shortly; "a set of plagues, the whole of 'em! Ef that there little gal was mine, I'd spank her while I could stand, and see ef *that* wouldn't take some of the nonsense out of her."

The last words did not reach the invalid's ear, and the little tempest-in-a-teapot retreated again to her corner, scowling darkly on Miss Jerusha, whom she evidently suspected of some sinister designs on her mother, which it was her duty to frustrate.

"Is she a play-acter, too?" said Miss Jerusha, after a sullen pause.

"Who? Georgia? Oh, yes; she plays juvenile parts, and dances and sings, and was a great favorite with the public. She has a splendid voice, and dances beautifully, and whenever she appeared she used to receive thunders of applause. Georgia will make a star actress if she ever goes on the stage again," said the woman, with more animation than she had yet shown.

"And do you want your darter to grow up a wicked good-for-nothing hussy of a play-acter?" said Miss Jerusha, sternly. "Mrs. Darrell, you ought for to be ashamed of yourself. Ef she was mine, I would sooner see her starve decently first."

The dying woman turned away with a groan.

"She won't starve here, though," said Miss Jerusha, feeling called upon to administer a little consolation; "there's trustees and selectmen, and one thing and another to look arter poor folks and orphans. She'll be took care of. And now, how did it happen you came here?"

"I came with the company to which I belong, and we stopped at a town about fifty miles from here. Georgia, as you can see, has a dreadful temper—poor little fiery, passionate thing—and the manager of the theater, being an insolent, overbearing man, was always finding fault with her, and scolding about something, whereupon Georgia would fly into one of her fits of passion, and a dreadful scene would ensue. I strove to keep them apart as much as I could, but they often met, as a matter of course, and never parted without a furious quarrel. He did not wish to part with her, for I—and it is with little vanity, alas! I say it—was his best actress, and Georgia's name in the bills never failed to draw a crowded house. I used to talk to Georgia, and implore her to restrain her fierce temper, and she would promise; but when next she would meet him, poor child, and listen to his insulting words, all would be forgotten, and Georgia would stamp and scold, and call him all manner of names, and sometimes go so far as to refuse appearing at all, and *that* last act of disobedience never failed to put him fairly beside himself with rage. I foresaw how it would end, but I could do nothing with her. Poor little thing! Nature cursed her with that fierce, passionate temper, and she could not help it."

"Humph!" muttered Miss Jerusha; "couldn't help it! That's all very fine; but I know one thing, ef *I* had anything to do with her, I'd take the fierceness out of her, or know for why—a ugly tempered, savage little limb!"

"One night," continued the sick woman, "Georgia had been dancing, and when she left the stage the whole house shook with the thunders of applause. They shouted and shouted for her to reappear, but I was sick that night, and Georgia was in a hurry to get home, and would not go. The manager ordered her in no very gentle tone to go back, and Georgia flatly and peremptorily refused. Then a dreadful scene ensued. He caught her by the arms, and dragged her to her feet, as if he would force her out, and when she resisted he struck her a blow that sent her reeling across the room.

"Aha! that was good for you, my lady!" said Miss Jerusha, with a grim chuckle, as she glanced at the little dancing girl.

"It was the first time any one had ever struck her," said Mrs. Darrell, in a sinking voice, "and a very fury seemed to seize her. A large black bottle lay on a shelf near, and with a perfect *shriek* of passion she seized it and hurled it with all her strength at his head."

"My gracious!" ejaculated the horrified Miss Jerusha.

"It struck him on the forehead, and laid it open with a frightful gash. He attempted to spring upon her, but some of the men interposed, and Georgia was forced off by the rest. Her brother Warren was there, and, almost terrified to death, he brought her home with him, and that very night we were told our services were no longer needed, and, what was more, Mr. B., the manager, refused to pay us what he owed us, and even threatened to begin an action against us for assault and battery, and I don't know what besides. I knew him to be an unprincipled, vindictive man, and the threat terrified me nearly to death, terrified me so much that, with my two children, I fled the next morning from the town where we were stopping, fled away with only one idea—that of escaping from his power. I had a little money remaining, but it was soon spent, and I was so weak and ill that but for my poor children I felt at times as if I could gladly have lain down and died.

"Coming from Burnfield to-night, we were overtaken by this storm, and must have perished had not Warren discovered this old hut. The exposure of this furious storm completed what sorrow and suffering had long ago begun, and I felt I was dying. It was terrible to think of leaving poor little Warren and Georgia all alone without one single friend in the world, and at last I sent Warren out to the nearest house in the hope that some hospitable person might come who would procure some sort of employment for them that would keep them at least from starving. *You* came, thank Heaven! but my poor Warren has not returned. Oh! I fear, I *fear* he has perished in this storm," cried the dying woman, wringing her pale fingers.

"Oh, I guess not," said Miss Jerusha, more startled than she chose to appear; "most likely he's gone some place else and stayed there to get warm; but you, *you*, what are we to do for you? It doesn't seem Christian like nor proper no ways to leave you to die here in this miserable old shed."

"Dear, kind friend, never mind me," said the invalid, gratefully; "my short span of life is nearly run, and oh! what does it matter whether for the few brief moments yet remaining where they are spent. But my children, my poor, poor children! Oh, madam, you have a kind heart, I know you have,"—(Miss

Jerusha gave a skeptical "humph!")—"do, *do*, for Heaven's sake, try if some charitable person will not take them and give them their food and clothing. Not so much for Warren do I fear, for he is quiet and sensible, very wise indeed for his age; but for the wild, stormy Georgia. Oh, madam, do something for her, and my dying thanks will be yours!"

"Well, there, don't take on! I'll see what can be done," said Miss Jerusha, fidgeting, and glancing askance at the wild eyed, tempestuous little spirit, "and though you don't seem to mind it much, still it don't seem right nor decent for you to die here like I don't know what," (Miss Jerusha's favorite simile), "so I'll jest step over to Deacon Brown's and get him to look arter you, and maybe he will hev an eye to the children, too."

"But you will be exposed to the storm," feebly remonstrated the dying woman.

"Bah! who keers for the storm?" said Miss Jerusha, glancing out of the window with a look of grim defiance. "Besides, its clarin' off, and Deacon Brown's ain't more than two miles from here. There, keep up your sperrits, and I'll be back in an hour or two with the deacon."

So saying, Miss Jerusha, who once she considered it her *duty* to do anything, would have gone through fire and flood to do it, stepped resolutely out to brave once more the cold, wintry blast.

The storm had abated considerably, but it was still piercingly cold, and Miss Jerusha's fingers and toes tingled as she walked rapidly over the hard, frosty ground. It had ceased snowing, and a pale, watery moon, appearing at intervals from behind a cloud, cast a faint, sickly light over the way. The high, leafless trees sent long black, ominous shadows across the road, and Miss Jerusha cast apprehensive glances on either side as she walked.

Not the fear of ghosts, nor the fear of robbers troubled the stout-hearted spinster; but the dread of seeing a slight, boyish form, stark and frozen, across her path. In mingled dread and remorse, she thought of what she had done and only the hope of finding him in the old cottage on her return could dispel for an instant her haunting fear.

Deacon Brown's was reached at last, and great was the surprise of that orthodox pillar of the church at beholding his un-looked-for visitor. In very few words Miss Jerusha gave him to understand the object of her visit, and, rather ruefully, the good man rose to harness up his old gray mare and start with Miss Jerusha on this charitable errand.

A quick run over the hard, frozen ground brought them to the cottage, and, fastening his mare to a tree, the deacon followed Miss Jerusha into the old house.

And there a pitiful sight met his eyes. The fire had gone out, and the room was scarcely warmer than the freezing atmosphere without. Mother and child lay clasped in each other's arms, still and motionless. With a stifled ejaculation, Miss Jerusha approached and bent over them. The child was asleep, and the mother was *dead*!

CHAPTER III.

A YOUNG TORNADO.

"She is active, stirring, all fire;
Cannot rest, cannot tire;
To a stone she had given life."

 was a bright, breezy May morning, just cool enough to render a fire pleasant and a brisk walk delightful. The sunshine came streaming down through the green, spreading boughs of the odorous pine trees, gilding their glistening leaves, and tinting with hues of gold the sparkling windows of Miss Jerusha's little cottage.

It was yet early morning, and the sun had just arisen, yet Miss Jerusha, brisk, resolute, and energetic, marched through the house, "up stairs, and down stairs, and in my lady's chamber," sweeping, dusting, scouring, scrubbing and scolding, all in a breath: for, reader, this was Monday, and that good lady was just commencing her spring "house-cleaning."

And Miss Jerusha's house-cleaning was something which required to be seen to be appreciated. Not that there was the slightest necessity for that frantic and distracting process which all good housekeepers consider it a matter of conscience to make their household suffer once or twice a year, for never since Miss Jerusha had come to the years of discretion had a single speck of dirt been visible to the naked eye inside of those spotless walls. But it was with Miss Jerusha the eleventh commandment and the fortieth article of the Episcopal creed, to go through a vigorous and uncompromising scouring down and scrubbing up every spring and fall, to the great mental agony and bodily torture of the unhappy little handmaiden, Fly, and her venerable cat, Betsey Periwinkle. Since the middle of April Miss Jerusha had shown signs of the coming epidemic, which on this eventful morning broke out in full force.

Any stranger, on looking in at that usually immaculate cottage, might have fancied a hurricane had passed through it in the night, or that the chairs, and tables, and pots, and pans, being of a facetious disposition, had taken it into their heads to get on a spree the night before, and pitch themselves in all sorts of frantic attitudes through the house. For the principal rule in Miss Jerusha's "house-cleaning" was first, with a great deal of pains and trouble, to fling chairs, and stools, and pails, and brooms in a miscellaneous heap through each room, to disembowel closets whose contents for the last six months had been a sealed mystery to human eyes, to take down and violently tear asunder unoffending bedsteads, and with a stout stick inflict a severe and apparently unmerited castigation on harmless mattresses and feather beds. This done, Miss Jerusha, who had immense faith in the hot water system, commenced with a steaming tub of that liquid at the topmost rafter of the cottage, and never drew breath until every crevice and cranny down to the lowest plank on the cellar floor had undergone a severe application of first wetting and then drying.

Awful beyond measure was Miss Jerusha on these occasions—enough to strike terror into the heart of every shiftless mortal on this terrestrial globe, could he only have seen her. With her sleeves rolled up over her elbows, her mouth shut up, *screwed* up with grim determination of conquering or dying in the attempt, with an eye like a hawk for every invisible speck of dust, and the firm, determined tramp of the leader of a forlorn hope, Miss Jerusha marched through that blessed little cottage, a broom in one hand and a scrubbing-brush in the other, a sight to see, not to hear of.

And then, having brushed, and scrubbed, and scoured, and polished everything, from the "best room" down to the fur coat of Betsey Periwinkle, until it fairly shone, all that could offend the sight was poked back into the mysterious closets again, another revolution swept through every room, returning things to their places, and the whole household was triumphantly restored to its former state of distressing cleanliness. And thus ended Miss Jerusha's house-cleaning.

"Them there three beds shill all hev to come down this morning," said Miss Jerusha, folding her arms, and regarding them grimly, "and every one of them blessed bedposts hev got to be scalded right out. You, Fly! is that there fire a-burning?"

"Yes, miss," answered Fly, who was tearing distractedly in and out after wood and water, and as nearly fulfilling the impossibility of being in two places at once as it was possible for a mere mortal to do.

"And is that biler of hot water a-bilin'?"

"Yes, miss."

"And did you tell Georgey to go down to Bunfield for some yaller soap?"

"Please, Miss Jerry, I couldn't find her."

"Couldn't find her, hey? What's the reason you couldn't find her?" said Miss Jerusha, in a high key.

"'Case she'd been and gone away some whars. Please, ole miss, dar ain't nebber no sayin' whar anybody can find dat ar young gal," replied Fly, beginning to whimper in anticipation of getting her ears boxed for not performing an impossibility.

"Gone away! arter being told to stay at home and help with the house-cleaning! Oh, the little shif'less villain. I 'clare ef I hadn't a good mind to give her the best switchin' ever she got next time I ketch holt of her. Told me this morning she wasn't going to be a dish-washing old maid like me! a sassy, impident little monster! Old, indeed! I vow to gracious only for she dodged I'd hev twisted her neck for her! Old! hump! a pretty thing to be called at my time o' life! Old, indeed! A nasty, ungrateful little imp!"

While she spoke, the outer gate was slammed violently to; a slight little figure ran swiftly up the walk, and burst like a whirlwind into the sacred precincts of the best room—a small, light, airy figure, dressed in black, with crimson cheeks, and dancing, sparkling, flashing black eyes, fairly blazing with life and health, and freedom, and high spirits—a swift, blinding, dark, bright vision, so quick and impetuous in every motion as to startle you—a "thing all life and light," a little tropical butterfly, with the hidden sting of a wasp, impressing the beholder with the idea of a barrel of gunpowder, a pop-gun, a firecracker, or anything else, very harmless and quiet-looking, but ready to explode and go off with a bang at any moment.

It was Georgia—our little Georgia; and how she came to be an inmate of Miss Jerusha's cottage it requires us to go back a little to tell.

On that very Christmas Eve, when with Deacon Drown she discovered the sleeping child and the ruined cottage, she was for a moment at a loss what to do. She knew the girl had fallen asleep, unconscious of the dread presence, and she had seen enough of her to be aware of the frantic and passionate scene that must ensue when she awoke and discovered her loss. She bent over her, and finding her sleeping heavily, she lifted her gently in her arms, and in a few whispered words desired the deacon not to remove the corpse, but to drive her home first with the orphan.

Wrapping the half-frozen child in her warm cloak, she had taken her seat, and was driven to the cottage without arousing her from her heavy slumber, and safely deposited her in Fly's little bed, to the great astonishment, not to say indignation, of that small, black individual, at finding her couch thus taken summary possession of.

It was late next morning when the little dancing girl awoke, and then she sprang up and gazed around her with an air of complete bewilderment. Her first glance fell on Miss Jerusha, who was bustling around, helping Fly to get breakfast, and the sight of that yellow, rigid frontispiece seemed to recall her to a realization of what had passed the preceding night.

She sprang up, shook back her thick, disordered black hair, and exclaimed:

"Who brought me here?"

"I did, honey," said Miss Jerusha, speaking as gently as *she* knew how, which is not saying much.

"Where is mamma?"

"Oh, she's—how did you sleep last night?" said Miss Jerusha, actually quailing inwardly in anticipation of the coming scene; for, with her strong nerves and plain, practical view of things in general, the good old lady had a masculine horror of scenes.

"Where is my mamma?" said the child, sharply, fixing her piercing black eyes on Miss Jerusha's face.

"Oh, she's—well, she ain't here."

"Where is she, then? You ugly old thing, what have you done to my mamma?"

"Ugly old thing! Oh, dear bless me! *there's* a way to speak to her elders!" said the deeply shocked Miss Jerusha.

"*Where's my mamma?*" exclaimed the child, with a fierce stamp of the foot.

"Little gal, look here! that ain't no way to talk to—"

"WHERE'S MY MAMMA?" fairly shrieked the little girl, as she sprang forward and clutched Miss Jerusha's arm so fiercely as to extort from her a cry of pain.

"Ah-a-a-a-a-a! Oh-h-h-h! you little crab-fish, if you ain't pinched my arm black and blue! Your mamma's dead, and it's a pity you ain't along with her," said Miss Jerusha, in her anger and pain, giving the girl a push that sent her reeling against the wall.

"Dead!"

The word fell like a blow on the child, stunning her into quiet. Her mamma dead! She could not realize—she could not comprehend it.

She stood as if frozen, her hand uplifted as it had been when she heard it, her lips apart, her eyes wide open and staring. Dead! She stood still, stunned, bewildered.

Miss Jerusha was absolutely terrified. She had expected tears, cries, passionate grief, but not this ominous stillness. That fixed, rigid, unnatural look chilled her blood. She went over and shook the child in her alarm.

"Little girl! Georgey! don't look so—*don't*! It ain't right, you know!"

She turned her eyes slowly to Miss Jerusha's face, her lips parted, and one word slowly dropped out:

"Mamma!"

"Honey, your ma's dead, and gone to heaven—I *hope*," said Miss Jerusha, who felt that common politeness required her to say so, although she had her doubts on the subject. "You mustn't take on about it, you—Oh, gracious! the child's gone stark, staring mad!"

Her words had broken the spell. Little Georgia realized it all at last. With a shriek,—a wild, terrific shriek, that Miss Jerusha never forgot—she threw up her arms and fell prostrate on the ground.

And there she lay and *shrieked*. She did not faint. Miss Jerusha, with her hands clasped over her bruised and wounded ear-drums, wished from the bottom of her heart she *would*; but Georgia was of too sanguine a temperament to faint. Shriek after shriek, sharp, prolonged, and shrill, broke from her lips as she lay on her face on the floor, her hands clasped over her head.

Miss Jerusha and Fly, nearly frantic with the ear-splitting torture, strove to raise her up, but the little fury seemed endowed with supernatural strength, and screamed and struggled, and *bit* at them like a mad thing, until they were glad enough to go off and leave her alone. And there she lay and screamed for a full hour, until even *her* lungs of brass gave way, and shrieks absolutely refused to come.

Then a new spirit seemed to enter the child. She leaped to her feet as if those members were furnished with steel springs, and made for the door. Fortunately, Miss Jerusha had locked it, somehow anticipating some such movement, and in that quarter she was foiled. She seized the lock and shook the door furiously, stamping with impotent passion at finding it resist all her efforts.

"Open the door!" she screamed, with a stamp, turning upon Miss Jerusha a pair of eyes that glowed like those of a young tigress.

The old lady actually shrank under the burning light of that dark, passionate glance, but composedly sat still and knit away.

"OPEN THE DOOR!" shrieked the mad child, shaking it so fiercely that Miss Jerusha fairly expected to see the lock come off before her eyes.

But the lock resisted her efforts. Delirious with her frantic rage, the wild girl dashed her head against it with a shriek of foiled passion—dashed it against it again and again, until it was all cut and bleeding; and then she flew at the horrified Miss Jerusha like a very fury, sinking her long nails in her face and tearing off the skin, like a maniac as she was.

That at last aroused all Miss Jerusha's wiry strength, and, grasping the child's wrists in a vise-like grip, she held her fast while she struggled to free herself in vain, for the fictitious strength given her by her storm of passion had exhausted itself by its very violence, and every effort now to free herself grew fainter and fainter, until at last she swayed to and fro, tottered, and would have fallen had not Miss Jerusha held her fast.

Lifting her in her arms, Miss Jerusha bore her upstairs and laid her in her own bed. And then over-charged nature gave way, and, burying her face in the pillow, Georgia burst into a passionate flood of tears, sobbing convulsively. Long she wept, until the fountains of her tears were dry, and then, worn out by her own violence, she fell into a dreamless sleep.

"Well, my sakes alive!" said Miss Jerusha, drawing a long breath and getting up, "of all the children ever I seen I never saw any like that there little limb. 'Clare to gracious! there's something bad inside that young gal—that's my opinion. Sich eyes, like blazin' coals of fire! My conscience! I really don't feel safe with her in the house."

But Georgia awoke calm and utterly exhausted, and thus passed away the first violence of her grief, which like a blaze of straw, burned up fiercely for a moment and then went out in black ashes. Still grave and unsmiling the little girl went about, with no life in her face save what burned in her great wild eyes.

Her mother was buried, and so Miss Jerusha with some inward fear and trembling ventured to tell her at last; but the child heard it quietly enough. She need not have feared, for it was morally and physically impossible for the little girl to ever get up another passion-gust like the last.

One source of secret and serious anxiety to Miss Jerusha was the fate of the little boy, Warren Darrell. Since that night when she had turned him from the door, nothing had ever been heard of him; no one had seen him, no traces of him could be found, and one and all came to the conclusion that he must have perished in the storm that night. Miss Jerusha too, had to adopt the same belief at last, and in that moment she felt as though she had been guilty of a murder. No one knew he had come to the cottage, and she had her own reason for keeping it a secret, and for politely informing Fly she would twist her neck for her if she ever mentioned it; and in dread of that disagreeable operation, Fly consented to hold her tongue.

Feeling as if she ought to do something to atone for the guilt of which her conscience, so often referred to by herself, accused her, Miss Jerusha resolved, by way of the severest penance she could think of, to adopt Georgia. Several of the "selectmen" offered to take the child and send her to the workhouse, but Miss Jerusha curtly refused in terms much shorter than sweet, and snappishly requested them to go and mind their own affairs and she would mind little Georgia Darrell.

And so, from that day the little dancer became an inmate of the lonely seaside cot. For the first few weeks she was preternaturally grave and still—"in the dumps" Miss Jerusha called it; then this passed away—like all the grief of childhood, ever light and short-lived—and *then* Miss Jerusha began to realize the trouble and tribulations in store for her, and the life of worry and vexation of spirit the restless elf would lead her.

In the first place, Miss Georgia emphatically and decidedly "put her foot down," and gave her *guardianess* (if such a word is admissible) to understand, in the plainest possible English, that she had not the remotest or faintest idea of doing one single hand's turn of work.

"I never had to work," said the young lady, drawing herself up, "and I ain't a-going to begin now for anybody. I don't believe in work at all, and I don't think it proper, no way."

In vain Miss Jerusha expostulated; her little ladyship heard her with the most provoking indifference. Then the old lady began to scold, whereupon Georgia flew into one of her "tantrums," as Miss Jerusha called them, and, springing to her feet, exclaimed:

"I *won't*, then, not if I die for it! I've always done just whatever I liked, and I'm going to keep on doing it—I just *am*! And I ain't going to be an old pot-wiper for anybody—I just *ain't*, old taffy candy!"

And then the sprite bounced out, banging the door after her until the house shook, leaving Miss Jerusha to stand transfixed with horror and indignation at this last "most unkindest cut of all," which referred to the candy Miss Jerusha was in the habit of making and selling in Burnfield.

And thus the wild, fearless child kept the old lady in a constant series of tremors and palpitations by the dangers she ran into headlong. Not a tree in the forest she would not climb like a squirrel, and often the dry frozen branches breaking with her, she would find it impossible to get down again, and have to remain there until Miss Jerusha would get a ladder and take her down. And on these occasions, while the old lady scolded and ranted down below, the young lady up in her lofty perch would be in convulsions of laughter at her look of terror and dismay. Not a rock on the beach, slippery and icy as they were, she had not clambered innumerable times, to the manifest danger of breaking her neck.

It was well for her she could climb and cling to them like a cat, or she would most assuredly have been killed; as it was, she tumbled off two or three times, thereby raising more bumps on her head than Nature ever placed there. Then she made a point of visiting Burnfield every day, and making herself acquainted generally with the inhabitants of that little "one-horse town," astonishing the natives to such a degree by the facility with which she stood on her head, or made a hoop of herself by catching her feet in her hands and rolling over and over, that some of them had serious doubts whether she was real, or only an optical delusion. And then her dancing! The first time Miss Jerusha saw her she came nearer fainting than she had ever done before in her life.

"Oh, my gracious!" said Miss Jerusha, in tones of horror, when afterward relating the occurrence, "I never see sich onchristian actions before in all my born days. There she was a-flinging of her legs about as if they belonged to somebody else, and a-twistin' of her arms about over her head, and a-jigging back and forward, and a-standin' onto one blessed toe and spinnin' round like a top, with the other leg a stickin' straight out like a toastin'-fork. I 'clare it gave me sich a turn as I hain't got over yit, and never expects to. Oh, my conscience! It was railly orful to look at the onnatural shapes that there little limb could twist herself into. And to think of her, when she got done, a-kneelin' down on one knee as if she was sayin' of her prayers, as she ought for to do, and then take and blow me up for not applaudin', as she called it. A sassy little wiper!"

Georgia's daily visits to Burnfield were a serious annoyance to Miss Jerusha; for there were some who delighted in her wild antics, just as they would in the mischievous pranks of a monkey, encouraged her in her willfulness, and exhorted her to defy the "Old Dragon," as Miss Jerusha was incorrectly styled. And such a hold did these counsels take on the mind of the young girl, that she really began to look upon Miss Jerusha in the light of a domestic tyrant—a sort of female Bluebeard, whom it would not only be right and just to defy and put down, but morally wrong *not* to do it. But though this was Georgia's inward belief, yet, to her credit be it spoken, a sort of chivalrous feeling led her always to defend Miss Jerusha on these occasions; and if any one went too far in sneering at her, Georgia's little brown fist was doubled up, and the offender, unless warned by some prudent friend to "look out for squalls," stood in considerable danger.

Then, too, the chief delight of the Burnfieldians was in watching her dance; and Georgia, nothing loth, would mount an extempore platform, and whirl, and pirouette, and flash hither and thither, amid thunders of applause from the astonished and delighted audience. Her singing, too—for Georgia had really a beautiful voice, and knew every song that ever was heard of, from Casta Diva to Jim Crow—was a source of never-failing delight to the townfolks, who were troubled with very few amusements in winter; and Georgia was never really in her element save when dancing, or singing, or showing off before an audience.

And so the little explosive grenade became a well known character in Burnfield, and Miss Jerusha's injunctions to stay from it went the way of all good advice—that is, in one ear and out of the other. No sort of weather could keep the sprite in the house. The fiercer the wind blew, Georgia's high spirit only rose the higher; the keener the cold, the more piercing the blast, it only flashed a deeper crimson to her glowing cheeks and lips, and kindled a clearer light in her bright black eyes, and she bounded like a young antelope over the frozen ground, shouting with irrepressible life. Out amid the wildest winter storms you might see that small dark figure flying along with streaming hair, bending and dipping to the shrieking blast that could have whirled her light form away like a feather, flying over the icy ground that her feet hardly seemed to touch.

Georgia, wild, fervid child, vowed she *loved* the storms; and on tempestuous nights, when the wind howled, and raved, and shook the cottage, and roared through the pines, she would clap her hands in glee, and run down through it all toward the high rocks near the shore, and bend over them to feel the salt spray from the white-crested waves dash in her face. Then, coming back, she would scandalize Miss Jerusha, and terrify Fly nearly into fits, by protesting that the white caps of the waves were the bleached faces of drowned men holding a revel with the demons of the storm, and that whenever *she* died, she was determined to be buried in the sand, for that no grave or coffin could ever hold her, and she knew she would have splendid times with the mermaids, and mermen, and old Father Neptune, and Mrs. Amphitrite, and the rest of them, in their coral grottoes down below.

Now, Miss Jerusha was by no means strait-laced in spiritual matters herself, but such an ungodly belief as this would shock even her, and, with a deeply horrified look, she would lay down her knitting and begin:

"Oh, my stars and garters! sich talk! Don't you know, you wicked child, that there ain't no sich place as that under the sun? There's nothing but mud, and fish-bones, and nasty sharks like what swallered Joner down there. No, you misfortunate little limb, folks allers goes to heaven or t'other place when they die, and it's my belief you'll take a trip downward, and sarve you right, too, you wicked little heathen you!"

"See here, Miss Jerusha," said Georgia, curiously, "Emily Murray says there's another place—sort of half-way house, you know, with a hard name; let's see

—pug—pug—no, *purgatory*, that's it—where people that ain't been horrid bad nor yet horrid good goes to, and after being scorched for awhile to take the badness out of them, they go up to heaven and settle down there for good. Is that so, Miss Jerusha?"

"There!" said Miss Jerusha, dropping her knitting in consternation, "I allers said no good would come of her going to Burnfield and taking up with unbelievers and other wagrants. Oh, you wicked, drefful little gal! *No*; there ain't no sich place; in course there ain't. If you had read that pretty chapter I gave you in the Bible last Sunday instead of tying Betsey Perwinkle's tail to her hind leg and nearly setting of her crazy, you wouldn't be such a benighted little heathen as you are."

"Well, I didn't like it—there! All about two ugly great bears eating a lot of children for calling somebody names. I don't like things like that. There ain't no fun in reading about them, and I'd a heap sooner read Robinson Crusoe; *he* was a nice old man, I know he was. And when I grow up to be a big woman, I'm going to find out his island and live there myself—you see if I don't."

Miss Jerusha gave a contemptuous snort.

"*You* grow up, indeed! As if the Lord would let a wicked little wretch like you, that believes in gods and goddesses and purgatory and such abominations grow up. No; if you ain't carried off in a flash of fire and brimstone, like King Solomon or some of them, you may think yourself safe, my lady."

"Well, I don't care if I am," said Georgia. "I *do* believe in mermaids, because I've seen them often and often, and I know they live in beautiful coral grottoes under the sea, because I've read all about it. And I know there are witches, and ghosts and fairies, because I've read all about *them* in the 'Legends of the Hartz Mountains,' the nicest book that ever was, and some Hallow Eve I'm going to try some tricks—you see if I don't."

The little girl's eyes were sparkling, and she was gesticulating with eager earnestness. Miss Jerusha held up her hands in horror.

"My-y conscience! only hear her! Oh, what *ever* will become of that there young gal? Why, you wicked child, where do you expect to go when you die?"

"To heaven," said Georgia, decidedly.

"Humph!" said Miss Jerusha, contemptuously. "A nice angel *you'd* make, wouldn't you? More likely the other place. I shill hev to speak to Mr. Barebones to take you into his Bible class, for I believe in my soul it ain't safe to sleep in the house with such an unbeliever."

"Well, you may speak to him as fast as you like, but I sha'n't go. A sour, black old ogre, all skin and bones, like a consumptive red herring! I'm going with Emily Murray to that nice church where they have all the pretty pictures, and that nice old man, Em's uncle, with no hair on his head, and all dressed up so beautifully. And old Father Murray is just the dearest old man ever was, and hasn't got a long, solemn face like Mr. Barebones. Come, Bets, let you and I have a waltz."

And seizing Betsey Periwinkle by the two fore-paws, she went whirling with her round the room, to the great astonishment, not to say indignation, of that amiable animal, who decidedly disapproved of waltzing in her own proper person, and began to expostulate in sundry indignant mews quite unheeded by her partner, until Miss Jerusha angrily snatched her away, and would have favored Georgia with a box on the ear, only the recollection of the theatre manager returned to her memory, and her uplifted hand dropped. And Georgia, laughing her shrill, peculiar laugh, danced out of the room, singing a snatch from some elegant ditty.

"Was there ever such a aggravating young 'un?" exclaimed Miss Jerusha, relapsing into her chair. "I sartinly *shill* hev to speak to Mr. Barebones about her. Gracious! what a thing it is to be afflicted with children!"

True to her word, Miss Jerusha did speak to Mr. Barebones, and that zealous Christian promised to take Georgia in hand; but the young lady not only flatly refused to listen to a word, but told him her views of matters and things in general, and of himself in particular, so plainly and decidedly, that, in high dudgeon, the minister got up, put on his hat, and took himself off.

And so Miss Georgia was left to her own devices, and stood in a fair way of becoming a veritable savage, when an event occurred that gave a new spring to her energies, and turned the current of her existence in another direction.

CHAPTER IV.

GEORGIA MAKES SOME NEW ACQUAINTANCES.

"His boyish form was middle size,
For feat of strength or exercise
    Shaped in proportion fair;
And hazel was his eagle eye,
And auburn of the darkest dye
    His short and curling hair.
Light was his footstep in the dance,
    And firm his stirrup in the lists—
And, oh, he had that merry glance
    That seldom lady's heart resists."—SCOTT.

 ss Jerusha's memorable "house-cleaning" was over, and the cottage having been polished till it shone, and everything inside and outside reduced to the frightfully clean state that characterized everything belonging to that worthy lady, she was prepared to sit down and enjoy the reward of her labors, and the pleasure of an approving conscience. Fly and Betsey Periwinkle, who had been in an excessively damp and limber state for the last few days, and whom Miss Jerusha had kept tearing in and out and up and down like a couple of comets, were at last permitted to dry out, and might now safely venture to call their souls their own again.

Georgia, who rather liked a fuss than otherwise, quite enjoyed the house-cleaning, and spent an unusually large portion of her valuable time at the cottage while that domestic revolution was in full blast; now that it was over, she began to resume her slightly vagabondish habit of roaming round the country, always up to her eyes in business, yet never bringing about any particular result excepting that of mischief. When Georgia wished to enjoy the pleasures of solitude, which was not often, she strolled off to the beach, where, perched on top of a high rock, she meditated on the affairs of the State, or whatever other subject happened to weigh on her mind at the moment.

One morning she started off for her favorite seat in order to have a quite read, having inveigled Miss Jerusha out of the "Pilgrim's Progress" for that purpose, in lieu of something more entertaining. Now this beach being so far removed from Burnfield, its solitude was rarely, if ever, disturbed; therefore, great was Georgia's surprise upon reaching it, to find a shady spot under her own favorite rock already occupied.

Miss Georgia came to a sudden halt, and, standing on tiptoe, gravely surveyed the new-comer, herself unseen.

Under the shadow of the overhanging rock, on the warm sands, lay a tall, slight, fashionably dressed youth, of sixteen or thereabouts, with handsome, regular features, a complexion of feminine fairness, a profusion of brown, curling hair, a high forehead, and unusually and aristocratically small hands and feet, the former as white as a lady's. The predominating expression of his face was a mixture of indolence and drollery; and as he lay there, with his half closed eyes, he looked the very picture of the *dolce far niente*.

"Well, now," thought Georgia, "I wonder who *you* are, and where you came from. I'll just go and ask him, though I do believe he's asleep. If he is, I reckon I'll wake him in double-quick time."

And Georgia, not being in the slightest degree troubled with that disease incident to youth, previous to the days of Young America, yclept bashfulness, marched up to the intruder, and planting herself before him, put her arms akimbo, and assuming a look of stern investigation, began:

"Ahem! See here, *you*, where did you come from?"

The young gentleman thus addressed leisurely opened a pair of large, dark eyes, and quietly surveyed his interrogator from head to foot, without disturbing himself in the slightest degree, or betraying the smallest intention of moving.

Very properly provoked at this aggravating conduct, Georgia's voice rose an octave higher, as she said, authoritatively:

"Can't you speak? Haven't you a tongue? I suppose it's the last improvement in politeness not to answer when you're spoken to."

This speech seemed to bring the young gentleman to a proper sense of his errors. Getting up on his elbow, he took off his hat and began:

"My dear young lady, I beg ten thousand pardons, but really at the moment you spoke I was just debating within myself whether you were a veritable fact or only an optical illusion. Having now satisfied myself on that head, I beg you will repeat your questions, which, unfortunately, in the excitement of the moment, I did not pay proper attention to, and any information regarding myself personally and privately, or concerning the world at large, that it lies in my power to offer you, I shall be only too happy to communicate."

And with this speech the young gentleman bowed once more, without rising, however, replaced his hat, and getting himself into a comfortable position, lay back on the sands, and supporting his head on his hands, composedly waited to be cross-examined.

"Humph!" said Georgia, regarding him doubtfully. "What is your name?"

"My name is Norval; on the Grampian hills—that is, it might have been Norval, only it happened to be Wildair—Charley Wildair, at your service, noted for nothing in particular but good-nature and idleness. And now, having satisfied your natural and laudable curiosity on that point, may I humbly venture to ask the name of the fascinating young lady who at this particular moment honors me with her presence?"

"Well, you may. My name's Georgia Darrell, and I live up there in that little cottage. Now, where do *you* live?"

"Miss Darrell, allow me to observe that it affords me the most dreadful and excruciating happiness to make the acquaintance of so charming and accomplished a young lady as yourself, and also to observe, that in all my wanderings through this nether world, it has never been my good fortune before to behold so perfectly fascinating a cottage as that to which you refer. Regarding my own place of residence, I cannot inform you positively, being a —'in point of fact,' as my cousin Feenix has it—a wanderer and vagabond on the face of the earth, with no fixed place of abode. My maternal ancestor resides in a place called Brooklyn, a younger sister of New York city, and when not doing up my education in the aforesaid city, I honor that venerable roof-tree with my presence. At present, if you observe, I am vegetating in the flourishing and intensely slow town of Burnfield over yonder, with my respected and deeply venerated uncle, Mr. Robert Richmond, a gentleman chiefly remarkable for the length of his purse and the shortness of his temper."

"Squire Richmond's nephews! I heard they had come. Are you them?" inquired Georgia, stepping back a pace, and speaking in a slightly awed tone.

"Exactly, Miss Darrell. With your usual penetration and good genius, you have hit the right thing exactly in the middle; only, if you will allow me, I must insinuate that I am not his nephews—not being an editor, I have not the good fortune to be a plural individual; but with my Brother Richard we do, I am happy to inform you, constitute the dutiful nephews of your Burnfield magnate, Squire Richmond."

"Hum-m-m!" said Georgia, looking at him with a puzzled expression, and not exactly liking his indolent look and intensely ceremonious tone. "You ain't laughing at me, are you?"

"Laughing at you! Miss Darrell, if you'll just be kind enough to cast an eye on my countenance you'll observe it's considerably more serious than an undertaker's, or that of a man with a sick wife when told she is likely to recover. Allow me to observe, Miss Darrell, that I suffered through the 'principles of politeness' when I was an innocent and guileless little shaver, in checked pinafores, and I hope I know the proprieties better than to laugh at a lady. A fellow that would laugh at a young woman, Miss Darrell, deserves to be—to be—a—a mark for the finger of scorn to poke fun at! Yes, Miss Darrell, I repeat it, he deserves to be a—I don't know what he doesn't deserve to be!" said Mr. Wildair, firmly.

"Well," said Georgia, rather mollified, "and what did you come up here for, anyway, eh?"

"Why, you see, Miss Darrell, the fact was, I was what you call expelled,—which being translated from the original Greek into plain slang, the chosen language of young America,—means I was politely requested to vamose."

"Oh," said Georgia, puckering up her lips as though she were going to whistle, "you mean they turned you out?"

"Pre-cisely! exactly! They couldn't properly appreciate me, you know. Genius never is appreciated, if you observe, but is always neglected, and snubbed, and put upon, in this world. Look at Shakespeare, and Oliver Goldsmith, and all those other old fellows that got up works of fiction, and see the hard times and tribulations they had of it."

"And how long are you going to stay here?" asked Georgia.

"That depends upon as long as I behave nicely, and don't endeavor to corrupt the minds of the rising generation of Burnfield, I suppose. I've been a perfect angel since I came, and would be at all times if they didn't aggravate me. My mother was very disagreeable."

"My mother was not—mamma never was disagreeable," said Georgia.

"Indeed! Wonderful old lady she must have been then! Is she living?"

"No: she's dead," said Georgia, looking down with filling eyes.

"Ah! excuse me. I didn't know," said the boy, hastily. "And your father?"

"Dead, too."

"Possible! With whom do you live?"

"Miss Jerusha."

"Miss Jerusha—who?"

"Skamp. She lives up in that cottage."

"Skamp! There's a pretty name to talk about! Old-lady, is she?"

"Yes; old and ugly."

"Ah! I guess I sha'n't mind an introduction, then. And what brings you down here, Miss Darrell? It's my time to ask questions now."

"Why, I came down here to read; and now, look here, I wish you wouldn't keep on calling me Miss Darrell; it sounds as if you were laughing at me. Say Georgia."

"With all my heart. Georgia be it—on one condition."

"Well, what is it?"

"That you call me Charley."

"Of course I'll call you Charley," said Georgia, decidedly; "I intended to all along. You didn't expect I'd say mister, did you?"

"Of course I didn't; I never indulge in absurd expectations. And may I ask the name of the book so fortunate as to find favor in your eyes, Miss Georgia?"

"Well, it's the 'Pilgrim's Progress.' I don't think much of it either—all about a man going on a journey, and getting into all sorts of scrapes. I don't believe it ever happened at all, for my part. And now, as you seem to like taking things easy, I guess I will too; so here we go!" said Georgia, as, shoving the book into her pocket, she made a spring forward, and by some mysterious sleight of hand, only understood by cats, monkeys, sailors, and depraved youths given to mischief, she clambered up the steep side of the high, smooth rock, and perched herself in triumph on the top, like a female Apollo on the apex of Mount Parnassus.

The young gentleman on the sands lifted himself on his elbow and stared at the little girl in a sort of indolent wonder at this energetic proceeding.

"Eh, what? you're up there, are you? May I ask, Miss Georgia, if it is your custom to perch yourself up there, like Patience on a monument, whenever you wish to appreciate the beauties of literature? Oh! the amount of unnecessary trouble people put themselves to in this world! Now why—I simply ask as a matter of courtesy—what possible object can you have in risking your neck in order to be slightly elevated above your fellow-mortals, eh?"

"Just for fun," said Georgia, as standing on one toe she cut a pigeon-wing, at the imminent danger of tumbling off and breaking her neck.

"For fun! Well, it's singular what perverted notions of amusement some people have. Now I—I'm about as fond of that sort of a thing, I may safely say, as any other youth; yet you'll excuse me when I say I really cannot see the point of that joke at all."

"*You* couldn't do it," said Georgia, exultingly; "bet you any thing you could not."

"Well, now, I don't know about that," said the youth, surveying the rock slowly with his large, indolent eyes; "of course, it's not polite or proper to contradict a lady, or else I should beg leave to differ from you in that opinion. There are precious few things, Miss Georgia, that I ever attempted and failed to execute, though I say it. I'm what you may call a universal genius, you know, equal to a steep rock, or any other emergency, up to anything, ancient or modern, or, to use another favorite and expressive phrase of Young America, a class to which I am proud to belong—I am, in every sense of the word, 'up to snuff.'"

"Bother!" exclaimed Georgia, to whom this homily, like all the lad's speeches, was Greek, or thereabouts. "It's all very fine to lie there like a lazy old porpoise, and talk such stuff, but you can't climb this rock, say what you like—now then."

"Can't I though!" exclaimed Master Charley, flinging away his cigar and springing up with more energy than might have been expected from his previous indolence, which, however, was more than half affected. "By Jove! then, here goes to try. Miss Georgia, if in my efforts in your service I turn out to be a case of 'Accidentally killed,' you'll see that the coroner's inquest is held properly, and that all my goods and chattels, consisting of a cigar-case, a clean shirt, and a jackknife, are promptly forwarded to my bereaved relative. Now then, here goes! '*Dieu et mon droit!*'"

So saying, the lad, with a great deal more skill and agility than Georgia had given him credit for, began climbing up the high rock. It was no easy task, however, for the sides were quite perpendicular and almost perfectly smooth, only suited to sailors and other aquatic monsters used to climbing impossible places.

Georgia clapped her hands and laughed her shrill elfish laugh at his desperate efforts, and, taunted by this, the boy made a sudden spring at the top, missed his footing, and tumbled off backward on the sands below.

With a sharp exclamation of alarm, Georgia, with one flying leap, sprang clear off the beetling rock, and alighted, cat-like, on her feet by his side. The lad lay perfectly still, and Georgia, terrified beyond measure, bent over and tried to raise him, and not succeeding in this, suddenly bethought herself of

Miss Jerusha's infallible plan for all distresses, mental and bodily, and, catching him by the shoulder, gave him a sound shaking.

This vigorous proceeding had the effect of completely restoring Master Charley, who had been for the moment stunned by the force of the fall, and, opening his eyes, he slowly raised himself and looked with a slightly bewildered glance around.

"Well, I knew you couldn't do it," cried Georgia, who, now observing that he was not killed, recovered all her aggravating love of teasing.

"Ugh! you tantalizing little pepper-pod! that's the sort of remorse you feel after nearly depriving the world of one of its brightest ornaments. 'Pon my word, I never was so nearly extinguished in all my life. Ain't you ashamed of yourself, Miss Georgia, now that you've been and gone and done and made me put my foot in it so beautifully? And speaking of feet reminds me that I have given my ankle a twist, and must see whether it is to be relied upon or not for the journey home, two miles being no joke, even at the best times."

So saying, Mr. Wildair got on his feet and attempted to walk, an experiment which resulted in his making a very wry face—and uttering something like a subdued howl, and finally sinking back in his former position.

"Well, here's a precious go, and no mistake!" was the exclamation jerked out of him by the exigency of the case; "here's my ankle has thought proper to go and sprain itself, and now I'll leave it to society in general if I'm not in just the tallest sort of a fix. Yes, you may stare and look blank, Miss Georgia, but I'll repeat it, you've used me shamefully, Miss Georgia, yes, abominably, Miss Georgia, and if you keep on like this, you stand a fair chance of sharing my own elevated destiny. You perceive I'm a fixture here, and may as well take up my quarters where I am for life, for out of this I can't go."

"Whatever will you do?" exclaimed Georgia, in dismay.

"Why, come to anchor here, of course; walking's out of the question. If you would be so obliging as to hunt me up a soft rock to sleep on, and where I could compose myself decently for death, it would be more agreeable to my feelings than to scorch here in the sand. Attempt to walk I positively can't and won't, traveling on one foot not being the pleasantest or speediest mode of locomotion in the world."

"Now, I declare, if it ain't too bad. I'm real sorry," said Georgia, whose sympathies were all aroused by the good-humor with which Master Charley bore his painful accident.

"Well, I wouldn't take it too much to heart if I were you, Miss Georgia; it might have been worse, you know—my neck, for instance."

"I'll tell you what," said Georgia, "I've got an idea."

"Pshaw! you're only joking," said Charley, incredulously.

"No, I ain't; I'll go for Miss Jerusha, and make her come here and help you up. You wait."

"Really," began Charley, but without waiting to hear him, Georgia bounded off, and clambering up the bank with two or three flying leaps reached the high road, and rushed impetuously along toward the cottage.

"There's an original for you," said the proprietor of the sprained ankle, looking after Georgia. "Well, this sprained ankle is mighty pleasant, I must say. If the old lady comes down she'll have to carry me on her back, for walk I won't."

Georgia, meanwhile, on charitable thoughts intent, rushed along where she was going, and the consequence was that she ran with stunning force against some person or persons unknown advancing from the opposite direction.

"Heads up!" said a pleasant voice; and Georgia, who betrayed symptoms of an insane desire to pitch head over heels, was restored to her center of gravity. "Rather an energetic mode of doing business this, I must say."

Georgia looked up, and jerked herself from the grasp of the stranger, a young man, dressed in a student's plain suit of black, who stood looking at her with a smile.

"What did you run against me for?" said Georgia, with one of her scowls, instantly taking the offensive.

"Run against *you*! Why, you are reversing cases, madam. Allow me to insinuate that you ran against *me*."

"I didn't, either! I mean I shouldn't if you hadn't poked yourself right in my way." Then, as a sudden idea struck her, she breathlessly resumed: "Oh, yes; you'll do better than Miss Jerusha! Come along with me to the beach, and help him up!" said Georgia, gesticulating with much earnestness.

"Help who up, my impetuous little lady?" said the young man, with a smile.

"Why, *him*, you know! He tumbled off—I knew he would all along—and went and sprained his ankle, and now he can't get up. It hurts him, I know, though he don't make a fuss or nothing, but talks and looks droll—nice fellow, I know he is! Help him up to our house, and Miss Jerusha'll fix him off, she will! Come! come along, can't you?"

All this time Georgia had stood, with sparkling eyes, gesticulating eagerly, as was her habit when excited; and now she caught him by the arm and pulled him vigorously along.

The stranger, with a laugh, allowed himself to be borne on by this breathless little whirlwind; and in less than ten minutes after she had left him, Georgia stood beside Charley Wildair on the beach.

Charley looked up as they approached, and glancing at her companion, exclaimed:

"Hallo, Rich! Well, here's a slice of good luck, anyway. How in the world did you scare *him* up, Miss Georgia?"

"Why he ran against me," said Georgia, "and nearly knocked my brains out. Do you know him?"

"I should think I did—rather!" said Charley, emphatically. "Here, Rich, come and help me up, there's a good fellow!"

"What have you been at now?" said Rich, as he obeyed. "Some piece of nonsense, I'll be bound."

"No, sir, I haven't been at nonsense. I was attempting to treat myself to a rise in the world by climbing up that rock, and, losing my equilibrium, the first thing I knew I was gracefully extended at full length on the sands, with one limb slightly dislocated, as completely floored an individual as you ever clapped your eyes on. For further particulars, apply to Miss Georgia here. And that reminds me, you haven't been duly presented to that young woman. Allow me to repair that error before proceeding to business. Miss Darrell, let me have the pleasure of presenting to your distinguished notice, my brother, Mr. Richmond Wildair, a young man chiefly remarkable for a rash and inordinate attachment for musty old books, and—having his own way. Mr. Wildair, Miss Georgia Darrell, a young lady whose many estimable qualities and aggravating will of her own require to be seen to be appreciated. Ahem."

And having, with great *empressment* and pomposity, delivered himself of this "neat and appropriate" speech, Mr. Charles Wildair drew himself up with dignity—which, as he was obliged to stand on one foot, with the other elevated in the air, hardly made the impression it was intended to make.

Mr. Richmond Wildair held out his hand to Georgia with a smile, and, after looking at it for a moment, in evident doubt as to the propriety of shaking hands with him, she at last consented to do so with a grave solemnity quite irresistible.

And thus Richmond Wildair and Georgia Darrell met for the first time. And little did either dream of what the future had in store for them, as they stood side by side on the sands in the golden light of that breezy, sunshiny May morning.

CHAPTER V.

"LADY MACBETH."

"Who that had seen her form so light,
For swiftness only turned,
Would e'er have thought in a thing so slight,
Such a fiery spirit burned."

"

d now what am I expected to do next?" said Richmond, looking at his two companions. "I am entirely at your service, monsieur and mademoiselle."

"Why, you must help him up to our house," said Georgia, in her peremptory tone, "and let Miss Jerusha do something for his lame ankle."

"And after that you must transport yourself over to Burnfield with all possible dispatch, and procure a cart, car, gig, wagon, carriage, wheelbarrow, or any other vehicle wherein my remains can be hauled to that thriving town, for walking, you perceive, is a moral and physical impossibility."

"All right!" said Richmond. "Here, take my arm. How will you manage to get up this steep bank? Do you think you can walk it?"

"Nothing like trying," said Charley, as leaning on his brother's arm he limped along, while Georgia went before to show them the way. "Ah, that was a twinge. The gout must be a nice thing to have if it is at all like this. I never properly felt for those troubled with that fashionable and aristocratic disease before, but the amount of sympathy I shall do for the future will be something terrifying. Here we are; now then, up we go."

But Master Charley found that "up we go" was easier said than done. He attempted to mount the bank, but at the first effort he recoiled, while a flush of pain overspread his pale features.

"No go, trying to do that; get up there I can't if they were to make me Khan of Tartary for doing it. Ah—h—h! there's another twinge, as if a red-hot poker had been plunged into it. The way that ankle can go into the aching business requires to be felt to be appreciated."

Though he spoke lightly, yet two scarlet spots, forced there by the intense pain, burned on either cheek.

Richmond looked at him anxiously, for he loved his wild, harum-scarum, handsome young brother with a strong love.

"Oh, he can't walk; I know it hurts him; what *will* we do?" said Georgia, in a tone of such intense motherly solicitude that, in spite of his painful ankle, Charley smiled faintly.

"I know what *I* shall do," said Richmond, abruptly. "I shall carry him."

And suiting the action to the word, the elder brother—older only by two or three years, but much stronger and more compactly built than the somewhat delicate Charley—lifted him in his arms and proceeded to bear him up the rocks.

"Why, Richmond, old fellow," remonstrated Charley, "you'll kill yourself— rupture an artery, and all that sort of thing, you know; and then there'll be a pretty to do about it. Let go, and I'll walk it, in spite of the ankle. I can hold out as long as it can, I should hope."

"Never mind, Charley; I'm pretty strong, and you're not a killing weight, being all skin and bone, and nonsense pretty much. Keep still, and I will have you up in a twinkling."

"Be it so, then, most obliging youth. Really, it's not such a bad notion, this being carried—rather comfortable than otherwise."

"Now, don't keep on so, Charley," said Georgia, in a voice of motherly rebuke. "How is your ankle? Does it hurt you much now?"

"Well, after mature deliberation on the subject, I think I may safely say it *does*. It's aching just at this present writing as if for a wager," replied Charley, with a grimace.

Georgia glanced at Richmond, and seeing great drops of perspiration standing on his brow as he toiled up, said, in all sincerity:

"See here, you look tired to death. *Do* let me help you. I'm strong, and he ain't very heavy looking, and I guess I can carry him the rest of the way."

Richmond turned and looked at her in surprise, but seeing she was perfectly serious in her offer, he repressed his amusement and gravely declined; while Charley, less delicate, set up an indecorous laugh.

"Carry me up the hill! Oh, that's good! What would Curtis, and Dorset, and all the fellows say if they heard that, Rich? 'Pon honor, that's the best joke of the season! A little girl I could lift with one hand offering to carry me up hill?"

And Master Charley lay back and laughed till the tears stood in his eyes.

His laughter was brought to a sudden end by an unexpected sight. Little Georgia faced round, with flashing eyes and glowing cheeks, and, with a passionate stamp of her foot, exclaimed:

"How *dare* you laugh at me, you hateful, ill-mannered fellow? Don't you ever dare to do it again, or it won't be good for you! If you weren't hurt now, and not able to take your own part, I'd *tear your eyes out!*—I just would! Don't you DARE to laugh at me, sir!"

And with another fierce stamp of her foot, and wild flash of her eyes, she turned away and walked in the direction of the cottage.

For a moment the brothers were confounded by this unexpected and startling outburst—this new revelation of the unique child before them. There was in it something so different from the customary pouting anger of a child— something so nearly appalling in her fierce eyes and passionate gestures, that they looked at each other a moment in astounded silence before attempting to reply.

"Really, Georgia, I did not mean to offend," said Charley, at last, as they by this time reached the high-road, and the exhausted Richmond deposited him on his feet. "I am very sorry I have angered you, but I'm such a fellow to laugh, you know, that the least thing sets me off. Why I'd laugh at an empress, if she did or said anything droll. Come, forgive me, like a good girl!" and Charley, looking deeply penitent, held out his hand.

But Georgia was proud, and was not one to readily forgive what she considered an insult, so she drew herself back and up, and only replied by a dangerous flash of her great black eyes.

"Come, Georgia, don't be angry; let's make up friends again. Where's the good of keeping spite, especially when a fellow's sorry for his fault? One thing I know, and that is, if you don't forgive me pretty soon, I'll go and heave myself away into an untimely grave, in the flower of my youth, and then just think of the remorse of conscience you'll suffer. Come, Georgia, shake hands and be friends."

But Georgia faced round, with a curling lip, and turning to Richmond, who all this time had stood quietly by, with folded arms, surveying her with an inexplicable smile, which faded away the moment he met her eye, she said, shortly:

"You had better come along. I'll go on ahead and tell Miss Jerusha you're coming." And then, without waiting for a reply, she walked on in proud silence.

She reached the cottage in a few minutes, and, throwing open the door with her accustomed explosive bang, went up to where Miss Jerusha sat sewing diligently, and facing that lady, began:

"Miss Jerusha, look here!"

Miss Jerusha lifted her head, and, seeing Miss Georgia's flushed cheeks and sparkling eyes, the evidence of one of her "tantrums," said:

"Well who hev you bin a-fightin' with *now*, marm?"

"I haven't been fighting with any one," said Georgia, impatiently, for a slight skirmish like this was nothing to pitched battle she called fighting; "but there's a boy that has sprained his ankle down on the beach, and his brother's bringing him here for you to fix it."

Now, Miss Jerusha, though not noted for her hospitality at any time, would not, perhaps, on an ordinary occasion make any objection to this beyond a few grumbles, but on this particular morning everything had gone wrong, and she was in an (even for her) unusually surly mood, so she turned round and sharply exclaimed:

"And do you suppose, you little good-for-nothing whipper-snapper, I keep an 'ospital for every shif'less scamp in the neighborhood? If you do, you are very much mistaken, that's all. If he's sprained his ankle, let him go sommer's else, for I vow to Sam he sha'n't come here!"

"He *shall* come here!" exclaimed Georgia, with one of her passionate stamps: "you see if he sha'n't. I told him he could come here, and he shall, too, in spite of you!"

"Why, you little impident hussy you!" said Miss Jerusha, flinging down her work and rising to her feet, "how dare you have the imperance to stand up and talk to me like that? We'll see whether he'll come here or not. *You* invited him here, indeed! And pray what right have you to invite anybody here, I want to know? You, a lazy, idle little vagabone, not worth your salt! Come here, indeed! I wish he may; if he doesn't go out faster than he came in it won't be my fault!"

"Just you try to turn him out, you cross, ugly old thing! If you do I'll—I'll *kill* you; I'll set fire to this hateful old hut, and burn it down! You see if I don't. There!"

The savage gleam of her eyes at that moment, her face white with concentrated passion, was something horrible and unnatural in one of her years. Miss Jerusha drew back a step, and interposed a chair between them in salutary dread of the little vixen's claw-like nails.

At that moment the form of Richmond Wildair appeared in the door-way. Both youths had arrived in time to witness the fierce altercation between the mistress of the house and her half-savage little ward, and Richmond now

48

interposed.

Taking off his hat, he bowed to Miss Jerusha saying in his calm, gentlemanly tones:

"I beg your pardon, madam, for this intrusion, but my brother being really unable to walk, I beg you will have the kindness to allow him to remain here until I can return from Burnfield with a carriage. You will not be troubled with him more than an hour."

Inhospitable as she was, Miss Jerusha could not really refuse this, so she growled out a churlish assent; and Richmond, secretly amused at the whole thing, helped in Charley, while Georgia set the rocking-chair for him, and placed a stool under his wounded foot, without, however, favoring him with a single smile, or word, or glance. She was in no mood just then either to forget or forgive.

"And now I'm off," said Richmond, after seeing Charley safely disposed of. "I will be back in as short a time as I possibly can; and meantime, Miss Georgia," he added, turning to her with a smile as he left the room, "I place my brother under your care until I come back."

But Georgia, with her back to them both, was looking sullenly out of the window, and neither moved nor spoke until Richmond had gone, and then she followed him out, and stood looking irresolutely after him as he walked down the road.

He turned round, and seeing her there, stopped as though expecting she would speak; but she only played nervously with the hop-vines crowning the walls, without lifting her voice.

"Well, Georgia?" he said inquiringly.

"I—I don't want to stay here. I'll go with you to Burnfield, if you like. Miss Jerusha's cross," she said, looking up half shyly, half defiantly in his face.

A strange expression flitted for an instant over the grave, thoughtful face of Richmond Wildair, passing away as quickly as it came. Without a word he went up to where Georgia stood, with that same light in her eyes, half shy, half fierce, that one sees in the eyes of a half-tamed and dangerous animal when under the influence of a master-eye.

"Georgia, look at me," he said, laying one hand lightly on her shoulder.

She stepped back, shook off the hand, and looked defiantly up in his face. It was not exactly a handsome face, yet it was full of power—full of calm, deep, invincible power—with keen, intense, piercing eyes, whose steady gaze few could calmly stand. Child as she was, the hitherto unconquered Georgia felt

49

that she stood in the presence of a strong will, that surmounted and overtopped her own by its very depth, intensity and calmness. She strove to brave out his gaze, but her own eyes wavered and fell.

"Well?" she said, in a subdued tone.

"Georgia, will you do me a favor?"

"Well?" she said, compressing her lips hard, as though determined to do battle to the death.

"My brother is alone, he is in pain, he did not mean to offend you, he is under *your* roof. Georgia, I want you to stay with him till I come back."

"He laughed at me—he made fun of me. I *won't*! I hate him!" she said, with a passionate flush.

"He is sorry for that. When people are sorry for their faults, a magnanimous enemy always forgives."

"I don't care. I *won't* forgive him. I was doing everything I could for him. I would have helped him up hill if I could, and he *laughed at me*! I won't stay with him!" she exclaimed, tearing the hop branches off and flinging them to the ground in her excitement.

He caught the destructive little hands in his and held them fast.

"Georgia, you *will*!"

"I *won't*! not if I die for it!" she flashed.

"Georgia!"

"Let me go!" she cried out, trying to wrench her hands from his grasp. "I never will! Let me go!"

"Georgia, do you know what hospitality means?"

"Yes."

"Well, he is your guest now. Have you ever read about the Arabs of the desert, my proud little lady?"

"Yes."

"Well, you know once their most deadly enemy entered their house, they treated him as though he were the dearest friend they had in the world. Now, Georgia, you will be a lady some day, I think, and——"

"I will stay with your brother till you come back," she said, proudly; "but I *won't* be his friend—never again! I liked him then, and I wanted to do everything I could for him. I would have had *my* ankle sprained if it would have made his well. I was so sorry, and—he—laughed at me!"

In spite of all her evident efforts her lips quivered, and turning abruptly, she walked away and entered the house.

Richmond Wildair stood for an instant in the same spot, looking after her, and again that nameless, inexplicable smile flitted over his face.

"*Conquered!*" he said, with a sort of exultation in his voice; "and for the first time in her life, I believe. Strange, wild child that she is. I see the germs of a fine but distorted character there."

He walked down the road, whistling "My love is but a lassie yet," while Georgia re-entered the house, and with a dark cloud still on her face, walked to the window and looked sullenly after the retreating figure of Richmond.

Master Charley, who had a taste for strange animals, had been devoting his time to drawing out Miss Jerusha, practicing all his fascinations on her with a zeal and determination worthy of a better cause, and at last succeeded in wheedling that deluded lady into a recital of her many and peculiar troubles, to all of which he listened with the most sympathizing, not to say painful attention, and with a look so intensely dismal that it quite won the old lady's heart. But when he praised Betsey Periwinkle, and stroked her down, and spoke in terms of enthusiastic admiration of a pair of moleskin pantaloons Miss Jerusha was making, bespeaking another pair exactly like them for himself, his conquest was complete, and he took a firm hold of Miss Jerusha's unappropriated affections, which from that day he never lost. And on the strength of this new and rash attack of "love at first sight," Miss Jerusha produced from some mysterious corner a glass of currant wine and a plate of sliced gingerbread, which she offered to her guest—a piece of reckless extravagance she had never been guilty of before, and which surprised Fly to such a degree that she would have there and then taken out a writ of lunacy against her mistress, had she known anything whatever about such a proceeding. Master Charley, being blessed with an excellent appetite of his own, which his accident had in no way diminished, graciously condescended to partake of the offered dainties, and launched out into such enthusiastic praises of both, that the English language actually foundered and gave out, in his transports.

And all this time Georgia had stood by the window, silent and sullen, with a cloud on her brow, and a bright, angry light in her eyes, that warned both Miss Jerusha and Charley Wildair that it was safer to let her alone than speak to her just then. For though the girl's combustible nature was something like a blaze of tow, burning fiercely for a moment and then going out, she did not readily forgive injuries, slights, or affronts, or what she considered such. No, she brooded over them until they sank deep among the many other rank things that had been allowed to take root in her heart, and which only the spirit of true religion could now ever eradicate.

The child had grown up from infancy neglected, her high spirit unchecked, her fierce outbursts of temper unrebuked, allowed to have her own way in all things, ignorant of all religious training whatsoever. She had heard the words, God, heaven and hell—but they were *only* words to her, striking the ear, but conveying no meaning, and she had *never* bent her childish knee in prayer.

What wonder then that she grew up as we find her, proud, passionate, sullen, obstinate, and vindictive? The germs of a really fine nature had been born with her, but they had been neglected and allowed to run to waste, while every evil passion had been fostered and nurtured.

Generous, frank, and truthful she was still, scorning a lie, *not* because she thought it a sin, but because it seemed *mean* and cowardly; high-spirited, too, she would have gone through fire and flood to serve any one she loved; *but*, had that one offended her, she would have hurled her back into the fire and flood without remorse.

Ingratitude was not one of her vices either, though from her conduct to Miss Jerusha it would appear so; but Georgia could not love the sharp, snappish, though not bad-hearted old maid, and so she believed she owed her nothing, a belief more than one in Burnfield took care to foster.

Not a vice that child possessed that a careful hand could not have changed into a real virtue, for in her sinning there was at least nothing mean and underhand; treachery and deception she would have scorned and stigmatized as *cowardly*, for courage, daring, bravery, was in the eyes of Georgia the highest virtue in earth or heaven.

Richmond Wildair understood her,   because he possessed an astute and powerful intellect, and mastered her, because he had a *will* equal to her own, and a mind, by education and cultivation, infinitely superior.

Georgia, almost unknown to herself, had a profound admiration and respect for *strength*, whether bodily or mental; and the moment Richmond Wildair let her see he could conquer her, that moment he achieved a command over the wild girl he never lost.

Yet it galled her, this first link in the chain that was one day to bind her hand and foot; and, like an unbroken colt on whom the bridle and curb are put for the first time, she grew restive and angry under the intolerable yoke.

"What right has he to make me stay?" she thought, with a still darkening brow. "What business has he to order me to do this or that? Telling me to stay with his brother, as if he was my master and I was his servant! I don't see why I did it; he had no *business* to tell me so. I have a good mind to run away yet, and when he comes he'll find me gone—but no, I promised to stay, and I will. I wouldn't have stayed for anybody else, and I don't see why I did for him. I won't do it again—I never will; the very next thing he asks me to do I'll say no, and I'll *stick* to it. I won't be ordered about by anybody!"

And Georgia raised her head proudly, and her eye flashed, and her cheek kindled, and her little brown hand clenched, as her whole untamed nature rose in revolt against the idea of servitude. Some wild Indian or gipsy blood must have been in Georgia's veins, for never did a lord of forest rock or river resolve to do battle to maintain his freedom with more fierce determination than did she at that moment.

Her resolution was soon put to the test. Ere another hour had passed Richmond Wildair returned with a light gig, and entered the house.

Georgia saw him enter, but would not turn round, and Charley, getting up, bade Miss Jerusha a gay good-by, promising to come and see her again the first thing after his ankle got well. Then, going over to Georgia, he held out his hand, saying:

"Come, Georgia, I am going away. *Do* bid me good-by."

It was hardly in human nature to resist that coaxing tone; so a curt "good-by" dropped out from between Georgia's closed teeth; but she would neither look at him nor notice his extended hand.

And with this leave-taking Charley was forced to be content; and, leaning on Richmond, he went out and took his place in the gig.

Then Richmond returned, and bowing his farewell and his thanks to Miss Jerusha, slightly surprised at the mollifying metamorphosis that ancient lady had undergone, he went up to Georgia, saying, in a low tone:

"Come with me to the door, Georgia; I have something to say to you."

"Say it here."

He hesitated, but Georgia looked as immovable as a rock.

"Well, then, Georgia, I want you to forgive my brother before he goes."

Georgia planted her feet firmly together, compressed her lips, and, without lifting her eyes to his face, said, in a low, resolute tone:

"Richmond Wildair, I won't!"

"But, Georgia, he is sorry for his fault; he has apologized; you *ought* to forgive him."

53

"I won't!"

"Georgia, it is wrong, it is unnatural in a little girl to be wicked and vindictive like this. If you were a good child, you would shake hands and be friends."

"I won't!"

"Georgia, for *my* sake—"

"*I won't!*"

"Obstinate, flinty little thing! Do you like me, Georgia?"

"No!"

"You don't? Why, Georgia, what a shame! You don't like me?"

"No, I don't! I hate you both! You have no business to tease me this way! I won't forgive him—I never will! I'll *never* do anything for you again!"

And, with a fierce flash of the eyes that reminded him of a panther he had once shot, she broke from his retaining grasp and fled out of the house.

He was foiled. He turned away with a slight smile, yet there was a scarcely perceptible shade of annoyance on his high, serene brow, as he took his place beside his brother and drove off.

"What took you back, Rich?" asked Charley.

"I wanted to bid good-by to that unique little specimen of girlhood in there, and get her to pardon you."

"And she would not?"

"No."

"Whew! resisted *your* all-powerful will! The gods be praised that you have found your match at last!"

Richmond's brow slightly contracted, and he gave the horse a quick cut with the whip that sent him flying on.

"And yet I will make her do it," he said, with his calm, peculiar, inexplicable smile.

"Eh?—you will? And how, may I ask?"

"Never you mind—she shall do it! I have conquered her once already, and I shall do it again, although she *has* refused this time. I did not expect her to yield without a struggle."

"By Jove! there's some wild blood in that one. There was mischief in her eyes as she turned on me there on the hill. I shall take care to give her a wide berth, and let her severely alone for the future."

"Yes, she is an original—all steel springs—a fine nature if properly trained," said Richmond, musingly.

"A fine fiddlestick!" said Charley, contemptuously; "she's as sharp as a persimmon, and as sour as an unripe crab-apple, and as full of stings as a whole forest of nettle-trees."

"Do you know, Charles, I fancy Lady Macbeth might have been just such a child?"

"Shouldn't wonder. The little black-eyed gipsy is fierce enough in all conscience to make a whole batch of Lady Macbeths. May all the powers that be generously grant I may not be the Duncan she is to send to the other world."

"If she is allowed to grow up as she is now, she will certainly be some day capable of even Lady Macbeth's crime. Pity she has no one better qualified to look after her than that disagreeable old woman."

"Better mind how you talk about the old lady," said Charley; "she and I are as thick as pickpockets. I flattered her beautifully, I flatter myself, and she believes in me to an immense extent. As to the young lady, what do you say to adopting her yourself? You'd be a sweet mentor for youth, wouldn't you?"

"You may laugh, but I really feel a deep interest in that child," said Richmond.

"Well, for my part," said Charley, "I don't believe in vixens, young or old, but you—*you* always had a taste for monsters."

"Not exactly," said Richmond, untying a knot in his whip; "but she is something new; she suits me; I like her."

CHAPTER VI.

TAMING AN EAGLET.

"In her heart
Are sown the sparks that kindle fiery war;
Occasion needs but fan them and they blaze."

COWPER.

"Mind's command o'er mind,
Spirits o'er spirit, is the clear effect
And natural action of an inward gift
Given by God."

 l that day little Georgia went wandering aimlessly, restlessly, through the woods, possessed by some walking spirit that would not let her sit still for an instant. She had kept her vow; she had resisted the power of a master mind; she had maintained her free will, and refused to do as he commanded her. Yes, she felt it as a command. She had thrown off the yoke he would have laid on her, and she ought to have exulted in her triumph—in her victory. But, strange to say, it surprised even herself that she had *not*; she felt angry, sullen and dissatisfied. The consciousness that she was wrong and he was right— that she ought to have done as he told her—would force itself upon her in spite of her efforts. How mean and narrow her own conduct did look now that she came to think it over, and the fever of passion had passed away; had she been brave and generous she felt she would have forgiven him when he so often apologized; it was galling to be laughed at, it was true, but when he was sorry for his fault she knew she ought to have pardoned him. How they both must despise her; what a wicked, ugly, disagreeable little girl they must think her. How she wished she had been better, and had made up friends, and not let them go away thinking her so cross and sullen and obstinate.

"Miss Jerusha says I'm ugly and good for nothing and bad-tempered, and so does every body else. Nobody loves me or cares for me, and every body says I've got the worst temper they ever knew. People don't do anything but laugh at me and make fun of me and call me names. Mamma and Warren liked me,

56

but they're dead, and I wish I was dead and buried, too—I do so! I'll never dance again; I'll never sing for anyone; I'll go away somewhere, and never come back. I wish I was pretty and good-tempered and pleasant, like Em Murray: every body loved her; but I ain't, and never will be. I'm black and ugly and bad-tempered, and every one hates me. Let them hate me, then—I don't care! I hate them just as much; and I'll be just as cross and ugly as ever I like. I was made so, and I can't help it, and I don't care for any body. I'll do just as I like, I will so! I can hate people as much as they can hate me, and I will do it, too. I don't see what I was ever born for; Miss Jerusha says it was to torment people: but I couldn't help it, and it ain't my fault, and they have no business to blame me for it. Emily Murray says God makes people die, and I don't see why he didn't let me die, too, when mamma did. Mamma was good, and I expect she's in heaven, but I'm so bad they'll never let me there I know! I don't care for that either. I was made bad, and if they send me to the bad place for it, they may. Em Murray'll go to Heaven, because she's good and pretty, and Miss Jerusha says *she'll* go, but I don't believe it. If she does, *I* sha'n't go even if they ask me to, for I know she'll scold all the time up there just as she does down here. If they do let her in, I guess they'll be pretty sorry for it after, and wish they hadn't. I 'pose them two young gentlemen from New York will go, too, and I know that Charley fellow will laugh when he sees me turned off, just as he did this morning. I don't believe I ought to have made up with him, after all. I won't either, if his brother says I *must*. If he lets me alone I may, but I'll never offer to do anything for him again as long as I live. Oh, dear! I don't see what I ever was born for at all, and I do wish I never had been, or that I had died with mamma and Warren."

And so, with bitterness in her heart, the child wandered on and on restlessly, as if to escape from herself, with a sense of wrong, and neglect, and injustice forcing itself upon her childish uncultivated mind. She thought of all the hard names and opprobrious epithets Miss Jerusha called her, and "unjust! unjust!" was the cry of her heart as she wandered on. She felt that in all the world there was not such a wicked, unloved child as she, and the untutored heart resolved in its bitterness to repay scorn with scorn, and hate with hate.

It was dark when she came home. She had had no dinner, but with the conflict going on within she had felt no hunger. Miss Jerusha's supper was over and long since cleared away, and, as might be expected, she was in no very sweet frame of mind at the long absence of her *protegee*.

"Well, you've got home at last, have you?" she began sharply, and with her voice pitched in a most aggravating key. "Pretty time o' night this, I must say, to come home, after trampin' round like a vagabone on the face o' the airth all the whole blessed day. You desarve to be switched as long as you can stand, you worthless, lazy, idle young varmint you! Be off to the kitchen, and see if Fly can't get you some supper, though you oughtn't to get a morsel if you were rightly served. Other folks has to toil for what they eat, but you live on other folks' vittals, and do nothing, you indolent little tramper you!"

Miss Jerusha paused for want of breath, expecting the angry retort this style of address never failed to extort from the excitable little bomb-shell before her, but to her surprise none came. The child stood with compressed lips, dark and gloomy, gazing into the fading fire.

"Well, why don't you go?" said Miss Jerusha angrily. "You ought to take your betters' leavin's and be thankful, though there's no such thing as thankfulness in you, I do believe. Go!"

"I don't want your supper; you may keep it," said Georgia, with proud sullenness.

"Oh, you don't! Of course not! it's not good enough for your ladyship, by no manner of means," said Miss Jerusha, with withering sarcasm. "Hadn't I better order some cake and wine for your worship? Dear, dear! what ladies we are, to be sure! Is there anything particularly nice I could get for you, marm, eh? P'raps Fly'd better run to Burnfield for some plum puddin' or suthin', hey? Oh, dear me, ain't we dainty, though."

Georgia actually gnashed her teeth, and turned livid with passion as she listened, and, with a spring, she stood before the startled Miss Jerusha, her eyes glaring in the partial darkness like those of a wild-cat. Miss Jerusha, in alarm, lifted a chair as a weapon of defense against the expected attack; but the attack was not made.

Clasping her hands over her head with a sort of irrepressible cry, she fled from the room, up the stairs into her own little chamber, fastened the door, and then sank down, white and quivering, on the floor of the room.

How long she lay there she could not tell; gusts of passion swept through her soul. Wild, fierce, and maddening raged the conflict within—one of those delirious storms of the heart—known and felt only by those whose fiery, tropical veins seem to run fire instead of blood.

She heard Miss Jerusha's step on the stairs, heard her approach her door and listen for a moment, and then go to her own chamber and securely lock the door.

In that moment the half crazed child hated her; hated all the world; feeling as though she could have killed her were it in her power. Then this unnatural mood passed away—it was too unnatural to last—and she rose from the floor, looking like a spirit, with her streaming hair, wild eyes, and white face. She went to the window and opened it, for her head throbbed and ached, and leaning her forehead against the cool glass, she looked out.

How still and serene everything was! The river lay bright and beautiful in the dark bright starlight. The pine trees waved dreamily in the soft spring breeze, and the odor of their fragrant leaves came borne to where she sat. The silence of the grave reigned around, the lonesome forest seemed lonelier than ever to-night, and so deep was the stillness that the plaintive cry of the whip-poor-will, as it rose at intervals, sounded startlingly loud and shrill. She lifted her eyes to the high, bright, solemn stars that seemed looking down pityingly upon the poor little orphan child, and all her wickedness and passion passed away, and a mysterious awe, deep and holy, entered that tempest-tossed young heart. The soft, cool breeze lifted her dark elf locks, and lingered and cooled her hot brow like a friend's kiss. Georgia had often looked at the stars before, but they never seemed to have such high and holy beauty as they possessed to-night.

"God made the stars," thought Georgia; "I wonder what He made them for? Perhaps they are the eyes of the people that die and go to heaven. I wonder if mamma and Warren are up there, and know how bad I am, and how wicked and miserable I feel? I guess they would be sorry for me if they did, for there is nobody in the world to like me now. Some people pray; Emily Murray does, for I've seen her; but I don't know how, and I don't think God would listen to me if I did, I'm so dreadful bad. She taught me a pretty hymn to sing; it sounds like a prayer; but I've forgot it all but the first verse. I'll say that anyway. Let's see—oh, yes! I know two."

And, for the first time in her life, she knelt down and clasped her hands, and in the light of the beautiful solemn stars, she softly whispered her first prayer.

> "Oh, Mary, my mother, most lovely, most mild,
> Look down upon me, your poor, weak, lonely child;
> From the land of my exile, I call upon thee,
> Then Mary, my mother, look kindly on me.
> In sorrow and darkness, be still at my side,
> My light and my refuge, my guard and my guide.
> Though snares should surround me, yet why should I fear?
> I know I am weak, but my mother is near.
> Then Mary, my mother, look down upon me,
> 'Tis the voice of thy child that is calling to thee."

Georgia's voice died away, yet with her hands still clasped and her dark mystic eyes now upturned to the far-off stars, her thoughts went wandering on the sweet words she had said.

"'Mary, my mother!' I wonder who that means. My mamma's name was not Mary, and one can't have two mothers, I should think. How good it sounds, too! I must ask Emily what it means; she knows. Oh, I wish—I do wish I was up there where all the beautiful stars are!"

Poor little Georgia! untaught, passionate child! how many years will come and go, what a fiery furnace thou art destined to pass through before that "peace which passeth all understanding" will enter your anguished, world-weary heart!

When breakfast was over next morning, Georgia took her sun-bonnet and set off for Burnfield. She hardly knew herself what was her object in passing so quickly through the village, without stopping at any of her favorite haunts, until she stood before the large, handsome mansion occupied and owned by the one great man of Burnfield, Squire Richmond.

The house was an imposing structure of brown stone, with arched porticoes, and vine-wreathed balconies. The grounds were extensive, and beautifully laid out; and Georgia, with the other children, had often peeped longingly over the high fence encircling the front garden, at the beautiful flowers within.

Georgia, skilled in climbing, could easily have got over and reached them, but her innate sense of honor would not permit her to steal. There was something mean in the idea of being a thief or a liar, and meanness was the blackest crime in her "table of sins." Perhaps another reason was, Georgia did not care much for flowers; she liked well enough to see them growing, but as for culling a bouquet for any pleasure it could afford her, she would never have thought of doing it. While she stood gazing wistfully at the forbidden garden of Eden, a sweet silvery voice close behind her arrested her attention with the exclamation:

"Why, Georgia, is this really you?"

Georgia turned round and saw a little girl about her own age, but, to a superficial eye, a hundred times prettier and more interesting. Her form was plump and rounded, her complexion snowy white, with the brightest of rosy blooms on her cheek and lip; her eyes were large, bright and blue, and her pale golden hair clustered in natural curls on her ivory neck. A sweet face it was—a happy, innocent, child-like face—with nothing remarkable about it save its prettiness and goodness.

"Oh, Em! I'm glad you've come," said Georgia, her dark eyes lighting up with pleasure. "I was just wishing you would. Here, stand up here beside me."

"Well, I can't stay long," said the little one, getting up beside Georgia.

"Mother sent me with some things to that poor Mrs. White, whose husband got killed, you know. Oh, Georgia! she's got just the dearest little baby you ever saw, with such tiny bits of fingers and toes, and the funniest little blinking eyes! The greatest little darling ever was! Do come down with me to see it; it's splendid!" exclaimed Emily, her pretty little face all aglow with enthusiasm.

"No; I don't care about going," said Georgia, coolly. "I don't like babies."

"Don't like babies!—the dearest little things in the world! Oh, Georgia!" cried Emily, reproachfully.

"Well, I don't, then! I don't see anything nice about them, for my part. Ugly little things, with thin faces all wrinkled up, like Miss Jerusha's hands on wash-day, crying and making a time. I don't like them; and I don't see how you can be bothered nursing them the way you do."

"Oh, I love them! and I'm going to save all the money I get to spend, to buy Mrs. White's little baby a dress. Mother says I may. Ain't these flowers lovely in there? I wish we had a garden."

"Why?"

"Oh, because it's so nice to have flowers. I wonder Squire Richmond never pulls any of his; he always leaves them there till they drop off."

"Well, what would he pull them for?"

"Why, to put on the table, of course. Don't you ever gather flowers for your room?"

"No."

"You don't! Why, Georgia! don't you love flowers?"

"No, I don't love them; I like to see them well enough."

"Why, Georgia! Oh, Georgia, what a funny girl you are! Not love flowers! What *do* you love, then?"

"I love the stars—the beautiful stars, so high, and bright, and splendid!"

"Oh, so do I; but then they're so far off, you know, I love flowers better, because they're nearer."

"Well, that's the reason I *don't* like them—I mean not so much. I don't care for things I can get so easy—that everybody else can get. Anything I like I want to have all to myself. I don't want anybody else in the world to have it. The bright, beautiful stars are away off—nobody can have them. I call them mine, and nobody can take them from me. I like stars better than flowers."

"Oh, Georgia! you are queer. Why, don't you know that's selfish? Now, if I have any pleasure, I don't enjoy it at all unless I have somebody to enjoy it with. I shouldn't like to keep all to myself; it doesn't seem right. What else do you like, Georgia?"

"Well, I like the sea—the great, grand, dreadful sea! I like it when the waves rise and dash their heads against the high rocks, and roar, and shriek, and rage as if something had made them wild with anger. Oh! I *love* to watch it then, when the great white waves break so fiercely over the high rocks, and dash up the spray in my face. I know it feels then as I do sometimes, just as if it should go mad and dash its brains out on the rocks. Oh, I do love the great, stormy, angry sea!"

And the eyes of the wild girl blazed up, and her whole dark face lighted, kindled, grew radiant as she spoke.

The sweet, innocent little face of Emily was lifted in wonder and a sort of dismay.

"Oh, Georgia, how you talk!" she exclaimed: "love the sea in a storm! What a taste you have! Now I like it, too, but only on a sunny, calm morning like this, when it is smooth and shining. I am dreadfully afraid of it on a stormy day, when the great waves make such a horrid noise. What queer things you like! Now I suppose you had rather have a wet day like last Sunday than one like this?"

"No," said Georgia, "I didn't like last Sunday; it kept on a miserable drizzle, drizzle all day, and wouldn't be fine nor rain right down *good* and have done with it. But I like a storm, a fierce, high storm, when the wind blows fit to tear the trees up, and dashes the rain like mad against the windows. I go away up to the garret then and listen. And I like it when it thunders and lightens, and frightens everybody into fits. Oh, it's splendid then! I feel as if I would like to fly away and away all over the world, as if I should go wild being caged up in one place, as if—oh, I can't tell you how I feel!" said the hare-brained girl, drawing a long breath and keeping her shining eyes fixed as if on some far-off vision.

"Well, if you ain't the queerest, wildest thing! And you don't like fine days at all?"

"Oh, yes, I do—of course I do; not so much days like this, cold, and clear, and calm, but blazing hot, scorching August noondays, when the whole world looks like one great flood of golden fire—*that's* the sort I like! Or freezing, wild, frosty winter days, when the great blasts make one fly along as if they had wings—*they're* splendid, too!"

"Well, I don't know, I don't think so. I like cool, pleasant days like this better, because I have no taste for roasting or freezing," said Emily, laughing. "Oh, I must tell mother about the droll things you like! Let me see what else. Like music?"

"Some sorts. I like the band. Don't care much for any other kind."

"And I like songs and hymns better. And now, which do you prefer—men or women?"

"Men," said Georgia, decidedly.

"You do! Why?"

"Oh, well—because they're stronger and more powerful, and braver and bolder; women are such cowards. Do you know the sort of a man I should like to be?"

"No; what sort?"

"Well, like Napoleon Bonaparte, or Alexander the Great. I should like to conquer the whole world and make every one *in* the world do just as I told them. Oh, I wish I was a boy!"

"I don't, then," said Emily, stoutly. "I don't like boys, they're so rude and rough. And these two conquerors weren't good men either. I've read about them. Washington was good. I like *him*."

"So do I. But if I had been him I would have made myself King of America. I wouldn't have done as he did at all. Now, where are you going in such a hurry?"

"Oh, I shall have to go to Mrs. White's. I've been here a good while already. I wish you would come along."

"No," said Georgia decidedly, "I sha'n't go. Good-by."

Emily nodded and smiled a good-by, and tripped off down the road. Georgia stood for a moment longer, looking at the stately mansion, and then was about to go away when a hand was laid on her and arrested her steps.

Close to the wall some benches ran, hidden under a profusion of flowering vines, and Richmond Wildair had been lying on one of these, studying a deeply exciting volume, when the voices of the children fell upon his ear. Very intently did he listen to their conversation, only revealing himself when he found Georgia was about to leave.

"Good-morning, Miss Georgia," he said, smilingly; "I am very glad to see you. Come, jump over the fence and come in; you can do it, I know."

Now, Georgia was neither timid nor bashful, but while he spoke she recollected her not very courteous behavior the previous day, and, for the first time in her life, she hung her head and blushed.

He appeared to have forgotten, or at least forgiven it, but this only made her feel it all the more keenly.

"Come," he said, catching her hands, without appearing to notice her confusion; "one, two, three—jump!"

Georgia laughed, disengaged her hands, and with the old mischievous spirit twinkling in her eyes, with one flying leap vaulted clear over his head far out into the garden.

"Bravo!" cried Richmond; "excellently done! I see you understand gymnastics. Now I would offer you some flowers only I heard you say you did not care for them, and as for the stars I regret they are beyond even my reach."

Georgia looked up with a flush that reminded him of yesterday. "You were listening," she said disdainfully; "that is mean!"

"I beg your pardon, Miss Georgia, I was not listening intentionally; I am not an eavesdropper, allow me to insinuate. I was lying there studying before you came, and did not choose to put myself to the inconvenience of getting up and going away to oblige a couple of small young ladies, more particularly when I found their conversation so intensely interesting. Very odd tastes and fancies you have, my little Lady Georgia."

Georgia was silent—she had scarcely heard him—she was thinking of something else. She wanted to ask about Charley, but—she did not like to.

"Well," he said, with a smile, reading her thoughts like an open book, "and what is little Georgia thinking of so intently?"

"I—I—of *nothing*," she was going to say, and then she checked herself. It would be a falsehood, and Georgia as proud of never having told a lie in her life.

"And what does 'I—I' mean?"

"I was thinking of your brother Charley," she said, looking up with one of her bright, defiant flashes.

"Yes," he said, quietly, "and what of him?"

"I should like to know how he is."

"He is ill—seriously ill. Charles is delicate, and his ankle is even worse hurt than we supposed. Last night he was feverish and sleepless, and this morning

64

he was not able to get up."

A hot flush passed over Georgia's face, retreating instantaneously, and leaving her very pale, with a wild, uneasy, glitter in her large dark eyes. Oh! If he should die, she thought. It was through her fault he had hurt himself first, and then she had been obstinate, and would not forgive him. Perhaps he would die, she would never be able to tell him how sorry she was for what she had done. She laid her hand on Richmond's arm, and, looking up earnestly in his face, said, in a voice that trembled a little in spite of herself: "Do—do you think he will die?"

"No," he said, gravely, "I hope—I think not; but poor Charley is really ill, and very lonely, up there alone."

"I—I should like to see him."

It was just what Richmond expected; just what he had uttered the last words to hear her say. *Her* eyes were downcast, and she did not see the almost imperceptible smile that dawned around his mouth. When she looked up he was grave and serious.

"I think he will be able to sit up this afternoon. If you will come up after dinner you shall see him. Meantime, shall I show you through the grounds? Perhaps you have never been here before."

He changed the subject quickly, for he knew it would not do to particularly notice her request. Georgia had often before wished to wander through the long walks and beautiful gardens around, but now her little dark face was downcast and troubled, and she said, gravely:

"No—thank you!" The last words after a pause, for politeness was not in the little lady's line. "I will go home now, and come back by-and-by. You needn't open the gate; I can jump over the fence. There! don't mind helping me. Good-by!"

She sprang lightly over the wall, and was gone, and pulling her sun-bonnet far over her face, set out for home.

Miss Jerusha wondered that day, in confidence to Fly and Betsey Periwinkle, what had "come to Georgey," she was so still and silent all dinner-time, and sat with such a moody look of dark gravity in her face, all unusual with the sparkling, restless elf. Well, they did not know that the free young forest eaglet had got its wings clipped for the first time, that day, and that Georgia could exult no more in the thought that she was wholly unconquered and free.

Richmond Wildair was at his post immediately after dinner, awaiting the coming of Georgia. He knew she would come, and she did. He saw the small, dark figure approaching, and held the gate open for her to enter.

"Ah! you've come, Georgia!" he said. "That is right. Come along; Charley is here."

"Does he know I am coming?" asked Georgia, soberly.

"Yes, I told him. He expects you. Here—this way. There you are!"

He opened the door, and ushered Georgia into a sort of summer-house in the garden, where, seated in state, in an arm-chair, was Master Charley, looking rather paler than when she saw him last, but with the same half droll, half indolent, languid air about him that seemed to be his chief characteristic.

"My dear Miss Georgia," he began, with the greatest *empressement*, the moment he saw her, "you make me proud by honoring so unworthy an individual as I am with your gracious presence. You'll excuse my not getting up, I hope; but the fact is, this unfortunate continuation of mine being resolved to have its own way about the matter, can be induced by no amount of persuasion and liniment to behave prettily, and utterly scouts the idea of being used as a means of support. Pray take a seat, Miss Georgia Darrell, and make yourself as miserable as circumstances will allow."

To this speech, uttered with the utmost *verve*, and with the blandest and most insinuating tones, Georgia listened with a countenance of immovable gravity, and at its close, instead of sitting down, she walked up, stood before him, and said:

"Yesterday you laughed at me, and I was angry. You said you were sorry, and I—I came to-day to tell you I was willing to make up friends again. There!"

She held out one little brown hand in token of amity. With the utmost difficulty Charley maintained his countenance sufficiently to shake hands with her, which he did with due decorum, and then, without another word, Georgia turned and walked away.

No sooner was she gone than Charley leaned back and laughed until the tears stood in his eyes. While he was yet in a paroxysm Richmond entered.

"Has she gone?" asked Charley, finding voice.

"Yes, looking as sober as Minerva and her owl."

"Oh! that girl will be the death of me, that's certain. By George! it was good as a play. There she stood with a face as long as a coffin, and as dark and solemn as a hearse," and Charley went off into another fit of laughter at the recollection.

"She condescended to forgive you at last, you see."

"Yes, Miss Georgia and I have, figuratively speaking, smoked the pipe of peace. Touching sight it must have been to a third person. It was a tight fit, though, to get her to do it."

"I think I could manage that proud little lady, if she were a sister of mine. I shall conquer her more thoroughly yet before I have done with her. I have a plan in my head, the result of which you will see pretty soon. I expect she will struggle against it to the last gasp, but she shall obey me," said Richmond.

CHAPTER VII.

GEORGIA'S DREAM.

"The wild sparkle of her eye seemed caught
From high, and lighted with electric thought,
And pleased not her the sports which please her age."

o weeks passed. Charley was quite well again, and had left no effort untried to reinstate himself in the good graces of Georgia. As that young gentleman, in the profundity of his humility, had once told her he seldom failed in anything he undertook, and with his seeming genial good humor and handsome boyish face, he never found it a difficult task to make people like him, and Georgia was no more able to resist his influence than the rest of the world. And so they became good friends again—"brothers in arms" Charley said.

At first Georgia tried to resist his advances, and felt indignant at herself for allowing him to talk her into good humor and make her laugh; but it was all of no use, and at last the struggle was given up, and she condescended to patronize Master Wildair with a grave superiority that disturbed the good youth's gravity most seriously at times.

Richmond had not lost his interest in the unique child, and his influence over her increased every day. But still he was the only one who had any command over her; to the rest of the world she was the same hot, peppery, fiery little snap-dragon, defying all wills and commands that clashed with her own. And even *his* wishes, when *very* repugnant to her, she openly and fiercely braved; but, as a general thing, she began to be anxious to please her young judge, whose grave glance of stern disapproval could trouble her fearless little heart as that of no other in the world ever could. And, though she was too proud to openly let him see she cared for his approval or disapproval, still he *did* see it, and exulted therein.

Georgia had made her new friends acquainted with the pretty little Emily Murray, whom Charley unhesitatingly pronounced at first sight a "regular stunner," and these four soon became inseparable friends. At first Emily was shy and silent, which Charley perceiving, he also assumed a look of extreme timidity, not to say distressing bashfulness, which so imposed upon simple little Emily, that, pitying his evident embarrassment, she would timidly try to help him out by opening a conversation.

"Is it nice to live in New York?" Emily would say, hesitatingly.

"Yes'm," would be Charley's reply, in a tone of painful timidity.

"Nicer than here?"

"Yes'm—I—I think so."

"Won't your ma miss you a good deal?" Emily would insinuate, getting courage.

"No'm—I mean yes'm."

"Ain't Georgia nice?"

"Splendiferous!"

This long word being a puzzle to Emily she would have to stop a moment to reflect on its probable meaning before going on.

"So is your brother."

"Yes, but he's not near so nice as I am."

Again there would be a pause, during which Emily would look deeply shocked by this display of vanity—and then:

"It ain't nice to praise one's self," Emily would observe, seriously.

"Well, but it's *true*," Charley would begin, in an argumentative tone. "Now I ask yourself—don't you think I'm nicer than he is?"

Now, it was Miss Emily's private conviction that he decidedly *was*, she could not say no, and not wishing to commit herself by saying yes, she would look grave, and remain silent. But Charley, whose shyness generally passed away at this point, was not to be put off, and would insist:

"Now, Emily, just tell the truth, as every well-brought-up little girl should, and say, don't you like me twice as well as you do Rich?"

"Well, ye-es," Emily would reply, hesitatingly, "but I guess he knows more than you do; he looks awfully wise, anyway, and then Georgia minds him, and she don't mind you."

"That's because she isn't capable of appreciating solid wit and hidden genius —or, to use language more fitted for your uncultivated intellect, my young friend—she doesn't know on which side the bread's buttered. Any person with his senses about him would see at a glance I am worth a dozen of Richmond."

"No, you're not," would be Emily's decided answer; "you only think so yourself. I heard Uncle Edward saying your brother was wise for his age, and knew more than any young man he ever met, and he only laughed about you, and said you were a 'curled darling of nature,' whatever that means. So, then, I guess Uncle Edward knows better than *you*."

"Now, Miss Emily, I can't stand this; I positively can't you know. It's outrageous to expect me to lie up here and be abused in this shameful fashion, and told anybody's Uncle Edward knows more about me than I do myself. I've an immense respect for Father Murray, but still I won't permit him or anybody else to insinuate that they know more about Mr. Charles Wildair than I do. I've been acquainted with that promising youth ever since he was the size of a well-grown doughnut, and I am prepared to say, without mental reservation of any kind, that he is a perfect encyclopedia of all sorts of learning—a moving, living Webster's Dictionary, neatly bound in cloth. I've undergone grammar, declined verbs and other vicious parts of speech. I have suffered a severe course of geography, and can tell to an iota where Ireland, Kamtschatka, and lots of other aggravating places are situated; I have fought my way through French, and German, and Latin, and other dead languages; and when I go back to New York, I'm bound to have at them again, and have every single one of them, dead or alive, at my fingers ends. I have a taste for poetry and the fine arts, as I evinced in early life by a diligent perusal of that work of thrilling interest known as 'Mother Goose's Melodies', and by becoming a proficient on the Jew's-harp. I have a soul above the common, Miss Nancy, and can discover beauties in a tallow candle, and sublimity in a mug of milk and water. And now, if after this brief and inadequate exposition you don't acknowledge that my thing-um-bob-sentiments do me honor, then your intellect, like small beer in thunder, is something to be looked upon with pity and contempt!"

As Mr. Wildair, Jr., usually promulgated his sentiments to an admiring world in an exceedingly slow and leisurely manner, it took him some time to get to the end of this speech, and when he was done he found that Emily, overcome by the heat and his monotonous tone, was dropping asleep. Making a grimace, he was about to lounge back into his former lazy position, when Georgia, who had left them a moment before in full chase after a butterfly, accompanied by Richmond, returned, looking so woebegone and disconsolate that Charley, after a stare of surprise, felt called upon by the claims of common humanity to offer her consolation.

"May I ask, Miss Georgia, what awful mystery of iniquity has come to light, to make you look as if your last friend had been hung for sheep-stealing? You look about as intensely dismal now as a whole grove of weeping willows."

"Oh! it's my butterfly! my poor butterfly!" said Georgia, sorrowfully, holding up the dead insect, its bright colors all faded and gone.

"Oh, I see—as the blind man said—the insect has departed this life, leaving, no doubt, a large and bereaved circle of friends to mourn its untimely end. Funeral this evening, when friends and relatives are respectfully invited to attend—that's the newspaper style, eh? May I venture to inquire, Georgia, if the butterfly in question was a personal acquaintance of yours, that you look so afflicted at its death? Because if it was, I shall feel called upon to shed a few tears myself, out of regard for you."

"Oh, it was killed; and it was so pretty. Wasn't it pretty?" said Georgia, looking in real grief, amusing to witness, at the poor little crushed insect.

"Strangely beautiful," said Charley. "I remarked it at the time; every feature was perfect. Roman nose, intellectual forehead, well-formed head, with the bump of benevolence largely developed, blue hair, and curly teeth. And so it was killed, was it? Georgia, my friend, in the name of common humanity, in the name of the law, I ask you who was the cold-blooded assassin?"

"Poor little thing! Richmond killed it," said Georgia, too deeply troubled about the loss of the bright-hued insect to notice Charley's highfalutin tones.

"Blood-thirsty monster! let him beware! the day of retribution is at hand!" exclaimed Charley, in tones so tragic that it would have made his fortune on the stage. "Yes, the day is at hand when the oppressed and downtrodden race of butterflies will rise in arms against such tyrants as he, and Mr. Richmond Wildair will probably find himself knocked into a cocked hat. But how did it happen? Explain the horrid deed. I have steeled my soul, and nothing can move me more."

And Master Charley struck his forehead with his fist, and assumed an expression so frightfully despairing that an artist wishing to paint a patriot beholding the ruin of his country would have given all the spare change he might have for a glimpse of that agonized face.

"Why," said Georgia, "I couldn't catch it, and Richmond was determined to do it. So he struck his hat down over it, and when he took it off it was dead, and all its beautiful colors faded and gone; poor little thing!"

"Oh, my wretched country!" exclaimed Charley, raising his hands and eyes, "and it is under the shadow of thy laws such barbarous atrocities are committed; in the face of open day crimes such as these, that make the blood run down one's back like a pail of cold water, are perpetrated! And man— black-hearted man—is the author of these deeds! What other animal would perpetrate such a crime? Would a horse, or a cow, or even a donkey, now, with malice aforethought, malice at which we shudder as if we had taken a dose of castor oil, take off its hat and smash all to pieces an upright member of society—like that dilapidated butterfly, who at the time was probably thinking of his happy wife and children at home—that is, supposing it wasn't an old bachelor? I ask you again what other—but perhaps we have hardly time to do the subject justice at present," said Charley, changing his tone with startling abruptness, from one of the deepest anguish to the indifferent one of every-day life. "Where's Rich, Georgia?"

"Here, *mon frere*," replied Richmond himself, as he came up and threw himself carelessly on the grass. "Come, Georgia, throw away that dead insect, and don't stand looking so pitiously at it. There are plenty more butterflies where that came from. Why, Emily, you're not falling asleep, are you?"

Emily started up, blushing deeply at being caught in the act, and put on a wide-awake look indeed, as if to utterly repudiate the idea of such a thing.

"I hope your dreams were pleasant—eh, Em?" asked Charley.

"I didn't dream," said Emily, blushing.

"*I* dreamed last night," said Georgia, soberly.

"About me, wasn't it?" said Charley, briskly.

"About *you*" said Georgia, contemptuously. "No; I ain't such a goose! It was a dreadful dream—ugh!" and Georgia shuddered.

"Oh, Georgia, tell us—what was it about?" exclaimed Emily, eagerly.

"Do, Georgia, and I'll be the Joseph who will interpret it," said Charley.

Georgia looked grave and dark, and was silent.

"Come, Georgia, tell us," said Richmond. "I should like to hear this dream of yours."

"Oh, it was awful!" said Georgia, speaking in a hushed tone of awe. "I thought I was walking on and on through a dark, gloomy place, following some one who made me come on. The ground was full of sharp stones and hurt my feet, and they bled dreadfully; but he wouldn't let me stop, but pulled me on and on, till the ground where I walked was all covered with blood."

"Hard-hearted monster!" said Charley; "should admire to be punching that fellow's head for him!"

"As we went on," continued Georgia, looking straight before her with a dark kind of earnestness, and speaking in the tone of one describing events then passing, "the ground grew sharper and sharper, and the blood flowed so fast that at last I screamed out for him to let me go, that I couldn't walk any farther. But he only laughed at me, and pulled me on."

"The scoundrel!" broke in Charley. "If I had been there, I would have made him laugh on the other side of his mouth."

"Then, all of a sudden, we came to a great, red-hot blazing fire, that looked like burning serpents with tongues of flame. All was fire, fire, fire, on every side, red-hot blazing flames, that crackled and roared, and made everything as red as blood. I screamed out and tried to break away, but he held me fast and pushed me into the fire. I felt burning, scorching, roasting. I screamed out, and fell all burned and blazing on the ground; and then I woke, and I was sitting up in bed screaming out, and Miss Jerusha was standing over me holding me down."

Georgia paused, and there was something in her blanched face, horror-dilated eyes, and deep, awe-struck tones that for a moment sent a superstitious thrill to every heart. It was for a moment, and then Charley carelessly remarked:

"Nightmares *are* pleasant quadrupeds I know; I made the acquaintance of one after eating half a mince pie and three pigs' feet one night before going to bed; but for constant exercise I must say I should decidedly prefer riding Miss Jerusha's Shanghai rooster to trying the experiment again."

"Did you recognize the man who was with you?" asked Richmond.

"Yes," said Georgia, in a low voice.

"You did, eh?" said Charley; "who was it?"

"I sha'n't tell you."

"Oh, now, you wouldn't be so cruel. Come, out with it."

"I won't," said Georgia, with one of her sharp flashes; "but it's true—every word of it."

"You mean it will come true?" said Richmond.

"Yes."

"Why, Georgia, do you believe in dreams?" said Emily. "Oh, that's wicked; mother says so."

"Wicked! it's no such thing. What do people dream for if they're not to come true?"

"So you believe you are destined to be burned up?" said Richmond.

"Yes," said Georgia, unhesitatingly.

"Oh, I haven't the slightest doubt of it," said Charley; "if you miss it in this world, you'll——"

"Now, Charley, be quiet," said Richmond, soothingly; "you have no experience in different sorts of worlds, so you are not capable of judging. Georgia, you are the most silly-wise child I ever met in all my life."

"What!" said Georgia, with a scowl.

"You are so unnaturally precocious in some ways, and so childishly simple in others. You know the most unexpected things, and are ignorant of the commonest facts that any infant almost comprehends. You are morbid and superstitious—but I knew that before. A little learning is a dangerous thing. Georgia, you ought to go to school."

Now, school was Georgia's pet abomination. Miss Jerusha, partly to be rid of her and partly for the propriety of the thing, had often wished to send her; but the idea of being cooped up a prisoner within the walls of a school-room, and obliged to obey every command, was abhorrent to the free, unfettered, untamed child. Go to school, indeed! Not she! She laughed at the notion. Richmond had never spoken of it before to her, and now, conscious of his power over her, and trembling for her threatened liberty, all the old spirit of daring and fierce defiance flashed up in her bold black eyes, and, springing to her feet, she confronted him.

"I *won't*! I'll never go to school! I hate it!"

Georgia never said "I can't" or "I don't like to," but her dauntless, defiant "I *will*" and "I *won't*," bespoke her nature. Emily said the former; Georgia, never.

Richmond expected exactly this answer, therefore he only smiled slightly, and carelessly asked,

"Why?"

"Because I won't be shut up in a nasty old school-house, and not be able to speak or move without asking leave. I'll not go for *any one!*" she said, flashing a threatening glance at him.

"Every one else does it, Georgia."

"I don't care for every one else."

"*I* did it, Georgia."

"Well, I don't care for you!"

"Whew!" whistled Charley. "Sharp shooting, this."

"Then you prefer to grow up a—"

"What?"

"A dunce, and be laughed at."

"Let them laugh at me! let them dare do it!" cried Georgia, fiercely.

"And dare do it they will. Pooh, Georgia, have sense. You can't roll up your sleeves and go to fisticuffs with the whole world. What else can you expect but to be laughed at when you are a woman if you know nothing but what you do now? Wait till you see the wise little woman Emily here is going to be. Why, your friends will be ashamed of you, Georgia, by and by, if you don't learn something."

"Let them, then! I don't care for them!"

"Oh, don't you? I thought that as they cared so much for you, you might care a little for them. I am sorry it is not so, Georgia; I am very sorry my little friend is selfish and ungrateful."

"I am *not* ungrateful," said Georgia, passionately, but her lips quivered.

"Then prove it by doing something to please your friends. Think how they have tried to please you, and just ask yourself what you have done in return to please them. Come, Georgia, be reasonable. You will think better of this when you come to reflect on it."

"That's right, Rich," cried Charley; "go in and win! I always knew you had a native talent for teaching young ideas how to shoot. Splendid parson you'd make."

"I *have* tried to please them! I have tried to please *you!*"

"Well, did I ever ask you to do any thing but what was your *duty* to do? I am afraid you have not a good idea of what that word means. I am your friend, you know, Georgia, am I *not?*" he said gently.

"I don't know," she said, with a trembling lip.

"But I am your true friend. What difference can it make to me whether you grow up learned and accomplished, or as ignorant as your little servant, Fly?"

"A great deal, if she know but all," muttered Charley.

"But I hate school! I should *die* if I was kept in," said Georgia with a sort of cry.

"Nonsense! You would do no such thing! Do you remember the bird I caught for you and put in a cage? Yes! well, it struggled to get out, and beat its wings against the bars of the cage until you thought it would have beat itself to death, yet now it is a willing captive."

"Yes, it is like a wooden bird, without life; it lies in the bottom of the cage and hardly ever sings or moves; it isn't worth having now," said Georgia, her lip curling with a sort of scorn.

"Well, it will be different with you; you are ambitious, Georgia, and in trying to pass your schoolmates you will feel a delight and pride you never experienced before. A new world will be opened to you; you will like it. *Do go, Georgia; if I were not your friend, if I did not like you very much, I should not ask you.*"

Charley, with his head bent down whistling "Yankee Doodle," was shaking with inward laughter.

"Oh, Georgia, do come," pleaded Emily.

Georgia, with her lips compressed, her glittering black eyes burning into the ground, stood silent, motionless, turned to iron.

"Well, Georgia?"

No reply.

"*Georgia!*" Richmond cried, anxiously.

She lifted her eyes.

"Well?"

"Georgia, will you go—I want you to—you don't know how deeply grieved I shall be if you refuse; so deeply grieved that we shall be friends no longer. Georgia, I am going away from here soon—I may never come back—never see you again, and I should be sorry we should part bad friends. Georgia, will you go?"

"Yes."

It was a hard-wrung assent. The word dropped from her lips as though it burned them.

Charley's whistle at that moment spoke volumes. Emily looked delighted, and the face of Richmond Wildair lit up with triumph and exultation. Once that "yes" had been uttered he knew her word would be sacredly kept. How he exulted that moment in his power.

"Thank you, Georgia," he cried, springing to his feet, and holding out his hand, "we are fast friends forever now."

Georgia shook hands, but the fingers she gave him were little rigid bars of steel—no life—no warmth there.

"When will you go?" said Richmond, following up his advantage, on the principle of striking while the iron was hot.

"On Monday."

"Oh, Georgia, I'm so glad! Oh, Georgia that's so nice!" exclaimed Emily, dancing round delightedly, and clasping her hands.

Georgia's face was a blank—cold and meaningless.

"That is right! Georgia, you are a good girl!"

"If I had refused to do as you told me I would have been a selfish, ungrateful thing—I understand!" said Georgia, turning away with a curling lip.

Richmond started. There was the look of a woman in her childish face at that moment. It was one of her precocious turns.

"Now, don't be cross, Georgia; it's real nice to go to school after you get used to it," said Emily, in her pretty, coaxing way, putting her arms round her waist.

"I must go home—Miss Jerusha will want me," said Georgia, by way of reply, as she resolutely, almost rudely, unclasped Emily's clinging arms.

"Shall I go with you?" said Richmond, making a step forward.

"*No!*" exclaimed Georgia, with one of her peculiar sharp, bright flashes, as she turned away in the direction of the cottage.

Richmond and Emily sauntered back to Burnfield together, chatting gayly. As Richmond entered the grounds of his uncle's stately residence he saw his brother standing in the threshold humming a classical ditty.

"Bravo, Richmond, old boy!" cried Charley, giving him a sounding slap on the shoulder; "you deserve a leather medal! Do you think any of the blood of your namesake of evil memory has descended to you?"

"Pshaw, Charley! don't be a fool!" said Richmond, impatiently.

"I don't intend to, my dear brother," said Charley, dryly; "but the scales fell from my eyes to-day. What a world we live in!"

"Tush! will you never learn to talk sense, Charles?" said Richmond, biting his lips to maintain his gravity, as he shook off his hand and passed into the house.

CHAPTER VIII.

"COMING EVENTS CAST THEIR SHADOWS BEFORE."

"A look of pride, an eye of flame,
A full drawn lip that upward curled,
An eye that seemed to scorn the world."

e little town of Burnfield contained but one school, within the old brown walls and moss-grown eaves of which the "fathers of the hamlet" for many a generation had sat at the feet of some worthy pedagogue, or pedagoguess, as the case might be, to catch the wisdom that fell from their lips. In summer woman held her sway there, but in winter man reigned supreme on the throne of learning, and "boarded round," a custom not yet obsolete.

Once every year came the great anniversary of the school, the last day of April, when the "master's" term expired, and he left the town to the dominion of the new school-marm. Then took place the great public examination, in which lanky youths, weighed down with the consciousness of their responsibility and first tail-coats, and cherry-cheeked girls, bursting out of their hooks and eyes, showed off before the admiring Burnfieldians, and received their rewards of merit, more highly prized by them than the Cross of the Legion of Honor would be by some old French veteran. A new innovation had lately been introduced by one of the teachers—that of speaking dialogues at these distributions, and wonderful was the delight young Burnfield took in these displays. The more strait-laced of the parents at first objected to this, as smacking too much of "play acting," but young Burnfield had a decided will of its own, and looked contemptuously on the "slow" ideas of old Burnfield, and finally, in triumph, carried the day.

The great day arrived, and the anxious parents who had young ideas at school, were crowding rapidly toward the large old-fashioned school-house under the hill. Among them, in grim, unbending majesty, stalked Miss Jerusha Skamp, resplendent in what she was pleased to term her new "kaliker gound," a garment which partook of the nature of its forerunners in being exceedingly short and exceedingly skimpy, and the gorgeous patterns of which can be likened to nothing save a highly exaggerated rainbow. But Miss Jerusha, happy in the belief that nothing like it had appeared in modern times, walked majestically in, upsetting some loose benches, half a dozen small boys, and other trifles that lay in her way, and took her seat on one of the front benches. The boys, gorgeous in blue and gray homespun coats, with brass buttons of alarming size and brightness, were ranged on one side, and the girls, arrayed in all the hues of a flower-garden, on the other. Miss Jerusha's eyes wandered to the side where the girls sat, and rested with a look of evident pride and self-complaisance on one—a look that said as plainly as words, "There! look at that! there's *my* handiwork for you."

And certainly, amid the many handsome, blooming girls there, not one was more worth looking at than she on whom Miss Jerusha's eyes rested. The tall, slight, but well-portioned form had none of the awkwardness common to girls in their transition stages. The queenly little head was poised superbly on the sloping neck; the clear olive skin, with its glowing crimson lips and cheeks, was the very ideal of dark, rich, southern beauty; the jet-black shining hair, swept off the broad forehead in smooth silken braids, became well the scarlet ribbons that bound it, as did also the close-fitting crimson dress she wore.

Georgia (for of course every reader above the unsuspecting age of three years knows who it is), without being at all aware of it, always fell into the style of dress that best suited her and harmonized with her warm, tropical complexion —dark, rich colors, such as black, purple, crimson, or, in summer, white. The two years that have passed since we saw her last have changed her wonderfully; but the full, proud, passionate, flashing eyes are the same in their dark splendor; the short, curling upper lip and curved nostril tell a tale of pride, and passion, and daring, and scornful power—tell that time may have softened, but has not eradicated, the temper of our stormy little essence of wild-fire.

Yes, she sits there, leaning listlessly back in her seat, her little restless brown hands folded quietly enough in her lap, her long black lashes vailing her darkly glancing eyes, cast down by a sort of proud indolence; but it is the calm that precedes the tempest, the dangerous spirit of the drowsy and beautiful leopard, the deep, treacherous stillness that heralds the bursting sheets of fire from the volcano's bosom, the white ashes that overlie consuming flames hidden beneath them, but ready at any moment to burst forth. And there she sat, known only to those present as the "smart little girl," the star scholar of the school, good-looking, bright, generous, and warm-hearted, too, but "ugly tempered."

The dark, bright, handsome eyes of the girl of fifteen had already carried unexampled desolation into more than one susceptible breast, and some of the unhappy youths were so badly stricken as to be guilty of the atrocity of perpetrating soul-harrowing "pote"-ry to those same dangerous optics. But these were only the worst cases, and even they never tried it but in the first delirium of the attack, and, like all delirious fevers, it soon passed away, died out like a hot little fire under (to use a homely simile) the wet blanket of her cool, utter indifference, and they returned to their buckwheat cakes, and pork, and molasses with just as good an appetite as ever.

One by one the people came in until the school-house was filled, and then the exercises commenced. The premiums were arranged on a table, and on a desk beside it stood the master, who rose and called out:

"First prize for general excellence awarded to Miss Georgia Darrell."

There was a moment's profound silence, while every eye turned upon Georgia, and then, as if by general impulse, there was an enthusiastic round of applause, for her warm, ardent nature, and many generous impulses, made her schoolmates like her in spite of her ebullitions of temper. And in the midst of this Georgia rose, with a flashing eye and kindling cheek, and, advancing to where the teacher stood, received the first prize from his hand, courtesied, and, with head proudly erect, and cheeks hot with the excitement of triumph, walked back to her seat.

Then came the other premiums, for grammar, for geography, history, and astronomy; the first prize was still awarded to "Miss Georgia Darrell," until the good folks of Burnfield began to knit their brows in anger and jealousy, and accused the master of being swayed, like the rest, by a handsome face, and unjustly depriving their offspring for the sake of this "stuck-up Georgia Darrell," who—as Deacon Brown remarked, in a scandalized tone—seemed to despise the very "airth she walked on."

The distribution was over at last, and then came the dialogues. And here Georgia's star was in the ascendant again. She, and the teacher, perhaps, knew what acting was—not one of the rest had the remotest idea—and they held their very breath to listen, as losing her own identity her eyes blazed and her cheeks burned, and she strode up and down, declaiming with such vehement gestures, that they looked at one another in a sort of terror, wonder, and admiration. And once, when she and another were repeating a selection from Tamerlane, where she took the character of Bajazet, and Tamerlane, in a sort of wonder and admiration, says:

"The world! 'twould be too little for thy pride!
Thou wouldst scale heaven!"

Georgia's eyes of lightning blazed, and raising her hand with a passionate gesture, she strode over and fiercely thundered:

"I WOULD! Away! my soul
Disdains thy conference!"

The Tamerlane of the moment recoiled in terror, and there was an instant of
death-like silence, while every heart thrilled with the knowledge that the dark,
wild girl was not "acting," but speaking the truth.

It was all over at last, and, with a few words from the teacher, the assembly
was dismissed. As Georgia gathered up her armful of prizes and put on her
bonnet, the teacher came over, and, to the jealousy of the other pupils, held
out his hand to her, who had from the first been his favorite.

"Good-by, Bajazet," he said, smiling; "you electrified the good people of
Burnfield to-day."

Georgia laughed.

"Do you know you were not acting just now, Georgia? Do you know you are
ambitious enough to scale heaven? Do you know that you have within you
what hurled Lucifer from heaven?"

"Yes, sir," she said, lifting her eyes boldly; "I know it."

"And do you not fear?"

"No, sir."

"Do you know you are composed of elements that will make you either an
angel or a—*demon*?"

"Miss Jerusha says I'm the latter *now*, sir," she said, with a light laugh.

He looked at her with a smile half fond, half sad.

"Georgia, take care."

"Of what, sir?"

"Of *yourself*—your worst enemy."

"Father Murray says everyone is his own worst enemy."

"You are not like everyone. You are a little two-edged sword in a remarkably
thin sheath, my little sprite. Take care."

"Well, I know I'm thin," said Georgia, who was in one of her unserious
moods; "but that is my misfortune, Mr. Coleman, not my fault. Wait a little
while, and you'll see I'll turn out to be a female pocket edition of Daniel
Lambert."

"Georgia!"

"Well, sir."

"Promise me one thing."

"What is it, first?"

"That you will study very hard till I come back next winter?"

"Of course I will, sir. I made that promise once before."

"Indeed? To whom? Miss Jerusha?"

"Miss Jerusha!" said Georgia, laughing. "I guess not! To a friend of mine—a young gentleman."

And the girl of fifteen glanced up from under her long lashes at the dignified man of forty.

"Pooh, Georgia! stick to your books, and never mind the *genus homo*. You're a pretty subject to be advised by young gentlemen. It was good advice, though, and I indorse it."

"Very well, sir; but why am I to attend to my studies more than any of the rest of your pupils—Mary Ann Jones, for instance?"

"Humph! there is a wide difference. Mary Ann Jones will go home and help her mother to knit stockings, scrub the floor, make pumpkin pies, and eat them, too, without even a thought of mischief, while you would be breaking your neck or somebody else's, setting the iron on fire, or bottling thunderbolts to blow up the community generally. As there is more truth than poetry in that couplet of the solemn and prosy Dr. Watts, wherein he assures us—

"'Satan finds some mischief still
For idle hands to do,'

on that principle you need to be kept busy. Between you and Mary Ann Jones there is about as much difference as there is between that useful domestic fowl, a barnyard goose, and that dangerous, sharp-clawed, good-for-nothing thing, a tameless mountain eaglet; and you may consider the comparison anything but complimentary to you. Mary Ann is going to be a merry, contented, capital housekeeper, and you—what are *you* going to be?"

"A vagabones on the face of the airth," said Georgia, imitating Miss Jerusha's nasal twang so well that it nearly overset the good teacher's gravity.

"Ah, Georgia! I see you are in one of your wild moods to-day, and will not listen to reason. Well, good-by—be a good girl till I come back."

"Good-by, sir. I don't think I will ever be a good girl, but I will be as good as I can. Good-by, and thank you, sir."

There was something so darkly earnest in her face, that Mr. Coleman looked after her, more puzzled than he had ever before been by a pupil. She had always been an enigma to him—she was to most people—and to-day she was more unreadable than ever.

"I declare to skreech, Georgy!" said Miss Jerusha, as they walked home together, "you like to skeered the life out o' me to-day, the way you talked and shouted. Clare to gracious! ef it wasn't parfectly orful, not to say downright wicked. Talk about scalin' heaven! there's sense for you now! And it's not only sinful, as Deacon Brown remarked, but reglir onpossible. Where could a ladder, now, or even a fire escape be got, long enough to do it? Pah! it's disgustin', such nonsense! I wonder a man like that there Mr. Coleman would 'low of sich talk in his school hus, it's rale disgraceful—that's what it is!"

Georgia laughed. Georgia was more patient with Miss Jerusha than she used to be, and had her hot temper more under control. This was in a great measure owing to the instructions and gentle exhortations of good Mrs. Murray, little Emily's mother, who had taught her that instead of conferring a favor on the old maid by living with her, she owed her a debt of gratitude she would find it difficult to repay. And Georgia, whose faults were more of the head than of the heart, saw Mrs. Murray was right, and consented to try and "behave herself" for the future. Georgia found *self*-control a *very* difficult lesson to practice; and the impulses of her nature very often rose and mastered her good resolutions yet. Still it was something for her even to try, and it had such an effect on Miss Jerusha, that the vinegar in that sour spinster's composition became perceptibly less acid, and the ward and "dragon" got along much better than formerly. So true it is that every effort to do good is rewarded even here.

When Georgia got home she found her friend Emily Murray awaiting her. Despite the wide difference in their dispositions Emily and Georgia were still fast friends. Emily did not go to the public school, but was taught at home by her mother. But they saw each other every day, and Emily's sunny disposition helped not a little to soften down our savage little wild-cat into her present state of comparative civilization. Still the same rounded little lady was Emily, perhaps an inch or two higher than when thirteen years old, but still nothing to speak of, with the same smiling, rosy, sunshiny little face peeping out from its wealth of tangled yellow curls—for Emily's hair would persist in curling in spite of all attempts to comb it straight and respectable looking, and persisted in having its own way, and openly rebelling against all established authority.

"Oh, Georgia! I'm so glad!" exclaimed Emily, throwing her arms around Georgia's neck, and administering a dozen or two short, sharp little kisses that went off like the corks out of so many ginger-beer bottles. "I'm *ever* so glad that you got all the prizes! I knew you would; I said it all along. I knew you were dreadfully clever, if you only liked. And now I want you to come right over to our house and spend the evening with us. Mother told me to come for you. Oh, Georgia! we'll have a good time!"

"Well, there, Em, you needn't strangle me about it," said Georgia, laughingly releasing herself. "If Miss Jerusha doesn't want me particularly, I'll go."

Two years previously Georgia would no more have thought of asking Miss Jerusha's leave about any thing than she would of flying; but since she had come to a sense of her duty things were different. But as the leopard cannot change his spots, nor the Ethiope his skin, so neither could she entirely change her nature, and there was an involuntary defiant light in her eye and haughtiness in her tone when asking a favor, and a fierce bright flash and passionate gesture when refused.

Miss Jerusha looked undecided, and was beginning a dubious "Wal, raily, now—" when Emily's impulsive arms were around *her* neck, and her pretty face upturned.

"Ah, now, Miss Jerusha, please do; that's a dear! Do just let her come over this once. I want her so dreadfully! P-p-please now."

No heart, unless made of double-refined cast iron, could resist that sweet little face and pleading "please now;" so Miss Jerusha, who liked little Emily (as indeed nobody could help doing), accordingly "pleased," and Emily, giving her a kiss—of which commodity that small individual had a large stock in trade, that like the widow's cruse of old, never diminished—put on Georgia's hat, and, nodding a smiling good-by to Miss Jerusha, marched her off in triumph.

"I am so glad, Georgia, you got so many prizes. Oh! I knew all along you were real clever. I should like to be clever, but I'm not one bit; but you, I guess you're going to be a genius, Georgia," said Emily, soberly.

"Nonsense, Em! A genius! I hope I shall never be anything half so dreadful."

"Dreadful! Why, Georgia!"

"Why, Emily!" said Georgia, mimicking her, "geniuses are a nuisance, I repeat—just as comets, or meteors, or eclipses, or anything out of the ordinary course are. People make a fuss about them and blacken their noses looking through smoked glass at them, and then they are gone in a twinkling, and not worth all the time that was wasted looking at them. I know it is sacrilege and high treason to say so, but that doesn't alter my opinion on the subject, and so don't trouble that small, anxious head of yours, my dear little snow-flake, about my being a genius again."

"I know who thinks so as well as I do," said Emily.

"Who?"

"Why, Richmond Wildair. Do you recollect the day, long ago, he first told you to go to school?"

"Yes."

"Coming home that day he said he knew you were a little genius and should not hide your light under a bushel, but set it on the hill-top. I remember his words, because they sounded so funny then that they made me laugh."

"Pooh! what does he know about it? What a little simpleton I must have been to do everything he used to tell me to! Still, that was good advice about going to school, and I don't know but what, on the whole, I feel grateful to him for it. That was two years ago—wasn't it, Em? Why, it seems like yesterday."

"And that funny brother of his," said Emily, laughing at some recollections of her own, "he used to say things in such a droll way. I wonder if they'll ever come back."

"Why, what would bring them back, now that their uncle is gone away for his health? I wonder if traveling really *does* make sick people well?"

"Don't know, I'm sure. Isn't it a pity to have such a nice house as that shut up and so lonely and deserted looking?"

"I wish that house was mine," said Georgia. "I should like to live in a large, handsome place like that. I hate little old cramped places like our cottage—they're horrid."

"Why, that's coveting your neighbor's goods," said Emily. "Look out, Georgia."

"Well, then, I should like one as good as that. I wish I owned one just like it. I *shall*, too, some day," said Georgia, decidedly.

"Do tell," said Emily, "where are you going to get it? Are you going to rob a peddler?"

"No. I intend to be rich."

"You do? *How?*"

"I don't know yet; but I *shall*! I'm determined to be rich. I am quite sure I will be," said Georgia, in a tone of quiet decision.

"Well, really! But it's better to be poor than rich. 'It's easier for a camel—' You know what the Testament says."

"I'd risk it. Why, Emily, it's riches moves the world; the whole earth is seeking it. Poverty is the greatest social crime in the whole category, and wealth covereth a multitude of sins. Don't tell me! I know all about it, and I am determined to be rich—*I don't care by what means!*"

Her wild eyes were blazing with that insufferable light that always illuminated them when she was excited, and the stern determination her set face expressed as she looked resolutely before her startled timid little Emily.

"Oh, Georgia, I don't think it's right to talk so!" she said, in a subdued tone; "I'm sure it's not. I don't think riches make people happy; do you?"

"No," said Georgia, quietly.

"Oh, Georgia, then why do you wish for it? Why do you crave so for wealth?"

"Because wealth brings power!"

"But neither does power bring happiness."

"To *me* it would. Power is the life of my life. Knowledge is power—therefore I studied; but it is only a means to an end. Wealth will attain that end, therefore wealth I must and *will* have."

The look of resolute determination deepened. She looked at that moment like one resolved to conquer even fate, and to tread remorselessly under foot all that stood between her and the goal of her daring ambition.

"What would you do if you were rich?"

"I would travel, for one thing—I should like to see the world. I would visit England, and France, and Germany, and Italy—dear, beautiful Italy! that I love as if it were my fatherland. I would visit the Alps—Oh, Em! how I love great sublime mountains rearing their heads up to heaven. I would sail down the Rhine, the bright flowing Rhine! I would visit the demons of the Black Forest, and see if I happen to be related to them, in any way. I would cultivate the acquaintance of the Black Horseman of the Hartz Mountains—and finally I should settle down and marry a prince. Yes, I rather think I *shall* marry some prince, Em!"

"Oh, Georgia! you're a case!" said Emily, breaking into one of her silvery peals of laughter; "marry a prince! what an idea!"

"Well, I am good enough for any prince or emperor that ever wore a crown," said Georgia, with a flash of her black eyes, and a proud lift of her haughty little head, "and I should consider that the honor was conferred upon him, and not me, if I did marry one—now then!"

"Oh, what a bump of self-esteem you have, Georgia!" said Emily, still laughing; "what a notion to talk about getting married, any way! whoever heard of such a thing."

"Well, it's nothing strange! you didn't suppose I was going to be an old maid like Miss Jerusha, did you? *Of course* I'll get married! I always intended to!" said Georgia, decidedly, "and so will you, Emily."

"To another prince," said Emily, shyly.

"No, to—Charley Wildair!"

"I guess not! But here we are at home, and what would mother say if she heard us talking like this? It all comes of your reading so many novels, Georgia. Here, mother; here she is. I've got her," cried Emily, flying into the pretty little parlor, where Mrs. Murray, a pleasant little lady, a faded copy of her bright little daughter, sat sewing. Mrs. Murray kissed Georgia, and congratulated her on her success, and then went out to see about tea.

Later in the evening Father Murray, a benign-looking old man, with silver-white hair, and a look so patriarchal that it had suggested Charley Wildair's graphic description of his being like one of those "blessed old what's-their-names in the Bible," came in, and the conversation turned upon Georgia's success.

"I suppose you felt quite elated, Georgia, at carrying off the highest honors to-day?" he said, smiling.

"A little, only," said Georgia. "It wasn't much to be proud of."

"What! To vanquish all competitors not much to be proud of! Why, Georgia?"

"Well, neither it is, sir—*such* competitors," said Georgia, scornfully. "I should like a greater conquest than that."

"Georgia's ambition takes a bolder flight; she looks down on the common people of this world," said Mrs. Murray, with a peculiar smile.

Georgia colored at the implied rebuke, but her disdainful look remained. Father Murray looked at her half pityingly, half sorrowfully.

"It will not do, Georgia," he said kindly: "you will have to stop. The Mountain of High-and-Mighty-dom is a very dazzling eminence to be sure, but the sun shines brighter in the valley below."

At that moment Fly entered for her young mistress, and Georgia arose to go.

"Good-by, Mrs. Murray; good-by, Em; good-night, Father Murray."

"Good-night, Georgia," he said, laying his hand on her shining, haughty young head, "and Heaven bless you, my child!"

She folded her hands almost meekly to receive his benediction, and feeling as though that blessing were sorely needed, she passed out and was gone.

Gone! As for you and me, reader, the *child* Georgia has gone forever. Let the curtain drop on the first act in her drama of life, to rise when the child shall be a woman.

CHAPTER IX.

OLD FRIENDS MEET.

> "It was not thus in other days we met;
> Hath time and absence taught thee to forget?"

d three years passed away.

Elsewhere these three years might have wrought strange changes, but they made few in good old Burnfield. The old, never-ending, but ever new routine of births, and deaths, and marriages went on; children were growing up to be men and women—there were no young *ladies* and *gentlemen* in Burnfield— and other children were taking their place. The only marked change was the introduction of a railway, that brought city people to the quiet sea-coast town every summer, and gave a sort of impetus to the stagnating business of the place. Very dazzling and bewildering to the eyes of the sober-going Burnfieldians were those dashing city folks, who condescended to patronize them with a lofty superiority quite overwhelming.

One other change these three years had wrought—the girl Georgia was a woman in looks and stature, the handsome, haughty, capricious belle of Burnfield. Time had passed unmarked by any incident worth mentioning. Life was rather monotonous in that little sea-shore cottage, and Georgia might have stagnated with the rest but for the fiery life in her heart that would never be at rest long enough to suffer her to fall into a lethargy.

Georgia's physical and mental education had been rapidly progressing during these three years. She could manage a boat with the best oarsman in Burnfield; and often, when the winds were highest and the sea roughest, her light skiff—a gift from an admirer—might be seen dancing on the waters like a sea-gull, with the tall, slight form of a young girl guiding it through the foam, her wild black eyes lit up with the excitement of the moment, looking like some ocean goddess, or the queen of the storm riding the tempest she had herself raised.

Georgia braved all dangers because they brought her excitement, and she would have lived in a constant fever if she could; danger sent the hot blood bounding through her veins like quicksilver, and fear was a feeling unknown to her high and daring temperament. So when the typhus fever once, a year previously, raged through the town, carrying off hundreds, and every one fled in terror, she braved it all, entered every house where it appeared in its most malignant form, braved storm, and night, and danger to nurse the pest-stricken, and became the guardian-angel of the town. And this—not, reader, from any high and holy motive, not from that heavenly charity, that inspires the heroic Sister of Charity to do likewise—but simply because there was excitement in it, because she was fearless for herself and exulted in her power at that moment, and perhaps, to do Georgia justice, she was urged by a humane feeling of pity for the neglected sufferers. She watched by the dead and dying, she boldly entered lazar houses where no one else would tread, and she did not take the disease. Her high, perfect bodily health, her fine organization and utter fearlessness, were her safeguards. Georgia had already obtained a sort of mastery over the townfolks; that deference was paid to her that simple minds always pay to lofty ones; but now her power was complete. She reigned among them a crowned queen; the dark-eyed, handsome girl had obtained a mastery over them she could never lose; she had only to raise her finger to have them come at her beck; she was beginning to realize her childish dream of power, and she triumphed in it. And so, free, wild, glad, and untamed, the young conqueress reigned, queen of the forest and river, and a thousand human hearts; looked up to, as comets are—something to admire and wonder at, at a respectful distance.

Under the auspices of Father Murray her education had progressed rapidly. As his congregation was not very numerous, his labors were not very arduous, and he found a good deal of spare time for himself. Being a profound scholar, he determined to devote himself to the education of his little niece Emily, and at her solicitation Georgia also became his pupil. Poor, simple, happy little Emily was speedily outstripped and left far behind by her gifted companion, who mastered every science with a rapidity and ease really wonderful. By nature she was a decided linguist, and learned French, and German, and Latin with a quickness that delighted the heart of good Father Murray. All the religious training the wild girl had ever received in her life was imbibed now, but even yet it was only superficial; it just touched the surface of her sparkling nature, nothing sunk in. She professed no particular faith; she believed in no formal creed; she worshiped the Lord of the mighty sea and the beautiful earth, the ruler of the storm and king of the universe, in a wild, strange, exultant way of her own, but she looked upon all professed creeds as so many trammels that no one with an independent will could ever submit to. Ah! it was Georgia's hour of highest earthly happiness then; she did not know how the heart of all atheists, infidels, and heretics cry out involuntarily to that merciful All Father in their hour of sorrow. Georgia was as one who "having eyes saw not, having ears heard not." In the summer time of youth, and health, and happiness she *would not* believe, and it was only like many others when the fierce wintry tempest beat on her unsheltered head, when the dark night of utter anguish closed around her, she fell at the feet of Him who "doeth all things well," offering not a fresh, unworldly heart, but one crushed, and rent, and consumed to calcined ashes in the red heat of her own fiery passions.

Georgia rarely went to church; her place of worship was the dark solemn, old primeval forest, where, lying under the trees, listening to the drowsy twittering of the birds for her choir, she would dream her wild, rainbow-tinted visions of a future more glorious than this earth ever realized. Ah! the dreams of eighteen!

It was a wild, blusterous afternoon in early spring, a dark, dry, windy day. Miss Jerusha, the same old cast-iron vestal as of yore, sat in the best room, knitting away, just as you and I, reader, first saw her on Christmas Eve five years ago, just looking as if five minutes instead of years had passed since then, so little change is there in her own proper person or in that awe-inspiring apartment, the best room. The asthmatic rocking-chair seems to have been attacked with rheumatism since, for its limbs are decidedly of a shaky character, and its consumptive wheeze, as it saws back or forward, betokens that its end is approaching. Curled up at her feet lies that intelligent quadruped, Betsey Periwinkle, gazing with blinking eyes in the fire, and deeply absorbed in her own reflections. A facetious little gray-and-white kitten (Betsey's youngest), is amusing itself running round and round in a frantic effort to catch its own little shaving-brush of a tail, varying the recreation by making desperate dives at Miss Jerusha's ball of stocking yarn, and invariably receives a kick in return that sends it flying across the room, but which doesn't seem to disturb its equanimity much. Out in the kitchen that small "cullud pusson," Fly, is making biscuits for supper, and diffusing around her a most delightful odor of good things. Miss Jerusha sits silently knitting for a long time with pursed-up lips, only glancing up now and then when an unusually high blast makes the little homestead shake, but at last the spirit moves her, and she speaks:

"It's abominable! it's disgraceful! the neglect of parents nowadays! letting their young 'uns run into all sorts of danger, and without no insurance on 'em neither. If that there little chap was mine, I'd switch him within an inch of his life afore I'd let him carry on with such capers. He'll be drowned just as sure as shootin', and sarve him right, too, a venturesome, fool-hardy little limb! You, Fly!"

Miss Jerusha's voice has lost none of its shrillness and sharpness under the mollifying influence of Old Father Time.

"Yes, Mist," sings out Fly, in a shrill treble.

"Ken you see that little viper yet, or has he got drownded?"

"He's a-driftin' out'n de riber, ole Mist; shill I run and tell his folks when I puts der biscuits in de oben?" says Fly, straining her eyes looking out of the kitchen window.

"No, you sha'n't do no sich thing! if his folks don't think he's worth a-lookin' arter thimselves, I ain't a-goin' to put myself out noways 'bout it. *Let* him drown, ef he's a mind to, and perhaps they'll look closer arter the rest. A young 'un more or less ain't no great loss. Don't let them ere biscuits burn, you Fly! or it'll be wuss for you! I wish Georgia was here; it's time she was to hum."

"*Quand un parle du diable on en voit le vue!*" says a clear, musical voice, and the present Georgia, a tall, superbly formed girl, with the shining eyes, and glossy hair of her childhood, but with a higher bloom and brighter smile than that tempestuous childhood ever knew, enters and stands before her, her dark hair blown out by the wind that has sent a deeper glow to her dark crimson cheeks, and a more vivid light to her splendid eyes.

"Oh, you've come, hev you?" says Miss Jerusha, rather crossly, "and a talkin' of Hebrew and Greek, and sich other ungodly lingo, again. It's suthin' bad, I know, or you wouldn't be a sayin' of it in thim onchristian langergers. I allurs said nothin' good would come of your heavin' away of your time and larning thim. I know it ain't right; don't sound as if it war. I feel it in my bones that it ain't. Where hev you bin?"

"Over to Emily's," Georgia said, laughingly, as she snatched up Betsey Periwinkle, junior, and stroked her soft fur. "What did you want me for when I came in?"

"Oh," said Miss Jerusha, "it's all along of that little imp, Johnny Smith, as has been and gone and went out in a boat, and I expect is upsot and gone to the bottom afore this."

Georgia sprang to her feet in consternation.

"What! gone out in a boat! to-day! that child! Miss Jerusha, what do you mean?"

"Why, just what I say," said Miss Jerusha, testily; "that there little cuss has a taste for drowndin', for he's never out of a boat when he can get into one, and I do b'lieve it's more'n half your fault, too, abringing of him out with you every day in your derned little egg-shell of a skiff. Ef he hain't got to the bottom before this it's a wonder."

94

"Oh, that child! that child! he will be drowned! Good Heaven, Miss Jerusha, why did you not send and tell his parents?"

"Well, 'taint my place to look arter other folks' young 'uns, is it?" said Miss Jerusha, shifting uneasily under the stern, indignant gaze bent upon her. "Let every tub stand on its own bottom, *I* say."

"Oh, Miss Georgia! Miss Georgia!" cried Fly, excitedly, "dar he is! run right into dat ar rock out'n de riber, an' now he can't get off, an' de tide is a risin' so fast he'll be swep' off pooty soon."

Georgia sprang to the window and looked out. The river, swollen and turbid by the spring freshets, and lashed into fury by the high winds, was one sheet of white foam, like the land in a December snow-storm. The boat had struck a high rock, or rather small island, out in the river, and there stood a lad of about ten years old with outstretched arms, evidently shrieking for help; but his cries were drowned in the uproar of the winds and waves. In ten minutes it was evident the sea would sweep over the rock, and then——

Georgia with a wild, frenzied gesture, turned and fled from the house, seized two light oars that lay outside the door, threw them over her shoulder, and sped with the lightness and fleetness of a mountain deer down the rocks to the beach.

"Oh, Miss Jerry! Miss Jerry! she's a-goin' arter him," shrieked Fly. "Oh, laudy! dey'll bof be drowned *dead*! Oh! Oh! Oh!" And shrieking, Fly rushed out and darted off toward the nearest house to tell the news.

New settlers had lately come to Burnfield, and Miss Jerusha's nearest neighbors, the parents of the venturesome little Smith, lived within a quarter of a mile of her. Mercury himself was not a fleeter messenger than Fly, and soon the Smiths and other people around were alarmed and hurrying in crowds to the beach. As Fly, still screaming out the news, was darting hither and thither, a hand was laid on her arm, and looking up, she saw a gentleman, young and handsome, muffled in a Spanish cloak, and with his hat pulled down over his eyes.

"What's all this uproar about, my good girl? Where are all these people hurrying to?" he asked, arresting her.

"Oh, to der beach! Miss Georgia will be drowned," cried Fly, breaking from him, and darting off among the crowd.

The stranger hurried on with the rest, and a very few minutes brought him to the beach, already thronged with the alarmed neighbors. On a high rock stood Miss Jerusha, wringing her hands and gesticulating wildly, and more wildly urging the men to go to Georgia's assistance, going through all the phrases of the potential mood, "exhorting, commanding, entreating," in something after the following fashion:

"Oh, she'll be drownded! she'll be drownded! I know she will, and sarve her right, too—a ventursome, undutiful young hussy! Oh, my gracious! what are you all a-standing here for, a-doing nothing, and Georgey drownding? Go right off this minit and git a boat and go after her. There! there! she's down now! No, she's up again, but she's sartin to be drownded, the infernally young fool! Oh, Pete Jinking! you derned lazy old coward! get out your boat and go arter her! Oh, Pete! you're a nice old man! do go arter her! There! now she's upsot! No, she's right end up agin, but the next time she sure to go! Oh, my conscience! won't none en ye go arter her, you miserable set of sneakin' cowards you! Oh, my stars and garters! what a life I lead long o' that there derned young gal!"

"There's no boat to be had," said "Pete Jinking," "and if there was, Miss Georgia's skiff would live where a larger one would go down. If *she* can't manage it, no one can."

"Oh, yes! talk, talk, talk! git it off your own shoulders, you cowardly old porpoise, you! afraid to venture where a delikay young gal does. Oh, Georgey, you blamed young pepper-pod, wait till I catch hold of you!" said Miss Jerusha, wringing her hands in the extremity of her distress.

"She has reached him! she has reached him! There, she has him in the boat!" cried the stranger, excitedly.

"And she has got him! she has got him! Hurra! hurra! hurra!" shouted the crowd on the shore, as they breathlessly shaded their eyes to gaze across the foaming waters.

Steering her light craft with a master hand, Georgia reached the rock barely in time, for scarcely had the lad leaped into the boat when a huge wave swept over the rocks, and not one there but shuddered at the death he had so narrowly escaped.

But the occupants of the skiff were far from safe, and a dead silence fell on all as they hushed the very beating of their hearts to watch. She had turned its head towards the shore, and bending her slight form to the oars, she pulled vigorously against the dashing waves. Now poised and quivering on the topmost crest of some large wave, now sinking down, down, far down out of sight until they feared it would never rise, yet, still re-appearing, she toiled bravely. Her long, wild, black hair, unbound by the wind, streamed in the breeze, drenched and dripping with sea-brine. On and on toiled the brave girl, nearer and nearer to the shore she came, until at last, with a mighty shout, that burst involuntarily from their relieved hearts, a dozen strong hands were extended, caught the boat, and pulled it far up on the shore. And then "Hurrah! hurrah! Hurrah for Georgia! hurrah for Georgia Darrell!" burst from every lip, and hats were waved, and the cheer arose again and again, until the welkin rang, and the crowd pressed around her, shaking hands, and congratulating her, and hemming her in, until, half laughing, half impatient, she broke from them, exclaiming:

"There, there, good folks, that will do—please let me pass. Mrs. Smith, here is your naughty little boy; you will have to take better care of him for the future. Uncle Pete, will you just look after my skiff, and bring those oars up to the house? My clothes are so heavy with the wet that they are as much as I can carry. Now, Miss Jerusha, don't begin to scold; I am not drowned, you see, so it will be all a waste of ammunition. Come along; I want to get out of this crowd."

Fatigued with her exertions, pale and wet, she toiled wearily up the bank, very unlike herself. The stranger, muffled in his black brigandish-looking cloak and slouched hat, stood motionless watching her, and Georgia glanced carelessly at him and passed on. Strangers were not much of a novelty in Burnfield now, so this young, distinguished looking gentleman awoke no surprise until she saw him advance toward her with outstretched hand. And Georgia stepped back and glanced at him in haughty amaze.

"Miss Darrell, you are a second Grace Darling. Allow me to congratulate you on what you have done to-day."

"Sir!"

"You will not shake hands, Miss Darrell? And yet we are not strangers."

"You labor under a mistake, sir! I do not know you! Will you allow me to pass?"

He stood straight before her, a smile curling his mustached lip at her regal hauteur.

"And has five years, five short years, completely obliterated even the memory of Richmond Wildair?"

"Richmond Wildair! *Who was he?*" she said, lifting her eyes with cool indolence, and looking up straight into the bronzed, manly face, from which the hat was now raised. "Oh, I recollect! How do you do, sir? Come, Miss Jerusha; let me help you up the bank."

He stood for a moment transfixed. Had he expected to meet the impulsive little girl he had left? Had he expected this scornful young empress, with her chilling "*who was he?*"

She did not notice his extended hand—*that* reminded him of the child Georgia—but, taking Miss Jerusha's arm, walked with her up the path, the proud head erect, but the springing step slow and labored.

He watched her a moment, and smiled. That smile would have reminded Georgia of other days had she seen it—a smile that said as plainly as words could speak, "You shall pay for this, my lady! You shall find my power has not passed away."

It was a surprise to Georgia, this meeting, and not a pleasant one. She recollected how he had mastered and commanded her in her masterless childhood—a recollection that filled her with angry indignation; a recollection that made her compress her lips, set her foot down hard, and involuntarily clinch the small hand; a recollection that sent a bright, angry light to her black, flashing eyes, and a hot, irritated spot burning on either cheek; and the dark brows knit as he had often seen them do before as he came resolutely up and stood on the other side of Miss Jerusha.

"And will *you*, too, disown me, Miss Jerusha?" he said, with a look of reproach. "Is Richmond Wildair totally forgotten by all his old friends in Burnfield?"

Miss Jerusha, who had not overheard his conversation with Georgia, faced abruptly round, and looked at him in the utmost surprise.

"Why, bless my heart if it ain't! Wall, railly now! Why, I never! Georgey, don't you remember the young gent as you used to be so thick 'long of? Wal, now! how do you do? Why, I'm rail glad to see you. I railly am, now!" And Miss Jerusha shook his hand with an *empressement* quite unusual with her in her surprise.

"Thank you, Miss Jerusha. I am glad *all* my friends have not forgotten me," said Richmond.

Georgia's lip curled slightly, and facing round, she said:

"Miss Jerusha, if you'll excuse me, I'll go on. I want to change this wet dress;" and without waiting for a reply, Georgia hurried on.

"What brings him here?" she said to herself, as she walked quickly toward the cottage. "I suppose he thinks he is to be my lord and master as of yore, that I am still a slave to come at his beck, and because he is rich and I am poor he can command me as much as he pleases. He shall not do it! he shall *not*! I will *never* forgive him for conquering me," flashed Georgia, clenching her hand involuntarily as she walked.

"And so you've come back! Wall, now, who'd a thought it? Is the square got well and come back, too?"

"My uncle is dead," said the young man, gravely.

"Do tell! Dead, is he? Wall, we've all got to go, some time or another, so there's no good making a fuss. What's going to come of the old place up there?"

"I am going to have it fitted up and improved, and use it for a country-seat."

"Oh—I see! it's your'n, is it? Nice place it is, and worth a good many thousands, I'll be bound! S'pose you'll be getting married shortly, and bringing a wife there to oversee the sarvints, and poultry, and things, eh?" and Miss Jerusha peered at him sharply with her small eyes.

"Really, Miss Jerusha, I don't know," he said, laughingly, taking off his hat and running his fingers through his waving dark hair. "If I could get any one to have me, I might. Do you think I could succeed in that sort of speculation here in Burnfield? The young ladies here know more about looking after poultry than they do in the city."

"Ah! they ain't properly brought up there," said Miss Jerusha, shaking her head; "it's nothin' but boardin' schools, and beaus, and theaters, and other wickednesses there; 'tain't ekil to the country noways. You'll get a wife though, easy enough; young men with lots of money don't find much trouble doing that, either in town or country. How's that nice brother o' your'n?" said Miss Jerusha, suddenly recollecting the youth who had by force possessed himself of so large a share of her affections.

"He is very well, or was when I heard from him last. He has gone abroad to make the grand tour."

"Oh—has he?" said Miss Jerusha, rather mystified, and not quite certain what new patent invention the grand tour was. "Why couldn't he make it at home?" Then, without waiting for an answer, "Won't you come in? do come in; tea's just ready, and you hain't had a chance to speak to Georgey yet, hey? You're most happy. Very well, walk right in and take a cheer. You, Fly!"

"Yes'm, here I is," cried Fly, rushing in breathlessly, and diving frantically at the oven.

"Where's your young mistress?"

"Up stairs."

"Well, you hurry up and get tea; fly round now, will you? Oh, here comes Georgey. Why, Georgey! don't you know who this is?"

Georgia gave a start of surprise, and her face darkened as she entered and saw him sitting there so much at home.

Passing him with a distant courtesy she said, with marked coldness:

"I have that pleasure. Fly, attend to your baking; I'll set the table."

Miss Jerusha was too well accustomed to the varying moods of her ward to be much surprised at this capricious conduct; so she entered into conversation with Richmond, or rather began a racking cross examination as to what he had been doing, where he had been, what he was going to do, and how the last five years had been spent generally.

To all her questions Mr. Wildair replied with the utmost politeness, but—he told her just as much as he chose and no more. From this she learned that he had been studying for the bar, and had been admitted, that his career hitherto had been eminently successful, that his uncle's death had rendered him independent of his profession, but that having a passion for that pursuit he was still determined to continue it; that his brother's health remaining delicate, change of scene had been recommended, and that therefore he had gone abroad and was not expected home for a year yet; that a desire to fit up and refurnish the "House," as it was called, *par excellence*, in Burnfield, was the sole cause of his leaving Washington—where for the past five years he had mostly resided—and finally, that his stay in this flourishing township "depended on circumstances."

It was late that evening when he went away. Georgia had listened, and, except to Fly, had not spoken half a dozen words, still wrapped in her mantel of proud reserve. She stood at the window when he was gone, looking out at the dark, flowing waves.

"Nice young man," said Miss Jerusha, approvingly, referring to her guest.

There was no answer.

"Good-lookin', too," pursued Miss Jerusha, looking reflectively at Betsey Periwinkle, "and rich. Hem! I say, Georgia—you're fond of money—wouldn't it be pleasant if you was to be mistress bime-by of the big house—hey?"

She looked up for an answer, but Georgia was gone.

CHAPTER X.

DREAMING.

"And underneath that face, like summer's ocean,
    Its lips as moveless and its cheek as clear,
Slumbers a whirlpool of the heart's emotions—
    Love, hatred, pride, hope, sorrow, all save fear."

HALLECK.

"

ll, this *is* pleasant," said Richmond, throwing himself carelessly on the grass, and sending pebbles skimming over the surface of the river; "this *is* pleasant," he repeated, looking up at his companion, as she sat drawing under the shadow of an old elm down near the shore.

Three months had passed since his return, and the glowing golden midsummer days had come. All this time he had been a frequent visitor at the cottage—to see *Miss Jerusha*, of course; and very gracious, indeed, was that lady's reception of the young lord of the manor. Georgia was freezing at first, most decidedly below zero, and enough to strike terror into the heart of any less courageous knight than the one in question. But Mr. Richmond Wildair was not easily intimidated, and took all her chilling hauteur coolly enough, quite confident of triumphing in the end. It was a drawn battle between them, but he knew he was the better general of the two, so he was perfectly easy as to the issue. In fact, he rather liked it than otherwise, on the principle of the "greater the trial, the greater the triumph," and, accustomed to be flattered and caressed, this novel mode of treatment was something new and decidedly pleasant. So he kept on "never minding," and visited the cottage often, and talked gayly with Miss Jerusha, and was respectful and quiet with Miss Georgia, until, as constant dropping will wear a stone, so Georgia's unnatural stiffness began to give way, and she learned to laugh and grow genial again, but remained still on the alert to resist any attempt at command. No such attempt was made, and at last Georgia and Richmond grew to be very good friends.

Georgia had a talent for drawing, and Richmond, who was quite an artist, undertook to teach her, and those lessons did more than anything else to put them on a sociable footing. Richmond liked to give his lessons out under the trees, where his pupil might sketch from nature, and Georgia rather liked it herself, too. It was very pleasant, those lessons; Georgia liked to hear about great cities, about this rush, and roar, and turmoil, and constant flow of busy life, and Richmond had the power of description in a high degree, and used to watch, with a sly, repressed smile, pencil and crayon drop from her fingers, and her eyes fix themselves in eager, unconscious interest on his face, as she grew absorbed in his narrative.

Dangerous work it was, with a pupil and master young and handsome, the romantic sea-shore and murmuring old trees for their school-room, and talking not forbidden either. How Miss Jerusha chuckled over it in confidence to Betsey Periwinkle—she didn't dare to trust Fly—and indulged in sundry wild visions of a brand-new brown silk dress and straw bonnet suitable for the giving away a bride in.

Little did Georgia dream of these extravagant peeps into futurity, or the lessons would have ended then and there, this new-fledged intimacy been unceremoniously nipped in the bud, and Miss Jerusha's castles in Spain tumbled to the ground with a crash! But Georgia was in a dream and said nothing. Richmond *did*, and laughed quietly over it in the shadow of the old ancestral mansion.

"Yes, this is pleasant," said Richmond, one morning, as he lay idly on the grass, and Georgia sat on the trunk of a fallen tree near, taking her drawing lesson.

She lifted her head and laughed.

"What is pleasant?" she said.

"This—this feeling of rest, of peace, of indolence, of idleness. I never sympathized with Charley's love for the *dolce far niente* before, but I begin to appreciate it now. One tires of this hurrying, bustling, jostling, uproarious life in the city, and then laziness in the country is considered the greatest of earthly boons. All work and no play makes Jack a dull boy, you know."

"And do you really like the country better than the city?" asked Georgia.

"I like it—yes—in slices. I shouldn't fancy being buried in the woods among catamounts, and panthers, and settlers hardly less savage. I shouldn't fancy sleeping in wigwams and huts, and living on bear's flesh and Johnny-cake; but I like *this*. I like to lie under the trees, away out of sight and hearing of the city, yet knowing three or four hours in the cars will bring me to it whenever I feel like going back. I like the feeling of languid repose these still, voiceless, midsummer noondays inspire; I like to have nothing to do; and plenty of time to do it in."

"What an epicure you are," said Georgia, smiling; "now it seems to me after witnessing the ever-changing, ever-restless life in Washington and New York, and all those other great cities, you would find our sober little humdrum Burnfield insupportably dull. I know I should; I would like above all things to live in a great city, life seems to be so fully waked up, so earnest there. I *shall*, too, some day," she said, in her calm, decided way, as she took up another pencil and went on quietly drawing.

"Indeed!" he said, slowly, watching the pebbles he sent skimming over the water as intently as if his whole life depended on them. "Indeed! how is that?"

"Oh! I shall go to seek my fortune," she said, laughingly, yet in earnest, too. "Do you know I am to be rich and great? 'Once upon a time there was a king and queen with three sons, and the youngest was called Jack.' I am Jack, and you know how well he always came out at the end of the story."

"Georgia, you are a—dreamer."

"I shall be a worker one of these days. My hour has not yet come." And Georgia hummed:

> "I am asleep and don't waken me."

"What will you do when you awake, Georgia?"

"What Heaven and my own genius pleases; found a colony, find a continent, make war on Canada, run for President, teach a school, set fire to Cuba, learn dressmaking, or set up a menagerie, with Betsey Periwinkle for my stock in trade," she said, with one of her malicious, quizzical laughs.

"Georgia, talk sense."

"Mr. Wildair, I flatter myself I am doing that now."

"Miss Darrell, shall I tell you your future?"

"I defy you to do it, sir."

"Don't be too sure. Now listen. In the first place, you will get married."

"No, *sir-r!*" exclaimed Georgia, with emphasis: "I scorn the insinuation! I am going to be an old maid, like Miss Jerusha."

"Don't interrupt, Miss Darrel; it's not polite. You will marry some sweet youth with nice curling whiskers, and his hair parted in the middle, and you will mend his old coats, and read him the newspaper, and trudge with him to market, and administer curtain lectures, and raise Shanghai roosters, and take a prize every year for the best butter and the nicest quilts in the county; and finally you will die, and go up to heaven, where you will belong, and have a wooden tombstone erected to your memory, with your virtues inscribed on it in letters five inches long."

"Shall I, indeed! that's all you know about it," said Georgia, half inclined to be provoked at this picture; "no, sir; I am bound to astonish the world some of these days—*how*, I haven't quite decided, but I know I shall do it. As for your delightful picture of conjugal felicity, *you* may be a Darby some day, but I will never be a Joan."

"You might be worse."

"And will be, doubtless. I never expect to be anything very good. Emily Murray will do enough of that for both of us."

"Emily is a good girl. Do you know what she reminds one of?"

"A fragrant little spring rose, I imagine."

"Yes, of that, too; but she is more like the river just now as it flows on smooth, serene, untroubled and shining, smiling in the sunshine, unruffled and calm."

"And I am like that same river lashed to a fury in a December storm," said Georgia, with a darkening brow.

"Exactly—pre-cisely! though you are quiet enough now; but as those still waters *must* be lashed into tempests, just so certain will you—"

"Mr. Wildair, I don't relish your personalities," said Georgia, with a flushing cheek and kindling eye.

"I beg your pardon—it was an ungallant speech—but I did not know you cared for compliments. What shall I say you look like?—some gorgeous tropical flower?"

"No, sir! you shall compare me to nothing! Georgia Darrell looks like herself alone! There! how do you like my drawing?"

He took it and looked long and earnestly. It was rather a strange one. It represented a wintry sea and coast, with the dark, sluggish waves tossing like a strong heart in strong agony, and only lit by the fitful, watery, glimmer of a pale wintry moon breaking through the dark, lowering clouds above. Down on the shore knelt a young girl, her long hair and thin garments streaming behind her in the wind, her hands clasped, her face blanched, her eyes strained in horror far over the troubled face of the sea on a drowning form. Far out a female face rose above the devouring waves—*such* a face, so full of a terrible, nameless horror, despair and utter woe as no fancy less vivid than that of Georgia could ever have conceived. One arm was thrown up far over her head in the death struggle, and the eyes in that strange face were appalling to look on.

Richmond Wildair held his breath as he gazed, and looked up in Georgia's dark face in a sort of fear.

"Georgia! Georgia!" he said, "what in Mercy's name were you thinking of when you drew that?"

She laughed.

"Don't you like it, Mr. Wildair?" she said.

"Like it! You're a goblin! a kelpie! a witch! an unearthly changeling! or you would never have conjured up that blood-chilling face. Why, you have been painting portraits! Did you know it?"

"I did not when I commenced—I found I had when they were done."

"And life-like portraits they are, too. That kneeling girl is Emily Murray, though her sweet face never wore that look of wild horror you have pictured there. And that other ghastly, agonized countenance, that seems rent by a thousand fiends, is—"

"Myself."

"Oh, Georgia! what spirit possessed you to paint that awful face?"

"How do I know? The spirit of prophecy, perhaps," she said, in a tone of dark gloom.

"Georgia Darrell, do you know what you deserve?"

"No, sir."

"Then I shall tell you. You ought to be locked in an attic, and fed on bread and water for a month, to cool the fever in your blood."

"Thank you; I would rather be excused. And now I come to think of it, it *couldn't* have been the spirit of prophecy either that inspired me, for your brother Charles once told me that I would never be drowned."

"No? How did he know it?"

"He said a more elevated destiny awaited me—hanging."

"What if he turns out a true prophet?"

"I shall not be surprised."

"You will not?"

"Most certainly not. They hang people for murder, don't they?"

"Well?"

"Well!" she repeated, mimicking his tone, "I expect to be the death of somebody one of these days."

He knew she spoke lightly, yet suddenly there rushed to his mind the recollection of the conversation he had once held with his brother, in which he compared her to Lady Macbeth, and declared his belief in her capability of committing that far-famed lady's crime. Strange that it should come back to him so vividly and painfully then.

"Well, signor," said the clear, musical voice of Georgia, breaking in upon his reverie, "of what is your serene highness thinking so intently? Do you fear you are to be the future victim?"

"Georgia!"

"I listen, mynheer."

"Suppose you loved somebody very much—"

"A mighty absurd supposition to begin with. I never intend to do any such thing."

"Now, Georgia, be serious. Suppose you loved some one with all your heart, if you possess such an article, you flinty female anaconda, and they professed to love you, and afterward deceived you, what would you do?"

"Do!" her face darkened, her eyes blazed, her lips sprung quivering apart, her hands clenched; "do! I should BLAST them with my vengeance; I would live for revenge, I would *die* for revenge! I would track them over the world like a sleuth-hound. I would defy even death by the power of my own will until I had wreaked this doom on their devoted head. Deceive me! Safer would it be to tamper with the lightning's chain than with the heart that beats here."

She struck her breast and rose to her feet *transformed*! The terrific look that had started him in the pictured face, flamed up in her living one now, and she stood like a young Medusa, ready to blight all on whom her dark, scorching glance might rest.

He stood appalled before her. Was she acting, or was this storm of passion real? It was a relief to him to see one of his own servants approaching at that moment with a letter in his hand. The presence of a third person restored Georgia to herself, and, leaning against a tree, she looked darkly over the smiling, shining waters.

"From Charley!" was Richmond's joyful exclamation, as he glanced at the superscription of the letter and dismissed the man who brought it. "It is nearly six months since he wrote last, and we were all getting seriously uneasy about him. Will you excuse me while I read it, Georgia?"

Georgia bent her head in token of acquiescence, and taking up another piece of paper, began carelessly drawing a scaffold, with herself hanging, to horrify her companion. So absorbed did she become in her task, that she did not observe the long silence of her companion, until suddenly lifting her eyes, she beheld a startling sight.

With the letter clutched with a death-grip in his hand, his face livid, his brow corrugated, his eyes fixed, his whole form rigid and motionless, he sat with his eyes riveted on that fatal letter.

In all her life Georgia had never seen the calm, self-sustained Richmond Wildair moved, and now—oh, this was awful! She sprang to his side and caught his arm, crying out:

"Richmond! Richmond! oh, Richmond! what is the matter?"

He lifted his eyes with a hollow groan.

"Oh, Georgia!"

"Richmond! oh, Richmond! is Charley dead?"

"Dead? No! Would he were!" he said, with passionate bitterness.

"Oh, Richmond, this is terrible! What has your brother—"

"Brother! it is false!" he exclaimed, fiercely, springing to his feet; "he is no brother of mine!"

"Good gracious! Richmond, what has he done?"

"Done!" he repeated, furiously: "he has disgraced himself, disgraced us all—done what I will never forgive."

It was the first time Georgia had ever heard him utter such language. As a gentleman, he was not in the habit of staining his lips with expletives, and now even *her* strong nature shrank, and she shuddered.

"Oh, what has Charley done? What *can* he have done? He so frank, so kind, so warm-hearted? Oh he cannot have committed a crime! It is impossible," cried Georgia, vehemently.

"It is *not* impossible!—lost, fallen, degraded wretch! Oh, mercy! that I should have lived to see this day! Oh, who—who shall tell my mother this?"

"Richmond, be calm—I implore you. Tell me what he has done?"

"What you shall never know—what I shall never tell you!" he cried, passionately.

The color retreated from Georgia's very lips, leaving her white as marble.

"If it is murder—"

"Murder! *That* might be forgiven! A man may kill another in the heat of passion and be forgiven. Murder, robbery, arson, *all* might be forgiven; but this! Oh, Georgia, ask me not! I feel as if I should go mad."

What had he done, what awful crime was this that had no name, before which, in Richmond's eyes, even murder sank into insignificance?

Georgia stood appalled, while Richmond, with the fatal letter crushed in his hand, strode up and down as if he were indeed mad. Then, as his eye fell on the familiar hand-writing, his mood changed, and he passionately exclaimed:

"Oh, Charles! Oh, my brother! Would you had died ere you had come to this! Oh, Georgia! I loved him so! every one loved him so! and now—and *now!*"

He turned away and shaded his eyes with his hands, while his strong chest heaved with irrepressible emotion.

Every tender, womanly feeling in Georgia's heart was stirred, and she went over and took his hand in hers, and said, gently:

"Mr. Wildair, things may not be so bad as you suppose. I am sure they are not. I could stake my soul on the innocence of Charles Wildair. Oh, it is impossible, absurd, he can be guilty of any crime. The Charley Wildair I once knew can never have fallen so low. Oh, Richmond, I feel he is innocent. I *know* he is."

"Georgia, I thank you for your sympathy; it is my best consolation now; but I am not deceived; *he is guilty*; he has confessed all. And now, Georgia, I never want to hear his name mentioned again; never speak of him to me more. I must go home now: I must be alone, for this shock has quite unmanned me. Do not speak of this to any one. Farewell!"

He pressed her hand, pulled his hat down over his eyes, and started off in the direction of Burnfield.

Lost in amaze, Georgia stood watching him until he was out of sight, and then resumed her seat on the grass, to think over this strange scene, and wonder what possible crime Charley Wildair had committed. It was hard to associate with *any* crime the memory of the handsome, happy, generous boy she remembered; but it must be so. He confessed it himself; his brother, who passionately loved him, branded him with it; therefore it must be so. While she sat thinking, two soft hands were placed over her eyes, and a silky curl touched her cheek.

"Emily," said Georgia, quietly, without moving.

"Yes, that same small individual," said a sweet voice; and our fair Emily came from behind her, and threw herself down on the grass by her side.

"Where did you drop from?" asked Georgia, not exactly delighted at the interruption.

"Not from the clouds, Lady Georgia. I went to the cottage, and learned from Miss Jerusha that teacher and pupil had gone off sky-gazing and 'makin' pictures. At the risk of being *de trop*, I followed, and here I am. Where's Monsieur le Tutor?"

"Gone home," said Georgia, listlessly.

"And left you here all by yourself! How shockingly ungallant! Now, I thought better things of the lord of Richmond Hall. What do you think of him, Georgia?"

"Of whom?"

"Of whom! You know well enough. Of Mr. Wildair."

"I have formed no opinion on the subject."

"Well, that's odd. *I* have, and I think him a splendid fellow—so gentlemanly, and all that. I wonder what he thinks of us?"

"He thinks you are a good girl, and I am a dreamer."

"A good girl! Well, that's very moderate praise, blank and cool, but just as much as I want. And you are a dreamer—I knew *that* before. Will you ever awaken, Georgia?"

"I shall have to; I never wish it, though."

"Then the awakening will not be pleasant?"

"No; I feel a presentiment that it will not. Oh, Emily! I am tired of my present stagnant life; and yet, sometimes I wish I might never be anything but a 'dreamer of dreams,' without even realizing how *real* life is. I wish I were now like you, my little Princess Frostina."

"You and I can never be alike—never, Georgia; every element in our nature is as essentially different as our looks. You are a blaze of red sky-rockets, and I am a little insignificant whiff of down."

"No indeed; you are a good, lovable girl, with a warm heart, a clear head, and a cool temper, who will lead a happy life, and die a happy death. But I—oh,

Emily, Emily! what is to be my fate?"

She spoke with a sort of cry, and Emily started and gazed on her with a troubled, anxious face.

"Oh, Georgia, what is the matter? *Dear* Georgia! what is the matter? You look so dark, and strange, and troubled."

"I am out of spirits—a bad fit of the blues, Em," said Georgia, trying to smile. "I am a sort of monomaniac, I think; I do not know what is the matter with me. I wish I were away from here; I grow fairly wild at times. Emily, I shall *die* if I stay here much longer."

All that day something lay on her heart like lead. Perhaps it was the memory of that mysterious letter, and Charley's guilt, and his brother's anguish, that weighed it down. Miss Jerusha had long ago given up wondering at anything her eccentric *protegee* might see fit to do; but when all day long she saw her sit, dark and silent, with folded hands, at the window, gazing at the ever-restless, flowing river, she *did* wonder what strange thoughts were passing through her young heart, or, to use her own expression, what had "come to her." Fly gave it as her opinion, it was only a "new streak," in the already sufficiently "streaked" character of her young mistress. And Betsey Periwinkle, wondering too, but maintaining a discreet silence on the subject, came purring round her, while her more demonstrative offspring leaped into her lap and held up her head for her customary caress.

Unheeding them all, Georgia went early to her room, and leaning her head on her hand, gazed languidly out. The soft evening breeze lifted the damp, shining braids of her dark hair, and kissed softly her grave, beautiful face, and the evening star rose up in solemn beauty, and shone down into the dark eyes fixed so earnestly on the far-off horizon that seemed her prison wall. And Georgia looked up, and felt a holy calm steal into her heart, and forgot all her somber fancies, and her high heart-beating grew still in gazing on the trembling beauty of that solitary star.

CHAPTER XI.

SOMETHING NEW.

The faltering speech, and look estranged,
Voice, step, and life, and beauty changed;
She might have marked all this and known
Such change is wrought by love alone.—MOORE.

ere were great doings going on up at the "house." All Burnfield was in a state of unprecedented excitement about it. The last Presidential election, the debut of the new school-marm, or even the first arrival of the locomotive at the Burnfield Railway depot, had not created half such a sensation. Marvelous tales ran like wild-fire through the town, of carpets, of fine velvets, as Mrs. Tolduso, the gossip-in-chief, called it; of mirrors reaching from floor to ceiling in dazzling gilt frames; of sofas, and couches, and lounging-chairs, and marble-topped tables, and no end of pictures, and statues, and upholstery, and "heaps, and heaps of other things—oh! most splendid," said Mrs. Tolduso; "sich as must have cost an awful sight of money."

Then workmen came from the city, and the stately old mansion underwent a course of painting and varnishing, until it fairly glittered; and the grounds were altered, and fountains erected, and statues of Hebes, and Waterbearers, and Venuses rising from the sea-foam, and lions, with fountains spouting from their mouths and nostrils, and lots of other devices scattered everywhere. And then a prim little matron of a housekeeper, and an accomplished cook, and an aristocratic butler, and coquettish chambermaids in shaking gold ear-drops and pink bows, and a dignified coachman, and two fascinating young footmen, and a delightful old gardener, with beautiful white hair and whiskers, made his appearance, electrifying the neighborhood, and looking down with contempt on their open-mouthed, homespun neighbors.

The people stood a great deal more in awe of the aristocratic butler, and footman, and the rest of them, than they did of their young master, who was never stiff and pompous, but was given to pat the children on the head as he passed and throw them coppers, and touch his hat to the blooming, blushing, smiling country belles, and nod with careless condescension to their fathers and brothers. And then wild, mysterious rumors began to fly about that the young "squire" was going to marry some great city heiress, and bring her here to live, and those who were so fortunate as to be graciously noticed by any of the aristocratic flunkeys aforesaid, endeavored to "pump" them, but knowing nothing themselves they could only shake their heads and look mysterious unspeakable things, that said as plainly as words: "Of course we know all, but we have too great an esteem for the young gentleman in whose house we reside to betray his confidence;" so Mrs. Tolduso, and the rest of her set, had to coin their own news, and were still left to their own surmises.

Miss Jerusha, albeit not given to gossiping, could not help hearing these rumors, and the worthy spinster began to grow alarmed. She had never realized until now the immense distance between the rich young gentleman, Mr. Wildair, and the poor daughter of the poor actress, Georgia Darrell, who wore her poverty as a duchess might her coronet. Why, the very servants of the house, in their arrogance, would look down on the village girl; the fascinating young footmen would have considered her honored by a smile; and the chambermaids would lift their rustling silken robes and sweep past her mouseline de laine in lofty disdain. Georgia, the cottage girl, mistress of the great house and all those awe-inspiring young ladies and gentlemen who did Mr. Wildair's work for a "consideration!" Oh, Miss Jerusha, no wonder your chin drops as you think of it, and a sigh comes whistling through your pursed-up lips like a sough of wind in a mainsail.

Then there is that rumor of that haughty young city heiress he is to marry. Miss Jerusha groans in spirit when she thinks of it, and wishes Georgia was not so careless about it, for the only time that young lady had been "short" with Miss Jerusha, for ever so long, was on the occasion of asking her opinion about the same heiress, when Georgia told her curtly "she neither knew nor cared—Mr. Wildair and his heiresses were nothing to her." Yes, Miss Jerusha's brilliant visions of a brown silk dress and new straw bonnet were fast going the way of many another brilliant vision, and she sighed again over the evanishment of human hopes, and then consoled herself with her everlasting stocking and the society of the Betsey Periwinkles, mother and daughter. It was true Mr. Wildair was a daily visitor still at the cottage, but his walks with Georgia were altogether discontinued, and the drawing lessons completely given up.

Miss Jerusha did not know that this was by the cold, peremptory command of Georgia herself, and much to the dissatisfaction of the young gentleman; but she *did* know that the vivid crimson was paling in Georgia's cheek, the light dying out of her brilliant eyes, and the quick, elastic spring leaving her slow footsteps; knew it and marveled thereat. She saw, too, with suppressed indignation (for it doesn't pay to be angry with rich people) that Richmond saw it too, and seemed rather pleased than otherwise thereat, while Georgia was relapsing into her first mood, and invariably froze into a living iceberg the moment his light, firm step sounded on the threshold.

All this was very puzzling to Miss Jerusha, who soon after had the pleasure of hearing he was going to be married to somebody else—a report which he never even contradicted. And so matters were getting into a "pretty mess," as Miss Jerusha said; and things generally were in a very unsatisfactory state indeed, when one day Mr. Richmond Wildair transfixed Miss Jerusha by the polite request that she would do him the honor of coming and looking at his house. It was all finished now, he said, and he wanted her opinion of it.

"Lor', Mr. Wildair? what do you 'spose I know 'bout your fine houses, and your fol-de-rols and gimcracks that you've got into it. There ain't no good in my going," said Miss Jerusha knitting away, and looking as grim as old Father Time in the primer.

"Still, my dear Miss Jerusha, I should like your opinion of it, and you will really very much oblige me by coming," said Mr. Wildair, in tones of suave and stately courtesy. "If you will confer this pleasure on me, I will send my carriage for you any day you will be pleased to name."

"Oh, gracious, no!" ejaculated Miss Jerusha, in alarm, as the remembrance of the dignified coachman came over her; "not for the world. Still I *should* admire to see it, but—Georgey, what do *you* say? Do I look fit to go?"

"You may please yourself, Miss Jerusha," she said in a voice so cold and constrained, that Miss Jerusha looked at her and shifted uneasily in her seat.

"Let me answer for Miss Darrell," broke in Richmond. "You *do* look fit to go, and I shall consider it a direct personal hint that you do not want to see me here any more if you refuse. If you will not visit me, I will not visit you."

"Perhaps it would have been better if you *never* had," thought Emily Murray, who chanced to be present.

"Oh, well, I s'pose I'd better," said Miss Jerusha, shifting uneasily in her seat again; "but the fact is, Mr. Wildair, them there servants o' yourn, are a stuck-up set, and I—"

"Have no fear on that score, my dear madam," said Mr. Wildair; "my servants will keep their proper places, and treat my guests with becoming deference. And now, when am I to expect you?"

"Well, to-morrow mornin', I guess," said Miss Jerusha, who perhaps would not have gone but for the opportunity of humbling and snubbing the servants, one or two of whom had sneered at her in Burnfield, by letting them see she was the honored friend of their master.

"If Miss Murray and Miss Darrell would honor me likewise by accompanying you," he said hesitatingly.

Georgia started as if she had received a galvanic shock, and a flash like sheet-lightning leaped from her fierce eyes; but Emily touched her hand softly, and replied, quickly, before she could speak:

"Thank you, Mr. Wildair; you will excuse us. Georgia, you promised to show me that French book you were reading. Come with me now and get it."

Both arose, and, passing Mr. Wildair with a slight courtesy, swept from the room, leaving him in undisturbed possession of Miss Jerusha, but whether to his gratification or annoyance it would have taken a profound observer to tell, for his face wore its usual calm, unruffled expression. But his visit was shorter than usual that day, and in half an hour Miss Jerusha was alone.

Next morning, resplendent in her still new and gorgeous "kaliker gownd," Miss Jerusha set off for the "house." Opening the outer gate, she passed up a magnificent shaded avenue, where her eyes were greeted and electrified by glimpses of floral beauty hitherto unknown. Arriving at the hall-door, Miss Jerusha plucked up spirit and gave a thundering knock; for though there was a bell, the ancient lady knew nothing of any such modern innovations.

The unusual sound brought the two fascinating footmen and spruce chambermaids (who up to the present had had very little to do) to the door; and when it swung back and displayed the tall, lank form of Miss Jerusha in her astonishing dress, a universal titter ran from lip to lip.

"Well, old lady, what can we do for you to-day?" insinuated one of the footmen, thinking Miss Jerusha an appropriate subject to poke fun at.

"Where's your master?" said Miss Jerusha, sharply.

"Here, marm, this is him," said the fellow, pointing to his brother flunkey, who stood grinning, with his hands in his pockets.

"Yes, marm, I'm the high cockalorum; we hev'n't got anything for you to-day, though."

"Gess you mistook the door, old lady, didn't you?" said the first, with an insolent leer.

The man's words and looks so enraged Miss Jerusha that, lifting her hand, she gave him a slap in the face that sent him reeling half way across the hall.

"Why, you old tramp," exclaimed the other, making a spring at the undaunted Miss Jerusha, when an iron grasp was laid on his collar, and he was hurled to the other side of the long hall, and his master's voice exclaimed:

"You insolent puppy! if I ever hear you address any one in this style again, I'll not leave a whole bone in your body. Miss Jerusha, I beg ten thousand pardons for having exposed you to the insolence of these rascals, but I will take care it never happens again. Here, you fellows," said Richmond, turning

115

round; but the hall was deserted, and he and Miss Jerusha were alone.

"Never mind, Mr. Wildair," said Miss Jerusha, delighted at their discomfiture, "it ain't no matter; I guess they got as good as they brought, sir! What a big house this is, to be sure."

But when Miss Jerusha was led through it, and all its wonders and hitherto undreamed-of grandeur were revealed to her amazed eyes, speech failed her, and she stood astounded, transfixed, and awe-struck. Never in all her wildest visions, had she conjured up any thing like this, and she held her breath, and trod on tiptoe, and spoke in a stilled whisper, and wondered if she were not in an enchanted land, instead of simply in the sumptuous drawing rooms, boudoirs, and saloons of the "house."

Richmond watched her with an amused smile, and when she had been "upstairs, and downstairs, and in my lady's chamber," he insisted on her taking off her bonnet and shawl, and staying for dinner. So he rang the bell, and ordered the servant to serve dinner an hour earlier than usual, and send up Mrs. Hamm, the housekeeper. And in a few minutes, Mrs. Hamm, a very grand little woman indeed, in a black satin dress, and gold watch, and dainty little black lace cap, swept in, and was introduced to Miss Skamp, who felt rather fluttered by the ceremony, and would have given a good deal to have been back in her cottage just then, scolding Fly and kicking Betsey Periwinkle. But Mrs. Hamm was a discreet little lady, and had heard the episode of the two footmen, and was intensely gracious and polite—so much so, indeed, that it seriously discomposed Miss Jerusha, who made a thousand blunders during dinner, and did not breathe freely until she was fairly on her way home again, in the carriage, too, for Mr. Wildair would not hear of her walking back.

That was a triumph for Miss Jerusha Glory Ann Skamp! Here was an eminence she had never dreamed of attaining! Driving through her native town, amid the wondering eyes of all the inhabitants crowding to every door and window, in the magnificent carriage, with silk velvet cushions, drawn by two beautiful horses in silver-mounted harness, and driven by a gentleman looking like a lord bishop at the very least.

Oh! it was too much happiness! She the descendant of many Skamps, to be thus honored! What would her ancient "parients" say, could they look out of their graves and behold this glorious sight? Wouldn't she be looked up to in Burnfield for the future, and wouldn't she carry her head high though! Why, not one in all Burnfield but Mr. Barebones, the parson, had been invited to dine with the "Squire," and neither Mrs. nor Miss Barebones had ever seen, much less riden in, his carriage. That was the red-letter day in all Miss Jerusha's life. She was sorry, *very* sorry, when the carriage drew up before her own door, and the dignified coachman, touching his gold-banded hat to her, drove off, and left her with a heart swelling high with pride and exultation, to enter her dwelling.

She found Georgia sitting in her favorite seat by the window commanding a view of the river, a book lying listlessly between her fingers, her eyes on the floor, her thoughts far away—far away. Miss Jerusha entered, dropped into a seat, and then began a glowing harangue on the glories and splendor of Richmond House.

Georgia moved her chair, turned her head aside, and listened like one deaf and dumb. Long and eloquently did the old lady expatiate on its beauties and pomp, but Georgia answered never a word.

"Ah! that heiress, or whatever gets him, will have good times of it," said Miss Jerusha, shaking her head by way of a wind-up. "What do you think, Georgia, but I asked him if he was really a-goin' to be married."

There was no reply; but Miss Jerusha was too full of her subject to mind this, and went on:

"Says, I, 'I hear you're a-goin' to be married, Mr. Wildair,' and he larfs. 'Is it true?' says I, and he nods and begins eatin' peaches, and larfs again. 'To a heiress?' says I. 'Yes, to an heiress—'mensely rich,' says he. 'That's what I am a-goin' to marry her for.' 'Marry her for her money!' says I; 'oh, Mr. Wildair, ain't you ashamed?' 'No,' says he, larfing all the time, and giving me one of those queer looks out of them handsome eyes of his'n. 'Well, you ought for to be,' says I, rail mad. 'Is she good-looking?' says I. 'Beautiful,' says he; 'the handsomest gal you ever seen.' 'I don't believe it! I don't believe it!' says I. 'She *couldn't* be handsomer than my Georgie, no how; it's clean onpossible,' says I."

As if she had received a spear-thrust, Georgia sprang to her feet and turned upon Miss Jerusha such a white face and such fiercely blazing eyes that the good lady recoiled in terror, and the word died on her lips.

"*Did you dare?*" she exclaimed, hoarsely.

"Dare what? Oh, my dear! What hev I done, Georgia?" cried out Miss Jerusha, in dismay.

But Georgia did not reply. Fixing her eyes on Miss Jerusha's face with a look she never forgot, she turned and left the room.

"Awful sarpints! what *hev* I done?" said the dismayed Miss Jerusha. "I'm always a doing something to make Georgey mad without knowing it. Can't be helped. Gracious! if I only had a house like that!"

117

All through Burnfield spread the news of the visit extraordinary, and before night it was currently known to every gossip from one end of it to the other that young Squire Wildair, forgetting the ancient dignity of his house, was going to be immediately married to Georgia Darrell, and before long this rumor reached the ears of Miss Jerusha and Mr. Wildair himself. From the latter personage it provoked a peculiar smile, full of quiet meaning, but Miss Jerusha hardly knew whether to be pleased or otherwise.

For her own part, she would have considered the rumor an honor; but Georgia was so "*queer*," Miss Jerusha would not for all the world she should hear it. Other girls might not mind such things; but she was not like other girls, and the old maid had a vague, uneasy idea that something terrible would be the consequence if she heard it. But Georgia did *not* hear it. There was a quiet, conscious dignity about her of late years that made people keep their distance and mind to whom they were talking; and not even that most inveterate of gossips, Mrs. Tolduso, would have been hardy enough to put the question to the haughty reserved girl. Therefore, though Emily, and Richmond, and Miss Jerusha, and every one over the innocent age of three years old in Burnfield, knew all about the current report, Georgia, the most deeply interested of all, never dreamed of its existence.

And so matters were getting most delightfully complicated, and Miss Jerusha's dreams were growing "small by degrees and beautifully less," when, one evening, about a fortnight after her visit, Georgia, who had been out for a walk—a very unusual thing for her of late days—came suddenly in, so changed, so transfigured, that Miss Jerusha dropped her knitting and opened her mouth and eyes to an alarming wideness in her surprise. Her face was radiant, lighted, brilliant; her eyes like stars, her cheeks glowing; she seemed to have found the fabled elixir of youth, and life, and hope, and happiness.

"Why, Georgia! *My-y-y* conscience!" exclaimed Miss Jerusha, with a perfect shake on the pronoun in her surprise.

But Georgia laughed. Miss Jerusha could not remember when she had heard her laugh before, and the rosy color lighted up beautifully her beaming face.

"What on airth has come to you, Georgey?" exclaimed Miss Jerusha, more completely bewildered than she had ever been before in the whole course of her life. "Why, one would think you was enchanted or something."

Again Georgia laughed. It was perfect music to hear her, and fairly gladdened Miss Jerusha's old heart. She did not say what had "come to her," but it was evidently something pleasant, for no face had changed so in one hour as hers had.

"Never mind, Miss Jerusha; shall I set the table for tea? Here, Betsey, get out of the way. Come, Fly, make haste; Miss Jerusha wants her tea, I know."

"Well, gracious!" was Miss Jerusha's ejaculation, as she watched the graceful form flitting airily hither and thither, like an embodied sunbeam, "if that gal ain't got as many streaks as a tulip! What will be the next, I wonder?"

All tea-time Georgia was another being; and when it was over, instead of going straight to her room, as was her fashion, she took some needle-work that Miss Jerusha could not sew on after candle-light, and sat down to work and talk, while Miss Jerusha sat at her work, still digesting her astonishment, and not quite certain whether she had not gone out of her mind.

The clock struck nine. Miss Jerusha, who, from time immemorial, had made it a point of conscience never to sit up a moment later, began folding up her work. Georgia, who was standing with her elbow resting on the mantelpiece, her forehead dropped upon it, and her luminous eyes filled with a deep joy too intense for smiles, fixed on the green boughs on the hearth, now came over, and, to the great surprise of the venerable spinster, knelt down before her, and put her arms caressingly around her waist.

"Miss Jerusha," she said, softly, lifting her dark, beautiful eyes to her wrinkled face.

"Well, Georgey," said Miss Jerusha, in a subdued tone of wonder.

"It is nearly six years since you first took me here to live, is it not?" she asked.

"Nearly six yes," said Miss Jerusha.

"And since then I have been a very wild, wayward, disobedient girl; repaying all your kindness with ingratitude, have I not?"

"Why, Georgey!"

"I have been passionate, stubborn, and willful; saucy, impertinent, and ungrateful; I know I have, I feel it now. You were very good to take the poor little orphan girl, who might have starved but for you, and this was your reward. Oh, Miss Jerusha! dear, best friend that ever was in this world, can you ever forgive me?"

"Oh, Georgey!" said Miss Jerusha, fairly sobbing.

"I am sorry for what I have done; say you forgive me, Miss Jerusha," said Georgey, sweetly.

"Oh, Georgey! my dear little Georgey, I *do* forgive you," and, quite melted, Miss Jerusha sobbed outright.

"Dear Miss Jerusha, how I thank you. Lay your hand on my head and say 'Heaven bless you!' I have no mother nor father to bless me now."

"May the Lord in Heaven bless thee, Georgey!" and Miss Jerusha's hand, trembling with unwonted emotion, fell on the young head bent so meekly now, and two bright drops fell shining there, too.

Georgia's beautiful arms encircled her neck, and her lips touched those of her old friend for the *first time*, and then she was gone. And Miss Jerusha found that there was something new under the sun.

But Miss Jerusha discovered, when the morning dawned, that still another surprise awaited her.

CHAPTER XII.

RICHMOND HOUSE GETS A MISTRESS.

"Bride, upon thy wedding day
Did the fluttering of thy breath
Speak of joy or woe beneath?
And the hue that went and came
On thy cheek, like lines of flame,
Flowed its crimson from the unrest
Or the gladness of thy breast?"

eakfast was over. Georgia, blushing and smiling beneath Miss Jerusha's curious scrutiny, had gone back to her room, and Miss Jerusha, sitting in her low rocking-chair, was left alone with the bright morning sunshine that lay in broad patches on the floor to the special delectation of Mrs. and Miss Betsey Periwinkle.

Miss Jerusha was thinking of a good many things in general, but Georgia's unaccountable freaks in particular, when a well-known step sounded on the threshold, and the tall, stately form of Richmond Wildair stood before her.

Miss Jerusha was always pleased to have the rich young squire visit her, because it added to her importance in the eyes of the villagers; so she got up with a brisk, delighted "how d'ye do," and placed a chair for her visitor.

"All alone, Miss Jerusha?" said Mr. Wildair, taking up Betsey Periwinkle the second, who came purring politely around him, and stroking her mottled coat.

"Wall, not exactly," said Miss Jerusha. "Georgia's up stairs, for a wonder. I'll call her down, if you like."

"No—never mind," said Mr. Wildair. "Miss Georgia doesn't always seem so glad to see me that she should be disturbed now on my account."

"Wall, Mr. Wildair, Georgey's *queer*; there's never no tellin' what she'll do; if you 'spect her to do one thing you may be pretty certain she'll do 'xactly t'other. Now, yesterday afternoon she went out as glum as a porkypine"— Miss Jerusha's ideas of porcupines were rather vague—"and, bless my stars!

121

if she didn't come in a smilin' like a basket of chips. My 'pinion is," said Miss Jerusha, firmly, "that something's come to her; you needn't believe it if you don't like too, but *I* do."

A smile full of curious meaning broke over Mr. Wildair's face.

"On the contrary, my dear madam, I *do* believe it most firmly. Not only do I *think* something came to her yesterday, but I *know* it from positive observation."

"Hey?" said Miss Jerusha, looking up sharply.

Mr. Wildair put down little Betsey Periwinkle, got up, and leaning his arm on the mantel, with that same strange smile on his face, stood looking down on Miss Jerusha.

"What is it?" asked the old lady, with a puzzled look answering that smile, as if he had spoken.

"My dear Miss Jerusha, I have a favor to ask of you this morning, a *great* favor, a *very* great favor, indeed," he said, with a light she had never seen before in his handsome eyes.

"Wall," said Miss Jerusha, looking most delightfully perplexed, "what is it?"

"I want you to give me something."

"You do! Why, my gracious! I ain't got nothing to give you."

"Yes, you have; a treasure beyond all price."

"Good gracious! where?" said Miss Jerusha, gazing round with a bewildered look.

"I mean—*Georgia*."

"Hey!"

Richmond laughed. Miss Jerusha had jumped as if she had suddenly sat down on an upturned tack.

"Miss Jerusha, Richmond House wants a mistress, and *I* want Miss Georgia Darrell to be that mistress."

"Oh, my gracious!" cried the overwhelmed Miss Jerusha, sinking back in her chair.

"You have no objections, I hope, my dear madam."

"Oh, my gracious! *did* you ever?" exclaimed Miss Jerusha, appealing to society at large. "Marry my Georgey! My-y-y conscience alive!"

Richmond stood smilingly before her, running his fingers through his glossy dark hair, waiting for her astonishment to evaporate.

"You ain't in airnest, now," said Miss Jerusba, resting her chin on her hand and peering up in his face with a look of mingled incredulity and delight, as the faded vision of the brown silk, and the new straw bonnet began again to loom up in the distance.

"Never was so much so in my life. Come, Miss Jerusha, say I may have her."

"Why, my stars and garters! 'tain't *me* you ought for to ask, it's Georgey. Why didn't you ask *her*?"

"I have already done so. I asked her last evening."

"Oh-h-h!" said Miss Jerusha, drawing in her breath, and sending out the ejaculation in a perfect whistle of astonishment at the new light that dawned upon her. "I see now. That's what did it! Well, I never! And what did she say?"

"She said what I want you to say—yes."

"But, look here," said Miss Jerusha, to whom the news seemed a great deal too good to be true, "how about that there heiress, you know—hey?"

"What heiress?" said Richmond, with a smile.

"Why, you know—that one everybody said you were a-goin' to be married to —that one from the city."

"Don't know the lady at all—never had the pleasure of seeing her in my life, Miss Jerusha."

"Well, now, it seems to me there's suthin' wrong somewhere," said Miss Jerusha, doubtfully; "why, you told me yourself, Mr. Wildair, you were going to marry a heiress—'mensely rich, you said. I recommember your very words."

"And so I am; but Georgia was the heiress I meant—immensely rich in beauty, and a noble, generous heart."

"Humph! poor sort o' riches to get along in the world with," said Miss Jerusha, rather cynically. "If you meant Georgey all along, what made you let folks think it was to somebody else—that there young woman from the city?"

Richmond laughed, and shook back his dark clustering hair.

"From a rather unworthy motive, I must own, Miss Jerusha. I wanted to make Georgia jealous, and so be sure she liked me."

"Wal, I never! that tells the whole story. She *was* jealous, and that is what made her as cross as two sticks. Well, to be sure! if it ain't funny! he! he! he!"

And Miss Jerusha indulged in a regular cachinnation for the first time that Richmond ever remembered to hear her.

"I am glad it seems to please you. Then we have your consent?"

"Why, my gracious, *yes*! I hain't the least objection. I guess not. What do *your* folks say about it?"

"My 'folks' will not object. I am my own master, Miss Jerusha. I have written to tell my mother, and I know she will not disapprove of any step I see fit to take," said Richmond, composedly.

"Well, railly! And when is it a-goin' to come off?"

"What?"

"Why, the weddin', to be sure."

"Oh, there is no use for unnecessary delay. I spoke to Georgia on the subject, and proposed Tuesday fortnight; but she seems to think that too soon—in fact, was preposterous enough to propose waiting until next year. Of course, I wouldn't listen a moment to any such proposition."

"Of course not," said Miss Jerusha, decidedly, thinking of her brown silk, which she had no notion of waiting for so long.

"Do *you* think Tuesday fortnight too soon?"

"Gracious, no! I can get the two dressmakers, and have everything ready before that, quite easy."

"Thank you, Miss Jerusha," said Richmond, gratefully; "and as suitable things cannot be obtained here, one of the dressmakers you mention will go with Mrs. Hamm to the city and procure a bridal outfit for my peerless Georgia. Neither shall you, my dear, kind friend, be forgotten; and, believe me, I shall endeavor to reward you for all your kindness to my future bride. And now for my plans. Immediately after we are married we depart for New York, and remain for some time with my mother there. We will return here and remain until the fall, when we will depart for Washington, and there spend the winter. Next year we will probably travel on the Continent, and after that—sufficient unto the day is the evil thereof," he said, breaking off into a smile. "And now, if you like, you may call Georgia; we must reason her out of this absurd notion of postponing our marriage. I count upon your help, Miss Jerusha."

So Georgia was called, and came down, looking a great deal more lovely, if less brilliant, in her girlish blushes, and smiles, and shy timidity than she had ever been when arrayed in her haughty pride. And Miss Jerusha attacked and overwhelmed her with a perfect storm of contemptuous speeches at the notion of putting off her marriage, quite sneering at the idea of such a thing, and Richmond looked so pleading that Georgia, half laughing, and half crying, and wholly against her will, was forced, in self-defense, to strike her colors, and surrender. She was so happy now, so deeply, intensely happy, that she shrank from the idea of disturbing it by the bustle and fuss that must come, and she looked forward shrinkingly, almost in terror, to the time when she would be a wife, even though it were *his*. But the promise was given, and Georgia's promises were never retracted, and so the matter was settled.

That afternoon the stately little housekeeper at Richmond House was told she was to have a mistress. Mrs. Hamm was altogether too well-bred, and too much of a lady, to be surprised at anything in this world; yet, when she heard her young master was going to marry a village girl, a slight, a very slight, smile of contempt was concealed behind her delicate lace-bordered handkerchief, but she quietly bowed, and professed her willingness to start for New York at any moment. And the very next morning, accompanied by the dressmaker Miss Jerusha had spoken of, she took her departure, with orders to spare no expense in procuring the bridal outfit.

Never was there a more restless, eccentric, tormenting bride-elect than Georgia. From being positively wild, she became superlatively wildest, and drove Miss Jerusha and Mr. Wildair daily to the verge of desperation for the next two weeks. She laughed at him, fled from him, refused to take a walk with him or sing to him, and made herself generally so provoking, that Richmond vowed she was wearing him to a skeleton, and threatened awful vengeance at some period fast forthcoming. And Georgia would laugh the shrill elfish laugh of her childhood, and fly up to her room, and lock herself in, and be invisible until he had gone.

Georgia wanted Emily to be her bride-maid, but when Emily heard that the Rev. Mr. Barebones was to officiate on the occasion, she refused. Georgia, who was not particular who performed the ceremony of "enslaving her," as she called it, asked Richmond to allow Father Murray to unite them; but, to her surprise, Richmond's brow darkened, and he positively refused. Georgia was inclined to resent this at first; but then she considered it might arise from conscientious scruples, and though she had none of her own, yet she respected them in others, and so she yielded, and Miss Becky Barebones, a gaunt damsel, whose looks were faintly shadowed forth in her name, gladly consented to "stand up" with her; while a young gentleman from the city, a brother lawyer of Richmond's, was to perform the same office for him.

And so old Father Time, who jogs on unrestingly and never harries for weddings or funerals, kept on his old road, and brought the bridal morning at last. A lovely morning it was—a gorgeous, golden September day, with hills, and river, and valleys all bathed in a golden haze; just the sort of a day our tropical, wild-eyed bride liked.

At early morning all Burnfield was astir, and crowding toward the little sea-side cot, to catch a glimpse of the elegant bridal carriage and gayly decked horses, and, perhaps, be fortunate enough to obtain a peep at the happy pair.

Inside the cottage all was bustle and excitement. Out in the kitchen (to begin at the beginning, like the writer of the "House that Jack Built,") Fly had been ignominiously deposed, to make way for the accomplished cook from Richmond House, who for the past week had been concentrating his stupendous intellect on the bridal breakfast, and had brought that *dejeuner* to a state of perfection such as the eye, nor heart, nor palate of man had ever conceived before. There were also the two fascinating young footmen, making themselves generally useful with a sort of lofty condescension and dignified contempt for everything about them, except when they met the withering eye of Miss Jerusha, and then they wilted down, and felt themselves dwindling down to about five inches high. There was Mrs. Hamm, in black velvet, nothing less, and so stately, and so politely dignified, that the English language is utterly unable to do justice to her grandeur. There was Miss Jerusha, in rustling brown satin, her wildest dreams realized, perfectly awful in its glittering folds, enough to strike terror into the heart of a Zouave, with a flashing ruby brooch, and a miraculous combination of lace and ribbons on her head, all broke out in a fiery eruption of flaring red flowers, which were in violent contrast to her complexion—that being, as the reader is already aware, decidedly, and without compromise, yellow. And, lastly, there were our two friends, the Betsey Periwinkles, looking very much astonished, as well they might, at the sudden change that had taken place around them; and, evidently considering themselves just as good as anybody there, they kept poking themselves in the way, and tripping up the company generally, and the two fascinating footmen in particular, invoking from those nice individuals "curses, not loud but deep." There was the Rev. Mr. Barebones, gaunt and grim in his piety; and the Rev. Mrs. Barebones, a severe female, with a hard jaw and stony eye; and there was Mrs. Tolduso, whom Miss Jerusha admitted just to dazzle with her brown satin; and there were ever so many other people, until it became a matter of doubt whether the bridal party would have room to squeeze through.

In the hall stood Richmond Wildair, looking very handsome and very happy indeed, while he waited for Georgia to descend. Mr. Curtis, his friend, resplendent in white vest and kids, lounged against the staircase, caressing his mustache, and inwardly raging that that flagstaff of a Becky Barebones was to be his *vis-a-vis*, instead of sweet, blooming little Emily Murray.

Up stairs in her "maiden bower" was our Georgia, under the hands of Emily, and Becky, and one of the spruce dressmakers, being "arrayed for the sacrifice," as she persisted in calling it. And if Georgia Darrell, in her plain cottage dress, was beautiful, the same Georgia in her white silk, frosted with seed pearls, enveloped in a mist-like lace vail, and bearing an orange wreath of flashing jewels on her regal head, was bewildering, dazzling! There was a wild, glittering light in her splendid oriental eyes, and a crimson pulse kept beating in and out like an inward flame on her dark cheek, that bespoke anything but the calm, perfect peace and joy of a "blessed bride."

Was it a vague, shadowy terror of the new life before her? Was it distrust of him, distrust of herself, or a nameless fear of the changes time must bring? She did not know, she could not tell; but there was a dread, a horror of she knew not what overshadowing her like a cloud. She tried to shake it off, but in vain; she strove to strangle it at its birth, but it evaded her grasp, and loomed up a huge misshapen thing between her mirror and the shining beautiful image in its snowy robes there revealed.

Little Emily Murray, quite enchanting in a cloud of white muslin, and no end of blue ribbons, kept fleeting about, hardly knowing whether to laugh or cry, and alternately doing both. She was so glad Georgia was going to be a great lady, and so sorry for losing the friend she loved that it was hard to say whether the laughing or crying had the best of it. And there, on the other side, stood Miss Barebones, as stiff and upright as a stove-pipe, in a crisp rattling white dress and frozen-looking white lilies and petrified rosebuds in her wiry yellow hair, with all the piety and grimness of many generations of Barebones concentrated in her.

And now all is ready, and, "with a smile on her lip and a tear in her eye," Emily puts her arm around Georgia's waist and turns to lead her down stairs, where her lover so impatiently awaits the rising of his day-star, and Miss Barebones and the trim little dressmaker follow. And Georgia involuntarily holds her breath, and lays her hand on her breast to still her high heart-beating that can almost be heard, and goes down and finds herself face to face with the future lord of her destiny. And then Emily kisses and relinquishes her, and she looks up with the old defiant look he knows so well in his handsome young face, and he smiles and whispers something, and draws her arm within his and turns to go in. And then Mr. Curtis swallows a grimace, and offers his arm to Miss Barebones, and that wise maiden gingerly lays the tips of her white kid glove on his broadcloth sleeve, and with a face of awful solemnity is led in, and the ceremony commences. And all through it Georgia stands with her eyes burning into the floor, and the red spot coming and going with every breath on her cheek, and hardly realizes that it has commenced until it is all over, and she hears, "What God hath joined together let no man put asunder." And then there is crowding around and a great deal of unnecessary kissing done, and Emily and Miss Jerusha are crying, and Mr. Curtis and Mr. Barebones, and the rest are shaking hands and calling her "Mrs. Wildair," and then, with a shock and a thrill, Georgia realizes she is married.

Georgia Darrell is no more; the free, wild, unfettered Georgia Darrell has passed away forever, and Georgia Wildair is unfettered no longer; she has a master, for she has just vowed to obey Richmond Wildair until "death doth them part." And her heart gives a great bound, and then is still, as she lifts her eyes in a strange fear to his face, and sees him standing beside her smiling and happy, and looking down on her so proudly and fondly. And Georgia draws a long breath, and wonders if other brides feel as she does, and then she tries to smile, and reply to their congratulations, and the strange feeling gradually passes away, and she becomes her own bright, sparkling self once more.

And now they are all sitting down to breakfast, and there is a hum of voices, and rattling of knives and forks, and a clatter of plates, and peals of laughter, and everybody looks happy and animated, and Miss Jerusha and Emily dry their tears and laugh too, and the fascinating footmen perform the impossibility of being in two or three places at once, and speeches are made, and toasts are drank, and Mr. Wildair gets up and replies to them, and thanks them for himself and his wife. His wife! How strange that sounds to Georgia. Then she sees through it all, and laughs and wonders at herself for laughing; and Mr. Curtis, sitting between Miss Barebones and Emily Murray, totally neglects the former and tries to be very irresistible, indeed, with the latter, and Emily laughs at all his pretty speeches, and doesn't seem the least embarrassed in the world, and Miss Barebones grows sourer and sourer until her look would have turned milk to vinegar; but nobody seems to mind her much. She notices, too, that Mr. Barebones perceptibly thaws out under the influence of sundry glasses of champagne, to that extent that before breakfast is over he refers to the time when he first met the "partner of his buzzum," as he styles Mrs. B., and shed tears over it. And Mrs. Hamm, in her black velvet and black lace mits, hides a sneer in her coffee cup at him, or at them all, and Miss Jerusha is looking at her with so much real tenderness in her eye that Georgia feels a pang of remorse as she thinks how ungrateful she has been, and how much Miss Jerusha has done for her. And then she thinks of her mother, and her brother Warren—her dear brother Warren—of whose fate she knows nothing, and of Charley Wildair and his unknown crime, and heaves a sigh to their memory. And then Betsey Periwinkle the second comes purring round her, and Georgia lifts her up and kisses the beauty spot on her forehead, and a bright tear is shining there when she lifts her head again, and Betsey purrs and blinks her round staring eyes affectionately, and then everybody is standing up, and Mr. Barebones, hiccoughing very much, is saying grace, and then she is going up to her room and finds herself alone with Miss Jerusha and Emily, who are taking off her bridal robes and putting on her traveling-dress.

And there she is all dressed for her journey, and Miss Jerusha holds her in her arms, and is kissing her, and sobbing as if her heart would break; and little Emily is sobbing, too, and Georgia feels a dreary, aching pain at her heart, at the thought of leaving her forever—for though she is coming back, they can never be the same to one another again in this world that they are now—but her eyes are dry. And then Miss Jerusha kisses her for the last time, and blesses her, and lets her go, and she follows her down stairs, where Richmond awaits her, to lead her to the carriage. And then there is more shaking of hands, until Georgia's arm aches, and a great deal of good-bying and some more female kissing, and then she takes her husband's arm and walks down the graveled walk to the carriage. And on the way she wonders what kind of a person Mrs. Wildair, Richmond's mother, may be, and whether she will like her new daughter, and whether that daughter will like her. And now she is sitting in the carriage, waving a last adieu, and the carriage starts off, and she springs forward and looks after the cottage until it is out of sight. And then she falls back in her seat and covers her face with her hands, with a vague sense of some great loss. But that picture she never forgets, of the little vine-wreathed cottage, with its crowd of faces gazing after her, and Miss Jerusha and little Emily crying at the gate. How she remembers it in after days—in those dark, dreadful days, the shadow of whose coming darkness even then was upon her!

They are whirling away, and away. She takes her hands from her face and looks up. They are flying through Burnfield now, and she catches a glimpse of the stately arches and carved gables of Richmond House, her future home, and then that, too, disappears. They are at the station, in the cars, with a crowd of others, but she neither sees nor cares for their curious scrutiny now. The locomotive shrieks, the bell rings, and away and away they fly. She falls back in her seat, and Georgia has left the home of her childhood forever.

CHAPTER XIII.

AWAKENING.

"Her cheek too quickly flushes; o'er her eye
The lights and shadows come and go too fast,
And tears gush forth too soon, and in her voice
Are sounds of tenderness too passionate
For peace on earth."

believe the established and time-honored precedent in writing stories is to bring the chief characters safely through sundry "hair-breadth escapes by flood and field," annihilate the vicious, make virtue triumphant, marry the heroine, and then, with a grand final flourish of trumpets, the tale ends.

Now, I hope none of my readers will be disappointed if in this "o'er true tale" I depart from this established rule. My heroine is married, but the history of her life cannot end here. Perhaps it would be as well if it could, but truth compels me to go on and depict the dark as well as the bright side of a fiery yet generous nature—a nature common enough in this world, subject to error and weakness as we all are, and not in the least like one of those impossible angels oftener read of than seen.

Jane Eyre says a new chapter is like a new scene in a play. When the curtain rises this time, it discloses an elegantly furnished parlor, with pictures and lounges, and easy-chairs, and mirrors, and damask hangings, and all the other paraphernalia of a well-furnished room—time, ten o'clock in the morning. A cheerful fire burns in the polished grate, for it is a clear, cold December day, and diffuses a genial warmth through the cozy apartment.

In the middle of the floor stands a little round table, with a delicate breakfast-service of Sevres china and silver, whereon steams most fragrant Mocha, appetizing, nice waffles, and sundry other tempting edibles. Presiding here is a lady, young and "beautiful exceedingly," robed in a rich white cashmere morning wrapper, confined at the slender waist by a scarlet cord and tassels, and at the ivory throat by a flashing diamond breastpin. Her shining jet-black hair is brushed in smooth bands off her broad, queenly brow, and the damp braid just touches the rounded, flushed cheek. Very handsome and stately indeed she looks, yet with a sort of listless languor pervading her every movement, whether she lounges back in her chair, or slowly stirs her coffee with her small, dark hand, fairly blazing with jewels.

Opposite her sits a young gentleman of commanding presence and graceful bearing, who alternately talks to the lady, sips his coffee, and reads the morning paper.

"Do put away that tiresome paper, Richmond," said the lady, at last, half impatiently. "I don't see what you can possibly find to interest you in those farming details, and receipts for curing spasms in horses, and making hens lay. Of all stupid things those country papers are the stupidest."

"Except those who read them," said the gentleman, laughing. "Well, I bow to your superior wisdom, and obey, like a well-trained husband. And now, what are your ladyship's commands?"

"Talk," said the lady, yawning behind the tips of her fingers.

"Willingly, my dear. On what subject? I am ready to talk to order at a moment's notice."

"Well, I want to know if you have given up that Washington project? Are we to spend the winter in Burnfield?"

"I think so—yes," said Richmond, slowly. "It will be better, all things considered, that we should do so, and early in the spring we will start on our continental tour. Are you disappointed at this arrangement, Georgia?"

"Disappointed? Oh, no, no," said Georgia, with sparkling eyes. "I am so glad, Richmond. It seems so pleasant, and so much like home to be here, with no strange faces around us, and all those dreadful restraints and formalities at an end. I was *so* tired of them all in New York."

"And yet you used to long so ardently for life in those large cities some time ago, Georgia. New York was a Paradise in your eyes—do you remember?"

"Oh, yes," said Georgia, laughing; "but that was because I knew nothing about it. I was dreadfully tired of Burnfield, and longed so for a change. 'Tis distance lends enchantment to the view,' you know, and the anticipation was somewhat different from the reality."

"You did not like the reality?"

"No," said Georgia, with her usual truthful promptness.

"And yet I did everything to make you happy—you never expressed a wish that I did not gratify."

Tears sprang to Georgia's eyes at the implied reproach.

"Dear Richmond, I know it. It seems very ungrateful in me to talk so; but you know what I mean. I do not like strangers, and I met so many there; there were so many restraints, and formalities, and wearying ceremonies to be gone through, that I used to grow almost wild sometimes, and feel as if I wanted to rush out and fly, fly back to dear old Burnfield again, and never leave it. And then, those ladies were all so elegant and grand, and could keep on saying graceful nothings for hours, while I sat mute, tongue-tied, unable to utter a word of 'small talk,' and feeling awkward lest I should disgrace you by some dreadful *gaucherie*. Oh, Richmond, I was so proud, and fearless, and independent before I was married."

"*Too* much so, Georgia," he interrupted, gravely.

"And now," she went on, unheeding his words, save by the deeper flush of her cheek. "I am almost timid, for your sake. When I was among all those people in New York I did not care for myself, but I was so afraid of mortifying *you*. I knew they used to watch Richmond Wildair's country bride to catch her in some outlandish act; and, oh, Richmond, when I would think of it, and find so many curious eyes watching me, as if I were some strange wild animal, I used to grow positively nervous—I, that never knew what nerves were before, and I used to wish—don't be angry, Richmond—that I had never married you at all. You used to call me an eaglet, Richmond, and I felt then like one chained and fettered, and I think I should have *died* if you had made me stay there all winter."

There was a passionate earnestness in her voice that did not escape him, but he answered lightly:

"Died! Pooh! don't be silly, Georgia. I *did* see that you were painfully anxious at times, so much so that you even made *me* nervous as well as yourself. You must overcome this; you must learn to be at ease. Remember, those are the people with whom you are to mingle for the rest of your life—not the common folks of Burnfield."

"They are a stiff, artificial set. I don't like them!" said Georgia, impetuously.

Richmond's brow darkened.

"Georgia!" he said, coldly.

"Perhaps it is because I have not become accustomed to my new position. Any one suddenly raised from one sphere of life to another diametrically opposite, must feel strange and out of place. Why, Richmond," she said, smiling, "I am not even accustomed to that grand little housekeeper of yours yet. Her cold, stately magnificence overwhelms me. When she comes to me for orders, I fairly blush, and have to look at my diamonds and silks, and recollect I am Mrs. Wildair, of Richmond House, to keep my dignity. It is rather uncomfortable, all this; but time, that works wonders, will, I have no doubt, make me as stiff, and solemn, and sublimely grand, as even—Mrs. Hamm."

His face wore no answering smile; he was very grave.

"You are not angry, Richmond?" she said, deprecatingly.

"Not angry, Georgia, but annoyed. I do not like this state of things. My wife must be self-possessed and lady-like as well as handsome. You *must* lose this country girl awkwardness, and learn to move easily and gracefully in your new sphere. You *must* learn to sit at the head of my table, and do the honors of my house as becomes one whom I have seen fit to raise to the position of my wife."

"Raise!" exclaimed Georgia, with one of her old flashes, and a haughty lift of her head.

"In a worldly point of view, I mean. Physically, mentally, and morally, you are my equal; but in the eyes of the world, I have made a *mesalliance*; and that world whose authority I have spurned is malicious enough to witness with delight your rustic shyness, to call it by no more mortifying name. Georgia, I knew from the moment I first presented you to my mother that this explanation must come; but, knowing your high spirit, I had too much affection for you to speak of it sooner, and if I wound your feelings now, believe me, it is to make you happier afterward. You are too impulsive, and have not dissimulation enough, Georgia; your open and unconcealed dislike for some of those you met in town made you many enemies—did you know it?"

"Yes, I knew it; and this enmity was more acceptable to me than their friendship!" flashed Georgia.

"But not to me. It is better to have a dog fawn on you than bark at you, Georgia. I do not say to you to like them, but you might have concealed your *dis*like. A smile and courteous word costs little, and it might have saved you many a bitter sneer."

"I *cannot* dissimulate; I *never* dissimulated; I never did anything so mean!" said Georgia, passionately.

"There is no meanness about it, Mrs. Wildair, and you might have spared the insinuation that I could urge you to do anything mean. Common politeness requires that you should be courteous to all, and I hope you will not mortify me again by any public display of your likes and dislikes."

Georgia arose impetuously from the table, and, with a burning cheek and flashing eye, walked to the window. What words can tell of the storm raging within her wild, proud heart, as she listened to his authoritative tone and words?

"It is necessary, too, that you should by degrees grow accustomed to what you call your strange position," he calmly went on, "before you enter the fashionable world at Washington, where you will make what you may call your *debut*. For that reason, while in New York, I invited a party of friends here to spend Christmas and New Year's, and you may expect them here now in less than a week."

She faced round as if her feet were furnished with steel springs, every feeling of rebellion roused into life at last.

"You did? And without consulting me?"

"Certainly, my dear. Have I not a right to ask my friends to my house?"

She laid her hand on her breast, as if to keep the storm within from breaking forth; but he saw it in the workings of her face.

"Come, Georgia, be reasonable," he said quietly. "I am sorry this annoys you, but it is absolutely necessary. Why, one would think, by your looks and actions, I was some monstrous tyrant, instead of a husband who loves you so well that he is willing to sacrifice his own fondness for solitude and quiet, that you may acquire the habits of good society."

She did not speak. His words had wounded her pride too deeply to be healed by his gentle tone.

"Well, Georgia?" he said, after a pause.

She turned her face to the window, and asked, huskily:

"Who are coming?"

"My mother and cousin, the Arlinfords, Mrs. Harper and her two daughters, Colonel and Mrs. Gleason, and their two sons, Miss Reid, and Mr. Lester."

"All I dislike most."

"All you dislike most, Mrs. Wildair?" he said, coolly. "What am I to understand by that?"

"What I say. I have not yet learned to dissimulate," she said, bitterly.

"Really, Mrs. Wildair, this is pleasant. I presume you forget my mother."

Georgia was silent.

"Am I to understand, Mrs. Wildair, that my mother is included in the catalogue of those you dislike?"

Georgia did not speak.

"Mrs. Wildair," he said, calmly, "will it please you to reply? I am accustomed to be answered when I speak."

"Oh, Richmond, don't ask me. How can I help it? I tried to like your mother, but—"

Her voice choked, and she stopped.

He went over, and lifted the face she had covered with her hands, and looked into it with a smile.

"But you failed. You did not understand each other. Well, never mind, Georgia; you will like each other better by and by. You will have to do so, as she is going to live with us altogether."

"*What!*"

"My dear, be calm. How intensely excitable you are! Certainly, she will live here: she is all alone now, you know—she and my cousin; and is it not natural that this should be their home?"

"*Your cousin, too?*"

"Of course. Why, Georgia, you might have known it. They are my only relatives, for he who was once my brother is dead to us all. Georgia, is it possible you hate my mother and cousin?"

He spoke in a tone so surprised and grieved that Georgia was touched. Forcing a smile, she looked up in his grave face, and said:

"Oh, Richmond, I did not mean to hurt your feelings; forgive me if I have done so. I will try to like all your friends, because they are yours. I will try to tutor this undisciplined heart, and be all you could wish. It startled me at first, that is all. It was so pleasant here, with no one but ourselves, and I was so happy since our return, that I forgot it could not always last. Yes, indeed, Richmond, I *will* like your mother and cousin, and try to be as urbane and courteous to all our guests as even you are. Am I forgiven *now*, Richmond?"

Half an hour later, Georgia was alone in her own room, lying prostrate on a couch, with her face buried in the cushions, perfectly still, but for the sort of shiver that ran at intervals through her slight frame. It was their first quarrel, or anything approaching a quarrel, and Georgia had been crushed, wounded, and humiliated, as she had never been before in her life. It may seem a slight thing; but in her pride she was so acutely sensitive, that now she lay in a sort of anguish, with her hands clasped over her heart, as if to still its tumultuous throbbings, looking forward with a dread that was almost horror to the coming of all those strangers, but more than all, to the coming of her husband's mother and cousin.

All that day she was changed, and was as haughty and self-possessed as any of those fine ladies, her husband's friends. The calm, dignified politeness of Mrs. Hamm looked like impudence to her in her present mood, and when that frigid little lady came to ask about dinner, there were two burning spots on Georgia's cheeks, and a high, ringing tone of command in her voice that made Mrs. Hamm open her languid eyes in faint amaze, which was as far as she could ever go in the way of astonishment.

Late that evening, as she sat in the drawing-room, practicing her music lesson, —for she was learning music now,—Emily Murray was announced, and the next moment, bright, breezy, smiling, and sunshiny, she came dancing in, like an embodied sunbeam.

"Mother's been over spending the afternoon with Miss Jerusha," said Emily, "and I felt so lonesome at home that I overcame my awe of Richmond House and its grand inmates, and thought I would run up and see you. Hope, like Paul Pry, I do not intrude?"

Georgia's reply was a kiss. She had been feeling so sad all day that her heart gave a glad bound at sight of Emily.

"Why, what's the matter, Georgie? You look pale and troubled. What has happened?" said Emily, her affectionate eyes discovering the change in her friend's tell-tale face.

"Nothing; at least, not much. I am a little out of spirits to-day; everyone is at times," said Georgia, with a faint smile. "My moods were always changeable, you know."

"Well, I hope you will not acquire that anxious, worried look most housekeepers wear," said Emily, gayly. "You have it exactly now, and it quite spoils your beauty. Come, smile and look pleasant, and tell me all about your journey to New York. Did you have a good time?"

"Yes," said Georgia, coloring slightly; "I enjoyed myself pretty well. We went to the theater and opera almost every night, and I went to a great many parties of one kind and another. But Burnfield's *home* after all, and there was no Emily in New York city."

"Flatterer!" said Emily, laughing; "and did you see Mr. Wildair's relatives there, too?"

"Yes," said Georgia, in a changed tone. "He has no relatives but his mother and a certain Miss Richmond, a cousin of his, and an orphan."

"You forget his brother—our old friend Charley?"

"He is not at home now—I have not even heard his name mentioned for many a day."

"Indeed?" said Emily, surprised. "How is that? I feel an interest in him, you know," she added, laughing; "he was so handsome, and droll, and winning—twice as nice, with reverence be it said, as your grave, stately liege lord."

"Well, it appears he did something. I never heard what, but Richmond says he disgraced the family, and they have disowned him. What his fault is I do not know, but one of the effects of it is, that he has lost the inheritance Squire Richmond left him. You see the way it was, my husband inherited all the landed property and half the bank stock, and Charley the remaining half. Not a very fair division, you will say; but as Richmond bore the family name, and was more after his uncle's heart than his wilder brother, the old gentleman saw fit to leave him most. As the bank stock was large, however, Charley's fortune was no trifle; but to it certain conditions were annexed, namely: that he should marry this young lady cousin, Miss Richmond, and take the family name before he went abroad. Charley only laughed at it, and declared his perfect willingness to marry 'Freddy'—her name is Fredrica—who would be handy to have about the house, he said, to pull off his boots, sew on buttons, and sing him to sleep of an afternoon. Miss Richmond, on her part, made no objection, and that matter seemed settled; but whatever he has done, it has completely broken up the whole affair, and his share comes to Richmond along with his own. So, my dear little snow-flake, that is all I know of your handsome Charley," concluded Georgia, with her own bright smile.

"It is all very strange," said Emily, musingly; "and I cannot realize that the gay, careless, but ever kind youth that we knew, and whom everybody loved, has become fallen and degraded, as all this would seem to imply. What sort of a person is this Miss Richmond he was to marry?"

Georgia's beautiful lip curled with a scorn too intense for words.

"She is a—But, as I cannot tell my impressions of her without speaking ill of the absent, I will be silent. In a few days you will have a chance to see her for yourself, as she is coming here to live."

"Indeed!" said Emily, slowly, fixing her eyes anxiously on Georgia's face —"indeed! Would you not be happier without her?"

"That is not the question," said Georgia, in a tone of reserve, for she was too proud to let even Emily know how much she disliked this visit; "it will not do for Richmond and me to make hermits of ourselves altogether, you know, so a large party from the city are coming here to spend Christmas. And, Emily, I want *you* to come too; they are all more or less strangers to me, and it will be such a comfort to look on your dear, familiar face when I grow tired of playing the hostess to all those grand folks. Say, little darling, will you come?"

The dark eyes were raised with such a look of earnest entreaty to her face that Emily stooped down and kissed the pleading lips before she answered.

"Dear Georgia, I cannot; I would not be happy among so many strangers—I should feel like a fish out of water, you know. We can meet often when no strange eyes are looking on; they would not understand us, nor we them, Georgia. And now, good-by; Uncle Edward is coming to tea, so I must hurry home."

She was gone. The airy little form and bright face flashed out of the door, and Georgia felt as if all the sunshine in that grand, cold room had gone with her. Impatiently she rose from the piano, and with a rebellious rising in her heart, walked to the window and looked out with a darkening brow.

"She shrinks from meeting this crowd—so do I. She need not meet them, but I have to—I must. Oh! hateful word. If there was a single bond of sympathy between me and one of them—but there is not. They come here to criticise and sneer at Richmond Wildair's country bride—to have a good subject to laugh over when they go back to the city. Richmond says I am morbid on this subject, but I am not. And that cousin, too—that smooth silvery-voiced, oily little cheat. Oh! why, why did he invite her here? I hate her—I loathe her. I shrank from her the moment I first saw her, with her snake-like movements and fawning smile. And she is to live here; to spy upon me night and day; to drive me wild with her cringing servility, hiding her mockery and covert sneers. I think I could get along with his mother, with all her open scorn and supercilious contempt; galling as it is, it is at least open, and not mean, prying and treacherous; but this horrid, despicable cousin that I loathe even more than I hate—oh! I dread her coming; I shrink from it; it makes my flesh creep to think of it. Oh, Richmond! if you knew how I detest this earthworm of a cousin, would you ever have invited her here? Yes, I know he would. I feel he would. He would be shocked, horrified, indignant, if he knew how I feel on the subject; so he shall never know. He would think it my duty to overcome this sinful feeling, and insist upon my being doubly kind to her to atone for it. He likes her—so does his mother—so does every one else; they believe in her silky smile, her soft, treacherous voice, and cat-like step, and mean, underhand fawning; but I—I see through her, and she knows it. She dislikes me. I saw that through all her cringing, officious attentions and professions of affection, and only loathed her the more.

"Oh!" cried Georgia, pacing up and down the room, "this is, indeed, awakening from my delusive dream. Perhaps I am too sensitive—Richmond says I am; but I cannot help feeling so. I was so perfectly happy since our return, but now it is at an end. Our delicious solitude is to be invaded by those cold, unsympathizing worldlings, who come here to gratify their curiosity and see how the awkward country girl will do the honors of stately Richmond country-house. Oh! why am *I* not sufficient? Why need he invite all these people here? But I forget they are his friends; they are to him what Emily Murray is to me. Dear, loving, happy little Emily! with her calm, seraphic eyes, and pure, serene brow. *What* is the secret of her inward happiness? How different she is from me; even in childhood none of those storms of passion agitated her, that distracted my tempestuous youth. Can it be that Christianity, in which she so implicity believes, has anything to do with this perfect peace? *Is* there a heaven?" she said, going back to the window and looking gloomily out. "Sometimes I have doubted it; and yet there *ought* to be. Our best happiness in this world is so short, so feverish, so fleeting, and the earthly strife is so long, and wearisome, and sorrowful, that we need perfect rest and peace somewhere. Two short months ago I was so happy—oh, *so* happy!—and now, at this first slight trial, my heart lies like lead in my bosom. How false the dazzling glitter of this world is!"

And, as if involuntarily, she murmured the beautiful words of Moore:

> "This world is all a fleeting show,
>   For man's illusion given;
> The smiles of joy, the tears of woe
> Deceitful shine, deceitful flow,
>   There's nothing true but Heaven."

There was an unusual shadow on little Emily Murray's face too, that day, as she went home. She was thinking of Georgia. The eyes of affection are not easily blinded, and she saw that under all her proud, reserved exterior, her friend was unhappy.

"I know she dreads the coming of all those people from the city, Uncle Edward," she said that evening to Father Murray, as she sat busily sewing at the table.

"Poor child!" said the kind old clergyman. "I feared from the first this marriage would not contribute much to her happiness. Not that it is Mr. Wildair's fault; he means well, and really does all for the best; but your friend, Emily, is peculiar. She is morbidly proud and intensely sensitive, and has a dread amounting to horror of being ridiculed. People of her nature are rarely, if ever, perfectly happy in this world; they are self-torturers, and their happiness comes in flashes, to be succeeded by deeper gloom than before. Georgia always was in extremes; she was either wildly, madly, unreasonably joyful, or else wrapped in a dark, sullen gloom that nothing could alleviate."

The next three days Emily was not up at the Hall, but on the fourth afternoon she started to see Georgia. The train from the city had just reached Burnfield station, and two large sleighs, filled with ladies and gentlemen, were dashing up amid the jingling of bells and peals of silvery laughter toward Richmond House.

Emily paused and watched them until they disappeared up the avenue, and then, as she was about to turn away, she saw Mrs. Hamm, cloaked and hooded, advance toward her.

"Good-afternoon, Miss Murray," said the stately little dame, in a tone of lofty courtesy that would have become a duchess.

"Good-afternoon, Mrs. Hamm," said Emily, pleasantly; "I see you have visitors up at the house."

"Yes, friends of Mr. Wildair's, from New York—his mother, and cousins, and others—quite a large party. Excuse me, this is my way. Good-day, Miss Emily."

What inward feeling was it that made Emily turn and send such a look of pity up at the window of Georgia's room?

"Poor Georgia!" she said, as she turned away, feeling, she hardly knew why, a most uncomfortable sinking of her heart at the thought of her sensitive young friend amid all those unsympathizing strangers. "Poor Georgia! Poor Georgia!"

CHAPTER XIV.

A DREAM COMING TRUE.

"I had a dream which was not *all* a dream."

BYRON.

"And we saw Medea burning
At her passion-planted stake."

BROWNING.

chmond House at last was full of guests; every room was filled; peals of laughter, and silvery voices of ladies, and the deeper tones of gentlemen, made music through the long silent house, and scared the swallows from their homes in the eaves. The idle servants had enough to do now, and were tearing distractedly up stairs and down stairs, and here, and there, and everywhere with a terrible noise and clatter, and all was gay bustle and lively animation.

Georgia, superb as a young empress, in purple satin, with a brilliant flush on her cheek, and a streaming light in her eyes, had never looked so handsome as that day when she received and welcomed her husband's guests. And when this ceremony was over, they were shown to their rooms to dress for dinner, and Richmond, with a gratified smile, congratulated her on the elegant manner in which she had performed her part. Georgia listened, and her cheek flushed deeper, and her eye grew brighter as she replied to his smile with one that made her face fairly radiant, and inwardly resolved that to merit his approbation, she *would* try to dissimulate, and try to be amiable and courteous to all, even to the detestable Miss Richmond.

The great dining-room of Richmond House was all ablaze that evening, and the long table fairly glittered and flashed with its wealth of massive silver and cut-glass; and around it gathered all the gay guests from the city, and not a lady among them all was half so handsome or brilliant as the dark, bright girl, in her rich sheeny dress, who sat at the head of the table and did the honors.

A very select party they were whom Richmond Wildair had invited. There was Colonel Gleason, a tall, pompous-looking gentleman; and Mrs. Gleason, a stiff, frigid lady, not unlike Mrs. Hamm; then there was a Mrs. Harper, a buxom, jolly-looking matron; and her two daughters, dashing, stylish-looking girls, who had never been guilty of a blush in their lives. There, too, was Miss Reid, a silent, languid, delicate-looking young lady, reminding one of a fragile wax japonica; and a Mr. Lester, one of those irresistible bipeds known as "Broadway swells," who never pronounced the letter R. and had the nicest little bits of feet and hands in the world. There was Lieutenant Gleason, the Colonel's eldest son, remarkable for nothing but a ferocious mustache and a pair of long and slender legs; and there was Mr. Henry Gleason, a youth of eighteen, who stared at the company generally through an eye-glass, and gave it as his opinion that there never was such a rum old house, or such a jolly stupid old place as Burnfield in the world before. There was Miss Arlingford, a pale, dark-eyed, pleasant-looking girl, and her brother, Captain Arlingford, a handsome, dashing young sailor—frank, off-hand, and brave, as all sailors are. And last, but by no means least, there was Mr. Dick Curtis, who on a certain interesting occasion had "stood up" with Richmond, and now, resplendent in a white vest and excruciating neck-tie, was making most anxious inquiries about our friend Emily Murray, about whom he said his private opinion, publicly expressed, was, that she was a "real nice girl—a regular stunner, sir, and no mistake!"

"Aw—should like to see her—weally," lisped Mr. Lester; "this heaw Burnfield seems so good at that sort of thing, you know—waising handsome gals, eh?" And the exquisite glanced with what he fancied to be an unmistakable look at his hostess, whose haughty lip, in spite of every effort, curled while meeting Captain Arlingford's laughing eye; she had to smile, too.

"I say, Lester," called Mr. Henry Gleason from across the table, "that must have been the little beauty we saw standing in the road as we drove up. By Jove! she was a *screamer*, a regular out-and-outer, a tip-top, slap-up girl," said the youth, enthusiastically.

"Henry, my dear," said his mother, looking shocked, "how *can* you use such dreadful language? 'Slap-up!' I'm really astonished at you!"

"Well, so she *was* slap-up!" reiterated Master Henry, determinedly, "nothing shorter. Ask our Tom, or Lester, or any of the fellows, if you don't believe me."

"A true bill, Harry," replied his brother Tom, the hero of the ferocious moustache. "I say, Wildair, you'll have to present us."

"Couldn't, my dear fellow," said Mr. Wildair, laughing; "little Emily would fly in terror at sight of your gold lace and sword-knot. No chance of getting up a flirtation with *her*."

"Aw—couldn't expect anything bettah from a wustic; they ah not wuth the time spent in flirting, you know," drawled Mr. Lester, sipping his wine.

Georgia gave a sudden start, and, had looks the power to kill, poor obtuse Mr. Lester would never have murdered the king's English again. Glances were exchanged, and one or two malicious smiles curled sundry female lips. The gentleman looked down at their plates, and Richmond's mouth grew stern. Not one present but felt the words, save the noodle who had spoken, and that fast youth, Master Henry Gleason.

"Curtis is a goner, anyhow," said Master Henry, breaking the awkward silence; "he turned as red as a boiled lobster the moment he clapped his eyes on her. Eh, Curtis, you're a gone case, ain't you?"

"It's no use though, my dear fellow," said Richmond, recovering his bland look; "my little friend, Emily, wouldn't have you if you were President of the United States. Isn't that so, Georgia?" he said, gayly, appealing to his wife, who was conversing with Miss Arlingford and her brother, the only two whom she did not positively dislike.

"I really do not know," she said, gravely, for she did not exactly relish this free use of Emily's name.

"And why, Wildair?" said Curtis, so earnestly that all laughed.

"Simply, my dear fellow, because you and she have antagonistic views on many subjects."

A change of theme was soon after effected by the ladies rising and seeking the drawing-room. There they dispersed themselves in various directions. The eldest Miss Harper sat down at the piano, in the hope of attracting the attention of Miss Arlingford, whom she professed a strong attachment for, on the principle of "let me kiss her for her brother," to change the song a little. But Miss Arlingford, who had taken a deep interest in the proud young lady of the house, sat down beside her and began to converse. The rest gathered in groups to chat or listen to the music, or turn over prints, until the entrance of the gentlemen—for which they had not to wait long, as that fast young scion of the house of Gleason had moved a speedy adjournment to the drawing-room, pronouncing the talk over the "walnuts and the wine" awfully slow without the girls. And immediately upon their entrance Master Henry crossed over to where Georgia and Miss Arlingford sat, and drawing up an ottoman, deposited himself at their feet, and began opening a conversation with his young hostess, whom, he had informed Captain Arlingford, he considered the greatest "stunner" he had ever seen in his life, and that, in spite of all people said about it, his opinion was that Rich Wildair had showed his good taste and good sense by marrying her.

"Where's the other Mrs. Wildair—the dowager duchess, you know?" he said, by way of commencing.

"In her room," replied Georgia, with a smile. "She was rather fatigued after her journey, and would not come down to dinner. She will grace the drawing-room by her presence by and by."

"Horridly easily fatigued she must be," said Henry, who was one of those favored individuals who can say and do anything they like without giving offense. "Freddy Richmond's with her, I suppose?"

"Yes; she would not leave her aunt. Both will be here very shortly," replied Georgia.

Even as she spoke the drawing-room door opened, and a tall, hard-featured, haughty-looking, elderly lady entered, leaning on the arm of a small, wiry girl with little keen gray eyes, and hair which her friends *called* auburn, but which *was* red, and very white teeth, displayed by a constant, unvarying smile. A smiling face ought to be a pleasant one, but this freckled one was not. There was a cringing, fawning, servility about her which made most people, except those fond of flattery and adulation, distrust her, and which fairly *sickened* Georgia.

"Speak of the—," began Henry, sinking his voice *pianissimo*, and concluding the sentence to himself.

Georgia arose, and almost timidly approached them, and inquired of the elder lady if she felt better. Mrs. Wildair opened her eyes and favored her with a stare that was downright insolent; and then, before her slow reply was formed, Miss Freddy Richmond took it upon herself to answer, with a fawning smile:

"Thank you, yes—quite recovered. A night's rest will perfectly restore her."

Georgia turned her flashing eyes down on the smiling owner of the ferret optics and red hair, and a hot "I did not address myself to you—speak when you are spoken to," leaped to her tongue; but Georgia was learning to restrain herself since her marriage, and so she only bit her lip till the blood started, at the open slight.

"Can we not get on, Fredrica?" said Mrs. Wildair, impatiently.

Georgia was standing before them, and now Miss Freddy, with her silkiest smile, put out her hand—a limp, moist, sallow little member—and gave her a slight push saying:

"Will you be kind enough, Georgia" (she had called her by her Christian name from the first, as if she had been a maid-of-all-work), "and let us pass. I see Mrs. Colonel Gleason over there, and Mrs. Wildair wants to join her."

Richmond, standing over Miss Harper, who was deafening the company with one of those dreadful overtures from "Il Trovatore," had not witnessed this little scene. Indeed, had he, it is probable he would have observed nothing wrong about it; but the gesture, the tone, and the insolent look—half supercilious, half contemptuous—that accompanied it, sent a shock through Miss Arlingford, brought a flush to her brother's cheek, and even made Master Henry mutter that it was a "regular jolly shame."

They brushed past Georgia as if she had been the housemaid, and she was left standing there before those who had witnessed the direct insult. Her head was throbbing, her face crimson, and her breath came so quick and stifled that she laid her hand on her chest, feeling as though she should suffocate. She forgot the curious eyes bent upon her—some in compassion, some in gratified malice—she forgot everything but the insult offered her by the worm she despised. With one hand resting on the table to steady herself, for her brain was whirling, and with the other pressed hard on her bosom, she stood where they had left her, until Miss Arlingford arose, and taking her arm, said, kindly:

"The heat has made you ill, Mrs. Wildair; allow me to lead you to a seat."

She did not resist, and Miss Arlingford conducted her to a remote seat somewhat in the shadow, if such a thing as shade it could be called in that brilliantly lighted room. And then the young lady began talking carelessly about the music, without looking at her, until Georgia's emotion had time to subside and, outwardly at least, she grew calm. Outwardly—but, oh! the bitterness that swelled and throbbed in that proud heart until it seemed ready to burst, that left her white even to the very lips, that sent such a dreadful fire into her dusky eyes as if all the life in her heart had fled and concentrated there.

She did not hear a word Miss Arlingford was saying, she scarcely knew she was beside her; she did not know what was going on around her for a moment, until, with one grand crash that might have smashed a more firm instrument, Miss Harper arose from the piano and sailed over to where the young captain and Henry Gleason were talking, and made herself quite at home with them at once. And then Georgia, whose eyes were fixed in a sort of terrible fascination on Miss Richmond, saw her led to the piano by her husband, and heard her singing, or rather *screeching* some terrific Italian song, and all the time she was combating a fierce, mad impulse to spring upon her and do—she did not know what—strangle her, perhaps. And then her song was ended—the final unearthly shriek was given, like to nothing earthly but the squeal of a steamboat, and she saw her approach, and, with her small, glittering, snaky eyes fixed upon her, in a voice audible to all, ask her—their hostess—to favor them next. Now she, as well as most there, knew Georgia could not play; but, wishing to have a little pleasure quizzing the "country girl," they came crowding around, and it was:

"Oh, *pray* do, Mrs. Wildair."

"*Don't* refuse us now."

"*Do* favor us, Mrs. Wildair; I am sure you sing beautifully."

"Of course Georgia will play; she knows it's not polite to refuse her guests," said Miss Richmond, winding up the chant and smiling insolently up in her face as she laid her hand on her arm.

Georgia started as if a viper had stung her, and, striking off the hand, arose white with concentrated passion.

Richmond, coming up at the moment, had just heard his cousin's silvery-toned request, and the startling way in which it had been received.

Miss Richmond and Miss Harper started back with two simultaneous little shrieks, and looked at Georgia as they would at a Shawnee savage, had one suddenly appeared before them, and a profound silence fell on all around.

Richmond's brow for one moment grew dark as night, and he caught and transfixed Georgia with a look that made her start as if she had received a galvanic shock. The next, with his strong self-command, his brow cleared, and, making his way through the startled group, he said, smiling:

"My wife does not play, Freddy. You forgot music teachers are not so easily obtained in Burnfield as in New York city. Why, Georgia, you are looking quite pale. Are you ill?"

She did not speak; she only lifted her eyes to his face with a look of such utter anguish that his anger gave way to a mingled feeling of compassion and annoyance.

"I am afraid Mrs. Wildair *is* indisposed," said Miss Arlingford. "We will leave her to your care, Mr. Wildair, while, if my poor efforts will be accepted, I will endeavor to take her place at the instrument."

As Miss Arlingford was known to be a beautiful singer, the offer was instantly accepted, and the kind-hearted young lady was followed to the piano by all present, who seated themselves near, while Richmond, Freddy, and Mrs. Wildair, who, with a frown on her brow, had just come up, gathered round Georgia.

"Really, Richmond, your wife has made a most extraordinary exhibition of herself this evening," said his mother, in a tone of withering contempt. "Are you quite sure she is perfectly sane? I do not ask from curiosity, but because Mrs. Gleason has been quite terrified."

Georgia started as if she would have sprung from the sofa, but Richmond held her down, while he said, coldly:

"You can tell Mrs. Gleason she need not alarm herself on the subject; the unusual excitement has been too much for her, that is all."

"The *unusual excitement*! Oh, I perceive," said Mrs. Wildair, with a smile more cutting than any words could have been. "Perhaps she had better retire to her room altogether, and I will endeavor to play the hostess to your guests."

"My dear Georgia," said Freddy, laying her hateful hand on Georgia's, and looking up in her face with a hateful smile, "I am afraid my request offended you. I am sure I quite forgot you could not play, and never thought you would have resented being asked; it is so common for people to play nowadays that one cannot realize another is ignorant of what every child understands. I really cannot leave you until you say you forgive me."

Georgia shuddered at the hateful touch, and her hands clinched as she listened, but Richmond's eye was upon her, and she only shook off the hand, and was silent.

"Do say you forgive me, Georgia, *do*, please, I am *so* sorry," fawned Freddy, with one arm around her neck.

"Oh, Richmond, take her away! Oh, Richmond, *do*!" she cried out, shrinking in loathing from her.

Freddy, with the sigh of deeply injured but forgiving spirit, got up and stood meekly before her.

"Really," began Mrs. Wildair, with haughty anger; but her son, with a darkened brow, said, hastily:

"Mother, leave her to me. Freddy, go; she does not know what she is saying; she will regret this by and by, and be the first to apologize. She is excited now; to-morrow you will see her in a very different frame of mind."

"I hope so, I am sure; it is very much needed, I must say," observed Mrs. Wildair, coldly, as, with a frown on her face, she drew Freddy's arm within hers and led her away.

"Oh, Richmond!" began Georgia, passionately lifting her eyes to his face.

And there she stopped, the words frozen on her lips. He did not speak, but catching her wrists in a steady grasp, he looked sternly and steadily in her eyes, until she sat shivering and trembling before him. And then he dropped her hands, and without a word drew her arm within his and led her down to where the rest were, and seated her on a sofa between Colonel Gleason and himself.

The song was finished, and amid a murmur of applause Miss Arlingford rose from the piano and came over to where Georgia sat, to inquire if she felt better. And then Captain Arlingford and Henry Gleason came, too, and Georgia was soon the center of a gay, laughing group, who strove to dissipate her gloom and restore the disturbed harmony of the evening. And Georgia, now that her evil genius was gone, remembering her husband's look, tried to smile and talk cheerfully with the rest, but, as she said herself, she had not yet learned to dissimulate. And the wild glitter of her eye and her marble-like face told a far different story, and her efforts to be at ease were so evident and so painful, that all felt it a relief when the hour came for retiring and they could seek their own rooms.

Mr. and Mrs. Wildair bade their last guest good-night, and then they were alone in the drawing-room.

Georgia sank down on a sofa, dreading even to look at him; and Richmond, his courteous smile totally gone and his face grave and stern, stood with his elbow leaning on the marble mantel, looking down on her with a stern, steady gaze.

"Mrs. Wildair!" he said, coldly.

"Oh, Richmond!" she cried, passionately.

"Well, this a delightful beginning, I must say," he observed, calmly. "Are you aware, madam, that you made both yourself and me ridiculous to-night?"

"Oh, Richmond, I could not help it! Oh, Richmond, I felt as if I should go mad!"

"It would not take much to convince our friends that you are that already, my dear. May I ask if it was Fredrica's simple and natural request that you would play for the company, that came so near driving you mad? I saw you drop her hand as if there were contamination in the touch."

"Oh, so there is! so there is!" she cried, in frenzied tones.

"Really, madam," said Mr. Wildair, in a tone of marked displeasure, "this is carrying your absurdity too far. Take care that *I* do not begin to believe you mad, as well as the rest. Are you aware that you grossly insulted my cousin before my guests this evening?"

"She insulted me!—the low, fawning hypocrite! Oh, that I should be obliged to live under the same roof with that *thing!*" exclaimed Georgia, wildly, wringing her hands.

There was a dead pause. It had more effect on Georgia than any words he could have uttered. She looked up, and saw him standing calm, stern, and deeply displeased, with his large, strong eyes fixed upon her in sorrow, surprise, and grave anger.

"Oh, Richmond! what shall I do? I am going crazy, I think. Oh, Richmond! I tried to do well, and not displease you, but she—— Oh! everything that is bad in my nature she rouses when she comes near me! Richmond! Richmond! I cannot *bear* to have you angry with me. Tell me—*do* tell me—what I shall do?"

"It is very plain what you must do, my love. You must apologize to Miss Richmond."

As if she had received a spear-thrust, Georgia bounded to her feet, her eyes blazing, her lips blanched.

"WHAT!"

"Nay, my dear; it is folly to excite yourself in this way. Be calm. Of course, you must apologize—there is no other way in which you can atone for your unparalleled madness."

"Never!"

"You *will not*? Georgia, do I understand you right? You mean you *will* apologize?"

"Never!"

"Georgia, you *will!*"

"I will NOT!"

There was another dead pause. Still he stood calm and coldly stern, while she stood with her full form drawn up to its full height, her eyes flashing sparks of fire, her brow corrugated, her lips white with passion and defiance.

"Georgia," he said, coldly, and his words fell like ice on the fire raging in her stormy breast, "once your boast was that you never told a lie; now you have *sworn* one. You vowed before God's minister to obey me, and yet the first *command* I have given you since, you passionately refuse to obey. I am no tyrant, Georgia, and I shall *never* request you to do anything for me again; but remember, madam, I shall not forget this."

He was turning away, but with a great cry she sprang after him and caught his arm.

"Oh, Richmond, unsay your words! Oh, I will do anything, anything, *anything* sooner than part with you in anger! Oh, Richmond, my heart feels as if it were breaking. I shall die if you do not say you forgive me!"

"Will you go to my cousin to-morrow, and beg her pardon for your insane conduct to-night?"

She shivered as one in an ague fit, while from her white lips dropped the hollow word:

"*Yes.*"

"That is my own brave Georgia. The insult was publicly given, and should be publicly atoned for; but I will spare you *that* humiliation. And now I feel that this lesson, severe as it is, will do you good. You will be more careful for the future, Georgia."

She lifted her head, and looked up in his face with a smile that startled him.

"It has come true, Richmond," she said.

"What has, my love?" he asked, uneasily.

"My dream. Do you not remember the dream I told you and Charley, long ago, when I first knew you?"

"Yes, I remember it. You told it so impressively I could not forget it. What of that dream, my dear?"

She laughed—such a mockery of laughter as it was!

"It was *you* I saw in that dream, Richmond; it was *you* who drove me, all wounded and bleeding, through the fiery furnace. You are doing it *now*, Richmond. But I did not tell you *all* my dream then. I did not tell you then that at last I turned, sprang upon my torturer, and STRANGLED him in my own death throes!"

Again she laughed, and looked up in his face with her gleaming eyes.

"My dear, you are hysterical," he said in alarm. "Be calm; do not excite yourself so. I always knew you were wild; but positively this is the very superlative of wildest. To-morrow you will feel better, Georgia."

"Oh, yes—to-morrow, when I shall have begged *her* pardon! Listen, 233Richmond, do you know what I wished to-night?"

"No, dear Georgia; what was it?"

"It was, Richmond, *that I had never married you!*"

CHAPTER XV.

SOWING THE WIND.

rry days those were in Richmond House, with the old halls resounding with music and laughter, and the hum of gay voices, from morning till night. Astonished and awed were the people of Burnfield by the glittering throng of city fashionables, who promenaded their streets and swept past them in the sweeping amplitude of flashing silks and rich velvets and furs. As for our city friends themselves, the ladies pronounced the place "horrid stupid;" but as the young gentlemen, with one or two exceptions, found the country girls exceedingly willing to be flirted with, they rather liked it than otherwise.

A proud man was the Reverend Mr. Barebones the first Sunday after their arrival, when the bewildering throng flashed into the meeting-house, and, with a great rustle of silks and satins, and an intoxicating odor of *eau de Cologne*, filled the two large front pews that from time immemorial had belonged to Richmond House. It was not religion altogether that brought them —at least, not all. Languid Miss Reid, for instance, went because the rest did, and it was less trouble to go than to form excuses for staying; and that quintessence of exquisiteness, Mr. Adolphus Lester, who was tender on that young lady, went because she did. Miss Harper went because Captain Arlingford was going, and Miss Freddy Richmond went because she was a very discreet young lady and it was "proper" to attend divine worship, and Miss Richmond never shocked the proprieties. Georgia went because she *had* to, and Lieutenant Gleason and his father went to kill time, which always hung heavy on their hands, on Sunday. Of the whole party, only Master Henry Gleason and Mr. Curtis were absent; Master Henry, having pronounced the whole establishment of Christian churches on earth and their attendant Christian ministers "horrid old bores," declared his intention of staying at home and having a "jolly good snooze."

Every one seemed to have enjoyed themselves the last week at Richmond House but its young mistress. There were rides, and drives, and excursions during the day, and sailing parties on the river in Mr. Wildair's yacht; and there were dancing, and music, and acting charades, and all sorts of amusements for the evening, into which all the young people entered with eager zest—all but Georgia.

Those days, few as they were, had wrought a marked change in her. The flush of her health and happiness had faded from her cheeks, leaving only two dark purple spots, that burned there like tongues of flame; her eye had lost its sparkle, her brow was worn and haggard, and her step was slow and weary.

She lived in daily martyrdom, such as none but a spirit so morbidly proud and keenly sensitive can comprehend. Slights, insults, insolence, and little galling acts of malice, "making up in number what they wanted in weight," were daily to be borne now from her supercilious mother-in-law and her malicious, insolent shadow and echo, Miss Richmond. And these were offered openly, in the presence of all; not an opportunity was allowed to escape of mortifying her; until sometimes, wild and nearly maddened, she would fly up to her room, and, alone and frenzied, struggle with the storm raging in her heart.

Richmond, absorbed in attending to the comfort and amusement of his guests, knew nothing of all this. It was not their policy to let him suspect their dislike —yes, *hatred* of his bride; and, as they well knew, the rest, who saw it all, would not venture to speak on so delicate a subject to their proud host. It is true, he saw the change in Georgia's face, and the freezing coldness her manners were assuming to all, even to him; but from some artfully dropped hints of immaculate Miss Freddy's, he set it down to stubborn sullenness. And believing her to be incorrigible in her disagreeableness and insubordination, he grew markedly reserved and cold when alone in her society; and thus the misunderstanding between them daily widened.

Georgia was too proud to complain of what she herself suffered and endured —she was dumb; and indeed if she had been inclined, she would have found it hard to make out a list of her grievances and relate them, for Miss Freddy's insults were offered in such a way that, keenly as they struck home, they dwindled into nothing when related to a third party. Had he not been so absorbed in the duties of hospitality, and striving to atone for his wife's neglect, he might have seen for himself; but he was blind and deaf to all, and only saw her uncourteous treatment of his friends and her wifely disobedience. And before long—no one scarcely knew how—Georgia was pushed aside, and Mrs. Wildair and Freddy began to take the place of hostess, and Richmond looked on and tacitly consented. All were consulted in their plans and amusements but Georgia; *she* was overlooked with the coolest and most insolent contempt; and if sometimes, as a matter of form, her opinion was asked by either of the ladies, it was worded in such a way or uttered in such a tone as made it even a more galling insult. And Georgia, with a swelling heart and with lips compressed in proud, bitter endurance, consented to bare her place usurped, without a word or attempt to regain it. With a heart that underneath all her calmness seemed ready to burst at such times, she would refuse to accompany them, pleading indisposition, or sometimes giving no reason at all; and Mrs. Wildair would turn away with an indifferent, "Oh, very well, just as you please," and Richmond would say nothing at the time, until he would find her alone, and then he would coldly begin:

"Mrs. Wildair, may I beg to know the reason you will not honor us with your company to-morrow?"

"Because I do not wish to," she would flash, with all her old defiance flaming up in her dusky eyes.

"*Because you do not wish to!* Insolent! Madam, I *insist* upon your accompanying us to-morrow!"

"You find my society so brilliant and agreeable, no doubt, that my absence will destroy your pleasure," she would say, with a bitter laugh that jarred painfully on the ear.

"No, madam, I regret to say that your fixed determination to disobey me, and be uncourteous and disagreeable, is carried out in the very letter and spirit. Still, I cannot allow my guests to be treated with marked discourtesy. *I* have some regard for the laws of hospitality, if you have not. Therefore, Mrs. Wildair, you will prepare to join our party to-morrow."

"And if I refuse?"

His eye flashed, and his mouth grew stern.

"You will be sorry for it! Do not attempt such a thing! You may disobey, but you shall not trifle with me."

She lifted her eyes, and he would see a face so haggard and utterly wretched that his heart would melt, and he would go over and put his arm around her, and say, gently:

"Come, Georgia, be reasonable. What evil spirit has got into you of late? Why will you persist in treating our friends in this way?"

"*Our* friends!—*your* friends, you mean."

"It is all the same; for my sake you ought to treat my friends differently."

Her heart swelled and her lip quivered. Yes, his friends might slight and insult her, but she was to put her head under their heels, and smile on those who crushed her.

"Well, Georgia, you do not speak," he would say, watching her closely.

"Mr. Wildair, I have nothing to say. Your mother and cousin are mistresses here; my part is to stand aside and obey them. If you *command* me to go to-morrow, I have no alternative. I am still capable of submitting to a great deal, sooner than willingly displease you."

"My mother and cousin undertook no authority here, Georgia, until you neglected all your duties as hostess, and they were obliged to do so. It is all your own fault, and you know it, Georgia."

She smiled bitterly.

"We will not discuss the subject, if you please, Richmond. I make no complaint; they are welcome to do as they please, and all I ask for is the same privilege. I cannot have it, it appears, and—I will go to-morrow, since you insist; my absence or presence will make little difference to your friends."

"Georgia, why *will* you persist in this absurd nonsense?" he would exclaim, almost angrily. "Really you are enough to try the patience of a saint. I wish some of this foolish, morbid pride of yours had been kept where it came from, and a little plain, practical common sense put in its place. You have taken a most unaccountable prejudice to my mother and cousin, which, if you had that regard for me you profess, you certainly would not pain me by displaying; in fact, you resolved from the first to dislike *all* I invited, and you have kept that promise wonderfully well I must say, except as regards the two Arlingfords, toward whom you evince a partiality that makes your neglect of the rest all the more glaring. It is certainly a pity you did not receive the education of a lady, Georgia, and then common politeness would teach you to act differently."

In silence, and with a curling lip and an unutterable depth of scorn in her beautiful eyes, Georgia would listen to this conjugal tirade, but her lips would be sealed; and Richmond, indignant and deeply offended, would leave the room, and the next moment, all smiles and suavity, rejoin his guests. And Georgia, left alone, would press her hand to her breast with that feeling of suffocation rising again until the very air of the perfumed room would seem to stifle her. And such scenes as this were of frequent occurrence now, and one and all sank deep in her heart, to rankle there in anguish and bitterness untold.

Perhaps it may seem strange that Mrs. Wildair and Miss Richmond should hate Georgia; but so it was. Mrs. Wildair was the haughtiest, the most overbearing, and the most ambitious of women. Her sons were her pride and her boast, in public as well as in private, and she had often been heard to declare that they should marry among the highest in the land, and perpetuate the ancient glory of the Richmonds. When Charley had disappointed all this expectation, and had become an alien from her heart and home, the shock, given more to her ambition than to her affections, was terrible, and when she recovered from it, all her hopes centered in her first-born, Richmond.

There was an English lady of rank, the daughter of an earl, at that time visiting an acquaintance of Mrs. Wildair in New York, and to this high-born girl did she lift her eyes and determine upon as her future daughter-in-law.

But before she had time to write to Richmond, and desire him to return home for that purpose, *his* letter came, and there she read the quiet announcement that, in a week or two, he was to be married in Burnfield to a young, penniless girl, "rich alone in beauty," he wrote.

Mrs. Wildair sat nearly stunned by the shock. Down came her gilded coroneted *chateau d'Espagne* with a crash, to rise no more. Her son was his own master; she knew his strong, determined, unconquerable will of old, to combat which was like beating the air. Nothing remained for her but to consent, which she did with a bitter hatred against the unconscious object that had thwarted her burning in her heart, and a determination to make her pay dearly for what she had done, which resolution she proceeded to carry into effect the moment she arrived in Richmond House.

"To think that she—a thing like that—sprang from the dregs of the city, for she is not even an honest farmer's daughter—should have dared to become my son's wife," she said, hissing the words through her clenched teeth; "a low wretch, picked up out of the slime and slough of the city filth, to come between me and my son. Oh! was Charley's act not degradation enough, that this must fall upon us too?"

"Let us hope, my dear aunt, that the place she has had the effrontery to usurp will not long be hers," murmured the dulcet voice of her niece, to whom she had spoken. "We have built up already a wall of brass between them, and I have a plan in my head that will transform it to one of fire. Recollect, aunt, divorces are easily obtained, and then your son will be free once more, and our queenly pauper will be ignominiously cast back into the slime she rose from."

Miss Freddy's hatred came from pretty much the same cause as Mrs. Wildair's. In any case, she would have considered it her duty to follow that lady's lead: but now she had her own private reasons for hating her with all the bitter intensity of a mean little mind.

Miss Freddy was to have married Charley, and was quite ready and willing to do so at a moment's notice, but in her secret heart she would have far preferred his elder brother. Differing from the rest of the world, Richmond, even "from boyhood's hours," had been her favorite; but when she saw his mother's hopes aspire to a coronet and a title, she was overawed, and made up her mind to be cast into the shade. To be rivaled by a lady like this could be borne, but that a peasant girl—a nameless, unknown girl—should win the prize for which she had sought in vain—oh! it was a humiliation not to be endured. So she entered heart and soul into all her aunt's plans, and won that lady's approbation for her dutiful conduct, while she carefully concealed her own motives. And this, then, was the secret of Georgia's persecutions.

The "wall of fire" the amiable young lady had referred to was to make Richmond jealous. Now, jealousy was never a fault of his, but artful people can work wonders, and Miss Freddy went carefully, but surely, to work, with Mrs. Wildair for her stanch backer. And Georgia, all unconscious, walked headlong into the snare laid for her.

As her husband had said, the Arlingfords were the only ones in the house whom Georgia could at all endure. The frank, genial, honest straightforwardness of brother and sister pleased her; and, indignant at the treatment so openly offered her, they devoted themselves in every way to interest and amuse her. And Miss Freddy seeing this, her little keen eyes fairly snapped with gratification, and by a thousand little devices and pretenses she would manage to dispose of the sister, and leave Georgia altogether to be entertained by the brother. And then the attention of the company would be artfully directed to the twain who were so much together, and Richmond would hear from one and another:

"What friends Mrs. Georgia" (so she was called to distinguish her from the other) "and captain Arlingford are!"

"How *very* intimate they are!"

"Yes, *indeed*; just see how she smiles upon him—don't you think her handsome when she smiles?"

"Very much so. Captain Arlingford seems to think so, too. What a pity he is the only one she will honor by one of them."

"Well, it is fortunate she has met some one who can please her—she seems so dull, poor thing!"

"A handsome man like Captain Arlingford does not find it very hard to be agreeable, I fancy; he is decidedly the best-looking young man here."

"Mrs. Georgia's opinion exactly," said Miss Harper, sending a spiteful glance at the unconscious objects of these remarks, who sat conversing on a sofa at some distance. "I asked her, yesterday, and she said, 'Yes, she thought he most decidedly was.'"

"Poor, dear Georgia!" chimed in Miss Freddy, looking tenderly toward her; "I am so glad she likes him; she seems to like so few, and indeed nobody could help liking him, he is so charming. What a nice nose, and lovely mustache, and sweet curling hair he has, to be sure!"

"And, by George! he shows his good taste, too, in flirting with the prettiest woman among you," exclaimed Harry Gleason, bluntly. "Arlingford knows what's what, I tell you; he'll go in and win, I'll bet!"

Now these remarks, though at first he paid no attention to them beyond what the words conveyed, jarred disagreeably on Richmond's mind. But as days passed on and they grew more frequent and more meaning in tone, and he saw the curious smiles with which they were regarded, and the expression of his mother's face as she watched them, and saw his cousin look first at them and then at him with a sort of anxiety and tender pity, he felt a growing disagreeable sensation of uneasiness for which he could hardly account. Even to himself, he was ashamed to own he was jealous of Georgia—his leal, true-hearted, straightforward Georgia, whom he had never known to be guilty of a dishonorable thought in her life. Fiery, rash, high-spirited she was, but treacherous, deceitful, *wicked* she was not. He could have staked his soul upon her truth, and yet—and yet by slow degrees the poison began to enter his mind, and he commenced to watch his wife with an angry, suspicious eye.

Oh, Richmond! Richmond! that you should fall so low as this! You, whom Georgia once regarded as a demi-god; you whom she still believes, in spite of your sorrowful misunderstanding, everything that is upright and true; you, whom, had heaven, and earth, and hades accused of infidelity, she would not have believed. And now, you are growing jealous of your rash but leal-hearted wife, whom you have completely neglected yourself, to attend to others. Oh, Richmond!

"Really, my dear, you are a jewel without price—worth a million in cash!" exclaimed Mrs. Wildair to Freddy, delighted at the success of her diabolical scheme. "Your plan has succeeded beyond all my expectations. I really did not think you could make Richmond jealous without alarming him, and putting him on his guard against us; but, positively, he is growing as jealous as a Turk, and never suspects either of us in the least."

Miss Freddy smiled her sinister and most evil smile.

"Poor Richmond! What a hard time he is going to have of it with that green-eyed monster! And how delightfully unconscious Mrs. Georgia walks into the pit with her eyes open! Really, it is as good as a farce! Oh! the stupidity of these earthworms!"

"Poor Rich! he *did* look so deliciously miserable to-night when he saw those two sitting together in a corner by themselves, turning over those prints, just as innocent as a couple of angels."

And both ladies leaned back in their seats and laughed immoderately.

Poor Georgia! the sky was rapidly darkening around her, though this, the blackest cloud, was still invisible to her eyes. Sometimes, in her desolation, it seemed to her as if she had not a single friend in the world, for Emily never ventured near Richmond House now, and she had only seen Miss Jerusha once since her return. She *could not* dissimulate. She had tried it in vain, and she would not bring her haggard face and anguished eyes to tell the tale her tongue was too proud to speak. So she did not visit the cottage, until at last Miss Jerusha grew seriously uneasy, and resolved to brave all obstacles, the impudent footman included, and go up to the house and see Georgia.

Until she was fairly gone, Miss Jerusha had never known how large a share of her heart her *protegee* had monopolized; and so, worthy reader, behold her arrayed in that respected "kaliker geownd" you are acquainted with, for brown silk could not be worn on a week-day, with the faded shawl, and a pink calico sun-bonnet, a recent addition to her wardrobe, knocking at the hall door of Richmond House.

It was some time in the afternoon, and the household were dressing for dinner, and so the servant told her, respectfully enough, for her first visit had taught them a lesson they did not soon forget.

"Dinner! you git out!" said Miss Jerusha, indignantly, "and it nigh onto four o'clock. Don't tell me no such stuff! Jist be off and tell Georgey I want to see her. Clear!"

The man hesitated; Miss Jerusha looked dangerous; he expected the dinner-bell to ring every moment, and his mistress was in her room; so while he stood hesitating, a rustling of silk was heard behind him, and the next moment Mrs. Wildair stood gazing in haughty surprise on the intruder.

Now, Mrs. Wildair knew well enough who Miss Jerusha was; her niece had pointed her out one day; but as this was an excellent opportunity for mortifying Georgia, she chose to be quite ignorant of the matter.

"What is this?" she said, stepping back haughtily. "What does she want? Wilson, how dare you allow beggars to enter the hall-door?"

"She—she ain't no beggar, ma'am," said Wilson, casting an apprehensive glance at Miss Jerusha, "she's——"

"I don't care what she is. Persons of her class should go round to the kitchen door. Send her out, and let her go there if she wants anything," exclaimed Mrs. Wildair, sharply.

Up to this point Miss Jerusha had stood fairly stupefied. She mistaken for a beggar! She—Miss Jerusha Glory Ann Skamp—whose ward was lady of this great house! For an instant she was speechless, with the blood of all the Skamps boiling within her, and then she burst out:

"Why, you yeller old lantern-jawed be-frizzled be-flowered, impident old woman, to call me a beggar! Oh, my gracious! to think I should be called that in my old ages o' life? *A beggar!* My-y-y conscience! If you hev the impidence to call me that agin, I'll—I'll——"

"Turn her out, she is crazy! turn her out, I tell you," said Mrs. Wildair, white with passion. "Do you hear me, Wilson? Turn this old wretch out."

The noise had now brought a crowd down into the hall, who stood gazing in mingled curiosity and amusement on this scene between the lady and the beggar, as they supposed her to be.

"Turn me out! Let them try it!" exclaimed Miss Jerusha, looking daggers at the startled Wilson.

"Do you hear me, sir? Am I to be obeyed? Turn this woman out," said Mrs. Wildair, stamping her foot.

"Touch her if you *dare!*" screamed a fierce voice; and Georgia, with blazing eyes and passionate face, rushed through the crowd, flashed past Mrs. Wildair, and stood, white, panting, and fierce, like a hunted stag at bay, beside Miss Jerusha. "Lay one finger on her at your peril! How *dare* you, madam!" she almost screamed, facing round so suddenly on the startled lady that she recoiled. "How dare you order her out—how *dare* you do it?"

"Really, young lady," said Mrs. Wildair, recovering her calm hauteur, "this is most extraordinary language addressed to me. I was not aware that persons of her condition were ever received in my son's house."

"Then learn it now," said Georgia, fiercely; "while I am here, this house shall be free to her in spite of you all. Perhaps you are not aware, madam, who she is?"

"Some of *your* relations, most probably," said Mrs. Wildair, with a withering sneer. "She looks like it."

"Mother! Georgia! What in the name of wonder is all this?" exclaimed a hurried, startled voice; and Richmond Wildair, pale and excited, made his way toward them.

"It means, sir, that I have been grossly insulted by your wife," said Mrs. Wildair, her very lips white with anger; "insulted, too, in the presence of your guests; spoken to as I never was spoken to before in my life."

"Mother, for mercy's sake, hush!" he said, in a fierce whisper, his face crimson with shame. "And, Georgia, if you *ever* loved me, retire to your room now, and make no exhibition before these people. Miss Jerusha, persuade her to go before I am eternally disgraced."

"Come, honey, come; I'll go with you," said Miss Jerusha, tremulously, quite nervous at this unexpected scene.

With heaving bosom and flashing eyes Georgia stood, terrible in her roused wrath, as a priestess of doom. Miss Jerusha put her arm around her and coaxingly drew her along, and passed with her into the empty breakfast parlor near. When she was gone, Richmond turned to his guests, who stood gazing at each other in consternation, and forcing a smile, said:

"My friends, you must be surprised at this extraordinary scene, but it will not appear so extraordinary when explained. The singular-looking person who was the cause of all this was a sort of guardian of my wife, and upon her entrance here my mother, deceived by her singular dress, mistook her for a beggar, and ordered her out. An altercation ensued, which my wife overheard, and, indignant at what she supposed a direct intentional insult to her old friend, rushed down, and in the excitement of the moment, thoughtlessly uttered the hasty words you have all overheard. Mother, I beg you will think no more about it; no one will regret them more than Georgia herself when she cools down. And now, there goes the dinner-bell; so, my friends, we will forget this disagreeable little scene, and not let it spoil our appetites."

With a faint smile he offered his arm to Mrs. Gleason and led the way to the dining-room, saying, as he did so:

"You will oblige me by presiding to-day, mother. Georgia, in her excitement, will not care to return to table, I fancy."

With a stiff bow Mrs. Wildair complied, and Richmond, beckoning to a servant, whispered:

"Go to the parlor and request Mrs. Wildair, with my compliments, to retire to her own room, and say I wish her to remain there for the evening."

"My dear cousin," said a low voice, and the small, sallow hand of Freddy was laid on his arm, "allow me to go. It would mortify our proud Georgia to death to have such a message brought by a servant. Remember, she only spoke hastily, and we *must* have consideration for her feelings."

"My dear, kind little cousin," said Richmond, with emotion, as he pressed her hand, "she does not deserve this from *you*. But go, lest she should make another scene before the servants."

With her silky smile Freddy glided out and opened the parlor door without ceremony. Sitting on a sofa was Miss Jerusha, while Georgia crouched before her, her face hidden in her lap, her whole attitude so crushed, desolate, and full of anguish, that it is no wonder Miss Jerusha was exclaiming between her sobs:

"There, honey, there! *don't* feel it so. I wouldn't if I was you. Where's the good of minding of 'em at all? Don't, honey, don't! It's dreful to see you so."

The malicious smile deepened and brightened on Freddy's evil face at the sight.

Miss Jerusha looked sharply up as she entered, and seeing her triumphant look, her tears seemed turned to sparks of fire.

"Well, what do *you* want?" she demanded.

Without noticing her by look or word, Freddy went over and laid her hand on Georgia's shoulder.

"Georgia," she said, authoritatively.

With a bound Georgia leaped to her feet, and with eyes that shone like coals of fire in a face perfectly white, she confronted her mortal enemy.

Freddy, with all her meanness, was no coward, else she would have fled at sight of that fearful look. As it was she recoiled a step, and her smile faded away as she said:

"My cousin sent me here to tell you to go to your room and stay there until he comes."

Slowly and impressively Georgia lifted her head, and keeping her gleaming, burning eyes fixed on the sallow face before her, pointed to the door.

"Go!" she said, in a hollow voice, "Go!"

Freddy started, and her face flushed.

"I have delivered my message, and intend to. If you don't do as my cousin orders you—take care, that's all."

"Go!" repeated the hollow tones, that startled her by their very calmness, so unnatural was it.

For the very first time in her life Freddy Richmond was terrified, and Miss Jerusha appalled. Without a word, the former glided past, opened the door, and vanished.

For a moment Georgia stood stock-still, like one turned to stone, and then, throwing up her arms with a great cry, she would have fallen had not Miss Jerusha caught her.

"Oh, my heart! my heart!" she cried, pressing her hands over it as though it were breaking. "Oh, Miss Jerusha, they have killed me!"

"Oh, Georgia!" began Miss Jerusha, but her voice choked, and she stopped.

"Oh, leave me! leave me! dear, best friend that ever was in this world, leave

163

me, and never come to this dreadful house again. Oh, Miss Jerusha, why did you not leave me to die that night long ago!"

Miss Jerusha essayed to speak, but something rose in her throat and stopped her. Nothing broke the silence of the room but her sobs and that passionate, despairing voice.

"Go! leave me! I cannot bear you should stay here; and never, never come back again, Miss Jerusha. Oh, me! oh, me! that I were dead!"

There was such painful anguish in her tones that Miss Jerusha could not stay to listen. Throwing her arms around her neck in one passionate embrace, she hurried from the house, sobbing hysterically, and startling the servant who opened the door.

Then Georgia reeled rather than walked from the room, up stairs, and into her own bedroom; and there, sinking down on the floor, she lay as still and motionless as if she were indeed dead. For hours she lay thus, as if frozen there, as if she would never rise again—crushed, humbled, degraded to the dust. Sounds of laughter and music came wafted up the stairs; she heard the voice she hated most singing a gay Italian barcarole, and now another voice joins in—*her husband's.*

Oh, Georgia, your hour of anguish has come, and where is your help now? Heaven and earth are dark alike; you did not look up when life's sunshine shone on you, and now, in your utter misery, there is no helper near.

Oh, Georgia, where, in your humiliation, is the pride, the independence that has supported you hitherto? Gone—swept away, like a reed in the blast, and you lie there prostrate on the earth, prone in the dust, a living example of human helplessness, unsupported by divine grace.

Hour after hour passed, and still she lay there. The door opened at last, but she did not move. The footsteps she knew so well crossed the threshold, but she was motionless. A voice pronounced her name, and a shiver ran through her whole frame, but the collapsed form was still. A hand was laid on her arm, and she was lifted to her feet and borne to a chair, and then she raised her sunken eyes and saw the stern face of her husband bent upon her.

CHAPTER XVI.

REAPING THE WHIRLWIND.

"Oh, woman wronged can cherish hate
More deep and dark than manhood may."

WHITTIER.

"And in that deep and utter agony—
Though then than ever most unfit to die—
She fell upon her knees and prayed for death."

 was not in human heart, much less in a heart that loved her still, to gaze on that death-like face unmoved; and Richmond's stern gaze relaxed, and his brow lost its cold severity, as he knelt beside her and said:

"Dearest Georgia, one would think you were dying. Deeply as you have mortified me, I have not the heart to see you thus wretched. Look up—smile —speak to me. What! not a word? Good mercy, how deeply you seem to feel these things!"

"Let me go, Richmond; I am tired and sick, and want to be alone."

"Yes, you are sick; the fiery spirit within you is wearing out your body. Oh, Georgia! when are these storms of passion to cease?"

She lifted her melancholy black eyes to his face with a strange, prolonged gaze.

"When I am dead."

"Oh, Georgia, sooner than that! Oh, *why* did you insult my mother, disgrace me, and horrify all these people to-day! Are you going crazy, Georgia?"

"No; I wish I were."

"Georgia!" he said, shocked as much by her slow, strange tone as by her words.

"Perhaps I *will be* soon; you are all taking a good way to make me so."

"Georgia!"

"It will be better for you, you know—you can marry a lady then."

"*Georgia!*"

"Oh, you can marry your cousin—she will never disgrace you, Richmond," she said, with a strange, short laugh.

"Georgia!"

"Oh, Richmond, why did you marry me? *Why* did you ever marry me?" she cried, suddenly changing her tone to one of piercing anguish, and wringing her pale fingers.

"Because," he said, flushing deeply, "I mistook you for a noble-hearted, generous girl, instead of the vindictive, rebellious one you have turned out to be. Because I made a mistake, as many another has done before me, and will do for all time. Are you satisfied now, my dear?"

She rose from her seat and paced up and down, wringing her hands.

"Oh, I thought I would have been so happy! You said you loved me, and I believed you. I did not know you wanted a wife to bear the brunt of your mother's sneers and your cousin's insults—some one to afford a subject of laughter to your friends. Oh, Richmond, I wish—I *wish* I had died before I ever met you!"

Richmond stood watching her in silence a moment, and the look of marked displeasure again settled on his face.

"Well, really, this is pleasant!" he said, slowly. "You can act the part of the termagant to the life, Mistress Georgia. I expected, and I believe so did all the rest, to see you knock my mother down a little while ago; that, I presume, will be the next exhibition. You have made out a long list of complaints against me during the past; take care that I do not turn the tables and accuse you of something worse than being a virago, my lady."

"Oh, I shall not be surprised. Say and do what you please; nothing will astonish me now. Oh, that it were not a crime to die!" she cried, passionately wringing her hands.

"Well, madam, you do not believe in hell, you know," he said, with a sneer, "so what does it matter?"

"Two months ago I did not, Richmond; now I *know* of it."

The frown deepened on his brow.

"What do you mean by that, Mrs. Wildair?" he said, hotly.

"Nothing," she replied, with a cold smile.

"Have a care, my lady; your taunts may be carried too far. It ill becomes you to take the offensive after what has passed this afternoon."

"After what has passed! By that you mean, I suppose, my preventing your mother from making the servants turn my best, my dearest friend, into the street like a dog," she said, stopping in her walk and facing him.

"My mother mistook her for a beggar. How was she to know she was anything to you?"

Georgia broke into a scornful laugh, and resumed her walk.

"Positively, Mrs. Wildair," said Richmond, flushing crimson with anger, "this insulting conduct is too much. If I cannot command your obedience, I at least insist on your respect. And as we are upon the subject, I beg in your intercourse with *one* of my guests you will remember you are a wedded wife. You seem to have forgotten it pretty well up to the present, both of you."

She had sunk on a sofa, her face hidden in the cushions, her hands clasped over her heart, as if to still the intolerable pain there. She made no reply to the words that had struck her ear, but conveyed no meaning, and after waiting in vain for an answer, he resumed, with a still deepening frown:

"You will not honor me with an answer, madam. Probably your smiles and answers are all alike reserved for the fascinating Captain Arlingford. How do you intend to meet my mother, Mrs. Wildair, after what has happened to-day?"

"Oh, Richmond, I do not know! Oh, Richmond, do, *do* leave me!"

"Madam!"

"I am so tired, and so sick. I *cannot* talk to-night!" she cried out, lifting her bowed head, and clasping her hands to her throbbing temples.

"Be it so, then, madam. I shall not intrude again," said Richmond, as, with a face dark with anger, he turned and left the room.

Next morning at breakfast Georgia did not appear. There was an embarrassment—a restraint upon all present, which deepened when the unconscious Captain Arlingford, the only one who ventured to pronounce her name, inquired for Mrs. Wildair.

A dusky fire, the baleful fire of jealousy, flamed up in Richmond Wildair's eyes. Freddy and his mother saw it, and exchanged glances, and the old evil smile broke over the former's face.

"She was indisposed last night," said Mr. Wildair, with freezing coldness, "and I presume has not yet sufficiently recovered to be able to join us at table. You will have the happiness of seeing her at dinner, Captain Arlingford."

There was something in his tone that made Captain Arlingford look up, and Mrs. Wildair, fearing a public disagreement, which did not suit her purpose at all, said hastily in a tone of the most motherly solicitude:

"Poor, dear child. I am afraid that little affair of yesterday has mortified her to death. Freddy, love, do go up to her room, and see how she is."

Now Miss Freddy, who was a most prudent young lady, for sundry good reasons of her own, would have preferred at first *not* bearding the lioness in her den, but after an instant's thought, the desire of exulting over her proved too strong for her fears, and she rose with alacrity from her seat, and with her unvarying smile on her face, passed from the room, and up stairs.

Upon reaching Georgia's door she halted, and discreetly peeped through the keyhole. Nothing was to be seen, however, and the silence of the grave reigned within. She softly turned the handle of the door, but it was locked, and after hesitating a moment, she rapped. Her summons was at first unanswered, and was repeated loudly three or four times before the door swung back, and Georgia, pale and haggard, with disordered hair and garments, stood before her. So changed was she that Freddy started back, and then, recovering herself, she drew a step nearer, folded her arms, and looked up in her face with a steady, insolent smile. But that smile seemed to have no effect upon Georgia, who, white, cold, and statue-like, stood looking down upon her from the depths of her great black eyes.

"Good-morning, my dear Georgia," she said, smiling. "*Captain Arlingford* sends his compliments, and begs to know how you are."

There was no reply to this insulting speech. The black eyes never moved in their steady gaze.

"What shall I tell the handsome captain, Georgia?" continued the little fiend. "He was inquiring most anxiously for you this morning. Shall I say you will relieve that anxiety by gracing our dinner table? Allow me to insinuate, in case you do, that it would be advisable to use a little rouge, or they will think a corpse has risen from the church-yard to take the head of Richmond Wildair's table. And, worse than all, the flame with which your red cheeks inspired the gallant captain will go out like a candle under an extinguisher at sight of that whitey-brown complexion. Say, Georgia, tell me in confidence how did you get up that high color? As you and I are such near friends you might let me know, that I may improve my own sallow countenance likewise."

No reply—the tail form was rigid—the white face cold and set—the black eyes fixed—the pale lips mute.

"Mrs. Wildair and Mrs. Colonel Gleason used to insist it was liquid rouge, but Captain Arlingford and I knew better, and told them all country girls had great flaming red cheeks just like that. We were right, were we not, Georgia?"

Still dumb. Her silence was beginning to startle even Freddy's admirable equanimity.

"And now, my dear Georgia, I must really tear myself away from you. When shall I say we are to be honored by your charming presence again?"

The white lips parted, one hand was slightly raised.

"Are you done?" she said, in a voice so husky that it was almost inaudible.

"Ye—yes," said Freddy, startled in spite of herself. "I only await your answer, my dear."

For all answer, Georgia stepped back, closed the door in the very face of the insolent girl, and locked it.

For one moment Freddy stood transfixed, while her sallow face grew sallower, and her thin lips fairly trembled with impotent rage. Turning a look of concentrated spite and hatred toward the door, she descended the stairs.

"Well, Freddy," said Mrs. Wildair, when she re-entered the parlor, "how is Georgia?"

"Not very well, I should say, by her looks—how she felt, she did not condescend to tell me," unable for once to suppress the bitterness she felt.

Richmond, who was chatting with Miss Reid and Miss Harper, started, and a faint tinge of color shone on his cheek.

"When is she coming down?" asked Mrs. Wildair.

"My dear aunt, Mrs. Georgia, for some reason of her own, saw fit to answer none of my questions. She closed the door in my face by way of reply."

Richmond began talking rapidly, and with so much *empressement*, to his two companions that languid Miss Reid lifted her large sleepy-looking eyes in faint wonder, and a malicious smile curled the lips of Miss Harper.

A sleighing party was to be the order of the day, and, after breakfast, the ladies hurried to their rooms to don their furs and cloaks; and Richmond, seizing the first opportunity, hurried to Georgia's room and knocked loudly and authoritatively at the door.

It did not open; all was silent within.

"Georgia, open the door, I command you!" he said, in a voice of suppressed passion. "Open the door this instant; I insist."

It opened slowly, and he saw the collapsed and haggard face of his wife, but he was too deeply angry to heed or care for her looks at that moment. Entering the room, he closed the door, and with a light in his eyes and a look in his face that, with all his anger, he had never worn hitherto, he confronted her.

"Madam, what did you mean by your conduct to my cousin this morning?" he said, in a tone that he had never used to her before.

A spasm shot across her face, and she reeled as if she had received a blow.

"Oh, Richmond! oh, my husband! do not say that *you* knew of her coming this morning!" she cried in tones of such anguish as he had never heard before.

"I did know it, madam! And when she was generous and forgiving enough to forget your insolent treatment, and come to ask how you were, she should have been treated otherwise than having the door slammed in her face," he said in a voice quivering with passion.

She did not speak—she could not. Dizzily she sat down with her hands over her heart, always her habit when the pain there was most acute.

He knew, then, of this last deadly insult—*he* sanctioned it—he encouraged it. His cousin was all the world to him—*she* was nothing. It only needed this to fill the cup of her degradation to the brim. Her hands tightened involuntarily over her heart, she could not help it; she felt as though it were breaking.

"And now, madam, since you *will* persist in your insolent course, listen to *me*. You shall *not* any longer slight the guests, who do you too much honor—yes, madam, I repeat it, who do you too much honor, by residing under the same roof with you. Since my requests are unheeded, listen to my commands! We are all now going out to drive; in four hours we will return, and see that you are dressed and in the drawing-room ready to receive us when we come. I do not ask you to do this. I *command* you, and you refuse at your peril! Leave off this ghastly look, and all the rest of your tantrums, my lady, and try to act the courteous hostess for once. Remember, now, and try to recall your broken vow of wifely obedience for the first time; for, as sure as Heaven hears me, if you dare disobey you shall repent it! I did not wish to speak thus, but you have compelled me, and now that I have been aroused you shall learn what it is to brave me with impunity. Madam, look up; have you heard me?"

She lifted her eyes, so full, in their dark depths of utter woe, of undying despair.

"*Yes.*"

"And you will obey?"

"Yes."

"See that you do! And remember, no more scenes of vulgar violence. Chain your unbridled passions, and behave as one in your sane mind for once. You shall have to take care what you are at for the future, mistress!"

And with this last menace, he departed to join his guests in their excursion.

For upward of three hours after he left her, she lay as she had lain all that livelong night, prostrate, rigid, and motionless. Others in her situation might have shed tears, but Georgia had none to shed; her eyes were dry and burning, her lips parched; natures like hers do not weep, in their deadliest straits the heart sheds tears of blood.

She arose at last, and giddily crossed the room, and rang the bell. Her maid answered the summons.

"Susan," she said, lifting her heavy eyes, "make haste and dress me. I am going down to the drawing-room."

"What will you please to wear, madam?" said Susan, looking at her in wonder.

"Anything, anything, it does not matter, only make haste," she said, slowly.

Susan, thus left to herself, arrayed her mistress in a rich crimson satin, with heavy frills of lace, bound her shining black hair around her head in elaborate plaits and braids, fastened her ruby earrings in her small ears, clasped a bracelet set with the same fiery jewels on her beautiful rounded arm, and then, finally, seeing even the crimson satin did not lend a glow to the deadly pale face, she applied rouge to the cheeks and lips, until Georgia was apparently as blooming as ever before her. And all this time she had sat like a statue, like a milliner's lay figure, to be dressed, unheeding, unnoticing it all, until Susan had finished.

"Will you please to see if you will do, ma'am," said Susan, respectfully.

Georgia lifted her languid eyes to the beautiful face and form in its dark, rich beauty and fiery costume, and said faintly:

"Yes; you have done very well. You can go now."

The girl departed, and Georgia sat with her arms dropped listlessly by her side, her heavy lashes sweeping her cheek unconscious of the flight of time. Suddenly the merry jingle of many sleigh-bells dashing up the avenue, mingled with silvery peals of laughter, broke upon her ear, and she started to her feet, pressed her hand to her forehead, as if to still the pulse so loudly beating there, and then walked from the room, and descended the stairs.

As she reached the hall, the whole party laughing and talking, with flushed cheeks, and sparkling eyes, flashed in, and the next instant, like one in a dream, she felt herself surrounded, listening to them all talking at once, without comprehending a word.

"Of course she is better. See what a high color she has," said the voice of Freddy Richmond, the first she clearly distinguished amid the din.

"I strongly disapprove of rouging," said Mrs. Wildair, in an audible whisper, to Mrs. Gleason, as they both swept up stairs with a great rustling of silks.

"What a bewildered look she has," said Miss Harper, with a slight laugh, as she too, brushed past; "one would think she was walking in a dream."

"Here comes Captain Arlingford, Hattie, dear," as she tripped after her; "she will awake now."

Poor Georgia! she did indeed feel like one in a dream; yet she heard every jibe as plainly as even the speakers could wish, but replied not.

"My dear Mrs. Wildair, I am rejoiced to see you again, and looking so well too," said the frank, manly voice of Captain Arlingford, as he shook her hand warmly. "I trust you have quite recovered from your late indisposition."

"Quite, I thank you," said Georgia, trying to smile. Every voice and every look she had lately heard had been so cold and harsh that her languid pulses gave a grateful bound at the honest, hearty warmth of the frank young sailor's tone.

Richmond Wildair had just entered in time to witness this little scene, and something as near a scowl as his serene brow could ever wear, darkened it at that very moment. Well has it been said that "jealousy is as cruel as the grave," it is also willfully blind. The very openness, the very candor of this greeting, might have disarmed all suspicion, but Richmond Wildair would not see anything but his earnest eagerness, and the smile that rewarded him.

Going up to Georgia, he brushed almost rudely past Arlingford, and, offering her his arm, he said coldly:

"You will take cold standing in this draught, my dear; allow me to lead you to the drawing-room."

At his look and tone the smile died away. He saw it, and the scowl deepened.

Placing her on a sofa, he stooped over and said in a hissing whisper in her ear:

"Do not *too* openly show your preference for the gallant captain this evening,

Mrs. Wildair. If you cannot dissimulate for my sake, try it for your own. People *will* talk, you know, if your partiality is too public."

A flash like sheet-lightning leaped from Georgia's eyes, as the insulting meaning of his words flashed upon her; she caught her breath and sprang to her feet, but with a bow and a smile he turned and was gone.

"Oh, mercy! that I were dead!" was the passionate cry wrung from her anguished heart at this last worst blow of all. "Oh, this is the very climax of wrong and insult! Oh, what, *what* have I done to be treated thus?"

How this evening passed Georgia never knew. As Miss Harper had said, she was like one in a dream, but it was over at last; and, totally worn out and exhausted, she was sleeping a deep dreamless sleep of utter prostration.

Next morning, at the breakfast table, Henry Gleason suddenly called out—

"Well, ladies and gentlemen, what's to be the bill of fare for to-day?"

"Somebody was talking of teaching us to skate yesterday," said Miss Harper. "I want to learn dreadfully. What do you say to going down to that pond we were looking at and giving us our first lesson."

"I'm there!" said Master Henry, whose language was always more emphatic than choice, "what do you say, all of you young shavers?"

"I second the motion for one," said Mr. Curtis

"And I for another," said Lieutenant Gleason, and a universal assent came from the gentlemen.

"And what says our host?" said Miss Harper, with a smile.

"That he is always delighted to sanction anything Miss Harper proposes," he said, with a bow.

"And what says our *hostess*?" said Captain Arlingford, turning to Georgia, who with her fictitious bloom gone, sat pale and languid at the head of the table.

"That she is afraid you will have to hold her excused," replied Georgia. "I scarcely feel well enough to accompany you."

"You are indeed looking ill," said Miss Arlingford, anxiously; "pray allow me to stay with you, then, as you are unable to go out."

"And me too!" sung out Henry Gleason so eagerly that the mouthful he was eating went the wrong way, nearly producing strangulation. "There is not much fun in teaching girls to skate; all they do is stand on their feet a minute, then squeal out, and flop down like a lot of bad balloons, and then get up and screech and go head over heels again. It's twice as jolly hearing Miss Arlingford sing."

Miss Arlingford laughed, and bowed her thanks for the compliment.

"And may I beg to stay too?" said Captain Arlingford; "I am really getting quite played out with so much exertion, and mean to take life easy for a day or two. Come now, Mrs. Wildair, be merciful to Harry and me?"

"I think you had better try to join us, Georgia," said Richmond, with no very pleased look; "the air will do you good."

"Indeed I cannot," said Georgia, who was half blinded with a throbbing headache; "my head aches, and I beg you will excuse me. But I cannot think of depriving any of you of the pleasure of going, though I thank you for your kind consideration."

"Now, Mrs. Wildair, I positively shall not take a refusal," said Miss Arlingford, who saw that it would do better not to leave Georgia alone with her morbid fancies. "I shall take it quite unkindly if you send me away. I shall try if I cannot exorcise your headache by some music, and I really must intercede, too, for my young friend, Master Harry here, who was delightful enough to compliment me a little while ago."

"And will no one intercede for me?" said the captain.

"*I* will," said Harry. "We three will have a real nice good time all to ourselves —— hanged if we don't! Oh, Miss Arlingford, you're a—a *brick*! you are so!" he exclaimed enthusiastically; "and Mrs. Georgia, I guess you'd better let Arlingford stay too. Three ain't company, and four *is*."

And "Do, Mrs. Wildair!" "Do, Mrs. Georgia," chimed in Captain and Miss Arlingford laughingly. And Georgia, unable to refuse without positive rudeness, smiled a faint assent.

For one instant a scowl of midnight blackness lingered on the face of Richmond, the next it was gone, and Georgia saw him, smiling and gay, set off with the rest on their skating excursion.

The dinner hour was past before they arrived. Georgia had spent a pleasanter morning than she had for many a day, and there was something almost like cheerfulness in her tone as she addressed some questions to her husband after his return. He did not reply, but turned on her a terrible look, that sent her sick and faint back in her seat, and then, without a word, he passed on and was gone.

That look was destined to overthrow all Georgia's new-found calmness for that day. She scarcely understood what had caused it. Surely he must have known she was ill, she thought, and not fitted to join in an excursion like that, and surely he could not be angry at her for staying at home while too sick to go out. Feeling that the gayety of the drawing-room that evening was like "vinegar upon niter" to her feelings, she quitted it and passed out into the long hall. The moon was shining brightly through the glass sides of the door, and she leaned her burning forehead against the cold panes and looked out at the bright stars shining down on the placid earth.

There was a rustle of garments behind her, a soft cat-like step she knew too well, and turning round she saw the hateful face with its baleful smile fixed upon her.

A flush of indignation covered her pale face. Could she not move a step without being dogged by this creature?

"Well, Mrs. Georgia," began Freddy, with a sneer, "I hope you had a pleasant time to-day with the gay sailor."

Georgia clinched her hands and set her teeth hard together to keep down her rising passion.

"Leave me!" she said, with an imperious stamp.

"Oh, just let me stay a little while," said Freddy, jeeringly. "What confidence he must have in you to make an appointment in the very face of your husband!"

"Will you leave me?"

"Not just yet, my dear cousin," Freddy said, smiling up in her face. "What a romantic thing it would be if we were to have an elopement in real life—how delightful it would be, wouldn't it?"

Georgia's face grew ghastly, even to her lips, and her whole frame shook with the storm of passion raging within. Freddy saw it, and exulted in her power.

"How delightfully jealous Richmond is, to be sure, of his pauper bride and her sailor lover; how his friends will talk when they go back to the city—and how Mrs. Wildair, of Richmond Hall, who is too much of a fool ever to know how to carry out an intrigue properly, will be laughed at. Ha! ha! ha! what delicious scenes have been witnessed here since we came, to be sure."

What demon was it leaped into Georgia's eyes at that moment—what meant her awful, calm, and terrible look?

"How will it read in the papers? 'We are pained to learn that the young and beautiful wife of Richmond Wildair, Esq., of Burnfield, eloped last night. The gay Adonis is Captain Arlingford, U. S. N., who was, we believe, at the time, the honored guest of the wronged husband. Mr. Wildair has pursued the guilty couple, and a duel will probably be the consequence of this sad affair.' Ha! ha! What do you think of my imagination, Georgia?"

No reply; but, oh! that dreadful look!

"Oh, the insolence of earthworms like you," continued Freddy, in her bitter gibing tone, "you dare to lift your eyes to one who would have honored you too much by letting you wipe the dust off his shoes. *You*, the parish pauper, reared by the bounty of a wretched old hag—*you*, the child of a strolling player, who died on the roadside like a dog—you, the——"

But she never finished the sentence. With the awful shriek of a demon—a shriek that those who heard could never forget, Georgia sprang upon her, caught her by the throat, and hurled her with the strength of madness against the wall.

With a faint cry, strangled in its birth, Freddy held up her hands to save herself; but she was as a child in the fierce grasp of the woman she had infuriated.

Ere the last cadence of that terrible shriek had ceased ringing through the house, every one, servants, guests and all, were on the spot. And there they saw Georgia standing like an incarnate fury, and Frederica Richmond lying motionless on the ground, her face deluged in blood.

CHAPTER XVII.

GONE.

> "Oh, break, break heart! poor bankrupt, break at once."
>
> SHAKESPEARE.

> "Break, break, break,
>   At the foot of the crags, O sea!
> But the tender grace of day that is dead
>   Will never come back to me."
>
> TENNYSON.

ere was an instant death-like pause, and all gazed, white with horror, on the scene before them. Freddy lay perfectly motionless, and Georgia, terrific in her roused wrath, stood over her like some dark priestess of doom. Not a voice dared to break the dreadful silence until Richmond Wildair, with a face from which every trace of color had faded, and with a terrible light in his eyes, strode over and caught Georgia by the arm.

"Woman! fiend! what have you done?" he said, hoarsely.

She looked up, wrenched her arm free from his grasp, sprang back and dauntlessly confronted him.

"Given her the reward for which she so long has been laboring," she said, in a voice awful from its very depth of calm.

His grasp tightened on her arm, tightened till a black circle discolored the delicate skin; his eyes were fixed on hers with a fearful look; but, with the tempest sweeping through her soul, she felt not his grasp, she heeded not his look.

"Yes," she said, folding her arms and looking down steadily on the senseless figure, "I have taught her what it is to drive me to desperation. A worm will turn when it is crushed, and I—oh! what I have endured in silence! And now let all beware!" she said, raising her voice almost to a shriek, "for if I must go down, I shall drag down with me all who have acted a part in my misery. Stand back, Richmond Wildair! for I shall be your slave no longer!"

No one there but actually quailed before the dark passionate glance bent upon them, save Richmond. Some Roman father about to sacrifice his dearest child on the altar of duty, might have looked as terribly stern, as ominously rigid and calm, as he did then.

Without a word, he strode over and grasped both her wrists in his vise-like hold, and looked full and steadily in her wild, flashing eyes.

"Georgia," he said; "come with me."

She strove again to wrench herself free, but this time she could not; he held her fast, and met her flashing defiant gaze with one of steady, immovable calm.

"You had better come. I do not wish to use force. If you do not come quietly you will be sorry for it."

His glance, far more than his words or voice, was conquering her. He felt the rigid muscles relax, and the fierce glance dying out before his own, and a convulsive shiver pass through her slight frame.

"Come, Georgia," drawing her toward the parlor; "dangerous maniacs should not be allowed to go at large. You will remain here until I come to you."

He opened the door, let her in, then came out, turned the key in the lock, and put it in his pocket.

All this had passed nearly in a moment. The others, spell-bound, had stood rooted to the ground, their eyes fixed on Georgia and Richmond, almost forgetting the very presence of Freddy.

Now he went over and raised her from the floor. Her arms hung lifeless by her side, her head fell over his arm, and a dark stream of blood flowed from a frightful wound in her forehead and trickled over her ghastly face.

A universal shriek from the ladies followed the sight, and some, overcome by seeing blood, swooned on the spot. Unheeding them all, Richmond made his way through the horrified group, entered the drawing-room, laid his burden on one of the sofas, and seizing the bell rope rang a peal that brought half a dozen servants rushing in at once.

"Here, one of you bring me some water and a sponge, instantly; and you, Edwards, be off for Dr. Fairleigh. Run! fly! lose not a moment."

The man darted off. Richmond, wetting the sponge, began carefully to wipe away the blood and bathe her temples, while the others gathered around, not daring to break the deep silence by a single word. There was something startling in Richmond Wildair's face—something no one had ever seen there before, underlying all its outward ominous calm—something in its still, dark sternness that overawed all.

In ten minutes the doctor arrived and proceeded to examine the wound, while all present held their very breath in expectation. Richmond stood with his arms folded over his chest during those moments of suspense, motionless as a figure of granite; but the knotted veins standing out dark and swollen on his brow, his labored breathing, and the convulsive clenching of his hands, bespoke the agony of suspense he was undergoing.

"Well, doctor," he said, huskily, when the physician arose, "will—will she *die*?"

"Die! pooh! No, of course she won't! What would she die for?" said the doctor, a jolly little individual, rejoicing in a very bald head and a pair of bandy legs; "it's nothing but a scratch, man alive! nothing more. We'll clap a piece of sticking-plaster on and have her all alive like a bag of grasshoppers in no time. Die, indeed! I think I see her at it."

And so saying, the little man drew the edges of the wound together, applied sundry pieces of court-plaster, and then pronounced the job finished.

"And now to bring her to," said the little doctor, proceeding to give the palms of her hands an energetic slapping; "and meantime, my dear sir, how in the world did she manage to smash herself up in this fashion?"

Richmond did not reply. The sudden reaction from torturing fears to perfect safety was too much even for him, and he stood at the window, his forehead bowed on his hand, his hard, stifled breathing distinctly audible in the silent room.

"Hey!" said the little doctor, looking up in surprise at his emotion. "Lord bless my soul! You didn't suppose she was going to die, really, did you! Well! well, well, well! the ignorance of people is wonderful! How *did* it happen, good folks?" said the doctor, making no attempt to hide his curiosity.

"An accident, sir," said Colonel Gleason, stiffly.

"Hum! ha! an accident!" said the doctor, musingly; "well, accidents will happen in the best of families, they say. Don't be alarmed, Squire Wildair; the young woman will be around as lively as a cricket in a day or two. Here, she's coming to already."

While he spoke there was a convulsive twitching around Freddy's mouth, a fluttering of the pulse, and the next moment she opened her eyes and gazed vaguely around.

"Here you are, all alive and kicking, marm," said the little country Galen; "no harm done, you know. Hand us a glass of water, somebody."

The water effectually restored Freddy, who was able to sit up and gaze about her with a bewildered air.

"My dearest Freddy, how do you feel? My darling girl, are you better?" said Mrs. Wildair, folding her in her arms.

"Of course she's better, marm," said the doctor, rubbing his hands gleefully; "right as ever so many trivets. There's a picture for you," he added, appealing to the company generally; "family affection's a splendid thing, and should be encouraged at any price. Let her keep on a low diet, and she'll be as well, if not considerably better than ever, in two or three days. Might have been killed dead as a herring, though, if she had struck her temple, instead of up there."

"What's your fee, doctor?" said Mr. Wildair, in a cold, stern tone, and a face to match, as he abruptly crossed over to where he stood.

"Dollar," said the doctor, rubbing his hands with a joyous little chuckle —"court-plaster—visit—advice"—

"There it is—good-evening, sir. Edward, show Dr. Fairleigh to the door," said Mr. Wildair, frigidly.

"Good-evening, *good*-evening," said the bustling little man, hurrying out. "Always send for me whenever any of you think proper to knock your heads against anything. GOOD-evening," repeated the doctor, as he vanished, with an emphasis so great as to pronounce the word not only in italics, but even in small capitals.

Richmond went over and took Freddy's hand.

"My dearest cousin, how do you feel?" he said.

"Oh, dreadfully ill," she said faintly; "my head does ache so."

"Perhaps you had better go to your room and lie down," said Richmond, his lips quivering slightly. "Mother, you will go with her."

"Certainly, my dear boy. Come, Freddy, let me assist you up stairs."

Putting her arm round Miss Richmond's waist, Mrs. Wildair led her from the room. And then every one present took a deep breath, and looked first at one another and then at their host, with a glance that said, "What comes next?"

But if they expected an apology from Mr. Wildair they were disappointed: for, turning round, he said, as calmly as if nothing had occurred:

"I believe we were to enact some pantomimes this evening—eh, Curtis! It is near time we were beginning, is it not, ladies?"

So completely "taken aback" were they by this cool way of doing business that a dead pause ensued, and amazed glances were again exchanged. Any one else but Richmond Wildair would have been embarrassed; but he stood calm and self-possessed, waiting for their answer.

"Really," said Mrs. Gleason, drawing herself up till her corset-laces snapped, "after the unaccountable scene that—ahem—has just occurred, you will have to excuse me if I decline joining in any amusements whatever this evening. My nerves have been completely unstrung. I never received such a shock in my life, and I must say——"

She paused in some confusion under the clear, piercing gaze of Richmond's dark eagle eye.

"Well, madam?" he said, with unruffled courtesy.

"In a word, Mr. Wildair," said the lady, stiffly, "I must say that I do not consider it safe to stay longer in the same house with a dangerous lunatic, for such I consider your wife must be. You will therefore excuse me if I take my departure for the city to-morrow."

In grave silence, Richmond bowed; and the offended lady, in magnificent displeasure, swept from the room.

"And, Mr. Wildair," said Miss Reid, languidly, "I too feel it absolutely necessary to return; violence is so unpleasant to witness. Good-night." And the young lady floated away.

Once again Richmond bowed, apparently unmoved, but the slight twitching of the muscles of his mouth showed how keenly he felt this.

"Aw, upon honnaw, Wildaih," lisped Mr. Lester, hastily, "though I regwet it— aw—exceedingly, you know—I weally must go back to New York to-morrow, too. Business, my deah fellow, comes—aw—befoah pleasure, and letters I ——"

"I understand; pray, do not feel it necessary to apologize," said Mr. Wildair, with a slight sneer; "allow me to bid you good night, Mr. Lester, and a pleasant journey to New York to-morrow."

Poor Mr. Lester! There was no use in trying to brave it out under the light of those dark, scornful eyes, and he sneaked from the room with much the same feeling as if he had been kicked out.

There was another profound pause when he was gone. Not an eye there was ready to meet the falcon gaze of their host. Mr. Wildair stepped back a pace, folded his arms over his chest, and looked steadily at them.

"Well, ladies and gentlemen," he said calmly, "who next?"

"Wildair, my dear old fellow," said Dick Curtis, with tears in his eyes, "I—I feel—I feel—I'll be hanged if I know *how* I feel. It's too bad—it's too darned bad for them to treat you this way, after all you've tried to do for them. It's abominable, it's *infernal*, it's a shame! I beg your pardon, ladies, for swearing,

182

but its enough to make a saint swear—I'll be shot if it's not!" said Mr. Curtis, looking round with a sort of howl of mingled rage and grief, and then seizing Richmond's hand and shaking it as if it had been a pump-handle.

"And I, too, Curtis," said the honest voice of Captain Arlingford, "am with you there. Mr. Wildair, you must not set us all down for Mr. Lesters."

"The mean little ass!—ought to be kicked from here to sundown!" said Lieutenant Gleason, in a tone of disgust.

"And so ought mother," said Henry, sticking his hands in his pockets and striding up and down in indignation: "and the nasty Lydia Languish Dieaway Reid, a be-scented, be-frizzled, be-flounced stuck-up piece of dry-goods. I wish to gracious the whole of them were kicked to death by hornbugs," said Henry, thrusting his hands to the very bottom of his pockets and glaring defiance round the room.

A low murmur of earnest sympathy came from all present, Miss Harper included; for as Captain Arlingford had joined the opposition party, like certain politicians of the present day, she found it no way difficult to change her tactics and go over to the enemy.

"My friends, I thank you," said Mr. Wildair, in a suppressed voice, as he abruptly turned and walked to the window; "but—you must excuse me, and allow me to leave you for the present. I feel—" he broke off abruptly, wheeled round, and with a brief "good night," was gone.

He passed up stairs and sank into a chair. His brain seemed on fire, the room for a moment seemed whirling round, and thought was impossible. The shame, the disgrace, the mockery, the laughter, the scenes in Richmond House must cause among his city friends, alone, stood vividly before him. He fancied he could hear their jeering laughs and mocking sneers whenever he appeared, and, half maddened, he rose and began to pace up and down like a maniac. And then came the thought of her who had caused all this—of her who had nearly slain his cousin, and the pallid hue of rage his face wore gave place to a glow of indignation.

He had seen Georgia leave the room that evening, and Freddy with her sweet smile rise to follow her, and his thought, had been, "Dear, kind little Freddy! what a generous, forgiving heart she must have to be so solicitous for Georgia's happiness, in spite of all she has done to her." And when he saw her lying wounded and bleeding, with his infuriated wife standing over her, he fancied she had merely spoken some soothing words, and that the demon within Georgia's fiery heart had prompted to return the kindness thus.

It is strange how blind the most wise of this world are when wisdom is entirely of this earth. Richmond Wildair, with his clear head and profound intellect, was completely deceived by his fawning, silk, silvery-voiced little cousin. In his eyes Georgia alone was at fault. Freddy was immaculate. She it was who had brought him to this—*she*, whom he had raised from her inferior position to be his wife—she, who, instead of being grateful, had commenced to play the termagant, as he called it, ere the honeymoon was over. And worse than that, she had proved herself that most despicable of human beings—a married flirt. Had she and Captain Arlingford not been together the whole day?—a sure proof that she had never cared much for him. Had she married him for his wealth and social position? Was it possible Georgia had done this? His brain for an instant reeled at the thought, and then he grew strangely calm. She was proud, ambitious, aspiring, fond of wealth and power, and *this* was the only means she had of securing them. Yes, it must be so. And as the conviction came across his mind, a deep, bitter, scornful anger filled his heart and soul, and drove out every other feeling. With an impulsive bound he sprang up, and with a ringing step he passed down stairs and entered the parlor where he had left her.

And she—poor, stormy, passionate Georgia! what had been her feelings all this time? At first, in the tumultuous tempest sweeping through her soul, a deep, swelling rage against all who were goading her on to desperation, alone filled her thoughts. She had paced up and down wildly, madly, until this passed away, and then came another and more terrible feeling—what if she had killed Freddy? As if she had been stunned by a blow, she tottered to a seat, while a thousand voices seemed shrieking in her ears, "Murderess! murderess!"

Oh! the horror, the agony, the remorse that were hers at that moment. She put her hands to her ears to shut out the dreadful sound of those phantom voices, and crouching down in a strange, distorted position, she struggled alone with all her agonizing remorse. How willingly in that moment would she have given her own life—a thousand lives, had she possessed them—to have recalled her arch enemy back to life once more. So she lay for hours, feeling as though her very reason was tottering on its throne, and so Richmond found her when he opened the door. She sprang to her feet with a wild bound, and flying over, she caught his hand and almost shrieked:

"Oh Richmond! is she dead? Oh, Richmond! in the name of mercy, speak and tell me, is she dead?"

She might have quailed before the look of unutterable scorn bent on her, but she did not. He shook her hand off as if it had been a viper, and folding his arms, looked steadily and silently down upon her.

"Richmond! Richmond! speak and tell me. Oh, I shall go mad!" she cried, in frenzied tones.

She looked as though she were going mad indeed, with her streaming hair, her pallid face, and wildly blazing eyes. Perhaps he feared her reason *was* tottering, for he sternly replied:

"Cease this raving, madam; you have been saved from becoming a murderess in act, though you are one in the sight of heaven."

"And she will not die?"

"No."

"Oh, thank heaven!" and, totally overcome, she sank for the first time in her life, almost fainting into her seat.

Richmond looked at her with deep, scornful eyes.

"*You* to thank Heaven!—*you* to take that name on your lips!—you, who this night attempted a murder! Oh, woman do you not fear the vengeance of that Heaven you invoke!"

"Oh, Richmond! spare me not. I deserve all you would say. Oh! in all this world there is not another so lost, so fallen, so guilty as I."

"You are right, there is not; for one who would attempt the life of a young and innocent girl must be steeped in guilt so black that Hades itself must shudder. Had you caused the death of Frederica Richmond, as you tried to, I myself would have gone to the nearest magistrate, had you arrested, and forced you off this very night to the county jail. I would have prosecuted you, though every one else in the world was for you; and I would have gone to behold you perish on the scaffold, and then—and then only—felt that justice was satisfied."

She almost shrieked, as she covered her face with her hands from his terrible gaze, but, unheeding her anguish, he went on in a calm, pitiless voice:

"You, one night not long since, told me you wished you had never married me. That you really ever wished it I do not now believe; for one who could commit a cold-blooded murder would not hesitate at a lie—a *lie*. Do you hear, Georgia? But I tell you now, that I wish I had been dead and in my grave ere I ever met Georgia Darrell!"

"Oh, Richmond! Spare me! spare me!" she cried, in a dying voice.

"No; I am like yourself—I spare not. You have merited this, and a thousand times more from me, and you shall listen now. That you married me for my wealth and for the power it would give you, I know only too well. You were an unnatural child, and I might have known you would be an unnatural woman; but I willfully blinded my eyes, and believed what you told me that accursed night on the sea-shore, and I married you—fool that I was! I braved the scorn of the world, the sneers of my friends, the just anger of my mother, and stooped—are you listening, Georgia?—and *stooped* to wed you. And now I have my reward."

"Oh, Richmond! I shall go mad!" she wailed, writhing in her seat, and feeling as if every fiber in her heart were tearing from its place, so intense was her anguish.

But still the clear, clarion-like voice rang out on the air like a death-bell, cold, calm, and pitiless as the grave:

"Once, in one of your storms of passion, madam, you asked me why I married you. Now I answer you: because I was mad, demented, besotted, crazed, or I most assuredly should never have dreamed of such a thing. Perhaps you wish I had not, for then the gallant sailor you admire so much might have taken it into his hair-brained head to do what I did in a fit of insanity—for which a life of misery like this is to atone—and married you. That I have deprived you of this happiness, I deeply regret; for, madam, much as you may repent this marriage, you can never, *never* repent it half as much as I do now."

She had fallen at his feet, whether from physical weakness, or whether she had writhed there in her intolerable agony, he did not know, and, at that moment, did not care. He stepped back, looked down upon her as she lay a moment, and went on:

"I fancied I loved you well enough then to brave the whole world for your sake; but that, like all the rest of my short brain-fever, has completely passed away. What feeling can one have for a murderess—for such in heart you are —but one of horror and loathing?"

She sprang to her feet with a moaning cry, and stood before him with one arm half raised; her lips opened as if to speak, but no voice came forth.

"Hear me out, madam," he interposed, waving his hand, "for it is the last time, perhaps, you will ever be troubled by a word from me. You have driven my guests from my house, you have eternally disgraced me, and, lest you should murder the very servants next, must not be allowed to go free. While a friend of mine resides under this roof you shall remain locked a close prisoner in your room, as a lunatic too dangerous to be at large. And if that does not subdue the fiend within you, one thing yet remains for me to do—that I may go free once more."

He paused, and the rage he had subdued by the strength of his mighty will all along, showed now in the death-like whiteness of his face, white even to his lips, like the white ashes over red-hot coals.

Again her arm was faintly raised, again her trembling lips parted, but the power of speech seemed to have been suddenly taken from her. No sound came forth.

"What I allude to will make me free as air—free as I was before I met you— free to bring another mistress to Richmond House before your very eyes. Money will procure it, and of that I have enough. I allude to a *divorce*—do you know what that means?"

Yes, she knew. Her arms dropped by her side as if she had been suddenly stricken with death, the light died out in her eyes, the words she would have uttered were frozen on her lips, and, as if the last blow she could ever receive had fallen, she laid her hand on her heart and lifted her eyes, calm as his now, to his face.

Some author has said, "Great shocks kill weak minds, and stir strong ones with a calm resembling death." So it was now with Georgia; she had been stunned into calm—the calm of undying, life-long despair. She had believed and trusted all along—she had thought he loved her until now—and *now*!

What was there in her face that awed even him? It was not anger, nor reproach, nor yet sorrow. A thrill of nameless terror shot through his heart, and with the last cruel words all anger passed away. He advanced a step toward her, as if to speak again, but she raised her hand, and lifting her eyes to his face with a look he never forgot, she turned and passed from the room.

And Richard Wildair was alone. He had not meant one-half of what he had said in the white heat of his passion, and the idea of a divorce had no more entered his head than that of slaying himself on the spot had. He had said it in his rage, none the less deep for being suppressed, and now he would have given uncounted worlds that those fatal words had never been uttered.

He went out to the hall, but she had gone—he caught the last flutter of her dress as she passed the head of the stairs toward her own room.

"I ought not to have said that," he said uneasily to himself as he paced up and down. "I am sorry for it now. To-morrow I will see her again, and then—well, 'sufficient unto the day is the evil thereof.' I cannot live this life longer. I will not stay in Burnfield. I cannot stay. I shall go abroad and take her with me. Yes, that is what I will do. Travel will work wonders in Georgia, and who knows what happiness may be in store for us yet."

He walked to the window and looked out. The white snow lay in great drifts on every side, looking cold and white and death-like in the pale luster of a wintry moon. With a shudder he turned away, and threw himself moodily on a couch in the warm parlor, saying, as if to reassure himself:

"Yes, to-morrow I will see her, and all shall be well—to-morrow—to-morrow."

There was a paper lying on the table, and he took it up and looked lightly over it. The first thing that struck his eyes was a poem, headed:

"To-morrow never comes."

Richmond Wildair would have been ashamed to tell it, but he actually started and turned pale with superstitious terror. It seemed so like an answer to his thoughts that startled him more than anything of the kind had ever done before.

To him that night passed in feverish dreams. How passed it with another beneath that roof?

At early morning he was awake. An unaccountable presentment of an impending calamity was upon him and would not be shaken off.

Scarcely knowing what he did, he went up to Georgia's room, and softly turned the handle of the door. He had expected to find it locked, but it was not so; it opened at his touch, and he went in.

Why does he start and clutch it as if about to fall? The room is empty, and *the bed has not been slept in all night.*

A note, addressed to him, lies on the table. Dizzily he opens it, and reads:

"MY DEAREST HUSBAND: Let me call you so for this once, this last time—you are free! On this earth I will never disgrace you again. May heaven bless you and forgive.

"GEORGIA."

She was gone—gone forever! Clutching the note in his hand, he staggered, rather than walked, down stairs, opened the door, and, in a cold gray of coming dawn, passed out.

All around the stainless snow-drifts seemed mocking him with their white blank faces, lying piled as they had been last night when he had driven his young wife from his side. Cold and white they were here still, and Georgia was—where?

CHAPTER XVIII.

THE DAWN OF ANOTHER DAY.

"Then she took up her burden of life again,
Saying only 'It might have been.'
God pity them both, and pity us all,
Who vainly the dreams of youth recall;
For of all sad words of tongue or pen,
The saddest are these, 'It might have been.'"

WHITTIER.

 the dead of night—of that last, sorrowful night—a slight, dark figure had flitted from one of the many doors of Richmond House, fluttered away in the chill night round through the sleeping town. A visitor came to Miss Jerusha's sea-side cottage that night, with a face so white and cold that the snow-wreaths dimmed beside it; the white face lay on the cold threshold, the dark figure was prostrate in the snow-drift before the door, and there the last farewell was taken while Miss Jerusha lay sleeping within. And then the dusky form was whirling away and away again like a leaf on a blast, another stray waif on the great stream of life.

Six pealed from the town clock of Burnfield. The locomotive shrieked, the bell rang, and the fiery monster was rushing along with its living freight to the great city of New York.

In the dusky gloom of that cold, cheerless winter morning the tall, dark form, all dressed in black and closely vailed had glided in like a spirit and taken her seat. Muffled in caps, and cloaks, and comforters, every one had enough to do to mind themselves and keep from freezing, and no one heeded the still form that leaned back among the cushions, giving as little sign of life as though it were a statue in ebony.

The sun was high in the sky and Georgia was in New York. She knew where to go; in her former visit she had chanced to relieve the wants of a poor widow living in an obscure tenement-house somewhere near the East River, and here, despairing of finding her way through the labyrinth of streets alone, she gave the cabman directions to drive. Strangely calm she was now, but oh, the settled night of anguish in those large, wild, black eyes!

The poor are mostly grateful, and warm and heartfelt was Georgia's welcome to that humble roof. Questions were asked, but none answered; all Georgia said she wanted was a private room there for two or three days.

Alone at last, she sat down to think. There was no time to brood over the past —her life-work was to be accomplished now. What next? was the question that arose before her, the question that must be promptly answered. How was she to live in this wilderness of human beings?

She leaned her head on her hands, forcibly wrenched her thoughts from the past and fixed them on the present. How was she to earn a livelihood? The plain, practical, homely question roused all her sleeping energies, and did her good.

The stage! She thought of that first with an electric bound of the pulse; she knew, she was certain she could win a name and fame there; but could she, who had become the wife of Richmond Wildair, become an actress? She knew his fastidious pride on this point; she knew the fact of her having been an actress in her childhood had never ceased to gall him more than anything else.

Georgia Darrell would have stepped on the boards and won the highest laurels the profession could bestow, but Georgia Wildair had another to think of beside herself. Much as she longed for that exciting life—that life for which nature had so well qualified her, physically and mentally, for which she had so strong a desire—she put the thought aside and gave it up.

Though she had wrenched asunder the chains that bound her to him, she still carried a clanking fragment with her, and, no longer a free agent, she must think of something else. Another reason there was why that profession could not be hers—she did not wish to be known or discovered by any she had ever known before; her desire was to be as dead to Richmond Wildair as if she had never existed—to leave him free, unfettered as he had been before this fatal marriage. And, to make the more sure of this, she had resolved to drop his name and assume another. She would take her mother's name of Randall; it was her own name, too—Georgia Randall Darrell.

But what was she to do? Females before now had won fame as artists, and Georgia had genius and an artist's soul. But she would have to wait and live on this poor widow's bounty meantime, and that was too abhorrent to her nature to be for a moment thought of. Nothing remained but to become a teacher or governess, and even in this she was doubtful if she could succeed. She knew little or nothing of music, and that seemed absolutely essential in a governess, but still she would try. If that failed, something else must be tried.

Drawing pen and ink toward her, she sat down and indited the following:

> WANTED—A situation as governess in a respectable private family, by one capable of teaching French, German, and Latin, and all the branches of English education. Address G. R., etc.

Next morning, among hundreds of other "wants," this appeared in the *Herald*, and nothing now remained for Georgia but to wait. The excitement of her flight, the necessity of immediate action, and now the fever of suspense, kept her mind from dwelling too much on the past. Had it been otherwise, with her impassioned nature, she might have sunk into an agony of despair, or raved in the delirium of brain-fever. As it was, she remained stunned into a sort of calm—white, cold, passionless; but, oh! with such a settled night of utter sorrow in the great melancholy dark eyes.

Fortunately for her, she was not doomed to remain long in suspense. On the third day a note was brought to her in a gentleman's hand, and tearing it eagerly open, she read:

> "ASTOR HOUSE, Jan. 12, 18—.

> "MADAM: Seeing your advertisement in the *Herald*, and being in want of a governess, if not already engaged, you would do well to favor me with a call at your earliest leisure. I will leave the city in two days. Yours,

> "JOHN LEONARD."

As she finished reading this, Georgia started to her feet, hastily donned her hat and cloak, with her thick vail closely over her face, and taking one of the widow's little boys with her, as guide, set out for the hotel.

Upon reaching it she inquired for Mr. Leonard. A servant went for him, and in a few minutes returned with a benevolent-looking old gentleman, with white hair and a kind, friendly face.

"You wished to see me, madam," he said, bowing, and looking inquiringly at the Juno-like form dressed in black.

"Yes, sir; I am the governess," said Georgia, her heart throbbing so violently that she turned giddy.

"Oh, indeed!" said the old gentleman, kindly; "perhaps we had better step up to my room, then; this is no place to settle business."

Georgia followed him up two or three flights of stairs, to an elegantly furnished apartment. Handing her a chair, he seated himself, and glanced somewhat curiously at her.

"You received my answer to your advertisement?" he said.

"Yes, sir," said Georgia, in a stifled voice.

"May I ask your name madam?" said Mr. Leonard, whose curiosity seemed piqued.

Georgia threw back her heavy vail, and the old gentleman gave a start of surprise at sight of the white, cold, beautiful face, and dark, sorrowful eyes.

"My name is Randall—Miss Randall," replied Georgia, while a faint red, that faded as quickly as it came, tinged her cheek at the deception.

Mr. Leonard bowed.

"I suppose you have credentials—your certificates from those with whom you have formerly lived?" said Mr. Leonard, hesitatingly, for he felt embarrassed to address this queenly looking girl, on whose marble-like face the awe-inspiring shadow of some mighty grief lay, as he would a common governess.

Georgia's eyes dropped, and again that slight tinge of color flashed across her face, and again faded away.

"No, sir; I have not. I never was a governess before; sudden reverses—adversity—"

She broke down, put her trembling hand before her face, and averted her head.

Mr. Leonard was an impulsive, kind-hearted old gentleman, and the sight of settled anguish in that pale young face went right home to his heart, and touched him exceedingly.

"Yes, yes, to be sure, poor child! I understand it all. There, don't cry—don't, now. You know there is nothing but ups and downs in this world, and reverses must be expected. I like you, I like your looks, and I rather guess I'll engage you *without* credentials. There, don't be cast down, my dear; don't, now. You really make me feel bad to see you in trouble."

Georgia lifted her head and tried to smile, but it was so faint and sad, so like a cold gleam of moonlight on snow, that it touched that soft heart of his more and more.

"Poor thing! poor thing! poor little thing!" he said, winking very rapidly with both eyes behind his spectacles; "seen a great deal of trouble, I expect, in her time, must have, to give her that look. I'll engage her; upon my life I will!"

"There may be one objection, sir," said Georgia, sadly. "I can't teach music."

"You can't—hum!" said Mr. Leonard, musingly. "Well, that doesn't make much odds, I guess. My daughters have a music-master now, and he can teach little Jennie, I reckon, too. Your pupils are two boys and a girl, none over thirteen; and as you teach French, and Latin, and grammar, and English, and all the other things necessary, music does not make much difference. And as for salary—well, I'll attend to that at the end of the quarter, and I think you will be satisfied. When can you come?"

"Now, if necessary, sir—any time you like."

"Well, to-morrow morning I start. I live forty miles out of New York, and if you will give me your address, I will call for you in the carriage."

"I thank you, sir, but it is too far out of your way. I will come up here," said Georgia, who did not wish to bring him to the mean habitation where she stopped. "I suppose that is all," she said, rising.

"All, at present, Miss Randall," said Mr. Leonard, rising, and looking at her in surprise as she started at the unusual name. "To-morrow at ten o' clock, I leave. Good-morning."

He shook hands cordially with her at parting, and then Georgia hurried out, feeling that one faint gleam of sunshine had arisen in her darkened life. In the desolate years of the weary life before her she would at least be a burden to no one, and for a few moments she felt as if an intolerable load had been lifted off her heart. But when she was alone again in her chamber and the reaction past, the awful sense of her desolation came sweeping over her. In all the wide world she had not one friend left. Sun, and moon, and stars all had faded from her sky, and night—dark, woeful night—had closed, and a night for which there was no morning. And, oh, worst of all, she felt it was her own fault, her own stormy, unbridled passions had done it all; and with a great cry, wrung from her tortured heart, she sank down quivering and white in the dusky gloom of that wild winter evening. There was no light in Georgia's despair; in happier days she had never prayed, and in the hour of her earthly anguish she *could not*. In this world she could look forward to nothing but a wretched, despairing life, and to her the next was a dull, dead blank. One name was in her heart, one name on her lips, one whom she had made her God, her earthly idol, and now he, too, was forever lost.

When the widow came in to awaken her the next morning, she was startled by the sight of the tall, dark form, wrapped in a shawl, sitting by the window, her forehead pressed to the cold pane, her face whiter than the snow-wreaths without. She had not laid her head on a pillow the livelong night.

The cold, pale sunshine of the short January day was fading out of the sky, when a sleigh, well supplied with buffalo robes and the merry music of jingling bells, came flying up toward a large, handsome country villa, through the crimson curtained windows of which the ruddy light of many a glowing coal fire shone. As it stopped before the door, a group from within came running out, and stood on the veranda, in eager expectation and pleasing bustle.

An old gentleman with white hair and a benevolent smile, answering to the cognomen of Mr. Leonard, got out and assisted a lady, tall and elegant, dressed in black, and closely vailed, to alight. Then, giving a few hasty directions to a servant who was leading off the horses, he gave the lady his arm and led her up to the house.

And upon reaching the veranda he was instantly surrounded, and an incredible amount of kissing, and questioning, and laughing, and talking was done in an instant, and the old gentleman was whisked off and borne into a large, handsomely furnished parlor, where the brightest of fires was blazing in the brightest of grates, and pushed into a rocking-chair and whirled up before the fire in a twinkling.

"Lord bless *my* soul!" said the old gentleman, breathlessly, and laying a strong emphasis on the pronoun; "what a lot of whirlwinds you are, girls! Where's Miss Randall, eh? Where's Miss Randall?"

"Here, sir," answered Georgia, as she entered the room.

"And pretty near frozen, I'll be bound! I know *I* am. Mrs. Leonard, my dear, this young lady is the governess—Miss Randall."

Georgia bowed to a little fat woman with restless, hazel eyes.

"And these are my two eldest daughters, Felice and Maggie," continued Mr. Leonard, pointing to two pretty, graceful-looking young girls, who nodded carelessly to the governess; "and these are your pupils," he added, pointing to two little boys, apparently between thirteen and ten, and to a little girl, who, from her resemblance to the younger, was evidently his twin sister. "Albert, Royal, Jennie, come up and shake hands with Miss Randall."

"Miss Randall! why, Licie, that's the name of that nice gentleman who brought you the roses last night, ain't it?" said little Jennie, looking up cunningly at her elder sister.

Miss Felice glanced at Miss Maggie and smiled and blushed, and began twisting one of her ringlets over her taper fingers, looking very conscious indeed.

"May I ask if you are any relation to young Mr. Randall, the poet, of New York?" said Mrs. Leonard, pushing up her spectacles and trying to see Georgia through the thick vail which still covered her face.

"Why, mamma, what a question! Of course she's not," said Miss Felice, rather pettishly; "he has no relatives, you know. There's plenty of the name."

Georgia threw back her vail at this moment, and stooped to kiss little Jennie, who came up and held her rosy mouth puckered for that purpose, as if she was quite accustomed to be treated to that sort of small coin.

"Oh, Felice, what a beautiful face!" exclaimed Miss Maggie, in an impulsive whisper.

"Ye-es, she's not bad-looking—for a governess," drawled Miss Felice. "They are generally so frightfully ugly. She's a great deal too pale though, and too solemn looking; it gives me the dismals to look at her; and she's ever so much too tall" (Miss Felice, be it known, was rather on the dumpy pattern than otherwise), "and too slight for her size, and her forehead's too high, and her —"

"Oh, Felice, stop! You'll try to make out she's as ugly as sin directly. Did you ever see such splendid eyes?"

"I don't like black eyes," said Miss Felice, in a dissatisfied tone; "they are too sharp and fiery. They do well enough for men, but I don't approve of them at all for women."

"Dear me, what a pity!" said Miss Maggie, sarcastically; "but you can't call hers fiery—they're dreadfully melancholy, I'm sure. Now ain't they, mamma?"

"What dear?" said Mrs. Leonard, not catching the whispered question.

"Hasn't Miss Randall got lovely melancholy black eyes?"

"Oh, bother her melancholy black eyes!" said Miss Felice, impatiently. "What a time you do make about people, Mag. And she only a governess, too. I should think you would be ashamed."

"Well, I ain't ashamed—not the least," said Maggie; "and no matter whether she's a governess or not, she looks like a lady. I'm sure she's very clever, too. I wonder who she's in black for."

"Ask her," said Miss Felice, shortly, as she picked up a French novel, and, placing her feet on the fender, sat down to read.

Miss Felice was blessed with a temper much shorter than sweet, and Miss Maggie, who was rather good-natured, took her curt replies as a matter of course, and, going over to Georgia, said pleasantly:

"Miss Randall, if you wish to go up to your room, I will be your *cicerone* for the occasion. Perhaps you would like to brush your hair before tea."

"Thank you," said Georgia, rising languidly, and following Miss Maggie from the room.

"This is to be your *sanctum sanctorum*, Miss Randall," said Maggie, opening the door of a small and plainly but neatly furnished bedroom, rendered cheerful by red drapery and a redder fire. "It's not very gorgeous, you perceive; but it's the one the governess always uses here. Our last one—Miss Fitzgerald, an Irish young lady—went and precipitated herself into the awful gulf of——"

"What?" said Georgia, with a slight start, caused by Miss Maggie's awe-struck manner.

"Matrimony!" said Miss Maggie, in a thrilling whisper. "Ain't it dreadful? Governesses, and ministers, and curates, and all sorts of poor people generally *will* persist in such atrocities, on the principle that what won't keep one, I suppose, will keep two. Don't you ever get married, Miss Randall. *I* never mean to—— Why, my goodness, what's the matter now?"

Georgia had given such a violent start, and a spasm of such intense anguish had passed over her face, that Miss Maggie jumped back, and stood regarding her with wide-open and startled eyes, the picture of astonishment.

"Nothing—nothing," said Georgia, leaning her elbow on the table, and dropping her forehead on it: "a sudden pain—gone now. Pray do not be alarmed."

"Oh, I ain't alarmed," said Miss Maggie composedly. "Do you think you will like to live out here? It's awful lonesome, I can tell you; a quarter of a mile almost to the nearest house. Licie and I want papa to stop in New York in the winter, but he won't—he doesn't mind a word we say. Papas are always the dreadfulest, most obstinate sort of people in the world—now, ain't they?—always thinking they know best, you know, and always dreadfully provoking. Oh, dear me!" said Miss Maggie, with a deep sigh, as she fell back in her chair, and held up and glanced admiringly at one pretty little foot and distracting ankle, "I don't know what we should ever do only papa comes from the city to see us, and that nice Signor Popkins, who was a count or a legion of honor, or some funny thing in France, and got exiled by that nasty Louis Napoleon, comes and gives Licie and me two music lessons every week. Oh! Miss Randall, he's got just the sweetest hair you ever saw; and mustaches—oh, my goodness! such mustaches—that stick out like two shaving-brushes; and splendid long whiskers, like a cow's tail. Felice don't care much for him, because she thinks she's caught that nice, clever Mr. Randall, your namesake, you know; but I guess she ain't so sure of him as she thinks. Oh! he does write the most divine poetry ever was—down right splendid, you know; and every lady is raving about him. He's travelled all over Europe, and Asia, and Africa, and the North Pole, and California, and lots of other nice places, and knows—oh, dear me, he knows a dreadful sight of things, and is a splendid talker. He only came from England two weeks ago, and everybody is making such a time about him. Felice met him at a party, and he came here last night with the divinest bouquet, and she thinks she has him, but *I* know better. Then some more gentlemen come here. Lem Turner, and Ike Brown, and Dick Curtis, but he's gone away somewhere to the country, to where some friend of his lives—— Hey? What now? Another pain, Miss Randall?"

"No—yes. Excuse me, Miss Leonard, I am very tired, and will lie down now. You will please to tell them I do not feel well enough to go down to tea."

"Well, there! I might have known you were tired, and not kept on talking so, but I am such a dreadful chatterbox. I'll tell Susan to bring up your tea. Good-by, Miss Randall; I hope you'll be quite well to-morrow, I'm sure." And the loquacious damsel bowed a smiling adieu, and retired.

Georgia *was* better the next morning, and able to join the family at breakfast, which meal was enlivened by a steady flow of talk from Miss Maggie, and a series of snappish contradictions and marginal notes from Miss Felice, who never got her temper on till near noon. Mr. and Mrs. Leonard took both daughters as matters of course, and seemed quite used to this sort of thing. On Georgia's part it passed almost in silence, as she sat like some cold, marble statue, with scarcely more signs of life.

After breakfast Miss Felice sat down to practice some unearthly exercises on the grand piano that adorned the drawing-room, and Miss Maggie Leonard bore off Georgia and the three juvenile Leonards to a large, high, severe-looking room, adorned with a dismal looking blackboard, sundry maps, with red, green, yellow splashes, supposed to represent this terrestrial globe. Four solemn-looking black desks were in the four corners, and one in the middle for the teacher. Books, and ink bottles, and slates, without end, were scattered about, and this, Mrs. Leonard informed Georgia, was the school-room, and after administering a small lecture to Messrs. Albert and Royal and Miss Jennie, the purport of which was that the world in general expected them to be good children and learn fast, and mind Miss Randall, she floated out, bearing off the unwilling Miss Maggie, and Georgia began her new life as teacher.

That day seemed endless to Georgia. Accustomed to uncontrolled freedom and wild liberty, she was fitted less for a teacher than for anything else in the world. That love of children which it is necessary every teacher should possess, Georgia had not, and before the wearisome day was done every feeling that had not been stunned into numbness rose in rebellion against the intolerable servitude.

At four o'clock the day's labor was over, and the children, glad to be released, scampered off.

Seating herself at the desk, Georgia dropped her throbbing head upon it, giddy and blind with one of her deadly headaches, which until the last month or two, she had never known.

Suddenly the door was flung open, and Miss Maggie's ringing voice was heard.

"Well, Miss Randall, how did you get on? Mamma wouldn't let me come up, and it was real mean of her. Why, what's the matter? Oh, my goodness! you look dreadful!"

"I have got a headache," said Georgia, pressing her hands to her throbbing temples dizzily.

"Oh, you have! Being in this hot room all day has caused it. Do let me bring you your things, and come out for a walk. It is a beautiful evening, though cold, and the air will do you good. Come. I'll go with you, Miss Randall: Shall I go and get your things?"

"You are very good," said Georgia, faintly; "I think I will; I feel almost suffocated."

Maggie bounded away, and the next moment came flying back, rolled up in a huge shawl, and her pretty face eclipsed in an immense quilted hood. She held another shawl and hood in her hands, and before Georgia knew where she was, she found herself all muffled up and ready for the road.

"Now, then!" said Miss Maggie, briskly; "come along! See if the wind won't blow roses into those white cheeks of yours!"

Passing her arm around Georgia's waist, Maggie drew her with her out of the house.

The day was cold, and clear, and bright, and windless; a frosty, sunshiny, cold afternoon. The sun, sinking in the west, shed a red glow over the snow-covered fields, and gave a golden brightness to the windows of the house.

Some of the old wild spirit, that nothing but death could ever entirely crush out of Georgia's gipsy heart, rose as the cold, keen frosty air cooled her fevered brow. The languid eyes lit up, and she started at a rapid walk that kept

Maggie breathless, and laughing, and running, and quite unable to talk.

"Oh, my stars!" said Maggie, at last, as she stopped, panting, and leaned against a fence. "If you haven't got the seven-league boots on, Miss Randall, then I should like to know who has? You ought to go into training for a female pedestrian, and you would make your fortune in twenty-five-cent pieces. I declare I'm just about tired to death."

"Why, how thoughtless I am!" said Georgia, whose excited pace had scarcely kept time with her excited thoughts; "I forgot you could not walk as fast as I can. Suppose you sit down and rest, and I will wait."

"All right, then," said Maggie, as she clambered with great agility to the top of the fence and sat down on the top rail; "but 'Hold, Macduff! who comes here?'"

A sleigh came dashing along the road, drawn by a small, spirited horse that seemed fairly to fly. It was occupied by a gentleman wearing a large black cloak, and a fur cap drawn down over his brow.

As he reached them he turned round and glanced carelessly toward the two girls. For one instant his face was turned fully toward them, the next he was whirling away out of sight.

"Oh, how handsome! oh, isn't he beautiful?" exclaimed Maggie, clasping her hands enthusiastically; "such splendid eyes, and such a pale, handsome face, and such a glorious driver. My! how I would like to be in that sleigh with him. I would—wouldn't you, Miss Randall?"

She turned to Georgia, and fairly leaped off the fence in amazement to see her standing rigid and motionless, with wildly distended eyes and white, startled face, gazing after the object of Maggie's admiration.

"Why, Miss Randall! Miss Randall!" said Maggie, catching her arms, "what's the matter? Do you know him?"

"Let us go back, Miss Leonard," said Georgia, passing her hand over her eyes as if to dispel some wild vision.

Know him! Yes, as if they had parted but yesterday. Could Georgia forget Charley Wildair?

CHAPTER XIX.

DESOLATION.

"And the stately ships go on
   To the haven under the hill,
But oh for the touch of a vanished hand,
   And the sound of a voice that is still."

TENNYSON.

l that night Georgia's thoughts ran in a new direction—Charley Wildair. Yes, she had been face to face with the living, breathing friend of her childhood once more. The mystery that surrounded him rose up in her mind, and again she found herself wondering what he had done, what crime he had committed. Evening after evening she walked out in the same place, in the hope of seeing him again, when she was determined to speak to him at all hazards; but in vain; he came not, no one knew, or could tell her anything of him who had passed that evening. As day after day wore on, she began to regard his appearance almost in the light of an apparition—something her disordered imagination had conjured up to mock her, and at last even the hope of seeing him again, faded away.

And so a month passed on. Oh! that dreary, endless, monotonous month, with nothing but the dull routine of the school-room day after day.

There were times when Georgia would start wildly up, feeling as though she were going mad; and evening after evening, when the last lesson was said, she would throw her shawl over her shoulders and hurry out into the cold wintry weather, and walk and walk for miles with dizzy rapidity, to cool the fever in her blood. Night after night, when, unable to lie tossing on her bed, she would spring up, and, heedless of the freezing air, pace her room till morning. The wild fire in her eye, even in the presence of others, bespoke the consuming fever in her veins that seemed drying up the very source of life in her heart. Had she been leading some exciting, turbulent life, it would have been better for her; but this stagnant monotony seemed in a fair way of making her a maniac before long. There were times when her very soul would cry out with passionate yearning for what she had lost—times when an uncontrollable impulse to fly, fly, far away from this place, to search over the world for him she had left, and, in spite of all that had passed, to cling to him forever, would seize her, and she would struggle and wrestle with the fierce desire until, from very bodily weakness, she would sink down in a very stupor of despair.

It seemed to her as if a dark doom had been hanging over her from childhood and had fallen at last—a widow in fate though not in fact, an outcast from all the world, and almost with the brand of murder on her brow. But oh, if she had sinned, was not the expiation heavier than it deserved? A life of desolation, a death uncheered by a single friendly face, to live forgotten and die forlorn, *that* was her doom. Poor Georgia! what wonder that, frenzied and despairing, the cry of her heart should be, "My punishment is heavier than I can bear."

The Leonards hardly knew what to make of Georgia. Mr. Leonard looked pityingly on the white face, so eloquent of wrong and misery, and expressed his opinion that she had come through more than people thought. Mrs. Leonard was rather puzzled about the young governess; when in her wild paroxysms she would hear startling legends of her walking through frost and snow for miles together, and would hear a quick, rapid footstep pacing up and down, up and down her chamber the livelong night, and would see the wild, lurid fire in her great black eyes, she would give it as her opinion that Miss Randall was not quite right in her mind; but when this mood would pass away, and reaction would follow, and when she would note the slow, weary step and pallid cheeks, and spiritless eyes, and lifeless movements, she would retract, and say she really did not know what to make of her.

Miss Felice snappishly said it was all affectation; the governess wanted to be odd, and mysterious, and interesting; and if she was her father she would put an end to her long walks, or know why. But these little remarks were prudently made when Georgia was not listening; for if the truth must be told, Miss Leonard stood more than slightly in awe of the dark, majestic, melancholy governess. Miss Maggie declared it was "funny," but she rather liked Georgia, though after the first week or two she voted her "awful tiresome, worse than Felice," and left her pretty much to herself. Her pupils liked her, but were rather afraid of her in her dark moods, and, like the rest of the household, stood considerably in awe of her, wrapped as she was in her dark mantle of unvarying gloom.

During this first month of her stay, Georgia had spoken to no one but the household. Visitors there were almost every day, but Georgia always fled at their approach, and both the Misses Leonard, conscious of her superior beauty, had no desire to be eclipsed by their queenly dependent, and were quite willing she should be invisible on these occasions. Since she had heard Dick Curtis was a friend of the family, she had dreaded the approach of every stranger, and always sent some excuse for not appearing at table at such times. Therefore, sometimes whole days would pass without her leaving her own room and the school-room.

As the children's study only comprised five hours each day, Georgia had a great deal of spare time to herself. This she had hitherto spent either in her long, wild walks or in her dark reveries; but now, of late, a new inspiration had seized her.

One day, to amuse little Jennie, she had seized her pencil and drawn her portrait, and the drawing proved to be so life-like that the whole family were in transports. The Misses Leonard immediately made a simultaneous rush for the school-room, and overwhelmed Georgia with praises of her talent, and pleadings to sketch theirs, too. And Georgia, feeling a sort of happiness in pleasing them, readily promised. The drawings were commenced and finished, and Georgia had unconsciously idealized and rendered them so perfectly lovely, yet so true to the originals, that they, in their ecstatic admiration, insisted that they should be perpetuated in oil. Finding the occupation so absorbing and so congenial, Georgia willingly consented, and sittings were appointed every day until the portraits were finished. And finished they were at last, and set in gorgeous frames, and with eyes sparkling with delight, the Misses Leonard saw themselves, or rather their etherialized counterfeits, hanging in splendor on the drawing-room walls, and calling forth the most enthusiastic praises of the unknown artist's skill from their guests, for Georgia had only painted them on condition that no one was to be told.

Then she voluntarily offered to paint Mr. and Mrs. Leonard and the three children, and at Jennie's earnest desire, her little tortoise-shell kitten was seduced into sitting still long enough to be taken too. This last was a labor of love, for, strangely enough, it brought back softened thoughts of the happy days spent in romping through the cottage by the sea with Betsey Periwinkle.

And a faint, sad, dreary smile broke over Georgia's face as she painted the little blinking animal, and thought of all the old associations it called forth. It brought back Miss Jerusha, and little Emily Murray—dear little Emily Murray, whose memory always came to her like the soft sweet music of an Eolian harp amid the repose of a storm. She wondered vaguely if *they* missed her much, and what they would think of her flight, and whether they would shudder in horror when they heard what she had done, or whether they would think lovingly of her still.

"Some day, when they hear I am dead, perhaps they will forgive me and love me again," she thought, with something of the simplicity of the *child* Georgia, as a gentler feeling came to her heart than had visited it for many a day. Somehow, Emily's memory always did soften her and bring back a gentler mood. In her wildest storms of anguish and remorse, in the darkest hour of her desolation, that sweet, calm, holy young face, with its serene brow and seraphic blue eyes, would arise and exorcise her gloom, and leave her calmer, softer feeling behind.

One day, on the occasion of Mrs. Leonard's birthday, the children had a holiday, and Georgia was left to herself. Seating herself at the window, she began to draw faces from memory. The first was a long, angular one, with projecting bones and sharp features, sunken eyes, and thin, compressed lips, the hair drawn tightly back and gathered in an uncompromising hard knot behind. An intelligent, dignified-looking cat sat composedly at her feet, deeply absorbed in thought. Any one could recognize, in these portraits, Miss Jerusha and our old friend Betsey Periwinkle.

"Dear Miss Jerusha! dear, good friend!" murmured Georgia, softly, as she gazed at the picture. "I wonder will I ever see you again. I wonder if you have grieved for my loss, and if you ever, these wild, stormy nights, think of your lost Georgey. Dear Miss Jerusha, may Heaven reward you for your kindness to the poor orphan girl."

The next was a fairer face, a small head set on an arching neck; a low, smooth, childish brow; small, regular, dainty features; sweet, wondering, wistful eyes; a little dimpled chin, and softly smiling lips, just revealing the pearly teeth within. It might have been the face of an angel had it not been Emily Murray's, spiritualized, as everything Georgia's magic pencil touched was. Such a lovely, child-like, innocent face as it was, smiling up from the paper with such a look of heavenly calm and serenity, that no breath of worldly passion had ever disturbed.

"Oh, dear little Emily! dear little Emily!" said Georgia, in a trembling voice. "My good angel! if I had only been like you. Calm, peaceful, happy little Emily! what will you think of me when you hear what I have done."

She hesitated a moment before she commenced the next, and then, as if a sudden inspiration had seized her, she rapidly began to sketch. Soon there appeared a noble, intellectual-looking head—a high, broad, princely brow— square eyebrows, meeting across the strongly marked nose—large, strong, earnest eyes—a fine resolute mouth, and square, resolute chin. Heavy waves of dark hair were shaken carelessly off the noble forehead, and it needed nothing now but the thick dark mustache, and the calm, handsome, kingly face of Richmond Wildair looked at her from the paper. In the seemingly fathomless eyes there shone a look of sorrowful reproach, and a sort of sad sternness pervaded the whole face. The very lips seemed to part and say, "oh, Georgia, what have you done?" and with a great cry of "oh, Richmond! Richmond! Richmond!" she flung down her pencil, then threw herself on her face on the couch, and for the first time in years, for the first time almost since she could remember, she wept, wept long, passionately, and bitterly.

It was a strange thing to see this stone-like Georgia weep. In all her misery she had shed no tears; in her stormy childhood she had wept not, and the tears of childhood are an easily flowing spring; yet now she lay, and wept, and sobbed, wildly, passionately, vehemently, wept for hours, until the very source of her tears seemed dried up, and would flow no longer.

And from that day Georgia grew calmer and more rational than she had ever been before. It was strange the consolation she derived from these "counterfeit presentments" of those she loved, and yet it was so. For hours she would sit gazing at them, and sometimes she would fancy Emily's smiling lips seemed saying, "Hope on, Georgia! before morning dawns night is ever darkest."

The Leonards, grateful for being made such handsome people, were quite solicitous in their efforts to make the governess comfortable. Georgia had a heart easily won by kindness, and as time passed on, she seemed, for the present at least, to grow reconciled to her lot. Perhaps the secret of this was that she had begun an achievement that had long been in her thoughts, and in which she was so completely absorbed as to be for a time quite insensible to outward things. This was a large painting of Hagar in the Wilderness, a wild, weird thing, on which she worked night and day in a fever of enthusiasm.

Had any one seen her, in the still, mystic watches of the night, bending over her easel, her dark hair flowing behind her, her wild eyes blazing, her whole face inspired—they might have taken her for the very genius of art descended on earth. She scarcely knew what was her design in painting this; probably, at the time, she had none, but a love of the work itself—a love that increased to a perfect fever, as it grew under her brush. None of the family knew aught of it, and they puzzled themselves in vain wondering what she could be doing to keep a light burning so late every night.

It was drawing toward the close of February that the severest snow storm that they had during the season fell. For nearly a week it raged with unceasing violence, and several gentlemen and ladies from the city were storm-bound at Mr. Leonard's. During their stay, Georgia, as usual, absented herself from the table and drawing-room, and the young ladies were so busy with their guests that even Miss Maggie found no time to visit her. Georgia did not regret this circumstance, as it gave her more time to devote to her painting, and secured her from interruption.

One wild, snowy evening, when it was too dark to paint and too soon to light the lamp, Georgia passed from her room and walked swiftly in the direction of the library in search of a book. She knew the library was seldom visited, especially in the evening, when other amusements ruled the hour, and so, not fearing detection, she went in, found the book she was in search of, and, seating herself within a deep bay-window, drew the crimson damask curtains close, and thus shut in on one side by red drapery and on the other by the clear glass, through which she could watch the drifting snow, she began to read.

It was a volume of poems by W. D. Randall, the young poet, whose fame was already resounding through the land. Such a sweet, dreamy, delicious volume as it was! Fascinated, absorbed, Georgia strained her eyes, and read and read on as long as one ray of light remained, unable to tear herself away from the enchanted pages, and feeling as if she were transported to some Arcadia, some fairy-land, by the magic power of the poet's pen.

At last it grew too dark to read another word, and then she closed the book and fell into a reverie of—the author. She knew he was a visitor at the house, and for once her curiosity was strongly excited. She resolved to see him. She would make Maggie point him out the next time he came, and see for herself what manner of man this young genius was. There had been a steel portrait of him in the book, but Miss Felice had carefully cut it out and preserved it for her own private use, as something not to be profaned by vulgar eyes, to the violent indignation of Miss Maggie.

While she still sat musing dreamily, she was startled by hearing the door flung open, and then a gleam of light flashed through the curtain. Hoping it might be some servant to light the gas, she glanced out between the folds and saw Miss Felice herself, standing beside a tall, handsome, distinguished-looking young man. Retreat was now out of the question. Georgia would not have encountered the stranger for worlds, lest he should happen to recognize her; and, trusting they only came for a book and would soon go away again, she resolved to sit still.

"And so you will translate 'Undine' for me, Mr. Randall," said Miss Felice, whose dress was perfection, and whose face was quite brilliant with smiles. "Oh, that will be charming. The children's governess teaches German, but I never could get her to read Undine."

This, then, was the poet. At any other time she would have become completely absorbed in looking at him, but the mention of "Undine" sent a pang to her heart, and she sank back in her seat and bowed her face in her hands. The sweet, sorrowful story of the German poet seemed so like her own —she was the Undine, Freddy Richmond was the base, designing Bertalda, and Huldbrand—oh, no, no! Richmond was not like him.

"It is a lovely tale. You do well to learn German, Miss Leonard, if only for the sake of reading 'Undine' in the original," said Mr. Randall.

"I have something else that is lovely here," said Miss Leonard, looking arch.

"Yes—yourself," said Mr. Randall.

"No, no; of course not—W. D. Randall's poems."

"And you call that lovely! Well, I gave you credit for better taste, Miss Felice."

"Oh, they are charming, sweet, *so nice*!" cried Miss Felice, clasping her hands in a small transport.

A smile broke over the handsome face of the poet. How pleasant it must be for a poet to hear his poems called *nice*.

"Well, never mind them; let us find 'Undine,'" said Mr. Randall.

"I'm sure I've sat up nights and nearly cried my eyes out over that beautiful poem 'Regina,' Did you ever see any one like the 'Regina' you described so delightfully?"

"Yes," said Mr. Randall, a sort of shadow coming over his face, "once, in my childhood, I saw such a one—a 'queen of noble nature's crowning;' one whose every motion seemed to say:

> "'*Incedo Regina*'—
> 'I move a queen.'"

"Dear me," said Miss Felice, "how nice! I really should like to see her. I suppose she will be Mrs. Randall some day," and Miss Felice, looking up between her ringlets, did the artless to perfection.

Mr. Randall smiled again; it was evident he read Miss Felice like a book.

"Hardly, I am afraid. I don't approve of the Regina style of woman for wives myself. Something less imposing would suit me better—a nice little thing like ——"

Miss Felice had cast down her long lashes, and stood looking as innocent and guileless as a stage angel; but here Mr. Randall most provokingly paused and began caressing a hideously ugly little Scotch terrier that had followed him into the room.

Georgia had to smile in spite of herself at the provoking nonchalance of the poet, more particularly as Miss Felice turned half pettishly away, and then, remembering that her *role* was to be sweet and simple, she gave him a smiling glance and returned to the charge.

"And those verses on Niagara are so pretty! Papa took Maggie and me to the Falls last summer, and I did like them so much! Oh, dear me! they are so sweet!"

Mr. Randall laughed outright. Miss Felice looked up in astonishment, but just at that moment little Jennie came running in with something in her hand.

"Oh Licie! look what I have got—such a lovely picture of the most beautiful lady ever was! Just look."

"What an angelic face!" impulsively exclaimed Mr. Randall; "a perfect Madonna! And only a pencil drawing, too! Why, Miss Leonard, this is something exquisite—a perfect little gem! I never saw anything more lovely."

"Where did you get it, Jennie?" said Miss Felice.

"In the hall; it's Miss Randall's—she dropped it coming out of the school-room. I'm going to ask her to give it to me; she can make plenty more."

"Is it possible the artist resides here? You don't mean to say that——"

"Oh, it's only the governess," said Miss Felice; "she draws and paints very well indeed. By the way, she's a namesake of yours, too, Mr. Randall. Yes, I see now it is one of her drawings; I could tell them anywhere."

The poet was gazing in a sort of rapture at the picture. The soft eyes and sweet, beautiful lips seemed smiling upon him—the face seemed living and radiant before him.

"Why, one would think you were enchanted, Mr. Randall," said Miss Felice, half pouting. "It's fortunate it's only a picture and not a living face, or your doom would be sealed."

"Oh, it is perfect, it is exquisite!" said the poet, under his breath; "a Madonna, a Saint Cecilia, a seraph! Why, Miss Leonard, do you know you have a genius under the roof with you?"

"Yes, sir—Mr. Randall," said Miss Felice, courtesying.

"Pshaw! I mean the artist. Come, is she the mysterious painter of those delicious portraits in the drawing-room that have attracted such crowds of admirers already?"

"Well, since you have guessed it, yes. It was her own wish it should not be known."

"Why, she must be the eighth wonder of the world—this governess. Who is she? What is she? Where does she come from?" said Mr. Randall, impetuously.

"She is Miss Randall—a governess, as I before told you, from New York city, and that is her whole biography as far as I know it, except that she is very strange, and wild, and solemn-looking, with oh, such immense black, haunting eyes!"

"Oh, Felice, she's really pretty!" said Jennie; "a great deal prettier than you or Mag. Now ain't she, Royal?"

"Who?" said Royal, entering at this moment.

"Our Miss Randall."

"Yes, I reckon she is. Miss Randall's a tip-top lady," said Royal, emphatically.

"I really should like to see her. Won't you present me to this genius, Miss Leonard? It is not fair to hide so brilliant a light under a bushel," said Mr. Randall. "I shall probably claim kindred with her, as we both have the same name."

"Well, I will ask," said Miss Felice, biting her lip. "I am not so sure, though, that she will consent, she is so queer. Here's 'Undine,' and now for the translation, Mr. Randall."

But Mr. Randall stood still, with his eyes riveted on the drawing.

"Dear me, Mr. Randall, hadn't you better keep that altogether?" said Miss Felice, pettishly. "One would think you had fallen in love with it."

"So I have," said Mr. Randall. "Come here, Miss Jennie; I have a favor to ask of you."

"What is it?" said Jennie.

"That if Miss Randall gives you this drawing, you will give it to me, and I will bring you the prettiest book I can find in New York in exchange."

"Will you, though? Isn't that nice, Royal? Oh, I'll get it from Miss Randall— she's real good—and I'll give it to you. May I tell her it's for you?"

"Just as you like; tell her anything you please, so as to get it for me. Won't you tell me how I can see this wonderful governess of yours, Miss Jennie?"

"Let's see. Come up to the school-room with mamma."

"By Jove! I will. But perhaps she wouldn't like me to intrude."

"Mr. Randall, they are waiting for us down stairs," said Miss Felice, stiffly. "Jennie—Royal—go out and go to bed."

Georgia caught a parting glimpse of the graceful, gallant form of the young poet as he held open the door for Miss Felice to go out, and drew a deep breath of relief when they were gone. Then, having assured herself that the coast was clear, she hurried out and sought her own room, and searched for Emily's portrait, but it was missing.

Next morning, as Georgia was about to enter the school-room, Miss Felice fluttered up stairs, in a floating white cashmere morning-gown, and with the drawing in her hand.

"Good-morning, Miss Randall," she said, briefly; "is this yours?"

"Yes," said Georgia, quietly.

"Will you be kind enough to give it to me?"

"It is the portrait of a very dear friend. I should be happy to oblige you were it otherwise, Miss Leonard," said Georgia, coldly.

"A portrait! that heavenly face! is it possible?" exclaimed the astounded young lady.

Georgia bowed gravely.

"But oh, do let me have it! do, please; you can draw another, you know," coaxed Miss Felice.

"Of what possible use can that portrait be to you, Miss Leonard?"

"Well, it's not for me, it's for a friend. Do oblige me, Miss Randall. Mr. Randall wants it so dreadfully."

"Mr. Randall! who is he?"

"The author, the poet that everybody is talking about. He saw it last night with Jennie, and took a desperate fancy to it, and, what's more, wants to be introduced to you."

"I would rather be excused," said Georgia, with some of her old *hauteur*. "I do not like to refuse you, Miss Leonard, and if any other picture——"

"Oh, any other won't do; I must have this. There, I shall keep it, and you can draw a dozen like it any time. And every one would not refuse to be introduced to Mr. Randall, I can tell you," said Miss Felice, half inclined to be angry; "he is immensely rich and ever so handsome, and as clever as ever he can be, and most young ladies would consider it an honor to be acquainted with him."

Georgia bowed slightly, and made an impatient motion to pass on.

"Well, I am going to keep it, Miss Randall," said Miss Felice, half inquiringly.

"As you please, Miss Leonard. Good-morning," and Georgia swept on to the school-room, and Miss Felice ran to give the poet the picture, and tell him their haughty governess refused the introduction.

CHAPTER XX.

FOUND AND LOST.

"There are words of deeper sorrow
Than the wail above the dead."

"An eagle with a broken wing,
A harp with many a broken string."

 was a pleasant morning in early spring. The sunshine lay in broad sheets of golden light over the fields, and tinted the tree-tops with a yellow luster. The fresh morning air came laden with the fragrance of sweet spring flowers, and the musical chirping of many birds from the neighboring forest was borne to Georgia's ears, as she stood on the veranda, her thoughts far away.

You would scarcely have recognized the flashing-eyed, blooming, wild-hearted Georgia Darrell in this cold, stately, stone-like Miss Randall, with cheek and brow cold and colorless as Parian marble, and the dark, mournful eyes void of light and sparkle.

It could scarcely be expected but that she would sink under the dreary monotony of her life here, so completely different in every way from what she had been accustomed to; and of late, she had fallen into a lifeless lethargy, from which nothing seemed able to arouse her. There were times, it was true, when, for an instant, she would awake, and her very soul would cry out under the galling chains of her intolerable bondage; but these flashes of her old spirit were few and far between, and were always followed by a lassitude, a languor, a dull, spiritless gloom, under which life, and flesh, and health seemed alike deserting her. Her "Hagar in the Wilderness" was finished, and she commenced drawing another, but lacked the energy to finish it.

It was an unnatural life for Georgia—the once wild, fiery, spirited Georgia, and it was probably a year or two, of such existence, would have found her in a lunatic asylum or in her grave, had not an unlooked-for discovery given a new spring to her dormant energies.

Nearly half a year had now elapsed since that sorrowful night when she had fled from home—six of the darkest months in all Georgia's life. For the first four she had heard no news of any of those she had left, not even of him who, sleeping or waking, was ever uppermost in her thoughts. But one morning, at breakfast, Mr. Leonard had read aloud that our "gifted young follow-citizen, Mr. Richmond Wildair, had returned from abroad, and having re-entered the political world, which he was so well fitted to adorn, had been elected to the legislature, where he had already distinguished himself as a statesman of extraordinary merit and profound wisdom, notwithstanding his extreme youth." Then there was another brief paragraph, in which a mysterious allusion was made to some dark, domestic calamity that had befallen the young statesman; but before Mr. Leonard could finish it he was startled to see the governess make an effort to rise from her seat and fall heavily back in her chair. Then there was a cry that Miss Randall was fainting, and a glass of water was held to her lips, and when, in a moment, she was her own calm, cold self again, she arose and hastily left the room.

But from that day Georgia made a point every morning, with feverish interest, to read the political papers in search of that one loved name. And in every one of them it continually met her eye, lauded to the skies by his friends and followers, and loaded with the fiercest abuse by his enemies. There were long, eloquent speeches of his, glowing, fiery, living, impassioned bursts of eloquence, that sent a thrill to the heart of all who heard him, and swept away all obstacles before the force of its own matchless logic.

A great question was then in agitation, and the young orator, as the champion of humanity and equal rights, flung himself into the thickest of the political *melee* and was soon the reigning demi-god of his party. It was well known he was soon to be sent as a Representative to Congress, and the knowing ones predicted for him the highest honors the political strife could yield—perhaps at some future day the Presidency of the United States. His name and fame were already resounding through the land, and morning, noon, and night, Mr. Leonard, who was the fiercest of politicians, was talking and raving of the matchless talents of this rising star.

And Georgia, how did she listen to all this. All she had hitherto endured seemed nothing in comparison to the anguish she felt in his evident utter forgetfulness of her. All the pride, and triumph, and exultation, she would have felt in his success was swallowed up in the misery of knowing she was forgotten—as completely forgotten as if she had never existed. And oh, the humiliation she felt, when in the papers of the opposition party, she saw *herself* dragged in as a slur, a disgrace, in his private life. The sneering insinuations that the wife of Richmond Wildair had deserted him—had eloped —had been driven from home by his ill-treatment; *these* were worse to her than death. She could almost fancy his cursing her in the bitterness of his heart when his eyes would fall on this, for having disgraced him as she had done.

On this morning, as she stood on the veranda, with a paper in her hand containing an unusually brilliant speech of the gifted young statesman, her thoughts wandering to the days long past when she had first known him, Miss Maggie came dancing out with sparkling eyes, and eagerly accosted her.

"Oh, Miss Randall! only think! papa is going to give a splendid dinner-party, and going to have lots of these political big-wigs here. You know, I suppose, that they, or rather that Mr. Wildair, has gained that horrid question about something or other the papers have been making such a time about?"

"Yes," murmured the white lips, faintly.

"Well, papa's been so dreadfully tickled about it, though why I can't see, that he is going to give this dinner-party, and have lots of those great guns at it, and at their head Mr. Wildair himself, the greatest gun of the lot. Only think of that!"

Georgia had averted her head, and Miss Maggie did not see the deadly paleness that overspread her face, blanching even her very lips, at the words. There was no reply, and shaking back her curls coquettishly, that young lady went on:

"I'm just dying to see Mr. Wildair, you know, everybody is making such a fuss about him; and I do like famous men, of all things. They say he is young and handsome, but whether he is married or not I never can rightly discover; some of the papers say he was, and that he didn't treat his wife well, and Mr. Brown from New York, who was here yesterday, says she committed suicide —isn't that dreadful? But I don't care; I'm bound to set my cap for him, and I guess *I* can manage to get along with him. I should like to see the man would make me commit suicide, that's all! But it may not be true, you know; these horrid papers tell the most shocking fibs about any one they don't like. I wish Dick Curtis were here; he knows all about him, I've heard, but he hasn't called for ever so many ages. Maybe I won't blow him up when I see him, and then I'll pardon him on condition that he tells me all about Mr. Wildair. He is going to be a senator one of these days, and a governor, and a president, and an ambassador, and ever so many other nice things, and there is nothing I would like better than being Madame L'Ambassadrice, and shining in foreign courts, though I *am* the daughter of a red-hot republican. Ha! ha! don't I know how to build castles in Spain, Miss Randall? Poor dear Signor Popkins! what *would* he say if he heard me?"

All this time Georgia had been standing as still and rigid, and coldly white as monumental marble, hearing as one hears not this tirade, which Miss Maggie delivered while dancing up and down the veranda like a living whirligig, too full of spirits to be still for an instant. All Georgia heard or realized of it was that Richmond was coming here—here! under the same roof with herself. Her brain was giddy; a wild impulse came over her to fly, fly far away, to bury herself in the depths of the forest, where he could never find her or hear her name again.

Miss Maggie, having waited in vain for some remark from the governess, was turning away, with a muttered "How tiresome!" when Georgia laid her hand on her arm, and with a face that startled her companion, asked:

"When—when do they come?"

"Who? Dear me, Miss Randall, don't look so ghastly! I declare you're enough to scare a person into fits."

"Those—those—gentlemen."

"Oh, the dinner-party. Thursday week. Papa's waiting till Mr. Wildair comes from Washington."

Georgia turned her face away and covered her eyes with her hand, with a face so agitated, that Maggie's eyes opened with a look of intense curiosity.

"Why, Miss Randall, you are so queer! What on earth makes you look so? Did *you* know Mr. Wildair, or any of them?"

With a gesture of desperation, Georgia raised her head, and then, through all the storm of conflicting feelings within, came the thought that her conduct might excite suspicion, and, without looking round, she said huskily:

"I do not feel well, and I do not like strangers—that is all. Don't mind me—it is nothing."

"Why, what harm can strangers do you? I never saw any one like you in my life, Miss Randall. Wouldn't you like to see Mr. Wildair? I'm sure you seem fond enough of reading about him. Papa told me to persuade you to join us at dinner that day."

"No! no! no! Not for ten thousand worlds!" cried Georgia, wildly. Then, seeing her companion recoil and look upon her with evident alarm, she turned hastily away, and sought refuge in the school-room.

Miss Maggie looked after her in comical bewilderment for a moment, and then setting it down to "oddity," she danced off to practice "Casta Diva," preparatory to taking Mr. Wildair's heart by storm singing it.

"I do hope he isn't married," thought Maggie, dropping on the piano stool, and commencing with a terrific preparatory bang; "he is *so* clever and *such* a catch! My! wouldn't Felice be mad!"

All the next week Miss Randall was more of a puzzle to the Leonards than ever before. Her moods were so changeable, so variable, so eccentric, that it was not strange that she startled them. Mrs. Leonard declared she was hysterical, or in the first stages of a brain fever; Miss Felice pooh-poohed the notion, and said it was only the eccentricity of genius, for Mr. Randall had said she was a genius, and he was infallible; while Miss Maggie differed from both, and set it down to "oddity." Fortunately, however, for Georgia, the whole house was in such an uproar of preparation, and new furnishing and cooking, and there was such distracting running up and down stairs from day-dawn till midnight, and the house was so overrun with milliners and dressmakers, and they were all so absorbed in those mysteries of flounces, and silks, and flowers, and laces wherein the female heart delighteth, that she was left pretty much to her own devices, and seldom ever disturbed.

At last the eventful day arrived. All the invitations had been accepted, and Mr. Wildair, and Mr. Curtis, and Mr. Randall, and all the rest were to come.

Through that whole day Georgia had seemed like one delirious. There was a blazing fire in her eye, and two dark crimson spots, all unusual there, burning on either cheek, bespeaking the consuming fever within. How she ever got through her school duties she could not tell, but evening came at last, and with it Georgia's excitement rose to a pitch not to be endured. She could not stay there and hear them, perhaps see them enter. She felt sure, even amid thousands, she would distinguish *his* step, hear *his* voice; and who knew what desperate act it might drive her to commit—perhaps to burst into the room, and in the presence of all to fall at his feet and sue for pardon.

Unable to sit still, with wild gusts of conflicting passions sweeping through her soul, she seized her hat and mantle and sought that panacea for her "mind deceased," a long, rapid, breathless walk.

It was a delightful May evening, soft, and warm, and genial as in June. There was an air of repose and deep stillness around; one solitary star hung trembling in the sky, and brought to her mind the nights long past, when she had sat at her little chamber window, and watched them shining in their tremulous beauty far above her. Everything seemed at peace but herself, and in her stormy heart was the Angel of Peace ever to take up his abode?

On, and on, and on she walked. It was strange the charm rapid walking had to soothe her wildest moods. Star after star shone out in the blue, cloudless sky, and the last ray of daylight had faded away before she thought of turning. Taking off her hat, and flinging back her thick, dark hair, that the cool breeze might fan her fevered brow, she set out at a more moderate pace for home.

It was a lonesome, unfrequented road especially after night. There was another, new road, which had of late been made the public thoroughfare, and this one was almost entirely deserted; therefore, Georgia was somewhat surprised to see a man approaching her at a rapid pace. He was a gentleman, too, and young and graceful—she saw that at a glance, but in the dim starlight she could not distinguish his features, shaded as they were by a broad-leafed hat. He stopped as he approached her, and hurriedly said:

"Can you tell me, madam, if this road leads to the Widow O'Neil's?"

That voice! it sent a thrill to Georgia's inmost heart, as, with her eyes riveted on his face, she mechanically replied:

"Yes; a little farther up there is a gate. Go through, and the road will bring you to it."

"Thank you; I shall take a shorter way," said the stranger, lifting his hat courteously, and turning rapidly away, but not before she had recognized the pale, handsome face and beautiful, dark eyes of Charley Wildair.

For an instant she stood, unable to speak. She saw him place one hand on the fence, leap lightly over, and disappear, then, with a sort of cry, she started after him. But ere she had taken a dozen steps some inward feeling arrested her, and she stopped. What would he think of her following him thus? He was no longer the boy Charley, any more than she was the child Georgia. Might he not think prying curiosity had sent her after him? Would he be disposed to renew the acquaintance? Perhaps, too, he had recognized her, as she had him, and gave no sign. The strange revelation of Richmond gave her a sort of dread of him, and after a moment's irresolution, she turned and walked back.

The whole house was one blaze of light when she reached it. On the dining-room windows were cast many shadows. Which among them was *his*? Did either brother dream he was so near the other? Did Richmond dream *she* was so near him, and yet so far off? She could not enter the house; her heart was throbbing so loudly that she grew faint and sick, and she staggered to a sort of summer-house, thick with clustering hop-vines, and sank down on a rustic bench, and buried her face in her hands.

How long she had sat there alone in her trouble, and yet so near him who had vowed to "cherish" her through all her trials until death, she could not tell. Footsteps coming down the graveled walk startled her. The odor of cigars came borne on the breeze, and then, with a start and a shock she recognized the voice of Dick Curtis saying, with a laugh:

"I wonder if Ringlets has got through that appalling howl on that instrument of torture, the piano, she was commencing when we beat a retreat? It's a mercy I escaped or I should have gone stark staring mad before the end."

"Come, now, Curtis, you're too severe," said a laughing voice, which Georgia recognized as Mr. Randall's. "Ringlets, as you are pleased to denominate Miss Felice, is only performing a duty every young lady considers she owes to society nowadays, deafening her hearers by those tremendous crashes and flourishes, and crossing her hands, and flying from one end of the piano to the other with dizzying rapidity."

"And it's a duty they never neglect, I'll say that for them," said Mr. Curtis. "And that's what they call fashionable music, my friend? Oh, for the good old days, when girls weren't ashamed to sing 'Auld Robin Gray' and the 'Bonnie Horse of Airlie.' The world's degenerating every day. Thank the gods, we have escaped the infliction, anyhow. Here's a seat; suppose we sit down, and, with our soul in slippers, take the world easy. Poor Wildair! he's in for being martyrized this evening."

"So much for being a lion," said Mr. Randall. "If he will persist in being a burning and shining light, he must expect to pay the penalty."

"Miss Maggie—little blue eyes, you know—has made a dead set at him. Did you observe?" said Mr. Curtis.

"Yes; but I can't say she has met with much success, so far. If report says true, she is not the only young lady who has tried that game of late."

"Poor Rich!" said Curtis. "If they knew but all, they would find how useless it was doing any thing of the sort. I suppose you heard of that sad affair that happened last winter?"

Oh, what would not Georgia have given to be a thousand miles off at that moment! She writhed where she lay; it was like tearing half-healed wounds violently open to sit there and listen to this. But move she could not without discovering herself to Curtis, so she was forced to remain where she was, and hear all.

"No, I can't say as I have," said Mr. Randall, in a tone of interest. "There are so many rumors afloat about his wife—suppose you allude to that—but one cannot even tell for certain whether he was ever married or not."

"Oh, he was; no mistake about it," said Curtis; "I was present—was groomsman, in fact. Such a magnificent creature as she was. I never saw a girl so splendid before or since! beautiful as the dream of an opium-eater, with a pair of eyes that would have made the fortune of half a dozen ordinary women. By George! that girl ought to have been an empress."

"Indeed! I should think Wildair *would* be fastidious in the choice of a wife. How came they to separate in so short a time? Did she not love him?"

"Yes, with her whole heart and soul; in fact, I believe, she loved nothing in earth or heaven but him, but then that is nothing strange, for Richmond is a glorious fellow, and no mistake! But you see, she was as poor as Job, and proud as Lucifer, with a high spirit that would dare and defy the Ancient Henry himself—one of that kind of people who will die sooner than yield an inch. Well, it appears his mother did not like the match, and persisted in snubbing her, and making little of her before folks and behind backs, in fact, treated her shamefully, until she drove the poor girl to the verge of madness."

"And Wildair allowed her to do this?" said Randall, indignantly.

"Well, I don't know how it was, but he was blind to all; but I think the truth of the matter is they deceived him, and only did it when he was absent. There was a cousin there, a little female fiend, whom I should admire to be putting in the pillory, who tried every means in her power to make him jealous, and succeeded; and you don't need to be told a jealous man will stop at nothing."

"Poor girl! poor Wildair! What an infernal shame."

"Wasn't it! You see, he had invited a party to his country-seat—Richmond Hall they called it—and I was there among the rest. Poor Mrs. Wildair had a wretched life of it, with them all set against her. If she had been one of your meek, spiritless little creatures, she would have drooped, and sunk under it, and died perhaps of a broken heart, and all that sort of thing; or if she had been a dull, spiritless young woman, she would have snapped her fingers in their faces, and kept on, never minding. Unfortunately, she was neither, but a sensitive, high-spirited girl, whom every slight wounds to the quick, and you would hardly believe me if I were to tell you the change one short week made in her—you would hardly have known her for the same person. What with her mother-in-law's insults, her cousin-in-law's sneers, her husband's jealousy and angry reproaches, and the neglects and slights of most of the company, a daily stretch on the rack would have been a bed of roses to it."

"Shameful! atrocious!" exclaimed Randall, impetuously. "How could Wildair have the heart to treat her so? He couldn't have cared much about her."

"Didn't he, indeed! That's all you know about it. If ever there was a man loved his own wife, that man was Rich Wildair; but when a man is jealous, you know, he becomes partially insane, and allowances must be made for him. One night, this little vixen of a cousin I mentioned somewhere before, began taunting Mrs. Wildair about her mother, telling her she was no better than she ought to be, and calling herself all sorts of scandalous names—one of the servants accidentally heard her—until she maddened the poor girl so that, in a fit of passion, she caught her and hurled her from her, with a shriek I will never forget to my dying day. Of course, there was the old—what's his name—to pay, immediately; but Freddy's injuries did not prove half so severe as she deserved, and a piece of court-plaster did her business beautifully for her. But you never saw any one in such a rage as Wildair was about it, knowing it would be all over town directly. Three or four of the mean crowd he had invited went off, declaring his wife was a lunatic, and that they were afraid to stay in the same house with her. Wasn't that pretty treatment, after his hospitality?"

"It's the way of the world, *mon ami*."

"And a very mean way it is. Well, Wildair went to his wife and said all sorts of cutting things to her, was as sharp as a bottle of cayenne pepper, in fact, and wound up by telling her he was going to apply for a divorce, which he had no more notion of doing than I have of proposing to one of the Misses Leonard to-morrow. She believed him, though, and, driven to despair by the whole of them, made a moonlight flitting of it, and from that day to this Richmond Wildair has never seen or heard of his wife."

"Poor thing! it was a hard fate. What do you suppose has become of her?"

"Heaven knows! She left a note saying she had gone and would never disgrace him more—these were her words—and bidding him an eternal farewell. Wildair nearly went crazy; he was mad, I firmly believe, for awhile, and it was as much as any one's life was worth to go near him. He searched everywhere, offered enormous rewards for the least trace of her, did everything man could do, in a word, to find her again; but it was of no use, no one had seen or knew anything of her."

"Could she have destroyed herself?"

"Just as likely as not; she was the sort of desperate person likely to do it, and she had no fear of death, or eternity, or anything that way. Well, he was frantic when he found she was lost forever, and would have given even every cent he was worth in the world for the least tidings of her, dead or alive, but it was all a waste of ammunition; and, maddened and despairing, he fled from the scene of disaster, sprang on board a steamship bound for Europe, and was off. But he couldn't stay away; he couldn't rest anywhere, so he came back, and plunged headlong into the giddy maelstrom of politics, and became the man of the people—the Demosthenes; the magnificent orator whose lips, to quote the *Political Thunderbolt*, 'have been touched with coals of living fire;' a pleasant simile, I should think. Poor Rich! they don't know the crucible of suffering from which this fiery, impassioned eloquence has sprung. Ambition will be to him for the rest of his mortal life, wife, and family, and home, for

219

he is not the man to dream for a second of ever marrying again."

"A sad story! And yet he can smile, and jest, and talk gayly, as I heard him half an hour ago, when he was the very life and soul of the company."

"He must—it is expected of him; a man of the people must please the people; and besides, he does it to drown thought; he tries to forget for a time the gnawing remorse that, if indulged, would drive him mad. He lives two lives—the inward and outward—and both as essentially different as day from night. He believes himself the murderer of his wife; in fact, an old lady who brought her up—for the girl was an orphan—told him so, and would not look at him or let him in her house. His mother, touched with remorse, confessed what she had done, and thus he learned all his wife had so silently suffered. It was enough to drive a more sober man insane, and that's the truth. Ah! there was more than one sad heart after her when she went. Poor little Emily Murray! the nicest, and best, and prettiest girl from here to sundown, was nearly broken-hearted. I offered her my own hand and fortune, though I didn't happen to have such an article about me, and she gave me my dismissal on the spot. Heigho! Burnfield's done for poor old Rich and me."

"What! Burnfield, did you say?" exclaimed Randall, with a start.

"Yes, Burnfield. You have no objections to it, I hope?"

"You—did you know—did you ever happen to hear of a widow and a little girl by the name of Darrell there?" said Mr. Randall, in an agitated voice.

"Well, I should think I did—rather!" said Curtis emphatically. "The widow died one night, and the little girl was brought up by one Miss Jerusha Skamp of severe memory, and it's of her I have been talking for the last half-hour, if you mean Georgia Darrell."

"What!" exclaimed Randall, wildly, as he sprang to his feet. "Do you mean to tell me that Georgia Darrell grew up in Burnfield, and was the wretched wife of Richmond Wildair?"

"Indeed I do," replied Curtis, with increasing emphasis. "Why, what the dickens is the matter with you? What does all this mean?"

"Mean! Oh, man! man! Georgia Darrell was my *sister*!"

CHAPTER XXI.

CHARLEY'S CRIME.

"By the strong spirit's discipline,
  By the fierce wrong forgiven,
By all that wrings the heart of sin,
  Is woman won to heaven."

th every nerve strained, every feeling wrought to the highest pitch of
excitement, Georgia had listened; but at this last moment the overstrung
tension gave way, and, for the first time in her life, she fainted.

On the wet grass where she had fallen she still lay when life and memory
came back. She raised herself on her elbow and looked wildly around, passed
her hand across her forehead, and tried to think. Gradually recollection
returned; one by one the broken chains of memory were reunited, and all she
had heard came back, flooding her soul with ecstatic joy. Beloved still, no
longer a cast-off wife, and her long-lost brother Warren restored!

She remembered him now; she wondered she had not done so at first, for
every tone of his voice was familiar. It was the name that had deceived her,
and yet he had his mother's name, too—Warren Randall Darrell. She rose up,
to find herself stiff and cold, lying on the wet ground, and her dress soaked
with the heavy dew. The garden was deserted, the house all dark, and with an
overpowering sense of loneliness she found herself locked out.

It would not do to disturb the family; she must wait till morning where she
was, so she resumed her seat and crouched down shivering with cold. The
new-born joy in her heart could not keep her from being chilled through and
through; and as the long hours dragged on, it seemed to her that never was
night so long as that. Benumbed with cold, sick, and shivering, she sank into
an uneasy slumber at last, with her head on the hard, wooden bench.

It was morning when she awoke. With difficulty she arose to her feet, and saw
a servant with lazy step and lack luster eyes come out and approach the
stables. As she arose, she found herself hardly able to walk from cold and
exposure, but she managed to stagger to the door and enter unobserved. It was
well for her she met no one, as they might have taken her for one newly risen
from the dead—for never did eye rest on such a deathly face as she wore that
morning. How she reeled to her room she did not know; how she managed to
take off her saturated garments and fling herself on her bed she could not tell;
but there she was lying, weak, prostrate, helpless, and chilled to the very

heart.

As the morning passed and she did not appear, a servant was sent to see what was the matter. Georgia tried to lift her head, but such a feeling of deadly sickness came over her that, weak and blinded, she fell back on her pillow. Every care was taken of her, but before night a raging fever had set in, and with burning brow and parched lips Georgia lay tossing and raving wildly in delirium. Alarmed now, the family physician was sent for, who pronounced it a dangerous attack of brain fever, from which he was extremely doubtful she could ever recover.

For days and days after that Georgia lay helpless as a child, with liquid flame burning in every vein. Sometimes she raved and shrieked madly of Freddy Richmond, calling herself a murderess, and trying to spring from those who held her. Sometimes she would plead pitifully with Richmond and implore him to forgive her, and she would never, never offend him again; and now she would forget all the past, and fancy herself talking to the children in the school-room, seemingly with no memory of anything but the present.

It was a golden, sunshiny June morning when consciousness returned, and she opened her eyes to find herself lying in her own room, with a strange woman sitting beside her. Youth, and a naturally strong constitution, had finally triumphed over the disease, but she lay there weak and helpless as an infant. She had a vague, confused memory of the past few weeks, and she turned with a helpless, bewildered look to the nurse.

"What is it? What is the matter? Have I been ill?" she asked, feebly.

"Yes, very ill; but you are better now," said the nurse, coming over and softly adjusting the pillow.

"How—how long have I been sick?" she said, passing her wasted hand across her forehead as if to dispel a mist.

"Three weeks," was the reply.

"So long!" said Georgia, drearily, and still struggling to recall something that had escaped her memory. "Who are you? I don't know you."

"I am your nurse," said the woman, smiling. "Mrs. Leonard hired me to take care of you, and look after things generally until she came back."

"Came back! Has she gone away, then?"

"Oh, dear, yes! the whole family, children and all; they were afraid of the fever, although the doctor said there was no danger."

"Where have they gone?" said Georgia, faintly.

"To New York. It's my opinion the young ladies were glad of any chance of getting back to town, and it was they, particularly Miss Felice, who insisted on leaving. Don't disturb yourself about them, my dear; you will soon be as well as any of them."

"Tell me," said Georgia, catching the woman's wrists in her thin, transparent hands, and looking earnestly in her face with the great black eyes so sunken and melancholy now—"tell me if you know whether a certain Mr. Randall who used to come here went with them? Perhaps you have heard?"

The woman shook her head.

"No, my dear, I have not. I have heard of him, though, often; they say he is very clever and going to be married to Miss Felice, but I don't know myself. Don't talk so much, Miss Randall; it is not good for you."

"One thing more," said Georgia. "I—I raved when I was out of my mind; will you tell me what it was I said?"

"That would be pretty hard to do," said the nurse, smiling; but then, seeing the look of desperate earnestness on her patient's face, she added: "Why, you know, my dear, you talked a great deal of nonsense—fever patients always do —about some one you called Richmond, and Freddy Richmond—some gentlemen, I expect," said the woman, with a meaning glance; "and you called yourself a murderess, and then you kept begging some one not to be angry with you, and you would never do so any more; and sometimes you would talk to the children, and fancy yourself in the school-room with them. In short, you know, you said all sorts of queer things; but that was to be expected."

From that day Georgia rapidly recovered, and in less than a fortnight was able to get up and sit for a few hours each day in an easy chair by the window, inhaling the fragrant summer air. Her first request was to call for the latest papers; but for some time the doctor said she was not equal to the exertion of reading them, and, in spite of her passionate eagerness, she had to wait.

To ask about Richmond she did not dare; but how eagerly she scanned the first paper she got, in search of his name! And there she learned that he had gone South on a summer ramble, wandering about from place to place with the strange restlessness that characterized him.

It was a blow to her at first, but when she came to think it over, she was almost glad of it. Somehow, she scarcely could tell why she did not wish to meet him yet; if ever she returned to him, it must be in a way different from what she had left. She wanted to find her brother first; she had a vehement desire to win wealth and fame, and return to Richmond Wildair as his equal in every way. During the long weary hours of her convalescence she had made up her mind to go to the city.

The monotonous life of the last six months here grew unendurable to her now; she would not have taken uncounted wealth and consented to spend six more like them. Life at least was not stagnant in the uproar and turmoil of the city, and solitude is not always a panacea for all sorts of people in trouble.

She had money—her half-year's salary had been untouched, and it was no inconsiderable sum, for Mr. Leonard had been as generous as he was rich. She had a vague idea of winning fame as an artist. She felt an inward conviction that her "Hagar in the Wilderness" would create a sensation if seen. She took it out from its canvas screen, and gazed long and earnestly upon it.

It was a wild, weird, unearthly thing, but strangely beautiful withal, and possessing a sort of fascination that would have chained you before it for hours. Never did eye look on a more gloriously beautiful face than that of the pictured Egyptian in its dark splendor and unutterable anguish. The posture, as she half-lay, half-writhed in her inward torture, spoke of the darkest depth of anguish and despair; the long, wild, purplish black tresses streamed unbound in the breeze, and the face that startled you from the canvas was white with woman's utmost woe. And the eyes that caught and transfixed yours, sending a thrill of awe and terror to most stoical heart—those unfathomable eyes of midnight blackness, where despairing love, fiercest anguish, and maddest desperation seem struggling for mastery. Oh! never could any, but one in the utmost depths of despair herself, have painted eyes like these. Lucifer hurled from heaven might have cast back one last look like that, so full of conflicting passion, but the superhuman agony shining and surmounting them all—eyes that would have haunted you like a frightful nightmare, long after you had first beheld them, eyes that would have made you shudder, and yet held you spell-bound, breathless, riveted to the spot.

All unknown to herself she had painted her own portrait; those flowing, lustrous tresses, that dark, oriental face, those appalling eyes, that posture of utter woe and unspeakable desolation, all were hers. The face was almost the fac-simile of the one that had once so startled Richmond Wildair that morning on the sea-shore, only the passionate, tortured form was wanting.

At a little distance lay the boy Ishmael, with all his mother's dark beauty in his face, but so serenely calm and childishly peaceful that the contrast was all the more startling.

It was a wonderful picture, and no wonder that Georgia's eyes fired up, and her color came and went and her countenance glowed with power, and triumph and inspiration as she gazed.

225

"It must succeed—it will succeed—it *shall* succeed," she vehemently exclaimed. "There has been a prize offered by the Academy of Art for the best painting from a native artist, and mine shall go with the rest. And if it succeeds—"

She caught her breath, and her whole face for an instant grew radiant with the picture she conjured up of the glory and fame that would be hers.

"Mr. Leonard shall take it for me; he has always been my friend, and the artist's name shall be unknown until the decision is announced. Yes, it shall be so; the paper says that all pictures for the prize must be delivered in three days from this, as the decision shall be given and the prize awarded in a fortnight. Yes, I will go at once."

And with her characteristic impulsive rapidity, Georgia made her preparations, and that very afternoon bade farewell to the house where the last six wretched months had been spent, and took the cars for New York.

Arrived there, her first destination was the widow's, where she had stopped before, and early next morning she set out for the hotel where the Leonards were stopping.

Mr. Leonard and his family were still there, and seemed quite overjoyed to see her. It was fortunate, Mrs. Leonard said, she had come when she did, for early in the next month she, and Mr. Leonard, and the girls were off for Cape May for a little tossing about in the surf, and would not return until quite late in the season, as, having been cooped up so long, they were determined to make the most of their holiday now. The children were to go back, and she, Miss Randall, was expected to go back with them, and oversee the household generally in their absence.

Great was the worthy lady's surprise when Georgia quietly and firmly declined. At first she was disposed to stand upon her dignity and be offended, but when Mr. Leonard declared emphatically Miss Randall was right, that she was by no means strong enough to resume the labor of teaching, that she needed rest and relaxation and amusement, and that the city, among her friends, was for the present decidedly the best place for her, she cooled down, and consented to listen to reason.

"And now, how are all your friends, Miss Leonard?" said Georgia, with a smile, yet with a sudden throbbing at her heart at the hope of hearing something of her brother.

"All well enough when we saw them last," said Miss Felice, in a dreary tone; "everybody's going away out of the city, but papa will insist on staying after every one else."

"Whom do you call everybody else, my dear?" said Mr. Leonard, looking over his paper good-humoredly. "If I don't mistake, you may see some thousands of people in New York every day still."

"Oh, yes, the nobodies stay, of course. I don't mean them," said Miss Felice, pettishly. "I hate people. Anybody that pretends to be anybody is going away."

"You're a nice republican—you are!" said Master Royal, who in one corner of the room was making frantic efforts to stand on his head, as he had seen them do in the circus the night before.

"Has your friend Mr. Randall gone, too?" said Georgia, still trying to smile, though there was a slight agitation in her voice in spite of all.

"Yes, of course he has. I wonder you didn't hear of it," said Miss Felice, looking dissatisfied.

"Hear of it! how could she?" broke in Maggie. "You see, Miss Randall, the queerest thing occurred while you were sick—just like a thing in a play, where everybody turns out to be somebody else. Mr. Randall had a sister once upon a time, and lost her somehow, and she grew up and married Mr. Richmond Wildair, and he lost her somehow, the lady evidently having a fancy for getting lost, and it was all found out through Dick Curtis. So Mr. Randall and Mr. Wildair had a great time about it, and now they have both gone to look for her again—one North and the other South, so if they don't find her it will be a wonder. Is it not romantic? I would give the world to see her—the wife and sister of two such famous men. Oh, Miss Randall! Mr. Curtis says she was quite splendid—so beautiful, you know, and,"—here Maggie lowered her voice to a mysterious whisper—"he thinks she has gone and killed herself."

"Oh, ma, look how pale Miss Randall is; she's going to faint if you don't look sharp," cried out Master Royal.

"No, it is nothing; pray do not mind," said Georgia faintly, motioning them away. "I am not very strong yet; allow me to wish you good-morning. Mr. Leonard, can I see you in private for a few minutes?"

"Certainly, certainly," responded Mr. Leonard, while the rest looked up, rather surprised, as they left the room.

In as few words as possible Georgia made known her request, and obtained from him a promise of secrecy. Mr. Leonard was not in the least surprised; he was perfectly confident about her taking the prize, and, having obtained her address, told her he would call for it on the morrow.

But when the old gentleman saw it he fairly started back, and gazed on it in a sort of terror and consternation that amused Georgia, breaking out at intervals with ejaculations of extreme astonishment.

"Eh? what? Lord bless my soul! Why, it's quite frightful—upon my life it is! Good gracious! what a pair of eyes that young woman has got! 'Hagar in the Wilderness.' Je-ru-sa-lem! I wouldn't be Abraham for a trifle, with such a desperate-looking wild-cat as that about the house. She's the born image of yourself, too; one would think you and Hagar were twin sisters. Well, Lord bless me! if it isn't enough to give a man fits to look at it! It's well I'm not nervous, or I'd never get over the shock of looking at it. Upon my honor, Miss Randall, I don't know what to make of you. You're the eighth wonder of the world—that's what you are!"

The painting was accordingly sent in, and three days after, the whole Leonard family departed—the children for home, and the elders of the house for Cape May—and now Georgia was left to solitude and suspense once more, until, as day after day was passed, and *the* day approached, she began her old fashion of working herself up into one of her fevers of impatience and excitement. Her usual antidote of a long, rapid walk was followed in the city as well as in the country, and often did people pause and look in wonder after the tall, dark-robed figure that flitted so rapidly by them, whose vailed face no one ever saw.

One night, as darkness was falling over the city, Georgia found herself suddenly among a crowd of people who were passing rapidly into a church. Borne along by the throng, she was carried in, too, and half-bewildered by the crowd, and by the crash of a grand organ, and the glitter of many lights, she found herself in a pew, among thousands of others, before she quite realized where she was. She looked, and, with a half-startled air, saw she was in one of the largest churches of the city, and that it was already filled to suffocation.

She heard some persons in a seat before her whisper that an eloquent young divine (she could not catch the name) was going to address them. While they yet spoke, a tall, slight figure, robed in black, came out of the vestry, passed up the stairs, and ascended the pulpit. A silence so profound that you could have heard a pin drop in that vast multitude reigned, broken at last by a clear, thrilling voice that rang out in deep tones with the awful words from Holy Writ:

"You shall seek Me and you shall not find Me, and you shall die in your sins."

A death-like pause ensued, and every heart seemed to stand still to catch the next words. But why does Georgia start as if she had received a spear thrust? Why do her lips spring white and quivering apart? Why are her eyes fixed so wildly, so strangely on the preacher? In that moment the mystery was solved, the secret revealed—the brother of her husband stands before her. The gay, the careless, the elegant, the thoughtless Charley Wildair is a clergyman. For awhile she sat stunned by the shock, conscious that he was speaking, yet hearing not a word. Then her clouded faculties cleared, and her ears were greeted by such bursts of resistless eloquence as she had never dreamed of before. In that moment rose before her, with terrific vividness, the despairing death-bed of the sinner and the awful doom that must follow. Shuddering and terrified, she sank back, shading her face with her hands, appalled by the awful fate that might have been hers. What—what was all earthly trouble compared with that dread eternity of misery she had deserved—that awful doom that might yet be hers? Still it arose before her in all its frightful horrors, exhibited by the clarion voice of the speaker, until, wrought up to the pitch of frenzy, her trembling lips strove to form the word "Mercy." And still, as if in answer, rang out that thrilling voice with that terrific sentence of eternal doom:

"You shall seek Me and you shall not find Me, and you shall die in your sins."

The sermon was over, the people were crowding out, and she found herself half senseless kneeling in the pew, with her face hidden in her hands. An uncontrollable desire to see, to speak to him she had just heard seized her, and she sprang up, and grasping some one who stood near her, said, incoherently:

"Where is he? I must see him! Where is he gone?"

"Who?" said the startled personage she addressed.

"He who has just preached."

"In there," said the man, pointing to the vestry. "Go in that way and you will see him."

Forcing her way through the throng, Georgia hurried on, passed into the sanctuary, and from thence to the vestry.

There she paused—restored to herself. Nearly a dozen clergymen were there, standing in groups, conversing with several ladies and gentlemen, who had come too late to get into the church, and had been forced to remain there to listen. All eyes were turned on the new-comer, whose pale, wild beauty made her an object of deep interest, as she stood startled and hesitating in the door-way. A little boy, standing near, looked up and said, curiously:

"Did you want anybody, ma'am?"

"Yes—Mr. Wildair. Is he here?" said Georgia, hurriedly.

"Yes'm, there he is," said the boy, pointing to where stood the man she was in search of, standing by himself, his forehead leaning on his hand, and a look of utter fatigue and weariness on his face.

All Georgia's eagerness returned at the sight. Passing rapidly through the wondering spectators she approached him, and, with an irrepressible cry of "Charley!" she stood before him.

Looking very much surprised, as well he might, the young clergyman lifted up his head and fixed his eyes full on her face; but there was no recognition in that look, nothing but the utmost wonder.

"Oh, Charley! don't you know me?—don't you know Georgia?" she cried out, passionately.

Instantly he started up.

"What! Georgia Darrell—little Georgia, my brother's wife!" he cried, eagerly.

Her eyes answered him.

"Is it possible? Why, Georgia, how little I expected to meet *you* here!" he said, holding out his hand, with a smile of mingled remorse and pleasure. "How came you here?"

"I do not know. Chance—Providence—something sent me here to-night."

"I would never have known you, it is so long since we met."

"Not so long as you think," she said, with one of her old rare smiles.

"No! How is that?"

"Do you remember the person you met on a country road, one night about a month ago, and asked the way to Widow O'Neil's?"

"Yes."

"I was that person."

"Indeed! And did you know me?"

"Certainly I did."

"Well, I never for an instant dreamed it was you; but no wonder—I never saw any one so changed," he said, looking in the pale wasted face, and contrasting it with the blooming happy one he had last seen.

"Trouble seldom changes people for the better, I believe," she said, with a sigh.

"Ah, I heard what you allude to; Curtis told me. I am very, very sorry indeed, Georgia; but do you know they imagine you dead?"

"Yes, I know it," she said, averting her face.

"And that Richmond has searched for tidings of you everywhere?"

"Yes."

"Well, Georgia," he said, anxiously, "what do you intend to do? You should return to your husband."

"I intend to," she said, looking up with a sudden bright smile, "but not just yet. And you—how little I ever expected to see you a clergyman—you, who, if your reverence will excuse my saying it, used to be such a rattlepate."

He laughed, the happy, careless laugh that reminded her of the Charley of other days, and shook back, with the old familiar motion, his thick, clustering, chestnut hair.

"Time works wonders, Georgia. Thank God for what it has done for me," he said, reverentially. "Did you know I was a clergyman?"

"Not until to-night. They never would tell me what became of you. They said you disgraced the family, committed some awful crime, but what it was I never could learn. Surely they did not mean that by becoming a clergyman you had disgraced your family?"

"They meant that, and nothing else," he said, emphatically.

"Ah, how much you gave up for the dictates of conscience—friends and family, wealth and worldly honors, and all that makes life dear; and yet you look happy," said Georgia, in a sort of wonder.

He laid his hand on hers and pointed up, while he said, in a low voice:

"'Amen, I say to you, there is no man that hath left home, or parents, or brethren, or wife, or children, for the kingdom of God's sake, who shall not receive much more in this present time, and in the world to come life everlasting.'"

She lifted her eyes in a sort of awe at the inspired tones. And his face was as the face of an angel.

A silence fell on them both, broken first by him.

"You must come to see me again, Georgia. I have a good deal to say to you that I have no time to say now. Here is my address while I remain in the city, which will not be long. You have suffered wrong, Georgia, but 'forgive that you be likewise forgiven.' I must go now. Good-night, and Heaven bless you!"

In her unworthiness she felt as if she could have sunk at his feet and kissed the hem of his garment. She bowed her once haughty head to receive his parting benediction, and hurried out.

Sitting in her room that night, she sank down to pray for the first time in years —almost for the first time in her life. Fervently, earnestly was that prayer offered; and a calmness, a peace hitherto unknown, stole into her heart. In the sighing of the wind she seemed to hear an angel voice softly saying, "Come unto me, all ye that labor and are heavy laden, and I will give you rest;" and dropping her forehead in her clasped hands, she sank down in the calm light of high, bright, solemn stars, and meekly murmured:

"Hear me, oh, Lord!"

CHAPTER XXII.

THE SUN RISES.

"Radiant daughter of the sun,
Now thy living wreath is won,
Crowned with fame! Oh! art thou not
Happy in that glorious lot?
Happier, happier far than thou,
With the laurel on thy brow,
She that makes the humblest
Lovely but to one on earth."

MRS. HEMANS.

e wise counsel and impressive instructions of her old acquaintance, the now calm, dignified, and subdued Rev. Mr. Wildair, soon brought forth good fruit. Georgia began to find the "peace which passeth all understanding." Now she looked forward with calm, patient expectation to her meeting with her husband, with the sweet promise ever in her mind, "seek first the kingdom of God, and all else shall be added unto you." With a sad heart Georgia noticed her old companion's thin, wasted face and form, the striking brilliancy of his eyes, the hectic flush of his pale cheek, and the short, hacking cough that impeded his speech, and felt that the inspired young missionary's days were numbered.

The day came at last when the decision regarding Georgia's picture was to be announced.

She tried to be calm and patient, but notwithstanding all her efforts in this direction, when Mr. Leonard started off to hear the decision that was to condemn or accept her picture, she was in a perfect fever of anxiety. She could not sit still, she could not taste breakfast; she walked up and down her room in irrepressible impatience, with two hot spots, all unusual there, burning on either cheek, and a wild, feverish light streaming from her eyes.

Noon came—twelve o'clock—Georgia looked at her watch unceasingly. He had promised to return between twelve and one, but one passed and he came not; two, and he was absent still; three, and in her burning impatience she was about to throw on her hat and shawl and hasten out in search of news, when the door was flung open, and Mr. Leonard, flushed, and panting, and perspiring, rushed in.

"Hurrah! you've done it! you've done it! you've got the prize, Miss Randall! Hagar's electrifying the whole of 'em and got herself to the top of the tree. If Abraham was around he'd feel pretty cheap just now, to see the fuss they're making about her. I knew you would get it, Miss Randall! Let me congratulate you! Hurrah!"

And Mr. Leonard, in his delight, waved his hat and gave a cheer that sent the widow shrieking into the room to see what was the matter. And there she found Mr. Leonard grasping Georgia by both hands, and shaking them with a zeal and vehemence quite startling, while Georgia herself, forgetting everything, even her success, in her sense of the ludicrous, was laughing until her cheeks were crimson.

Georgia smiled, but her cheek was flushed and her eye flashing with triumph. Never had she looked so beautiful before, and the old gentleman gazed at her with profound admiration as she stood like a triumphant young queen before him.

"You are right, Mr. Leonard, wonders never *will* cease. Some day, very shortly, I intend to give you a still greater surprise."

"Eh—how—what is it?" said the old man, puzzled by her radiant face.

"Never mind, sir. You shall know in good time. To-morrow I will go with you to 'receive my reward of merit.' I have never got one since I left school, but I don't know but that I rather like the idea after all."

As she spoke the door was opened, and the widow re-entered.

"Well?" said Georgia, inquiringly.

"There are two gentlemen in the next room who want to see you, if you please," she said.

"To see me!" said Georgia, in surprise.

"Yes'm; they asked for Miss Randall."

Georgia's heart throbbed, and her color came and went. A sudden faintness seized her, and she sank into a chair.

"Why, bless my heart! what's the matter?" said Mr. Leonard, in surprise; "it can't be the artists, you know, because they don't know your name or address. What *does* ail you, Miss Randall?"

"Show them in here. I will see them," said Georgia, faintly, raising her head and laying her hand on her heart to still its tumultuous throbbings.

Georgia's hour had come.

The door opened, and Georgia rose to her feet, deadly pale, with many emotions, as Dick Curtis and Mr. Randall entered.

"I was right—it *is* she!" cried Mr. Curtis, joyfully, as he sprang forward and caught both her hands in his. "Huzza! Oh, Mrs. Wildair, Mrs. Wildair! to think I should ever see you again!" said Dick, fairly ready to cry.

"*Mrs. Wildair!* Why, what the——"

Mr. Leonard, in his astonishment, made use of an improper word, reader, so you will excuse me for not repeating it.

"My dear Mr. Curtis, I am truly glad to see you again," said Georgia, in a faltering voice—"more rejoiced than I have words to say."

"And this gentleman! I'll bet you a dollar, now, you'll say you don't know him," said Mr. Curtis, rubbing his hands gleefully.

"Not so, sir," said Georgia, taking a step forward and looking up in the pale agitated face of Mr. Randall, every feature of which was familiar to her now. "My dear, my long-lost brother! My dearest Warren!" And with a great cry she sprang forward and was locked in her brother's arms.

"Georgia! Georgia! my sister!" was all he could say, as he strained her to his breast, and tears, which did honor to his manly heart, dropped on her bowed head.

"Huzza! hip, hip, hurrah! it's all right now!" shouted Mr. Curtis, as he flourished round the room in a frantic extempore waltz of most intense delight, and then, in the exuberance of his joy, he seized hold of the astounded Mr. Leonard and fairly hugged him, in his ecstacy:

"Help! help! murder! fire!" yelled Mr. Leonard, struggling frantically in what he supposed to be the grasp of a maniac.

"There! take it easy, old gentleman!" said Mr. Curtis, releasing him, and cutting a pigeon's wing. "Tol-de-rol-de-riddle-lol! Don't raise such an awful row! Ain't there a picture to look at, my hearty? Hurrah! Oh, how happy I feel! And to think that I should have been the means of bringing them together—I, Dick Curtis, that never did anything right before in my life!

Good gracious! Tol-de-rol—— Hello? Where are you going so fast, old gent?"

Mr. Leonard, the moment he found himself free, had seized his hat, and was about to decamp, in the full feeling that a lunatic asylum had broken loose somewhere, when Georgia, looking up, espied him, and said:

"Mr. Leonard, don't go. My best friend must stay and share in my joy this happy day. Can you guess who this is?" she said, laying her hand fondly on her brother's shoulder, and looking up in his face, with a smile shining through her tears.

"Guess!" said Mr. Leonard, testily—"I don't need to *guess*, young lady. I know well enough it's young Randall, and I must say, although he *is* a namesake of yours, it doesn't look well to see you flying into his arms and hugging him in that manner the moment he comes into the house. No more does it look well for Dick Curtis to take hold of me like a bear, and dislocate every rib I have in the world, as he has done."

"No, I haven't, Mr. Leonard," interrupted Dick; "there's Mrs. Leonard, your chief rib—I haven't dislocated her, have I?"

Mr. Leonard's look of deepest disgust was so irresistible that Dick broke off and burst into a fit of immoderate laughter, snapping his fingers, and throwing his body into all sorts of contortions of delight, and his example proving contagious, both Mr. Randall and Georgia followed it, and all three laughed without being able to stop for nearly five minutes, during which Mr. Leonard stood, hat in hand, looking from one to the other, with a look of solemn dismay unspeakably ridiculous.

"Do not be shocked, Mr. Leonard," said Georgia, as soon as she could speak for laughter, "though really you are not so without cause. Did I not tell you I would surprise you oftener than you thought? Mr. Randall is my own, my only, long-lost brother."

"Her brother! Oh, ginger!" muttered Mr. Leonard, completely bewildered. "I might have known two such geniuses must be related to one another."

"For all you have kindly done for my sister, Mr. Leonard, accept my thanks," said Mr. Randall, as he came forward, with a smile, and shook him heartily by the hand.

"Well, what a go this is, anyway!" said Mr. Curtis, meditatively. "Only to think of it! And all through me—or, rather, through little Emily's picture! Why, it's wonderful! downright wonderful!—ain't it, Mrs. Wildair?"

"Mrs. Wildair!" exclaimed Mr. Leonard, looking from Dick to Georgia with wide-open eyes. Then, as a sudden light broke in upon him. "Why, Heaven bless my soul!" he ejaculated. "Sure enough, they told me Randall's sister was Wildair's wife—the one that ran away. Great Jehosaphat! to think she should turn up again in such a remarkably funny way, and should prove to be our Miss Randall! I've a good mind to swear!—upon my life, I have!"

"And all through me, too, Mr. Leonard," said Mr. Curtis, exultingly; "if it hadn't been for me they might have gone poking round the world till doomsday and not found one another. If I don't deserve a service of tin plate, I shall feel obliged to you to let me know who does."

"Land of life and blessed promise!" exclaimed Mr. Leonard, who had originally come from "away down East," and when excited always broke out into the expletives of his boyhood, "how do you like it? Do tell, Curtis."

"Well, you see," began Mr. Curtis, with the air of one entering into an obtuse narrative, "Randall—*his* name's Darrell, but that's neither here nor there; 'what's in a name,' as that nice man, Mr. Shakespeare, says, or, rather, as he makes Miss Juliet Capulet say when speaking of young Mr. R. Montague, her beau. Randall, as I was saying, got hold of a picture of little Emily—I mean Miss Murray, a friend of mine—drawn by Mrs. Wildair there, while residing in your house and doing the governess dodge under the name of Randall too, which turns out to be a family name after all, and one day he accidentally showed it to me, and if I didn't jump six feet when I saw it, then call me a flat, that's all. Of course, I asked him no end of questions and found out where he got it, and then it was all as clear to me as a hole in a ladder, and I knew in a twinkling who 'Miss Randall' was. So we tore along here like a couple of forty-horse-power comets, and, after a whole day of most awful bother, we found out where she was. And here we came, and here we found her, and so, no more at present from yours respectfully, Dick Curtis." And Mr. Curtis made a feint of holding out an imaginary dress, like an old lady in a minuet, and courtesied profoundly to the company around.

"My dear Miss Ran—I mean my dear Mrs. Wildair, allow me to congratulate you," said Mr. Leonard, his face all in a glow of delight as he shook her warmly by the hand, "upon my life, I never was so glad in all my days. Good gracious! to think you should turn out to be such a great lady after serving as governess in our—— Well, well, well! And that you should find your brother the same day you took the prize for the best picture in the Academy of Art. G-o-o-d gracious!" said Mr. Leonard, with a perfect shake on the word.

"What! Georgia taken the prize? It can't be possible that *you* are the successful candidate whose wonderful picture everybody is talking about?" exclaimed her brother, whose turn it was to be astonished.

"Mr. Leonard says so," said she, smiling.

"Oh, Jupiter!" ejaculated Mr. Curtis, thrusting his hands into his pockets and uttering a long, low whistle, indicative of an unlimited amount of amazement, "and you really and truly painted 'Hagar in the Wilderness?'"

"Yes, I really and truly did," smiled Georgia.

"Well," said Mr. Curtis, in a tone of resignation, "all I have to say is that nothing will surprise me after this. And that reminds me, I've quite forgotten an engagement down town, and must be off. Randall, don't you come. I know you have lots of things to say to your sister. Mr. Leonard, you have an engagement, too—don't say no—I'm sure you have—come along. By-by, Randall, old-fellow; good-day, Mrs. Wildair. I'll drop in again in the course of the evening. Now, Mr. Leonard, off we go!" and Mr. Curtis put his arm through Mr. Leonard's and fairly dragged him away.

"And so, instead of a poor unknown governess, I have found in my sister one with whose fame the whole city is already ringing," said Mr. Randall, when they were alone, as he looked proudly and fondly in her beautiful face. "Dear Georgia, how famous you are."

CHAPTER XXIII.

OVER THE WORLD.

"They stood apart.
Like rocks which have been rent asunder,
A dreary sea now flows between,
But neither heat, nor frost, nor thunder
Shall wholly do away, I ween,
The works of that which once hath been."

COLERIDGE.

"

, Warren, what is fame compared to what I have found to-day?" she said, sweetly. "What is fame, and wealth, and all worldly honors, compared to a brother's love? But one thing more is needed now to make me perfectly happy."

"I know what you mean, Georgia—your husband. Is it possible you care for *him* still, after all he has made you suffer?"

She looked up in his face, and he was answered.

"Then, for your sake, I am sorry he has gone," he said slowly.

"Gone?" she repeated, with a paling cheek. "Gone where?"

"To France, on some important mission from government that no one can fulfill so well as himself, and—I have not the faintest idea of when he will return."

"Now that I have told you all that has befallen me," said Georgia, some half an hour later that same afternoon, as brother and sister sat side by side at the window, "I want to hear your adventures and 'hair-breadth 'scapes by flood and field' since that sad night long ago, when we parted last."

"I fear you are doomed to be disappointed, then, if you expect any such things from me," said her brother, smiling. "My life has been one of most inglorious safety so far, and I never had a hair-breadth escape of any kind, since I was born."

"How strange it is that I could ever believe you dead," said Georgia, musingly. "Miss Jerusha, too, to use her own words, constantly averred that you had 'got taken in somewheres,' and never would hear for a moment that you had perished in the storm."

"Well, Miss Jerusha was right," said Warren, "though really I need not thank her for it, as I am quite certain, from your description, she is the old lady that turned me out that same night. However, I forgive her for that, and owe her a long debt of gratitude besides, for all she has done for you. You remember, of course, Georgia, the company we used to act with?"

"Yes, perfectly. Don't I remember my own performances on the tight-rope and on horseback as the 'Flying Circassian?" she said, smiling.

"Well, when the old lady turned me off that night, I never felt more like despairing in all my life. I was wretchedly clad—if you don't remember it, *I* do—and it was bitterly cold. Still, I would not go back without help of some kind, so I staggered on and on through the blinding storm, until at last, benumbed and helpless, I sank down on the frozen ground, as I thought, never to rise again."

"Poor little fellow!" said Georgia, sadly, in whose mind the image of the slight, delicate boy he was then rose uppermost.

Warren laughed at the epithet applied to one who stood six feet without his boots, and went on:

"I suppose I had fallen into that sort of stupor which precedes freezing to death, and was unconscious; but when next I awoke to the realities of this exceedingly real world, I was in bed in a meanly furnished room, and the first face I beheld was that of Betsey Stubbs, Georgia—the one who used to figure on the bills as Eugenia De Lacy?"

"And always played the artless little girl, although she was thirty years old," said Georgia, laughing. "Oh, I remember her."

"Well, there she was, and there I was with her, and with the company again. It turned out that two of the men were passing along the road, returning to the village—what do you call it?—Burnfield, and stumbled over me, lying stiff and nearly frozen on the road. They knew me immediately, and carried me off to where the rest of them were; and it was resolved that they should decamp with me, for that old tyrant of a manager thought it too much of a good thing to lose three at once. So, in spite of my tears, and cries, and struggles and entreaties, I was forcibly carried off a little after midnight, when the storm cleared away, and brought back to the city.

"Well, Georgia, for nearly another year I remained at our old business, and with the old set, too closely watched to think of escaping, and to escape from them was now the sole aim of my life. The opportunity so long sought for came at last. One night a chance presented itself, and I was off; and fickle fortune, as if tired of making me a mark to poke fun at, came to my aid, and I made good my escape from my jealous guardians. For hours I wandered about through the city, until at last, worn out and exhausted, I curled myself up on the marble door-steps of an aristocratic mansion, and fell fast asleep.

"A hand grasping my shoulder and shaking me roughly awoke me after a time, and as I started up, I heard a gruff voice saying:

"'Hallo! you little vagrant, what are you doing here?'

"I rubbed my eyes and looked up. An old gentleman, who had just alighted from a carriage, stood over me, with no very amiable expression of countenance, shaking me as if he would shake a reply out of me by main force.

"I stammered out something—I don't know what—and terrified lest he should give me into the hands of a policeman, I tried to break away from him and fly; but the old gentleman held on like grim death, and seemed not to have the slightest intention of parting with me so easily.

"'You're a pickpocket, ain't you?' said he, sharply.

"'No, sir,' said I, half-angrily, and looking him full in the face, 'I am *not*.'

"'Then what brought you here,' persisted he, 'if you are not a juvenile thief?'

"'I was tired, sir,' said I, 'and I sat down here to rest, and so fell asleep.'

"The old gentleman kept his sharp eyes fixed on me as if he would read me through, with a strange look of half-recognition on his face.

"'Please to let me go, sir,' said I, again struggling to get free.

"'What's your name, boy?' said the old man, without heeding me in the slightest degree.

"'Warren Randall Darrell,' replied I.

"As if he had been struck, the old man loosened his hold and recoiled; and I, seizing the opportunity, darted off, but only to find myself in the grasp of a servant who stood holding the horses.

"'Not so fast, my little shaver,' said he, grinning; 'just you wait till Mr. Randall's done with you.'

"'Mr. Randall!' repeated I, and instantly a sort of conviction flashed across my mind that he might be my grandfather.

"At the same instant the old man approached me, and catching me by the arm, gazed long and steadily into my face, plainly revealed by the light of a street-lamp. I looked up in his agitated face quite as unflinchingly, and so we stood for nearly five minutes, to the great bewilderment of the coachman, who stared first at one and then the other, as if he thought we had both lost our senses.

"'Tell me,' said the old man, after a pause, 'what was your mother's maiden name?'

"'Alice Randall,' said I, my suspicion becoming certainty; 'and you are my grandfather.'

"'What!' he exclaimed, with a start. 'Do you know me? Who told you I was?'

"'No one,' said I; 'but I think so. My grandfather's name is Warren Randall, and that is the name on your door-plate there. I was called after him.'

"'You are right,' said he, in an agitated voice. 'I am your grandfather. My poor Alice! You have her eyes, boy—the same eyes that once made the light of my home. Where—tell me where is she now?'

"'I don't know,' said I, half-sobbing. 'She's dead, I'm afraid—she and Georgia.'

"'Who is Georgia?'

"'My sister.'

"'And your father?' he said, with a darkening brow.

"'Is dead, too; has been dead this long, long time.'

"'And so you are an orphan, and poor and friendless,' he said, speaking as much to himself as to me. 'Poor boy! poor little fellow! Warren, will you come and live with me—with your grandfather?'

"I thought for a moment, and then shook my head.

"'No,' said I, 'I can't. I must find my mother and Georgia.'

"'Where are they?' he said, eagerly. 'I thought you told me they were dead.'

"'I said I didn't know, and I don't. They may be dead, for it is over a year since I saw them last. I was carried away from them by force, and now I am going to seek for them.'

"'You!' said he. 'How can a little friendless boy like you find them? No, no,

Warren, stay with me, and let me search for your mother. I may succeed, but you will starve ere you find them, or be put in prison. Warren you *will* stay?'"

"And you did?" said Georgia.

"And I did. I answered that what he said was true, and that he was far more likely to succeed than I was. That night I slept in a princely home, with servants to come at my call—with every luxury to charm every sense around me. Was not that a sudden change, Georgia, from the miserable quarters of the players?"

"Yes, indeed," said Georgia. "And what change did it make in you? Did affluence spoil you?"

"It might have, if I had stayed long enough there," said Warren, smiling, "for I, with all my perfections—and if you want a list of them just ask Miss Felice Leonard—am not infallible. I gave him my history, and he dispatched a trusty messenger to Burnfield, and upon his return he told me that both my mother and sister were dead. I believed him then, but I have since thought that, finding you provided for, he wished to keep me all to himself, and make me his sole heir.

"I had so long thought, Georgia, that you and my mother were dead that the revelations did not take me by surprise, and though I grieved for awhile, the novelty of everything around me kept my mind from dwelling much on my bereavement. My grandfather told me he intended to send me to school, and, when he died, make me his sole heir, on condition that I would drop the detested name of Darrell and take his. Not being very particular about the matter, I readily consented, and two months afterward I was sent to old Yale, where he himself had been educated, there to be trained in the way I should go.

"Well, Georgia, I remained there four years, and won golden opinions from the big wigs of the institution, and delighted the heart of my kind old grandfather by my progress in the arts and sciences. A letter announcing his sudden death recalled me at last. I hurried back to New York in time to follow him to the grave, and, when the will was read, I found myself sole heir to his almost princely wealth.

"Then I went to Europe and Asia, and saw all the sights, from the pyramids of Egypt down, and wrote a book about my travels, as every one does now who goes three yards from his own vine and fig-tree. Then I came home, and lo! before I have been here three months, I find that my sister, who was dead, comes to life again, and so—*finis*!"

"You should add, 'And they lived happy for ever after,'" said Georgia, smiling, "only, perhaps, it would not be strictly correct. And now that you have found your sister, what do you mean to do with her?"

"Make her mistress of the palatial mansion of the Randalls," said Warren, promptly, "and settle one-half my fortune on her. *That*, Madam Wildair, is my unchangeable intention."

"Oh, Warren, dearest. I will never hear of such a thing!" said Georgia, vehemently.

"Well, if you will excuse me for saying so, I don't care in the least whether you will or not—I shall do it. Not a word now, Mistress Georgia; you will find that you will have to obey your brother, since you have found him, and do for the future exactly as he tells you. Besides, Georgia, Warren Randall's sister shall never go back penniless to her husband," he said, proudly; "he shall find her his equal in wealth, as in everything else."

"Oh, Warren!" she said, with filling eyes.

"Not a word about it now," he said, putting his fingers over her lips; "to-morrow the world shall know you as you really are."

"Warren, listen to me," she said, taking his hand. "Until I meet Richmond again, I intend to keep my *incognito*. Perhaps you may call it an odd fancy, but I really wish it. No one yet knows my secret but Mr. Curtis, Mr. Leonard, and Richmond's brother, and if I wish it they will keep it a secret. Let me still be Miss Randall until he comes."

"But when will he come?" broke in Warren, half impatiently; "who knows? It may be years or—Georgia," he added, suddenly, "suppose we go to *him*, eh? When the mountain will not come to Mahomet, Mahomet must go to the mountain—rather that style of thing, isn't it? What do you say to a trip to France, *ma belle?*"

"Oh, Warren!" she cried, catching her breath, her whole face growing radiant with delight.

"I am answered," he said, gayly; "this day week we start."

"For where, may I ask?" said Mr. Curtis, lounging in. "Your chateau in Spain? or on a wild-goose chase?"

"Something very like it," said Warren, laughing. "We are off to France, in search of one Richmond Wildair, plenipotentiary and ambassador extraordinary to the court of that distant and facetious region."

"Whew!" whistled Mr. Curtis, "I see, says the blind man. What a thing conjugal affection is, to be sure! When do you go?"

"This day week, in the Golden Arrow. And for some inscrutable feminine reason Georgia wishes you to preserve her secret inviolable until she returns. She is still Miss Randall; you understand? You and Mr. Leonard are not to mention she is Richmond Wildair's runaway wife."

"I'm dumb," said Mr. Curtis, shutting his lips as firmly as though they were never to be opened on earth again. "Neither tortures, nor anguish, nor bad pale ale shall tear from this lacerated heart the fearful secret. Are you going to see after that prize of yours to-morrow, Mrs. Wild—gee Whittaker! I mean Miss Randall," said he, dropping his tone of stage agony, and speaking in his natural voice.

"Most decidedly," said Georgia, smiling.

"And then you are going to throw yourself away on our painfully clever friend Wildair again, and leave all your friends here in Gotham to pine away, with tears in their eyes and their fingers in their mouths," said Mr. Curtis, in a lugubrious tone; "it's something I never expected of you, Mrs. Wil—pooh! I mean Miss Randall, and I must say I, for one, never deserved it."

"Mr. Curtis, you—you were in Burnfield since I was," said Georgia, hesitatingly, and coloring deeply; "how was Miss Jerusha and Emily Murray?"

"Well they were both in a state of mind—rather," said Mr. Curtis. "Miss Jerusha flamed up, and blew us all, sky high, in fact raised the ancient Harry, in a way quite appalling to a person of tender nerves—myself, for instance— and gave Richmond what may be called, without exaggeration, particular fits! As for little Emily," said Mr. Curtis, turning red suddenly, "she—she didn't scold anybody, but she cried and took on so that I felt—I felt a sort of all-over as it were—a very peculiar feeling, to use a mild phrase, if you observe."

"Dear little Emily," said Georgia, sighing.

"That's just what I said," said Mr. Curtis, eagerly "but she didn't pay any attention to it. I suppose you know I—I went—I mean I asked—that is I offered—pshaw! what d'ye call it—proposed," said Mr. Curtis, blushing, and squirming uneasily in his chair.

"No, I did not know it," said Georgia, with difficulty repressing a smile.

"But I did though, and she refused me—she did, by Jove!" said Mr. Curtis, dolorously.

"What bad taste the girl must have," said Mr. Randall.

"You're another," said Mr. Curtis, fiercely; "she's no such thing! How dare you insinuate such a thing, Mr. Randall? There never yet was born a man good enough for her; and if you dare to doubt it, I'll be hanged if I don't knock you into the middle of next week—now then!"

Mr. Curtis was as fierce as a Bengal tiger. Mr. Randall threw himself into a chair, and laughed immoderately.

"My dear fellow, I cry you mercy, and most humbly beg Miss Emily Murray's pardon. I look forward some day to being acquainted with her myself, and if I find her all that you say, I shall consider the advisability of making her Mrs. Warren Randall."

"You be—shot!" growled Mr. Curtis, striding savagely up and down. "She's not to be had for the asking, I can tell you; and after refusing *me*, it's not likely she'd have anything to do with you. Mrs. Wildair—oh, darn it!—Miss Randall, I mean, when you see your husband, tell him his mother is very ill, and if he does not hasten home soon he will not see her alive. A precious small loss that would be though," said Mr. Curtis, in parenthesis—"a stiff, sneering, high-and-mighty old virago! Don't see, for my part, what Rich meant by ever having such a mother!"

One week later, Warren Randall and his sister were on board the Golden Arrow, *en route* for Merrie England. Fair breezes soon wafted them to the white cliffs of that "right little, tight little" island, and Georgia for the first time set foot on a foreign shore.

But now, in her impatience to rejoin and be reconciled to her husband, she would consent to make no stay; so they immediately crossed the channel into France, and posted at once for Paris. And there the first news they heard from the American consul was that Mr. Wildair had left a fortnight before for St. Petersburg.

It was a disappointment to both, a bitter one to Georgia, and Warren felt it for her sake. To follow him was the first impulse of both, and they immediately started for the Russian capital.

But fortune still inclined to be capricious, and to doom Georgia's new-found patience to another trial. Mr. Wildair's political mission required dispatch, and a few days before their arrival he had gone. From the minister they learned that his first destination was a return to Paris, from thence to Baden Baden, and it was more than probable he would visit London and then return home.

"Well, Georgia," said Warren, "you see fate is against you, and has doomed you to disappointment. Nothing remains now but to make the best of a bad bargain and start on a regular sight-seeing tour, and 'do' Europe, as Curtis would call it. And, after all, perhaps it is for the best you did not meet him. He is now rapidly rising to political distinction, and his meeting with you might distract his thoughts, and would certainly keep him from entering heart and soul into the political arena as he does now. Besides, having lost you for so long, he will know how to value you all the more when you do return. Come, Georgia, what difference, after all, will a year or two make in a life? Don't think of returning now, but let us continue our tour."

"I am at your disposal, my dear Warren," said Georgia, with a smile and a sigh. "As you say, after all, a year more or less will not make a great deal of difference, and I am particularly anxious to continue our tour. Therefore, *mon frere*, do with me as you will."

With an account of that tour, dearest reader, I will not weary your patience— already, I fear, too much taxed. All "grand tours" are alike—the same sights are seen, the same incidents occur, the same scenery and pictures are looked at and gone into raptures over, and the same people are met everywhere. The summer was spent traveling slowly through France and Germany, and the winter was passed in Italy. Early in the spring they visited Switzerland; and, almost imperceptibly, two years passed away.

And where, meanwhile, was he whose willful blindness and haughty pride had brought on his own desolation? Where was he, widowed in fate though not in fact?—where was Richmond Wildair?

Home again, drowning thought and his intolerable remorse in the giddy whirl of political life. He had returned in time to close his mother's eyes, and hear her last words—a wild appeal for Georgia, the wronged Georgia, to forgive her. And then, with all the power of his mighty intellect, he had given himself up to the life he had chosen, that life for which Heaven and nature had so well qualified him—a great legislator—and that life became to him wife, and home, and all. Already he had taken his seat in the Senate, and, though perhaps the youngest there, stood foremost among them all, crowned with his lofty genius as with a diadem. The knowing ones whispered that at the next election he was certain of becoming Governor of his native State, and certainly, as far as popularity went, there could be little doubt of it. Never was there a young statesman, perhaps, who in so short a time had risen so rapidly to distinction, and won such "golden opinions" from all sorts of people.

Of almost all concerning his wife he was profoundly ignorant. One thing he knew, and that was that she, and no other, had painted the wonderful picture about which the artistic world was still raving. Hagar, in her mighty grief and dark despair, the wild, woeful, anguished form writhing yet majestic in her great wrongs, was Georgia as he had seen her last. And, as if to make

247

conviction doubly sure, the picture bore her initials. One consolation it brought to him, and that was that she still lived. Every effort in human power he had made to discover her, but all he could succeed in learning was that a tall, dark, majestic-looking lady, bearing the name of Miss Randall, had received the prize; but nothing more was known of her. Then he sought for her brother, and heard he had gone to Europe, but whether alone or not he could not discover. A score of times within the day would Dick Curtis be on the point of telling him all, until the recollection of his promise would stop him, and he would inwardly fume at not having made a mental reservation at the time. Still, these tortures of doubt, and uncertainty, and hope, and despair served Richmond just exactly right, he argued, and would teach him, if he ever did find Georgia, to treat her better for the future.

And so, while Georgia was roaming over the world, Richmond was rising to still higher fame and eminence in his native land; and neither dreamed how each had searched, and sought, and sorrowed in vain for the other.

CHAPTER XXIV.

AT LAST!

"And there was light around her brow,
 A holiness in those dark eyes,
Which showed, though wandering earthward now,
 Her spirit's home was in the skies."

o years had passed and gone.

It was drawing toward sunset of a clear, bright, breezy day, when a crowd of people "might have been seen," and were seen, too, hurrying down to one of the wharves of B——, to watch the arrival of the steamer from Europe. Throngs of people who had friends on board came trooping down, and watched with eager eyes the stately vessel as it smoked and puffed its way, like an apoplectic alderman, to the shore.

Among these lounged a young man, good-looking and fashionably dressed, and evidently got up regardless of expense. There was a certain air of self-complacency about him, as he stroked a pair of most desirable curling whiskers, that said, as plainly as words, he was "somebody," and knew it. Another young republican, puffing a cigar, stood beside him, and both were watching, with the careless nonchalance of sovereigns in their own right, the throng of foreigners that stood on the steamer's deck.

"A crowd there—rather!" remarked the hero of the cigar, as he fastidiously held it between his finger and thumb and knocked the ashes off the end. "Our European brethren have arrived in time to see the elephant to good advantage. Young America will be out in great force to-night."

"To cheer the new governor—ye-es," drawled the other, as he, too, lighted a cigar, and began smoking like a living Vesuvius.

"What a thing it is to be the people's favorite—a man of the people, that style of thing, you know—isn't it, Curtis?" said the first speaker.

"I believe you!" said Mr. Curtis, emphatically, for our old friend it was. "It is the sovereign people's pleasure to go mad about their favorite just now, and, like spoiled children, they must be humored. What a thing the mob is, to be sure! They would shout as heartily and with as good a will if Wildair were to be hung to-night as inaugurated. Since the days when they shouted 'Crucify Him! crucify Him! Release unto us Barrabas!' they have remained unchanged."

"I hope you don't mean to insinuate that there is any resemblance between the Jewish malefactor and the American governor—eh, Curtis?" said his friend, laughing.

"By no means, Captain Arlingford. Wildair deserves his popularity; he is a great statesman, a real friend of his admirers, the people, and with genius enough to steer the whole republic himself. He has fought his way up; he has fought for equal rights, liberty, fraternity, equality—the French dodge, you know—and deserves to be what he is, the people's idol. Never in this good Yankee town was a new governor greeted so enthusiastically; never did the mob shout themselves hoarse with such a right good will. By Jove! I envied him to-day, as he stood on the balcony of the hotel, with his hat off, while the sea of human beings below shouted and shouted, until they could shout no longer. It was a reception fit for a king; and never did a king look more kingly and noble than at that moment of triumph did he."

Captain Arlingford laughed.

"Whew! there's enthusiasm for you! My sober, steady-headed friend, Dick Curtis, starting off in this manner, and longing for public popularity! I confess I should like to have witnessed his triumphal entry to-day though. I have heard that the ladies absolutely buried him alive in the showers of bouquets from the windows."

"Didn't they!" said Mr. Curtis laughing at the recollection. "As his secretary, I sat in the carriage with him, and, 'pon my honor, I was half smothered under the load of fragrant favors. Such a waving of cambric handkerchiefs, too, and how the crowd doffed their hats and hurrahed! It excites me even yet to think of it; but there sat Wildair touching his chapeau, and bowing right and left, 'with that easy grace that wins all hearts,' to quote our friend and your admirer, Miss Harper, a little."

"That last bill about the people's rights did the business for him," said Captain Arlingford, meditatively; "what a strong case he made out in their favor, and what an excitement it created! Well, it's a famous thing to be clever, after all; I knew it was in him, but it might never have come out so forcibly, had it not been for that loss of his two years ago. And it appears *she* is a genius too. To think she should have painted that blood-chilling picture of Hagar, and found a brother in that poet, Randall. Don't things turn up strangely, Curtis? I

250

wonder where she has gone, and if she will ever come back."

"Don't know! Like as not," said Mr. Curtis, sententiously.

"Splendid-looking girl she was, wasn't she, Curtis?" continued Arlingford, pursuing his own train of thought.

"Magnificent eyes, a step like an empress, and the smile of an angel."

"Come, don't draw it quite so steep, my gallient saileur boy," said Curtis; "recollect you're speaking of another man's wife, and that man not a common mortal either, but the Governor of B—— and future President of these Benighted States. Besides, what would Miss Harper say?"

"Miss Harper be—hanged!" exclaimed Arlingford, with such impatient vehemence that Curtis laughed; "that's enough about her. Are you going to the inauguration ball to-night?"

"Of course—what a question! Do you think they could have a ball fit to be seen without the presence of the irresistible, the fascinating Richard Curtis, Esq., to keep it moving? Do you think any lady as is a lady would enjoy herself if I was absent? Echo answers, 'Of course, they wouldn't;' so don't harrow my feelings again by such another question."

"Well, I see humanity and vanity are not among your failings. I suppose all the *elite* of the city will be there?"

"You had better believe it. The *creme de la creme* of B——. All the beauty, and wit, and gallantry of the city, as the newspapers have it. I have engaged with the editor of the *Sky Rocket* to write him an account of the sayings and doings, for a 'consideration,' as the delicate phrase goes, which, being translated from the original Hebrew, means that he will puff our party on every occasion and no occasion, and if you don't see 'among the guests was the gallant young Captain A——, U. S. N., who paid during the evening the most marked attention to the lovely and accomplished Miss H——, whom it is whispered he is about to lead to the hymeneal altar——' Hello! stop that! I say, Arlingford, don't choke a fellow!"

"Confound you!" said Captain Arlingford, catching him by the collar, and fairly shaking the cigar out of his mouth; "will you forever continue harping on that string? I say, let's get out of this; I hate to make one in a crowd."

"No; wait," said Curtis, laughing and adjusting his ruffled plumage. "I want to see if there is any one I know on board the steamer; I expect some friends. Here come the passengers. What a wretched, sea-sick, sea-green-looking set. The amount of contempt I have for the ocean is something appalling."

"You had better mind how you express it before me," said Captain Arlingford, decidedly. "I—but look there, Curtis, at that lady! Oh, ye gods and little fishes! what a Juno! Eh? how? what? By the Lord Harry, Curtis!" he exclaimed, springing up excitedly, as the lady in question turned her face fully toward them; "if ever I saw Mrs. Georgia Wildair in my life, there she stands!"

"Where? where? where?" fairly shouted Curtis, catching him by the arm, and staring round in an excitement far surpassing his own. "Where? which? when?"

"Whither? why? wherefore?" said Arlingford, laughing in spite of his surprise and excitement. "*There*, man alive! don't you see? That tall lady in black on the deck beside that intensely foreign-looking young gentleman. Why, where are your eyes? don't you see?"

"I see! I see! It's she! Hip, hip, hurrah!" shouted Mr. Curtis, waving his hat, and electrifying the crowd around him, and then, before Captain Arlingford knew what he was about, he darted off, played in and out through the crowd, dug his elbows into the ribs of all around him, and so forced his way aboard the steamer, amid the stifled shrieks and groans, and curses of his victims.

"That's what you call a summary proceeding," said Captain Arlingford, laughing; "what a living galvanic battery that fellow is—a broad-clothed barrel of gunpowder; touch him and off he goes! Well, here's to follow his example."

So saying, but in a less impetuous manner, he made his way through the throng to where stood a lady, "beautiful exceedingly," and dressed entirely in black, after the fashion of the Spanish Creoles, for one of whom, in her dark, rich beauty, she might easily have been mistaken.

"Mrs. Wildair! Good gracious, Mrs. Wildair, how *do* you do?" exclaimed a breathless voice. "To think that you should come this day of all days! Oh, scissors! Well, I *am* glad to see you! Upon my word and honor, I am."

"Mr. Curtis!" exclaimed the lady, with a little cry of surprise and delight. "Why, what an unexpected pleasure to meet *you* here! Dear Mr. Curtis, how glad I am to see you!"

"So am I, just as glad!" said Mr. Curtis, seizing the little hand she extended, and wringing it until she winced. "Good gracious! to think of it. How *do* you do? Well, if it isn't the most unexpected—to think that you should come home to-day of all days! Good gra——— Hey? what now?"

A vigorous slap on the shoulder that staggered him, as well it might, had jerked the last words out of him, and turning fiercely round, he saw the laughing face of the lady's companion turned toward him.

"Why, Curtis, old fellow, have you a greeting for no one but Georgia? Come, you have shook her hand long enough; try mine now."

"Randall, my boy, how goes it? Well, I *am* glad, and no mistake. Good gracious! what the mischief kept you so long in those barbarous foreign parts, anyhow?"

"Don't know, really," said Mr. Randall, laughing at his vehemence; "the time passed almost imperceptibly. But you—what brings you here? I thought you were in New York."

"Well, I am not, though you mayn't believe it. Hello! Guess who this is, Mrs. Wildair?"

"Captain Arlingford!" exclaimed Georgia, delightedly, holding out her hand; then, as the recollections of the past arose, the color mounted for an instant to her very temples.

"Yes, marm; nothing shorter," said Curtis, rubbing his hands gleefully. "Jerusalem! only to think of it! Well, the astonishing way things *will* persist in turning up! Just to think of it. Why, it's like a thing in a play or a novel. Now, isn't it, Arlingford?"

"What! our coming home?" said Randall. "What do you see so extraordinary about that, Curtis?"

"No, it is not that," said Mr. Curtis, chuckling; "it's the remarkable coincidence of your coming to-day of all days—not you, but your sister. There, don't ask me now, everybody's looking—a set of ill-mannered snipes. Arlingford, run and call a coach, there's a good boy, and I'll tell Mrs. Wildair all about it. Good gracious! if it isn't the funniest thing!"

Mr. Curtis' excitement and delight, as he danced up and down, rubbing his hands and chuckling, were so irresistible that all three, after watching him an instant, burst into an immoderate fit of laughter, and, beholding his look of dismayed surprise, laughed until the tears stood in their eyes.

"Eh! why, what the—— what are you laughing at? Don't act so, don't; everybody's looking, and they'll think you're crazy," said Mr. Curtis, imploringly. "Wait a minute, I'll call a coach myself—you just hold on."

Off darted Mr. Curtis, leaving them still laughing and unable to stop, and ere five minutes he was back, and whipped them off like a living whirlwind— pushed them into a coach, jumped in after, and banged the door.

"Dixon's Hotel!" he bawled to the driver, and away they rattled over the pavement.

"Now we're comfortable," said Mr. Curtis, surveying them complacently, "and, only for me, you might have stood there all night, for coaches are in demand, and hardly to be got for love or money. Oh, Jehosaphat! just to think of it! why it's *droll!*" said Mr. Curtis, thrusting his hands into his pockets, and, as the absurdity of it struck him for the first time he leaned back in the carriage, and burst into a peal of laughter that was perfectly terrific, and from the effect of which he did not recover until they reached the hotel.

"It's lucky for you, in more ways than one, that you met me," said Mr. Curtis, as he got out and offered Georgia his arm, "for the city's full, and you wouldn't have got a room in a hotel from one end of it to the other—no, not if you went on your two blessed, bended knees and prayed for it. Here, these rooms were engaged for the governor and his suite, and this is mine, and is quite at your disposal, Mrs. Wildair."

"But, oh! Mr. Curtis, I cannot think of depriving you——"

"There—not a word! not a word!" said Mr. Curtis, briskly, as he ushered them into a sumptuously furnished apartment. "I'll camp with somebody else. And now the very first thing I want you to do is to dress and come to the ball to-night."

"The ball! What ball?" said Georgia, in surprise.

"Why the inauguration ball, to be sure! Oh, I forgot you did not know. Well, then, the astonishing news is, that Mr. Richmond Wildair has this day entered B—— as its governor! Now don't faint, Mrs. Wildair, because I won't understand your case. And, as usual, there is to be a ball, and I want you to come and be presented to his excellency the governor."

Georgia had no intention of fainting. A flush of pride, and triumph, and delight, lit up her face, and, with the step of a queen, she arose and paced up and down the room.

"And so he has been elected," said Mr. Randall, thoughtfully. "I knew he would rise rapidly."

"What says Georgia—will you go?"

"Yes," she said, with a radiant smile.

"Hooray!" exclaimed Mr. Curtis; "Mrs. Wildair, you're a brick! Maybe Mr. Wildair won't be astonished some, if not more, and a *leetle* delighted! It's getting dark fast, and I ought to be off to the executive mansion; but I'll let etiquette go be hanged for once, and wait for you. You had better have tea in your own room, Mrs. W.; sha'n't I ring? It will take you two or three hours to dress, you know—it always does take a lady that long, I believe. Here, my man, supper for four up here; be spry now."

It was impossible to be serious and watch Curtis, as he flew round impetuously, asking a thousand questions in a breath about what they had seen abroad, and then interrupting them in the middle of the answer to tell them something about Richmond, that had not the slightest bearing on the matter.

In his excitement he found it impossible to sit still, but kept flying round the room, rubbing his hands in an ecstacy of delight, and laughing uproariously as he thought of the surprise in store for the young governor. During supper he monopolized the whole conversation himself, and kept the others in fits of laughter, while his look of innocent astonishment at their mirth would, as Captain Arlingford said, "make a horn-bug laugh."

After tea the gentlemen took themselves off to dress, and Georgia's maid, who had arrived, remained to superintend her mistress' toilet. Those two years of absence had restored the bright bloom to Georgia's dark face, but the old flashing light had left her dark eyes, and in its place was a sweetness, subdued, gentle, and far more lovely. The haughtily curling lips were tender and placid, the queenly brow calm and serene, the dark, beautiful face almost seraphic with its look of inward peace. Oh, far more sweet, and tender, and lovable was the Georgia of to-day than the haughty, fiery, passionate Georgia of other years! As she stood before the mirror, in her rich, showy robe of gold-colored satin, under rare old point lace, with diamonds flashing in rivers of light around her curving throat, flashing in her small ears, gleaming in her midnight hair, and glittering and scintillating like sparks of fire on her rounded arms and small dark fingers, she looked every inch a princess, a "queen of noble Nature's crowning."

And so thought the gentlemen as they entered, in full dress—in "glorious array," as Mr. Curtis pompously said—if one might judge by her brother's look of pride and pleasure, Captain Arlingford's glance of intense admiration, and Mr. Curtis' burst of rapture.

"Why, you're looking splendid, absolutely splendid, you know; something quite stunning, Mrs. Wildair! Ah! I should like to be as good-looking as you. I never saw you looking so well before. Now, did you, Randall?"

"Georgia is looking her best," said Mr. Randall, smiling.

"Looking her best! I guess so! It's astonishing how handsome women can make themselves when they choose. Now, I might try till I was black in the face, and still I would be the old two-and-sixpence at the end. I wish I knew the secret. Suppose we go now; we're behind time three quarters of an hour as it is. The carriage is waiting, Mrs. Wildair."

"I am quite at your service, Mr. Curtis," said Georgia, flinging a shawl over her shoulders, and trying to smile, but her heart was throbbing so rapidly that she leaned against the table for a moment, sick and faint.

Who, when about to meet a dear friend from whom she had been long separated, does not feel a sort of dread mingling with her pleasure, lest she should find him changed, altered, cold, different from what she had known him in other years?

So felt Georgia as she took her seat in the carriage and was whirled as rapidly as the crowded state of the streets would admit toward the executive mansion. Her color came and went, now that the crisis was at hand, and the loud beating of her heart could almost be heard, as she lay back among the cushions, trembling with excitement and conflicting emotions.

A gay scene the streets presented that night. Never had a governor received such an ovation as had this young demi-god of the dear public. Every house was illuminated from attic to basement; flags were flying; arches had been erected for him to pass under, as if it were the reception of a prince. Thousands of gayly dressed people thronged the pavements, bands were out playing triumphant marches, and an immense crowd congregated around the governor's house, watching the different carriages as they passed, bearing their freight of magnificently dressed ladies on their way to the ball. But not to behold them was the dense crowd waiting, but to catch a glimpse of the young governor when he should arrive.

As the carriage conveying our party approached the arched gate-way of the executive mansion it was stopped, blocked up by a crowd of other carriages. The people had pressed before, and it was in vain they tried to get on. Drivers swore, and shouted, and vociferated, the mob laughed and bandied jokes, gentlemen in commanding tones gave orders that were either unheard or impossible to be obeyed, and a perfect Babel of confusion reigned.

"Come, this won't do, you know," said Mr. Curtis, "we must get on somehow. Here, you fellows," he said, thrusting his head out of the window, "get out of the way, I want to pass. I'm the governor's secretary, and must get on."

A derisive laugh from a group near followed, and a voice in the crowd inquired anxiously whether his mother had many more like him, and also whether that venerable lady was aware that he was out.

Mr. Curtis showed symptoms of getting into a passion at this, but his voice was drowned in a cry from a band of loafers near, who shouted:

"We want to see the governor! You won't pass till we see the governor!"

There was a plain dark carriage right in front of them, and now the glass was let down, and a clear, commanding voice, that rang out above all the din, calmly said:

"I am the governor! Stand aside, my friends, and let me pass!"

That voice! Georgia half-sprang from her seat, and then fell back.

Such a cry as arose—such a mighty shout, at the voice of their favorite! The crowd swayed to and fro in their struggles to get near. The driver whipped up his horses, a passage was cleared, and carriage after carriage passed on and entered the crowded court-yard.

"Hurrah for Wildair! Hurrah for Wildair! Hurrah! Hurrah! HURRAH for Wildair!" shouted the crowd, till the welkin rang.

"Hurrah for Richmond Wildair—the MAN OF THE PEOPLE!" exclaimed a loud voice, and instantly the cry was taken up, and "Hurrah! hurrah! hurrah!" rang out like the roar of the sea.

And now on the balcony, clearly revealed in the light of myriads of lamps, stood the kingly form of Richmond Wildair himself, his princely brow uncovered, his calm, commanding face looking down on them, as a king might on his subjects.

And then once again arose the mighty shout, "Hurrah for Wildair! Hurrah for Wildair! Hurrah for the Friend of the People!" until, hoarse with shouting, the swaying multitude relapsed into silence.

And then, clear, calm, and earnest, arose the commanding voice of their favorite, as he addressed them.

A dead silence fell on that great crowd the moment his first word was heard. Short, and well chosen, and to the point, was his speech; and hats flew off, and again and again the hoarse cheers of his listeners interrupted him. Having thanked them for the enthusiastic reception they had given him, he begged them to disperse for the present, and then, having bowed once more, he retired.

With three times three for the speaker they obeyed, and, save a few who remained to watch the brilliantly illuminated mansion and listen to the music of the band, the crowd soon dispersed through the thronged streets.

"There's popularity for you!" said Mr. Curtis, as with Georgia leaning on his arm he entered the brilliant ball-room, blazing with lights and crowded with splendidly attired ladies. "I should admire to see them cheering me that way. How would it sound, I wonder? Hurrah for Curtis! That's not bad, is it, Mrs. Wildair?"

She did not reply—she did not hear him. Her eyes were wandering through the glittering throng in search of one, the "bright, particular star" of the evening. Yes, there he was, at the upper end of the room, surrounded by a throng of the most distinguished there, bowing, and shaking hands, and smiling, and chatting with the ladies. She strove to calm herself and listen to what her companion was saying, but in vain, until the mention of Richmond's name attracted her attention.

"I won't bring you over among that crowd," he was saying; "I'll wait till he's a little disengaged. They'll begin dancing presently, and then the coast will be clear. Just see how everybody is looking at you and whispering to one another. I guess they would like to know who you are just now. Ah! what would you give to know?" said Mr. Curtis, making a grimace at the crowd.

And now an audible whisper might have been heard among the throng:

"Who is she? oh, who is she?—that beautiful girl with Mr. Curtis. I never saw her before."

"Nor I. Nor I. Who can she be?" ran around the room. "How *distingue* she is! how surpassingly beautiful! and how magnificently dressed! Oh, I must get an introduction. See, he is bringing her up now to present her to the governor. I'll ask him to introduce me. She is certainly destined to be the belle of the evening."

Meantime two or three quadrilles had formed, and the group surrounding the governor had thinned, and he was left as much alone as he was likely to be during the evening. Leaning against a marble pillar, he stood talking to a starred and ribboned foreigner, and when Curtis approached with Georgia, he was so engrossed with the topic they were discussing that he did not observe him until his voice fell on her ear.

"Mrs. Wildair, your excellency!" said Mr. Curtis, in the most emphatic of voices, standing right before him.

He started up, staggered back, grew deadly pale, and grasped the marble pillar for support.

Yes, there before him, radiant in her beauty, with serene brow and calm smile, stood his long-lost wife—face to face at last!

CHAPTER XXV.

"AFTER TEARS AND WEEPING, HE POURETH IN JOYFULNESS."

"Do not spurn me in my prayer,
    For this wand'ring ever longer, evermore,
Hath overworn me,
    And I know not on what shore
I may rest from my despair."

BROWNING.

om his pale lips dropped one word:

"Georgia!"

"Dearest Richmond," she said, looking up in his face with her radiant eyes.

"Oh, Georgia, my wronged wife, can you ever forgive me?" he cried, passionately.

"I have nothing to forgive, my husband," she said, sweetly. "It is I who should be forgiven."

"Oh, Georgia, where have you been? Do I really see you, or do I dream? So often have I dreamed you were restored, and woke to find it a dream. Is this a delusion like the rest?"

"Shake hands, and see."

She held out hers with a smile, and he took it, and gazed into her face with a doubtful, troubled look.

"Yes, it is Georgia; it must be she; the same, yet so different. You never looked like this in the days gone past, Georgia."

"I have been new-born since," she said, with a serene smile. "You shall learn all soon, Richmond. Do you know I have come to stay now?"

"See here, Mr. Wildair," said Curtis, giving him a poke "don't you keep looking so; everybody's staring and whispering, and our friend here,

Whiskerando," pointing to the starred foreigner, "looks as if he thought he had got into a lunatic asylum by mistake. You take Georgia—I mean Mrs. Wildair—off into that conservatory, for instance, where you can stare at her to your heart's content, and learn all the particulars since she cut her lucky—I mean since she ran off and left you in the lurch. Go; I know it will take you an hour, at least, to settle matters, and beg each other's pardon, and smoke the pipe of peace, and so on; and, meantime, as it is necessary the company should know who it is, I'll whisper it as a great secret into the ear of the first lady I meet, and get her to promise not to tell. There! vanish!"

Passing his hand across his eyes, as if to dispel a mist, Richmond offered her his arm and led her toward the conservatory, followed by the wondering eyes of the guests.

But Mr. Curtis had no need to tell. Miss Harper was there, and recognized her with a suppressed shriek; and in an instant after, like wild-fire, it ran through the room that this dark, beautiful stranger was the mysterious wife of Mr. Wildair.

Dancing was no longer thought of. Everybody flocked around Mr. Curtis, and such an avalanche of questions as was showered upon him human ears never listened to before. Had he possessed a thousand tongues he could hardly have answered one-half. But he did not try to answer them. Mr. Dick Curtis was a sensible young man, and never attempted impossibilities; so he only folded his arms and looked around him complacently, listening with the profoundest attention to all, but answering never a word; until, at last, when quite tired and breathless, there was a pause, he lifted up his voice and spoke:

"Ladies and gentlemen: On the present interesting and facetious occasion allow me to say—(ahem!)—to say——"

[Here a voice in the crowd, that of Mr. Henry Gleason, if you remember that young gentleman, reader, interrupted with, "You *have* said it! Push along, old boy!"]

"To say," pursued Mr. Curtis, casting a withering glance at the speaker, "as that very polite youth, whoever he may be, has falsely informed you I have already said, that Mr. Wildair, his excellency," said Mr. Curtis, with a dignified wave of his hand, "has commissioned me to say—I beg your pardon, sir; you're standing on that lady's dress—to say that the lady you beheld this evening is his wife, who has been indulging in a little trip to Europe with his—(ahem!)—full approbation, while he was seeing after the great, glorious, and immortal Union in Washington, and scattering political oats—to use a figure of speech—before that tremendous bird, the American eagle; and the lady arriving quite promiscuously, if I may be allowed so strong an expression, he was slightly surprised to see her—(ahem!)—as you all perceived, and has just gone to have a little friendly chat with her over family matters and kitchen cabinet affairs generally. And so, ladies and gentlemen," concluded Mr. Curtis, laying his kid glove on his heart and bowing gracefully, "I hope his temporary absence will not plunge you into *too* deep affliction, or cause you to feel too dreadfully cut up, but that you will set seriously to work and enjoy yourselves, while I represent his excellency, and during his absence receive your homage. And to conclude, in the words of Demosthenes, the great Latin poet, who beautifully observes, '*E Pluribus Unum*,' a remark which I hope none of you will consider personal, for I solemnly assure you it was not meant to be, as I haven't the remotest idea of what it means. If any further particulars are needed," said Mr. Curtis, drawing himself up, and casting another glance of withering scorn upon Mr. Henry Gleason, "I must refer you to the young gentleman who was good enough to interrupt me, and who stands there now, a mark for the finger of scorn to poke fun at. Ladies and gentleman, I have spoken! Long may it wave."

And with this last "neat and appropriate" quotation, Mr. Curtis bowed and blushingly retired, leaving his audience in convulsions of laughter, for his unspeakably droll look and solemn tone no pen can describe. It had the good effect, however, of diverting their attention from Mr. Wildair and his wife for the present; and Mr. Curtis the center of a laughing group, while his own face maintained its expression of most doleful gravity, became for the time being the lion of the hour. With edifying meekness did Mr. Curtis stand, "his blushing honors thick upon him," until getting rather tired of it, he made a signal to the band to strike up, and selecting Miss Arlingford for his partner, a quadrille was formed and dancing commenced with real earnestness, and the business of the evening might be said to have begun.

But when an hour passed and the lady whose *entree* had created such a sensation did not appear, impatient glances began to be cast toward the conservatory, and petulant whispers to circulate, and pouting lips wondered why they did not come. In vain Mr. Curtis was "funny;" his popularity was waning as fast as it had risen, and it was all a waste of ammunition. His jokes were unattended to, his puns were unlaughed at, his most dolorous looks had no effect on the risibles of any, except those who had a *very* keen sense of the ludicrous. At last, in disgust at the fickleness of public favor, he got dignified and imposing, and *that* had the effect of making sundry compressed lips smile right out loud, but it is uncertain whether even this would have lasted any time had not, suddenly, Richmond Wildair appeared with his wife leaning on his arm.

In an instant a profound hush of expectation reigned throughout the room; the music instantaneously stopped; the dancers one and all paused, and every eye was bent upon them. A low, respectful murmur of admiration ran round the room at her queen-like beauty, but it lasted only an instant, and all was again still.

"My friends," said the clear, powerful voice that a short time before had dispersed the surging crowd, "this lady, as you are all probably aware, is my wife. There is not one here who has not heard a thousand vague, floating rumors why we were separated, and now I feel it necessary to say a few words of explanation, and silence the tongue of scandal forever. A misunderstanding, slight and unimportant at first, such as will arise at times in all families, was the cause. No blame, not the faintest shadow of blame, attaches to this lady; if blame there be, it solely belongs to me. A mutual explanation and a perfect reconciliation have ensued, and if any one for the future shall canvass the motives which caused us for a brief time to part, I will consider that person my willful enemy. Ladies and gentlemen, let this pleasant but unexpected incident not interfere with the amusements of the evening, and as example is better than precept, I shall join you. Come, Georgia."

He motioned to the musicians, and the dancers again formed, with Mr. and Mrs. Wildair at their head. And then, when the quadrille was ended, all came flocking round to be presented to his beautiful wife, whose Juno-like beauty and grace was the theme of every tongue. And for the remainder of the evening "all went merry as a marriage bell." If anything were wanting to add *eclat* to the inauguration of the new governor this supplied it, and every one grew perfectly enthusiastic about the gifted young statesman and his beautiful wife. So romantic and mysterious as it all was, "just like something in a play or a novel," as Mr. Curtis said, that the excitement it created was perfectly unheard of, and when the ball broke up and the company dispersed, in the "wee sma' hours ayont the twal," they even forgot they were sleepy and tired, and talked away of the unexpected *denouement*, and electrified their friends when they got home with the wonderful news.

"And now, Georgia," said Richmond, "tell me what has changed you so. I can scarcely tell how it is, but it seems as if you were the Georgia I once knew etherealized—the spiritual essence of Georgia Darrell; as if you had cast off a slough and stepped forth radiant, serene, seraphic."

"Flatterer!" said Georgia, smiling, yet serious, too. "But oh, Richmond! I fear you will be angry when I tell you."

"Angry at anything that has made you just what *I* wanted, just what *I* tried to make you and failed! Not I, Georgia. Tell me what elixir of happiness and inward joy have you found."

"One without price, and yet one free to all—to the king and to the beggar alike."

"And yet hitherto it has been beyond my reach. Tell me what it is, sweet wife, that I may drink and live, too."

"Oh, Richmond, if you would—if you *only* would!" she said, catching her breath.

"Why should I not? Name it, Georgia."

"It is called *Faith*, Richmond."

He looked up reverentially, and his face was very grave.

"I think I know; and yet, hitherto it has been only a word to me. I have seen it personified in two—in your little friend Emily, and in—"

He paused and his face worked.

"In whom, Richmond?"

"In Charley. Oh, Charley! oh, my brother!" he cried, in passionate tones as he began pacing rapidly up and down.

The irrepressible cry reminded Georgia of that other day long ago when he had received the letter in which he learned all. At the mention of that name, Georgia too rose, pale and trembling, from her seat.

"And have you seen him? Oh, Richmond! have you seen him?"

"Yes," he said, hoarsely.

"And where is he? Richmond—oh, Richmond, do not look so! Charley, your brother—where is he, Richmond?"

"In heaven, Georgia."

She fell back in her seat, and covered her face with her hands.

"Dead! Oh, Charley! and I not there!" she cried, while her tears fell fast.

"Weep not, Georgia," said Richmond, gently removing her hands; "his death was the death of the just. May my last end be like unto his."

But still she wept hot, gushing tears that would not be stayed—tears that fell, not wildly, but that came from the heart, and were sanctified to the memory of the early dead. At last—

"Blessed are the dead who die in the Lord," she softly murmured, lifting her pale face; "God be merciful to his soul! Dear Charley!"

"He died like a saint, Georgia; he expired like a child falling asleep in his mother's arms, with a smile on his lips; death had no terror for him."

"Were you with him, Richmond?"

"Yes—thank God! Oh, Georgia, I had hardened my heart against him, and yet when I would pass him on the street—I did often pass him, Georgia—every feeling in my heart would be stirred, and no words can tell how I would yearn for him, my own, my only brother. I saw he was dying day by day, and yet pride—that curse, that bane that has dogged me like an evil spirit from childhood up—would not let me step over the barrier I myself had raised, and sue for forgiveness. At last came the news that he was sick unto death, and then I could hold out no longer. I went, Georgia—went in time to hear him forgive me, and to see him die. Oh, Georgia, I shall never forget it—never! Oh, Charley, my gay, thoughtless, light-hearted brother! to think you should be lying in that far-off church-yard, cold and dead."

"Grieve not, my husband," said Georgia, earnestly, as she laid her hand on his, "but look forward to a happy meeting in heaven. And now of others— your mother, Richmond?"

"Is dead, too. Oh, Georgia, she wronged you. Can you ever forgive her?"

"Yes, as freely and fully as I hope to be forgiven. May she rest in peace! And your cousin, Richmond."

She smiled slightly, and Richmond met her bright glance with a sort of honest shame.

"I feel like going down on my knees to you, Georgia, when *that* name is mentioned. She is well—or was when I saw her last—and safely married."

"Indeed! To whom, pray?"

Richmond laughed.

"Do you remember Mr. Lester, of foppish memory, who made one of that party to Richmond House two years ago—'Aw, weally such a boah'"—and Richmond mimicked him to perfection.

"What a shame!" said Georgia, laughing; "of course I remember him. Is it possible she has married that little dandy?"

"That she has, and a precious life she leads him, if all Curtis says be true, for I never go there myself. The gray mare in that stable is decidedly the better horse."

"So I should imagine. But where is Miss Reid? Mr. Lester used to be tender in that quarter, if I remember right."

"Oh, yes: but she married Gleason—Lieutenant Gleason, you know. That gallant officer proposed, and Miss Reid found it too much trouble to refuse, so she became Mrs. Gleason the second."

"Well, I wish them joy, all. How strangely things turn out in this world, don't they, Richmond?"

"Why, yes," said Richmond, laughingly, "rather so—your finding that unexpected brother, for instance. But you don't ask for your old friends in Burnfield—have you forgotten them, Georgia?"

"Forgotten them! Oh, Richmond."

"Well, don't look so reproachfully; you know I didn't mean it. You want to go and see them, I suppose?"

"Oh, indeed I do. Dear Miss Jerusha, and dear little Emily, and——"

"Dear little Betsey Periwinkle," interposed Richmond.

"Yes; just so," said Georgia, resolutely; "a really good friend of mine was Betsey, and very intimate we were. Yes, I want to see them all; when will you take me there, Richmond?"

"In one week from this, Georgia; I cannot get away before; and then, with your brother, we will make a pilgrimage to Burnfield, and you can look once more at the 'auld hoose at hame.' You will have to go down on your knees and intercede for me with Miss Jerusha, or she will never forgive me for the way I behaved to her darling."

"Oh, how I long to go back there again! Now that the time is near, I feel twice as impatient as I did before. A whole week! I wonder if it will ever pass."

But it did pass, and another, too, and busy weeks they were with the governor and his lady. The nine days' wonder of her appearance had scarcely yet passed away when Mr. and Mrs. Wildair and Mr. Randall left B——, en route for the little "one-horse" town of Burnfield.

A fairer day never came out of the sky than the one that heralded Georgia's return to Burnfield—dear old Burnfield! fairer in her eyes than Florence, the beautiful, brighter than Rome, the imperial, for her home was there. Nothing was changed. There stood Richmond House, the pride and boast of the town still, there was the pleasant home of Emily Murray, there was the old schoolhouse where her stormy girlhood had been spent.

As she gazed, she lay back amid the cushions of the carriage and put her hand before her face, that they might not see how deeply she was moved. Her brother looked out with mingled interest and curiosity, and with a dim recollection of the few wretched days and nights he had passed here. Richmond looked on the familiar objects with mingled gladness and remorse, and recollected, with many strange emotions, that the last time he had entered Burnfield it had been with his bride, as they returned from their brief city tour. Only two years since then, and what changes had taken place! Mr. Dick Curtis, who had insisted on making one of their party, and positively refused to take no for an answer, was of them all the only one perfectly unmoved, and sat looking at the familiar landmarks as they drove past, with a face of grave approval.

"Fine place, sir—fine place," said Mr. Curtis, with a wave of his hand; "considerable of a town is Burnfield, eh, Randall? Not equal to Paris, you know, or Lapland, or the great St. Bernard, or any of the other tremendous cities, but a pretty tall place considering, and a real, genuine Yankee town. And then the produce—I defy the world to raise such girls, and boys, and pumpkins as they do in Burnfield. I defy 'em to do it, sir! Look at that young lady there, in the pink sun-bonnet and red cheeks, round as a cask of lager beer, and sweet as a cart-load of summer cherries—there's a specimen of American ingenuity for you! Could they surpass that in Constantinople or the city of Dublin, or any other distant or impossible region? No, sir; they couldn't. I defy 'em to do it, sir! Yes, I repeat it," said Mr. Curtis, striking his knee with his hand, and glaring round ferociously at the company generally, "I defy 'em to do it, sir."

Mr. Curtis was as fierce as an African lion, so everybody immediately settled down and looked serious.

"The notion," said Mr. Curtis, folding his arms and surveying his three companions in haughty disgust, "that they can raise as good-looking people in any other quarter of the world as they can in these here blessed United States. Look at me now," said Mr. Curtis, drawing himself up till his suspenders snapped, "*I'm* a specimen! Mr. Randall, my young friend, you have traveled, you have crossed that small pond, the Atlantic, and have become personally acquainted with all the great guns of Europe, from the Hottentots of Portugal to the people of 'that beautiful city called Cork,' and now I ask you as an enlightened citizen and fellow sinner, did you ever, in all your wanderings, clap your two eyes on a better-looking young man than the individual now addressing you? Don't answer hastily—take time for reflection. You know you didn't—you know you didn't; the thing's impossible."

"Mr. Curtis must be the best judge of his own surpassing beauty," said Mr. Randall, politely; "if he will hold me excused, I would rather not give an opinion on the subject."

"Welcome to Richmond House," said Mr. Wildair, as the carriage rolled up the avenue. "And now, gentlemen, I will leave you here for the present, while Mrs. Wildair goes to see her former guardian, Miss Jerusha Skamp."

"Perhaps I had better go alone, Richmond," said Georgia, hesitatingly. "Our first meeting——"

"Had better be unwitnessed; that is true enough," said Richmond. "Well, John will drive you down. Shall I call for you in person?"

"If Miss Jerusha consents to forgive you, I shall send for you, if Fly is still in the land of the living," said Georgia, smiling. "Good-by, gentlemen;" and kissing her hand, and laughing at Mr. Curtis, who nearly turned a somerset in his profound genuflexion, she was whirled away toward the cottage.

Yes, there it stood still, the same old brown, low-roofed little homestead. How different was this visit to it to what had been her last. There was her own little room under the roof, and there, in the broad window-sill, basking in the broader sunshine, lay Betsey Periwinkle and one of her numerous family, lazily blinking their sleepy eyes.

Georgia's heart beat fast as she leaped out of the carriage and walked slowly toward the house. Gathering the sweeping folds of her purple satin dress in one hand, she rapped timidly, faltering at the door.

It was opened by Fly—yes, it was Fly, no doubt about it—who opened her eyes and jumped back with a screech when she saw who it was.

"Hush, Fly! How do you do?" said Georgia, tapping her black cheek. "Is Miss Jerusha in?"

But Fly, in her astonishment and consternation, was incapable of speech; and smiling at her stunned look, Georgia swept past and entered the "best room."

There it was, still unchanged, and there, in her rocking-chair in the chimney-corner, knitting away, sat Miss Jerusha, unchanged, too. Old Father Time seemed to have no power over her iron frame. She did not hear Georgia's noiseless entrance, and it was only when a bright vision in glittering robes of silk and velvet, with dark tearful eyes and sadly smiling lips, knelt at her feet, and two white youthful arms, with gold bracelets flashing thereon, encircled her waist, and a sweet, vibrating voice softly murmured, "Dear, dear, Miss Jerusha," that she looked up.

Looked up, with a wild cry, and half arose, then fell back in her seat, and flinging her arms round her neck, fell on her shoulder with one loud passionate cry of "Georgia! Georgia!"

267

CHAPTER XXVI.

"LAST SCENE OF ALL."

"I have seen one whose eloquence commanding,
  Roused the rich echoes of the human breast;
The blandishments of wealth and ease withstanding,
  That hope might reach the suffering and oppressed.

"And by his side there moved a form of beauty,
  Strewing sweet flowers along his path of life,
And looking up with meek and love-bent duty—
  I called her angel, but he called her wife."

ANON.

ng and cool lay the shadows on the grass, one by one the bright, beautiful stars arose in the sky, up and up sailed the "lady moon," smiling down with her serene face on the trio sitting in the moonlight in the humble parlor of that little cot by the sea.

No light but that of the cloudless moon, no light but the beaming glances from eyes bright with joy—no other light was needed. By Miss Jerusha's side sat Georgia—not Georgia, the radiant vision of the ball-room, Juno-like in her queenly beauty, but the humble, gentle loving girl, meek in her great happiness. One wrinkled yellow hand of the venerable spinster lay in the small dark hands blazing with gems, and held them fast as if she would have held them there forever, while her eyes never for an instant wandered from the sweet smiling face.

And at Georgia's feet knelt another—a vision in robes snowy white, with the sweetest, fairest face ever sun shone or moon beamed on—one who looked like a stray seraph in her white garments, and floating golden curls, and sweet, beautiful violet eyes. Dear little Emily Murray, sweeter and fairer than ever she looked nestling there, crying and laughing together, and clinging to Georgia as though she would never let her go again.

"And to think you should have seen so much, and come through such strange scenes!" sobbed Emily, laughing at the same time; "to think you should have found a brother, and traveled all over Europe, and then come back and found yourself the wife of the greatest man of the age! Oh, dear me!" said little Emily, laughing and swallowing a sob, "it is *so* funny and *so* strange to find our Georgia back here in the old cottage again."

"But it's very nice—now ain't it, Emily?" said Miss Jerusha, complacently.

"Nice! I guess it is," said Emily, clasping Georgia tighter. "Oh, Georgia! I've lain awake night after night, crying and thinking about you, and wondering what had become of you, and oh! so frightened lest you should be dead—drowned, or frozen, or something; and in the stormy nights all that long winter I never could sleep for fear you might be out in the frost and cold, without a home or friends. Oh, Georgia! I did feel so restless and miserable all that winter, for fear, while I was warm and sheltered, you might be lying in the bleak streets cold and dead." And little Emily sobbed.

"Dear little Emily!" said Georgia, kissing her.

"And, oh, it is so nice to think you have become a devout Christian," said Emily, changing from sobbing to laughing again, "and I am *so* glad. Oh, dear me! how funny everything happens, to be sure. And Charley Wildair, too," pursued Emily; "I am sure I never thought *he* would be a clergyman; but I am very, very glad. Oh, I am so happy," said Emily, laughing, and squeezing Georgia's waist, "that I don't know what to do with myself."

"Nor me neither, I don't now, railly," said Miss Jerusha, who was the very picture of composure.

"Dear Miss Jerusha," said Georgia caressingly, "and won't you forgive Richmond—he really does not merit your anger, and wants to be forgiven and be friends with you again so much. Please do."

"Oh, you must, Miss Jerusha, you know," said Emily, seizing her other hand, and putting her happy little face close up to hers, "it won't do to refuse a governor your pardon. You must forgive him, please—won't you, Miss Jerusha?"

"Well, now, I don't know," said Miss Jerusha, relentingly, "he did treat you dreffully, Georgey, but——"

"No, he didn't Miss Jerusha—just served her right," said Emily, "Georgia was naughty, I know, and didn't behave well. There, she forgives him—look, she's going to laugh. Oh, say yes, Miss Jerusha."

"Well, '*yes*' then; does that please you?" said Miss Jerusha, breaking into a grim smile.

"Dear Miss Jerusha, accept my best thanks for that," said Georgia, with radiant face, "and now, may I send Fly up for him to Richmond House, that he may hear your forgiveness from your own lips?"

"Well, yes, I s'pose so," said Miss Jerusha, rubbing her nose; "and see here, Georgey, while you're about it, I reckon you might as well send for that there brother o' your'n too; I turned him out o' doors once, and while I'm forgiving that there graceless husband o' your'n, I guess I'll get him to forgive *me*."

Georgia laughed, and went out to the kitchen to despatch Fly off on the errand.

"Perhaps I had better go," said Emily, timidly, "I—I think I'd rather. It's so long since I met Mr. Wildair that I don't like to now."

"Pooh, nonsense," said Georgia laughing, "don't like to meet Mr. Wildair, indeed! Not a step shall you go until they come, and besides, I want to make you acquainted with my poet brother, who is a handsome fellow!" and Georgia's eyes sparkled.

"Does he look like you, Georgia?" said Emily, meditatively.

"Not a bit; better looking," smiled Georgia. "And oh, Em, there's a particular friend of yours up at the hall, a certain Mr. Curtis, if you remember him."

"He's not a particular friend of mine," said Emily, pouting and blushing. "I don't know anything about him. I wish he hadn't come."

"How flattered he would feel if he heard that. You refused him, didn't you, Emily?"

"Oh, Georgia, don't tease," said Emily, springing up and turning half pettishly away.

Georgia laughed, and silence for awhile fell on all three, broken at last by the sound of carriage wheels, and the next moment two tall gentleman stood in the little moonlit parlor with their hats off, and one of them stepping up to Miss Jerusha, extended his hand, and said, with a smile:

"Well, Miss Jerusha, am I forgiven at last?"

There was no resisting that frank tone and pleasant smile. Miss Jerusha looked meditatively at his proffered hand a moment, and then grasped it with an energy that made the governor of B—— wince, as she exclaimed:

"Well now, I railly don't think I ought, but Georgey says I shall hev to, and I s'pose I've got to mind her. Mr. Wildair, how d'ye du? I'm rail glad to hear they've made a governor of you, and I hope you'll behave better for the future, and be good to Georgey."

"I shall certainly try to; but, Miss Jerusha, I was almost as much sinned against as sinning. That malicious little cousin of mine, you know——"

"Oh, I know; Georgey told me. Well, she won't interfere again, I reckon—a impident little whipper-snapper, speaking as sassy to Georgey as if she was mistress herself, and allers grinnin' like a chessy cat."

"And has Miss Jerusha no greeting for me? Has she forgotten the little boy who paid her a visit one stormy Christmas eve long ago?" said Warren, as he advanced smilingly, shaking back his dark, clustering hair.

"My conscience! you ain't he, are you? Tall as a flagstaff, I declare! Forget you—no I guess I don't. I did behave most dreadfully that night to turn you out; but gracious! I knew you wouldn't freeze or nothin', and neither you did, you see."

"No I am frost-proof," said Warren, laughing; "but I owe you a long debt of gratitude for the care you took of this wild sister of mine all those years, Miss Jerusha. Come," he said, extending his hand, "we shall be good friends now, shall we not?"

"That we shall," said Miss Jerusha, cordially shaking the hand he extended. "My, to think the little feller I turned out that night should come back sich a six-footer, and rail good-looking, too, now ain't he, Emily? Why, you weren't the size of a well-grown doughnut then, you know. Good gracious! jist to think how funny things *will* turn out. 'Clare to man, if it ain't the queerest world I ever heerd tell of!"

Miss Jerusha wiped her spectacles meditatively, and gave a small, mottled kitten who came purring round her a thoughtful kick.

"Hallo!" said Richmond, picking it up. "One of Betsey Periwinkle's. How is that intelligent domestic quadruped, Miss Jerusha? She and I used to be tremendous friends long ago, you know."

"Yes, I know; she was no ways proud, and made friends with most people," said Miss Jerusha, complacently; "that's Betsey's youngest. She's raised several small families since, and is beginning to fall into the old ages o' life now. Ah, well! sich things must be expected; everybody gets old, you know— even Betsey Periwinkle."

Very swiftly passed that evening. It seemed as if the old happy days had come back—those unclouded days, when no shadow of the darkness to come had yet risen on horizon. Only one face was needed there to complete the circle, one voice to complete the charm; but that bright young head lay low now, the tall grass waved over that familiar face, and that clear, spirited voice was silenced forever. Tears sprang to Miss Jerusha's hard gray eyes, as she listened to the tale of the noble life and early death of her light-hearted favorite, and little Emily sobbed.

"You must give up this little cottage, Miss Jerusha," said Richmond, before they left that evening, "and come and live with Georgia and me. Once upon a time you admired Richmond House, and now you must make it your home."

"Do, Miss Jerusha! Oh, dear Miss Jerusha, do!" cried Georgia, eagerly; "it will make me so happy to have you always near me. And you shall bring Fly and Betsey Periwinkle and all the little Betseys, and we will be ever so happy together."

But Miss Jerusha shook her head.

"Mr. Richmond, I'm obliged to you, and you, too, Georgey, but I sha'n't leave the old homestead while I live. My father and mother, and all our folks, since the time of the revolution long ago, hev lived and died here, and I don't want to be the first to leave it. I can see you every day as long as you're in Burnfield; and whether I went to live with you or not I wouldn't go with you to the city—a noisy, nasty place! So, I reckon I shall keep on living here; very much obliged to you both at the same time, as I said afore."

And from this resolution nothing could move her—no amount of coaxing could induce her to depart from it. The laws of the Medes and Persians might be changed, but Miss Jerusha Skamp's determination never!

It was late when they returned to Richmond House, where they found Mr. Curtis solacing himself with a cigar; his chair tipped back and his heels reposing on the low marble mantel, and yawning disconsolately as he glanced drearily over the *Burnfield Recorder.*

"Got back, have you?" he said, looking up as our party entered; "and time, I should say. What precious soft seats your excellency and the rest of you must have found in Miss Jerusha's. Quarter to twelve, as I am a sinner! I wonder Miss Skamp didn't turn you out. How is that ancient vestal?"

"In excellent health," replied Richmond, throwing himself on a lounge, "and perfectly unchanged since you saw her last. By the way, there was a young friend of yours there, Dick."

"Ah, was there?" said Mr. Curtis, twisting round suddenly in his chair, and turning very red. "Aw—Bob Thompson, I daresay."

"Yes, if Bob Thompson is five feet three inches high, and has blue eyes, pink cheeks, yellow curls, and white forehead, ditto a dress, and is in the habit of wearing gold bracelets, and answering to the pretty name of Emily."

"Ah—Miss Murray," said Mr. Curtis, thrusting his hands abruptly into his pockets, and beginning, without the smallest provocation, to whistle violently. "Nice little girl! How is *she?*"

"Ask Randall," said Richmond, with a slight laugh and a malicious glance toward the gentleman in question. "He had Emily pretty much to himself all the evening—took summary possession of the young lady, and the moment he was introduced began to be as fascinating as he knew how. Irresistible people are poets. Ask *him*."

Instead of asking him, however, Mr. Curtis favored the handsome poet with a ferocious scowl, and then, flinging away his Havana, stalked out of the room with tragic strides that would have made his fortune on the stage.

Mr. Wildair laughed, and Mr. Randall looked after him with a slight smile, but said nothing.

One week later Georgia learned his opinion. Emily had been spending the evening at the hall, and had just gone home.

"What a dear little angel she is!" exclaimed Georgia; "so sweet, so good, so gentle and loving. Her presence brightens the room the moment she enters, like a ray of sunshine. Darling little Emily! how I love her! I wish she were my sister."

Warren smiled, and placing a hand lightly on either shoulder, looked down in her flushed, enthusiastic face.

"Belle Georgia," he said, meaningly, "*so do I*."

And now let the curtain rise once more ere it falls again forever.

Five years have elapsed, but Burnfield and Richmond House are still the same; a little larger, a little more noisy, a little more populous, but nothing to speak of. The march of improvement does not get ahead very fast there.

There is a little brown cottage standing by the sea-shore, and sitting in the "best room" is an elderly lady knitting away as if the fate of kingdoms depended on it. Such a spotless best room as it is; not a speck of dust to be seen anywhere, the very covers of the "Pilgrim's Progress" and "Robinson Crusoe" fairly glitter with cleanliness, and it's absolutely dangerous for a person of weak eyes to look at the chairs and painted floor, so perfectly dazzling are they. The old lady herself, albeit a little stiff and prim in her dress, is as bright as a new penny, and although the said dress would at the present day be called somewhat skimpy, it is a calico, like Joseph's coat of many colors, and she is fairly gorgeous in it.

A demure, well-mannered, polite animal of the feline species reposes on a rug at her feet, and blinks a pair of intensely green eyes in the sunshine with a look of calm, philosophical happiness beautiful to see. Betsey Periwinkle, our early friend, has departed this life, deeply regretted by a large and respectable circle of acquaintances, and was buried in state at the bottom of the garden, and the one now introduced is a descendant of that amiable animal, and as such no doubt will be cordially welcomed.

Out in the kitchen is a "cullud pusson" of the female persuasion, whose black face glistens with happiness and a recent application of yellow soap, who sits chewing gum and sewing at a new turban with a look of contentment.

But there is one other inmate of that best room—a stranger to you, reader, whom I now hasten to introduce. It is a young lady of some three years old, who goes skipping along, alternately tumbling down, and after emitting one or two shrill yells, which she considers necessary to draw attention to the clever way in which the fall was managed, crawls up again and resumes her journey round the room, until she thinks proper to undergo another upset.

This small individual, not to be mysterious, is Miss Georgia Wildair, eldest daughter of his excellency, Richmond Wildair, of Richmond House. A pocket edition of our early friend Georgia she is, with the same hot, fiery temper, but never will it lead her into such trouble as her mother's has done, for the restraining hand of religion will hold her back, and little Miss Wildair, the heiress, will be taught what our Georgia never was, to "Remember her Creator in the days of her youth;" and this little lady is the pride and darling of Miss Jerusha's heart, and spends, while papa and mamma rusticate in Burnfield, a great deal more of her time in the cottage than in the hall, and enjoys herself hugely with Fly and Betsey Periwinkle.

And now, reader, to that worthy cat, to the sable handmaiden, to the little heiress, and to our old friend Miss Jerusha Glory Ann Skamp, you and I must bid farewell.

A new scene rises before us. A large and elegantly furnished parlor, where pictures, and statuary, and curtains, and lounges, and last, but not least, a genial fire, make everything at once graceful and home-like. A lady, young and beautiful, but with a calm, chastened sort of beauty, and a soft, subdued smile, sits in a low nursing-chair and holds a baby, evidently quite a recent prize, who lies making frantic efforts to swallow its own little, fat fists, and hitting its invisible little nose desperate blows in the vain endeavor. This young gentleman is Master Richmond Wildair, while in "nurse's" lap, at a little distance, his eldest brother Master Charley, a youth of some sixteen months, is jumping and crowing, and evidently having a heap of fun all to himself. These manifestations of delight at last grow so obstreperous that a handsome, stately gentleman who lies on a sofa near, reading the paper, looks up with a smile.

"What a noisy youth this boy of yours is, Georgia!" he says, looking at

Master Charley; "he is evidently bent on making himself heard in this world. Come Charley, be quiet; papa can't read."

But Charley, who had no intention of being bound over to keep the peace, no sooner hears papa's voice than, with a crow an octave higher than any of its predecessors, he holds out his arms and lisps:

"Papa, tate Tarley! papa, tate Tarley!"

"Now do put down that stupid paper, Richmond, and take poor 'Tarley,'" says Georgia, looking up with her bright smile. "Bring him over, nurse."

"Well, I suppose I must," Richmond says, resigning himself as a man always must in such cases, and holding out his arms to "Tarley," who, with an exultant crow, leaps in and immediately buries two chubby little hands in papa's hair. "Where's Georgia?"

"Oh, down at the cottage, of course," says the lady, laughing; "when is Georgia ever to be found anywhere else? Dear Miss Jerusha! it does make her so happy to have her there; so while we live in Burnfield we may as well let her stay there."

"Oh, certainly—certainly," replies Richmond, with tears in his eyes as Master "Tarley" gives an unusually vigorous pull to his scalp-lock. "And by the way, my dear, guess from whom I heard to-day?"

"Who—Warren?" inquires Georgia eagerly.

"No—Curtis," says his excellency, laughing. "Poor Dick's done for at last. Miss Maggie What's-her-name Leonard, the one with the curls and always laughing, has finished him. As the king in the play says, 'I could have better spared a better man.'"

"Why, you don't mean to say he has married her?" says Georgia, in extreme surprise. "Well, I *am* surprised. Where is he now?"

"Off in the South for a bridal tour, and then he will return and resume his duties as my secretary. There goes the tea-bell. Here, nurse, take Master 'Tarley.' Come, Georgia."

Look with me on another scene, reader. The beautiful moon rides high over the blue Adriatic; the bright cloudless sky of glorious Italy is overhead, that sky of which poets have sung, and artists have dreamed, and old, sweet romancers have pictured, and gazing up at its serene beauty with uncovered brow, stands a poet from a foreign land, with his blue-eyed bride. You know them both; you need no introduction; you cannot mistake them, for the lofty mien and gallant bearing of Warren, and the soft holy blue eyes and seraphic smile of Emily are unchanged. Some day, when they are tired wandering under the storied skies of the old world, they will come back to the land of their birth, but you and I will see them no more.

On the last scene of all let the curtain rise ere it drops again forever.

In a sunny corner of a sunny church-yard, where the sweet wild roses swing in the soft west wind, where trees wave and birds sing, and a little brook near murmurs dreamily as it flows along, is a grave, with a marble cross above, bearing the name of "Charles Wildair," and underneath the inscription, "Blessed are the dead who die in the Lord." Tread lightly, reader; hold your breath as you gaze. Kneel and pray in awe, for a saint lies there.

And now that the story is finished, I see the sagacious reader putting on his spectacles to look for the moral. Good old soul! With the help of a microscope he *may* find it; may Heaven aid him in his search; but lest he should fail, I must decamp. Reader, adieu!

THE END.